After Midnight

EXCURSIONS

TAM AHLBORN

PAGE PUBLISHING, INC.
Conneaut Lake, PA

First originally published by Page Publishing 2020

ISBN 978-1-64701-190-1 (pbk)
ISBN 978-1-64701-191-8 (digital)

Printed in the United States of America

CHAPTER 1

"I appreciate you fitting me in, Alana," Kristianna said as she sat down in the red hibiscus-patterned chair at A Weeks Adventure Travel Agency.

The entire office had the allure of a tropical getaway. There were colorful posters of exotic countries lining the walls. Silk-potted plants with tiny twinkle lights hidden in the branches separated each agent's desk. A blue-and-gold macaw stood on a wooden perch, cracking almond shells and bobbing his head while native drum music played discretely from unseen speakers. Against the back wall of the room, a Spanish colonial credenza hosted a carved wood tray of white-chocolate macadamia-nut cookies, a carafe of coffee, and bottles of sparkling water. The credenza was strategically placed by shelves of booklets enticing their magical parts of the world, to be explored.

Alana Weeks had spared no expense when she hired the decorator to remodel the drab musty building a year ago, Kristianna thought, as she continued looking around the office.

"Kristi dear, why on earth did you wait so long to decide on a cruise? You know, cruises are usually booked six to eight months in advance," Alana asked Kristi, never looking up from her computer screen.

"Alana, I am so sorry. I guess I am just impulsive," Kristianna said with a shrug. She really didn't want Alana Weeks, *the* travel agent / social butterfly in town to know she just wanted to get away from the snooty neighborhood women she and Alana lived near.

"Let see, there is a seven-day cruise to Cozumel, Grand Caymans, and the Bahamas the end of September, sailing out of Tampa Bay," Alana said, still staring at the screen.

"Don't you have anything sooner than September?" complained Kristi.

The beautifully carved wood door of the travel agency opened and in walked a drop-dead gorgeous guy in a surfer logo T-shirt, jeans, and deck shoes. Kristi's mouth fell open as she watched him shut the door behind him. He was at least six feet tall with dark hair and eyes. There was nothing awkward about the way he slowly moved into the room. He had just enough muscle on his tanned arms to be sexy. He could be her cabana boy any day, she thought.

"Hi, Zac, Doris will be with you in a few minutes," Alana said without looking up.

"No worries, I'm early," said the voice that belonged to the tantalizing dark-eyed guy.

"Oh my, I just found you the perfect vacation!" Alana said, bring Kristi back to reality. "Kristianna Romanoff, you are going to owe me big time. A couple just canceled an eleven-day cruise—land adventure in Alaska mid-May," Alana practically shouted as she clapped her hands together above her head.

"Really, Alana, tell me more," Kristi questioned, leaning forward in her chair. The middle of May could be good, actually perfect, Kristi started thinking. She could skip out on the end of tourist season gossipy parties in the neighborhood. She wouldn't have to listen to the plans for summer vacations in the Hamptons or European getaways from the heat of Florida.

"Your vacation would start in Vancouver, British Columbia, where you will board ship. The first day you will be cruising the inside passage, you know getting your sea legs after the long flight. You would spend a day in Ketchikan, Icy Strait Point, Juneau, Skagway, and then, another day cruising Hubbard Glacier. Your cruise ends and your land adventure begins when you leave ship in Seward. You will travel by coach to Anchorage. You will spend the night and next morning in Denali National Park. Here is a picture of the resort you will be staying at, very top-of-the-line, since you will be in the middle of six million acres of wilderness. From there, you will head to Fairbanks, where you will spend two days touring early gold mining settlements and taking in sights in and around the city of Fairbanks. Your land tour ends with your flight home from Fairbanks.

"The cost will be about six thousand five hundred dollars for single occupancy of a double room. It does not include air travel to Vancouver or your flight home from Fairbanks," Alana said. She was clearly proud of herself for finding the perfect last-minute cruise.

"It is a really exciting itinerary. But it does not include my air-fare, so that is quite expensive for one person," Kristi said with a frown.

"The rooms are double occupancy, and it is a portside balcony suite, which makes it a little more expensive. If you take someone with you, it would be cheaper for you. Do you have a man you could take?" Alana said as if it was no big deal. "But I have to tell you, this is a cancelation, so you have to jump on it immediately or it will be gone."

"Can I have twenty-four hours to think on it?" pleaded Kristi.

"Here, let me give you all the information on the cruise, the excursions available to you at each port, and the cost of air travel. I can only give you until tomorrow morning. So I will need an answer by then, or it will be back on the market. I'm sorry, that's the best I can do," Alana said.

"I understand and I appreciate your search. I will let you know tomorrow morning. Thanks Alana," Kristi said, extending her hand to Alana as she stood to leave.

Slowly Kristi walked to her car, thinking almost ten thousand dollars for a two-week escape from the neighbors seemed a little bit extreme. However, seeing the pictures of whales breaching in the Gulf of Alaska and moose grazing in meadows the size of Texas was very enticing. On the negative side, Kristi debated, it's dang cold up there, on any given day. Why, oh why, would she want to fly to Alaska when all she had to do was close the drapes and turn down the air conditioner if she wanted cold?

"Excuse me, miss, excuse me…can I talk to you?"

Kristianna turned as she reached her car to find Mr. Oh So Gorgeous, who had walked into the travel agency a while back, striding toward her. She looked down to see if she had dropped any of the hundred pamphlets, cruise line catalogs, and paperwork Alana had given her.

"I'm sorry, but I overheard your conversation with Alana. I know this may sound strange, but I might be able to help you."

"My conversation with Alana. What do you mean?" Kristi questioned as she dropped her armful of stuff onto the passenger's seat of her sports car.

"You're thinking about going to Alaska, but one person traveling in a double occupancy room is kind of expensive. I was in the travel agency thinking about booking a business vacation. If we split the cost of the room, it would help you. Plus it could give me some great ideas for changes I want to make in my business," said Mr. your eyes look like yummy dark chocolate.

"Did Alana put you up to this?" Kristi questioned.

"What? No, her daughter and my daughter graduated from high school together. That's how I know her. Anyway, a last-minute cruise could help me and cut down expenses for you at the same time. You see, I own a restaurant and am looking to change out menu items. I never thought about a cruise, but they have some of the finest chefs and spare no expense. Oh, by the way, my name is Zac, Zac Karas. And you are Kristi, if I heard Alana correctly call you?" Zac said, extending his hand.

"Yes," was all Kristi could mumble; she was sure it was due to brain overload.

"Yes, you are agreeing to the idea, or yes, your name is Kristi?"

"Yes, I'm Kristi. Actually my name is Kristianna," Kristi said, slamming the car door shut.

"Instead of standing here in the parking lot in the heat, there is a Mexican restaurant down the street and a couple of fast-food joints a couple of blocks away. We could go somewhere and discuss this. Or if you want to ask Alana, she will vouch that I am not a murderer, rapist, or thief," Zac said, nodding toward the travel agency.

"Well, you are right. Your idea does sound weird but…" Kristi looked down at her watch, stalling for time to think up some excuse not to leave the parking lot with this oh so gorgeous hunk of a guy. When she couldn't come up with anything at a moment's notice, she said, "Okay, I will meet you at Poncho's Patio, and we can discuss it."

Two hours later, after three bowls of salsa, at least a pound of tortilla chips, two enchiladas, and several sodas, Zac had explained to Kristi how he wanted to keep customers intrigued with his restaurant. He conveyed, by changing parts of the menu every so often, keeping up with the latest trends in food fusions and competition, it would keep customers returning. His passion for his restaurant was clearly seen with every hand gesture, every shrug, and at times, the faraway look in his eyes.

The conversation slowly shifted to food service on cruise liners and pubs in Alaska versus Florida and comfort foods while away from home. They discussed the idea of two strangers traveling together to Alaska for almost two weeks, which sounded totally ridiculous.

"From the looks of all the pamphlets and information on the shore excursions that Alana gave you, I'm sure you could be really busy playing tourist," Zac told Kristi.

"I know, did you see how many she gave me? The ship will sail before I can figure out which excursions I want," Kristi joked.

"Do you have an idea of what you would like to see and do in Alaska?"

"To tell you the truth, I never thought of Alaska as my vacation destination before Alana suggested it," Kristi said. "I envisioned the Bahamas or Jamaica but never Alaska."

"Is there a reason why you didn't consider Alaska?"

"I don't know, maybe because it is really cold there and on the other side of the continent!" Kristi shrugged. She really didn't want Zac to know she was just looking for a place to escape to.

Being single, in a neighborhood full of upper-class executive families, was sometimes brutal. Her neighbors on many occasions tried to out due each other. So when one or another saw Kristi lounging by her pool or grilling dinner, they tended to take turns migrating over. As dusk settled over the lower Manatee River and a couple of glasses of wine; their conversations sometimes turned to rants. Kristi had thought it was funny; most of their complaints were over how their other neighbors' lawns were mowed, which palms needed trimming, which neighbor changed hair salons or workout trainers. Since none of her neighbors cared for their green space personally, on occasion, Kristi pointed out which lawn services were not as good as others. But she never said the lawn companies her neighbors used were bad. She would inquire which workout trainer was increasing their clientele or who the best was. Yet again, she knew if she took any side, they would end up hating her for it.

Before Zac could probe deeper into her reasons for an impromptu vacation, Kristi asked, "Do you think you will be able to schedule appointments with the cruise ship chefs to discuss their various menus?"

"I don't know. I am going to check some of my connections to see the chain of command I will have to go through. Also, I will get some of Alana's pamphlets to see what culinary excursions are available. Or I can get the website from you later," Zac said. He was already making mental notes on ways to go about learning the cruise ship's latest culinary secrets.

"You know, this could be the perfect vacation," Kristi said thoughtfully.

"Just remember who suggested it," Zac said, grinning.

"The more we've talked, I realize that you have your own agenda and so do I. If you choose to hang out at all the 'off the beaten track' pubs south of the Arctic Circle, it is your choice," Kristi said.

"And if you want to sign up for every excursion, you can fit in and be the last person to return to the ship every evening, so be it," Zac said, smiling.

"And no one will complain that you are ruining their vacation."

It soon became very obvious to them the waitress wanted to settle up their bills before going off shift. Zac's signaling for the check.

"Could we have separate checks please?" Kristi said to their server when she came to see if they needed anything more from the kitchen. Kristi felt that it was only fair since it was a sort of business meeting.

"No. I'm paying for the meals. One bill please," he said to the server. "Kristi, it was my bizarre idea, and I invited you."

Kristi was too full of tortilla chips and salsa to continue the debate. Finally agreed.

"You know," Kristi said as she watched Zac sign the credit stub. "I think I am going back to the travel agency and let Alana book the cruise."

"I guess I have to go back too so I can pay for my half of the trip," Zac said with a heart-stopping grin.

Alana Weeks was just locking the door when Kristi drove into the parking lot of A Weeks Adventure Travel Agency, a second time that day. Once again, Kristi wondered how long it took for Alana to decide on that name for her business. Oh well, it was kind of catchy, and everyone trusted Alana with their travel arrangements. She was good at finding perfect deals at the last minute. Kristi had heard this from the scuttlebutt at some of the neighborhood parties. And now, it proved to be true.

"What brings you back? Did you have more questions for me, Kristi dear?" Alana asked from the door.

"No, I wanted to go ahead and book the cruise, but I see you are closing, I can come back tomorrow," Kristi said as she closed the door of her car, knowing Alana would never turn down a deal. She could practically see dollar signs in Alana's eyes.

"No, no. Since I gave you a time limit, let's just fill out the paperwork before someone tries to horn in on your adventure," Alana said, reopening the door, just as Zac pulled his car in the parking spot next to Kristi's car.

After seeing Alana's questioning facial expression as Zac walked across the parking lot, maybe Alana hadn't given him the nudge on the Alaska cruise idea after all, Kristi decided. In a few minutes, Kristi was sure she was going to shock the heck out of Alana.

The office was still exotic. The twinkle lights were more pronounced as the late afternoon sun dipped behind the building. There were no cookies on the credenza or rhythmic music; the bird was even dosing on his perch. Kristi again sat down on one of the tropical patterned chairs.

"I," she said.

"We," Zac emphasized.

"*We* would like to book the eleven-day cruise to Alaska," Kristi said, first looking at Alana, then turned her head to Zac.

"Yes, we have discussed it, and it would work out perfectly for both of our travel needs," Zac said, sounding more businesslike than a vacation hunting local, sitting down in the chair opposite of Kristi.

"Let me get the computer up and running, and we will get your adventure on the way," Alana said, clearly dumbstruck while trying to remain professional.

CHAPTER 2

Later that night, Kristi sat up in bed when the realization hit her. She was going on an eleven-day Alaskan cruise with a guy she didn't even know. What was she thinking? She needed her head examined. She had never done anything so impulsive and unpredictable in her life. Everything had always been planned and well thought out. What if Zac was an ax murderer? Wait, he might not own an ax, but he owned a restaurant; he probably had a meat cleaver instead. Great, chopped up and found a month later in an abandoned frozen meat locker in Alaska! Ridiculous, she thought, flopping back on her goose down pillows.

Barely able to see the sailboat oil painting on the far wall of her bedroom in the darkness, Kristi thought about how well she knew Alana. By tomorrow, everyone in a mile radius of Kristianna's house would know she was going off with a well-to-do divorced guy she hardly knew to Alaska of all places. Now, Kristi worried, instead of having to endure the endless bragging vacation plans of the upper-middle class, she would have to see the "I know what you have been doing" eyes of everyone on the street, even if she didn't do anything.

By 2:00 a.m., Kristi had emotionally gone from disbelief in her decision to go to Alaska with a guy she didn't know to frustration with herself to anger with her tongue-wagging neighbors. Chewing on her lip, Kristi tried to think of every pro and con to her impulsive plan. She was divorced. She was a thirty-nine-year-old healthy female. She lived a boring life. Why couldn't she go on a spontaneous adventure? Why couldn't she agree to an impromptu excursion in the Alaskan wilderness with a totally drop-dead gorgeous guy? It wasn't like he was interested in her. It was all about his restaurant business. They both had agreed, it was a mutual financial good idea.

By 3:00 a.m. and still staring at the sailboat painting in the dim light, Kristi decided she had nothing to wear in Alaska. She didn't have any boots. She had no cold weather clothes. She had cold-, cold-weather ski attire but not sort of cold-weather clothes. Alana had told her, it would be in the thirty to forty-degree temperatures at night and fifty- and sixty-degree temperatures during the day. She said to dress in layers so she could peel off the clothes as Kristi got warm during her off-ship excursions. Also, Alana encouraged Kristi to buy a good heavy-duty backpack. She explained, it was easier to stuff the top-layer clothes in the backpack rather than sling them over Kristi's arm or drag them along the way.

After taking stock of all her winter outfits scattered across her bed, lounge chair, and bathroom counter, Kristi confirmed her worst fears. The way-too-heavy, balky sweaters, dress trousers, sandals, and tennis socks lying around the room were not proper attire for late spring in Alaska.

At 4:00 a.m., Kristi was on her computer searching Vermont and Maine clothing store websites and catalogs for cold-weather apparel. Stores in Florida only had swimsuits and clothing that catered to the tourist population in April. She had cutesy boots, perfect for Florida at fifty degrees and ski boots she had worn on her Aspen ski trips several winters, years ago. But she had no mid-temperature kind of boots she would need for one of her chosen excursions to the Arctic Circle or hiking in Denali National Park. She had a dress black winter wool coat she wore to her father's funeral, but what she needed was a medium-weight waterproof jacket with a hood or a navy pea-coat. Kristi thought of her many pairs of lacy trouser socks. Nope, she needed socks, warm fuzzy socks. She kept adding things to the web shopping carts. After entering her credit card information, Kristi smiled, with a tap of the enter key on her computer, shopping in her pajamas had been a blast. Now all she had to worry about would be making sure her charged items were shipped on time.

Finally exhausted from all the worries and online shopping, Kristi pushed the discarded clothes from her wardrobe closet hunt off the bed and crawled between the sheets. She fell asleep only to wake a few minutes later. She ran down the stairs and into the den. Kristi found an ink pen, then searched for a piece of paper. "Don't forget to call a private investigator in the morning," she wrote. She would have a background check done on one Mr. Zac Karas. If there was anything she learned from her father, it was to be prepared. She decided she didn't need any surprises on her vacation on the other side of the continent.

Across town, standing looking out over Sarasota Bay from his penthouse high rise living room window, Zac didn't notice the sailboat motoring toward the open water of the Gulf of Mexico. Nor did he see the moon shining down on the boats in the yacht club marina or the lady standing on the dock, smoking a cigarette. His mind was reviewing the conversations of the last twenty-four hours.

After Kristi had left the travel agency a second time earlier that day, Zac stayed behind and spent a few minutes talking to Alana Weeks. First, they had discussed both of their daughters' lives post-high school graduation. College tuitions and changing degree majors midyear were usually the topic of ire for most parents of late teenage children. Zac didn't realize until Alana brought it up that she lived a couple of houses down the street from Ms. Romanoff. She said Kristi did a lot of volunteer work for Mote Marine and a local heart charity. She didn't know where Kristianna's money had come from, but Alana said Kristi lived in a very nice house and never caused problems in the neighborhood that she knew of. Alana did say that Kristi had a son, but he only visited on holidays. Maybe he lived with his father, she didn't know.

On the way home from signing the papers at Alana's office, logic had started setting in. Yes, Zac knew he could still back out of the trip. It would be a nasty trick to pull on someone. But for some reason, something Zac couldn't quite put his finger on nagged at him. Could his usual impulsive behavior finally be getting the better of him? As he turned onto Tamiami Trail, better known as US-41, thank goodness he decided to stop off at the office of an ex-Navy SEAL friend turned investigator. If anyone could find dirt or anything else on someone, it was Frank. He had the computer skills to search in places Zac didn't even know existed.

"Hey, my friend, long time, no see; how goes it?" Frank had said, welcoming Zac into his office. "Are you having trouble with some little ole lady who you once helped across the street? She's now following you wherever you go? Or one of those rich women from Sarasota who had too much botulism injections, you know, fish lips, stalking you?"

Zac smiled when he recalled Frank's fish lip pout. He had let Frank spend a few minutes ribbing him before he explained the situation with Kristianna Romanoff. Zac had expressed his desire for a background check to make sure she was not some crazy chick. He did not need someone to try and exploit him or his restaurant. Or a dangerous ex-husband who was out for revenge because of his loss.

Zac's thoughts then shifted to his daughter. She had been right. He hated to admit it, but he had been spending almost twenty hours a day, every day for the last eight months, at his diner. He really did need to get away. "Do something fun and explore life," was how Lacey had said it. But how could he do that? There were days when breathing even hurt. The restaurant was his comfort zone—the sizzle of food on the grills, the aroma of savory dishes leaving the kitchen, or the clink of silverware against the hand-painted plates. At The Mermaid Isle, he could block his feelings and focus on all that needed to be accomplished every minute of owning a very successful eatery. Yet what his daughter said was also a truism if ever there was one. He needed to seek out a life away from the restaurant, which brought his thoughts to his up and coming trip to Alaska. He technically was getting away from his place of business, even if it was to search for different ways to present exceptional cuisine and boost business.

Taking a sip of his Siesta Key Rum Spiced Siesta Coquito, Zac's thoughts circled back to the weird arrangement he made with Kristianna Romanoff. There was something intriguing about her. She had the basic goods, blond hair, blue eyes, not skinny but not fat, probably five feet six-ish tall and no visible tattoos. He had noticed she had a shy little smile that appeared often when they chatted at the Mexican restaurant. Yet she had looked so utterly sad when Alana asked if she had any male friends, she could take on vacation. For some reason, he felt it was necessary to rescue her from whatever made her unhappy. He hadn't taken the time to explore just why it seemed important to him. He didn't know if it was hopelessness that he saw in her eyes, but at the time, it seemed right to say he would split the cost of the land and sea cruise with her. Besides, maybe his daughter would be happy he was listening to her and taking a vacation. He would try to explore life in Alaska, not only culinary wise but for the adventure of spending almost two weeks away from the palm trees and the sugary white sand of Sarasota, Florida. But between now and leaving in less than three weeks, he had a lot of loose ends he needed to tie up.

The days until the adventure began were flying by. Kristi had so much to do as she looked at her calendar. She had taped notes to the refrigerator door of things she needed to buy for the trip, like travel-size shampoo, soap, and toothpaste. Her itinerary for the cruise and land tours were already set with the cruise line; however, she had chosen excursions in every port to add to the adventure. Kristi had decided since she was going to Alaska, she better fit in as many extra side trips as possible to her already exciting journey. She had printed out maps of each port to save time and footsteps in her travels. She had scratch paper notes taped to her computer of things she still wanted to research about Alaska. Things like where were the best shops and best photo opportunities in each port?

Packages from Kristi's midnight internet pajama shopping started arriving. George, the postman, at first dropped a box by the front door and rang the bell. But as days passed and one box plus another box plus another box arrived, George rang the bell to make sure Kristi was home to receive them. Kristi knew it was his way to help prevent doorstep-package theft. She also bet that although the postman was trying so hard to be professional; he was dying to find out where she was going. She had seen many neighbors who had stood at their mailboxes gabbing with the postal drivers, so it was better to thank him and let him get on with delivering the mail.

It was fun opening the parcels she was receiving; it felt like Christmas or birthdays as a child. The black turtleneck sweater would be warm enough for hiking or panning for gold, but with a touch of jewelry, it would look nice with black dress trousers for dinner on boardship. She loved the waterproof jacket with flannel lining that came about a week later. And as much as she wanted to take her white gloves and wooly scarf, she chose her black accessories instead since white would look dirty quickly. One afternoon, George, the postman, delivered yet another parcel. After thanking him, Kristi excitedly unboxed a pink wool sweater. She slipped it on over her purple tank top and stepped into the half bathroom by the back door leading to the pool. Looking at her reflection in the mirror, Kristi laughed until tears rolled down her face. The person staring back at her looked more like a wad of pink cotton candy from the county fair. What was she thinking? Maybe, because it looked so good on the model, she thought it would look good on her. Nope, that item was getting shipped back and right away!

Twenty-four hours closer to departure day, after dropping the ugly pink sweater at the post office for return, Kristi drove to a drab strip mall by the airport for her meeting with the private investigator she had hired to do a background check on Zac Karas. The place was just like in the movies, a real hole in the wall. The stucco building looked like it hadn't had a coat of paint in many years. The place was creepy looking even against the bright blue sky and sunny afternoon. It looked like the dead quiet of a hillside cemetery, no pun intended. The palm trees lining the front walkway looked like they were in dire need of a bucket or two of water. The two cars parked in the gravel parking lot baking in the midday sun even looked drab. As a plane took to the sky across the street, the glass windows facing the airport rattled and shook. Kristi stared at the building and wondered if it was part of the MO of private investigators to have a seedy-looking place of business. Maybe the place was better looking on the inside. Maybe she had made a huge mistake, about hiring a private investigator and taking Zac up on his offer. Maybe, she was just nervous about what the investigator had found. Kristi decided, if she had made a huge mistake, she could always fall back on plan B. And that would be to not take the cruise. She would lose the money invested in the trip. But she could drive to New Orleans or a hotel on the white sandy beaches in Panama City for two weeks.

Once inside the cool interior of the building, it took a moment or two to adjust from the brightness and heat from outside. To Kristi's relief, a very professional secretary led her to an office painted a creamy white with two high-backed leather chairs in front of a huge polished oak desk. A burgundy leather sofa was against one of the walls next to what looked like a bar cabinet. Amazing, Kristi thought as she waited in one of the chairs, how neat and organized the desk was. Just then a bearded man with gray hair and blue eyes walked in from a side door, extended his hand, and apologized for stepping out on the terrace for a bite to eat. He seemed to search her eyes like he was looking for something in the depth of her soul. But maybe that was the investigator in him, always searching for something.

Settling behind his desk, the private investigator opened a file, flipped through some pages. He stopped, looked up. Then he looked down again at a sheet of paper in the file. He studied something for a moment. Kristi couldn't tell what it was from the angle of her chair. He quietly closed the file and again looked at her. It was like sitting in her father's law office when she was eleven years old after breaking the neighbor's glass patio door when she was playing catch with a baseball. She just knew the floor was going to open, and she would be eaten by an alligator in a broken culvert below.

The soft-spoken PI let her know that Zachariah Karas was a widower with a college-age daughter.

Kristi never thought of Zac as a Zachariah. She kind of paused for a second and let his name drift through her mind. She must have missed it when Alana had said they had to make sure their names were typed the same on their tickets as how it was signed on their passports. She didn't remember Zac saying his full name. Maybe Alana didn't ask him and just typed it out.

The PI continued to read from the papers in the file. Zac owned a penthouse condo in Sarasota overlooking the marina and Sarasota

Bay. He received his culinary arts degree and master chef skills from one of the finest academies in Paris. He was the owner of a trendy restaurant downtown. The PI showed Kristi a couple of pictures of Zac and the mayor of Sarasota and pictures of Zac with some professional awards he had received. He continued to read off all of Zac's attributes, which ended with he had never had any criminal activity, not even a speeding ticket in the last ten years. As the PI pushed the file across the desk for Kristi to take with her, she again felt like he was trying to analyze her instead.

He said, "What use have you with this information I just gave you?"

Kristi took a deep breath, and even though it sounded kind of stupid to her ears, she said, "Zac offered to help me by paying half of my vacation. He really didn't have to extend the courtesy. The explained reason for the offer was as he said a win-win for both of us. He didn't need to do it, but he did. I still can hardly believe it. And usually, most people have ulterior motives for helping people. I just wanted to make sure he wasn't some psychopath."

"Ah, psychopath, Zachariah Karas is not," the PI said before bidding Kristi goodbye.

With Zac's background check clear of any dubious activities, Kristi relaxed a bit and could now look forward to her upcoming vacation. On a whim, instead of heading home after her meeting with the PI, Kristi turned her car south toward downtown Sarasota. Dropping in on Zac's restaurant might help her understand his passion for food more. She figured at this time in the afternoon, he would be busy with office work or dinner prep, or maybe he wouldn't even be there. She really didn't know what to expect. Was his establishment upscale or just a pub downtown with squeaky wood floors? The place was called The Mermaid Isle, she said to herself as she drove slowly down Pineapple Avenue, then Ringling Boulevard, then onto Orange Avenue—ah, there it was.

Kristi combed her hair in her car's sun-visor mirror. She applied some fresh lip gloss, then laughed and scolded herself at the same time because Zac Karas was only going to Alaska to get some fresh ideas for his restaurant. He had no interest in her.

Walking into The Mermaid Isle, Kristi was caught totally off guard. The place was absolutely beautiful. Sand color walls with framed coral artwork, huge fish aquariums with very-expensive-looking colorful fish separating seating areas. There were elegant mermaid statues placed, so they looked like they were lounging on outcropped rocks. These weren't the cheap-looking mermaid statues like in tourist souvenir shops with exposed breasts and ugly faces. These mermaids were mesmerizing, like the kind in the stories which caused the men on board ships to crash into the rocky shores.

"Would you like to be seated, or are you waiting for someone?" asked the hostess dressed totally in black.

"Oh, sorry, yes, I would like to be seated," Kristi stuttered, still in awe of the atmosphere of the restaurant. Why hadn't she heard of this place before now? She couldn't believe how it had been kept quiet in her neighborhood when the ambience, once she stepped inside, was so exquisite. Maybe the food was bad?

"Kristianna?"

As Kristi turned her head, not only was she surprised by the stunning attractiveness of Zac Karas but the fact he was standing in front of her. He was dressed in black, like the rest of the staff. With his blue-black hair, dark eyes, and wicked grin, she hoped he didn't notice her lean against the high-backed chair to steady herself. He was just as good-looking as she remembered from her first meeting of him at Alana's travel agency.

"You're here," Zac stated with an unmistakable tone of disbelief in his voice.

"Yes, I'm here," Kristi said, unable to think of anything intelligent to say.

"Let me cook for you. I will create for you something special. Do you like fish?" Zac questioned excitedly.

"No. Please, I mean yes, I love fish, but no, keep it simple. I just wanted to come see your place and have a bite to eat," Kristi pleaded with Zac.

"Okay, I will keep it light. Let me surprise you. I will be back," Zac said as he walked toward the kitchen area.

The hostess brought a crystal goblet of white wine and set it in front of Kristi. Kristi was stunned by the quizzical expression on the girl's face. Did she have lip gloss coloring on her teeth? Was there a spot on her shirt? She thought she dressed okay to come into the restaurant at this time of day.

Within a few minutes, Zac had returned with a silver platter. He said, "I have prepared for you grilled cherrystone clams with a white wine garlic sauce. I hope you will enjoy this."

"Oh my gosh, this looks fantastic, Zac. Please join me?" Kristi asked.

After Zac sat down, he scooped up three clams from the platter. He drizzled the silky-smooth sauce over the tender morsels of meat and set the china plate in front of Kristi. The aroma was rich with the scent of garlic and wine. He watched as Kristi placed the tender clam meat on her fork into her mouth.

"You are a superb chef. This is the most tender and flavorful clam I have ever eaten," Kristi said with awe in her voice.

"I am so glad you like it. And I am happy you came to my restaurant," Zac said.

"I now understand your passion. This place is beautiful and if everything is as tasteful as this," Kristi said gently placing another clam on her fork. "Then you should be proud."

Kristi could tell Zac was humbled by the praise of his culinary skills.

Changing the subject, Zac said, "So are you all packed and ready to board ship?"

"No, I'm still trying to decide what clothes to take. And you?" Kristi asked.

"Oh, I must tell you, I going to go to San Francisco for two days on business before the cruise. So I won't see you until we set sail from Vancouver. I'm sorry. But it is something I have to do for The Mermaid Isle before I can leave," Zac said with a frown.

"I understand. Not a problem," Kristi said with a shrug. "I am really looking forward to this trip. And I appreciate your help."

"I think it is going to work out well. Let me get started on your dinner," Zac said, starting to rise from the table.

"Please, something very light. The clams were so filling, and the flavor was fantastic. I don't think I could eat a huge meal."

"Okay, something totally you." And with that Zac headed back to the kitchen.

Kristi could tell the hostess and a couple of the servers were trying to figure out who she was and why Zac was giving her special attention. It was kind of fun to be the middle of their speculation but at the same time sad because there was no substance to it. She wasn't his secret mistress or lover or even new girlfriend. With a frown, Kristi realized she wasn't even gossip-worthy. It may be an exciting vacation to Alaska for eleven days for her, filled with adventures in the wilderness and shopping quaint shops. But for Zac, it was a means of finding new and better ideas for his business. She probably wouldn't see much of him at all.

Once again, Zac returned with a very expensive looking plate. He said with a flair of drama, "For the lady, I present two blackened grouper fish tacos with sriracha sour cream and coleslaw, a side of black beans, onions, jalapeno peppers and cilantro drizzled with sour cream and to compliment your meal, a mug of twisted coconut rum punch." Grinning, he set the beautifully plated meal and pewter mug in front of Kristi.

"When you said you would make something totally me, I didn't know what you meant," Kristi said with a laugh. "But this looks fantastic."

"I hope you like it. You said simple, and that is my most simple meal I know how to make," Zac said, sliding into the seat across from Kristi to watch her eat.

As Kristi lifted the scrumptious taco off the plate, a chef dressed in all white came and spoke into Zac's ear. Kristi watched as Zac's facial muscles tightened, and a frown appeared on his face. Within moments, Zac had encouraged Kristi to enjoy her meal with a dazzling smile that didn't quite radiate to his eyes. He excused himself and walked away. She felt bad that something could diminish someone's joy that fast. But in the service industry, drama sometimes happened in a flash.

After finishing the fantastic meal that Zac had prepared especially for her, Kristi asked for the bill. She had lots of last-minute things to check off her to-do list. She hadn't planned on this adventure down to Sarasota to see Zac's restaurant, but it had been so much fun. She now understood the excitement she saw in him when he talked about The Mermaid Isle. She wondered how Zac would find anything in Alaska to top the exquisite and powerful flavors he pulled from the foods he plated.

The hostess who first seated Kristi returned to the table. She said in an oddly cool professional tone, "There is no charge for your meal. Chef Karas prepared your dinner for your enjoyment. Is there anything else I can get for you?"

"No. Thank you. Please convey my thank you to Mr. Karas. The meal was superb," Kristi said in an equally aloof tone. She didn't understand the standoffish behavior of the hostess. However, thanks to the sometimes-rude remarks of her neighbors, she was well-schooled in detached conversations.

Leaving The Mermaid Isle, Kristi took one last look around the mesmerizing beauty of the restaurant. She was happy she ventured downtown to see it. And she wouldn't let someone else's personal issues dampen her own pleasure.

CHAPTER 3

Zac stood on the balcony of his childhood best friend, Mark's home in Santa Cruz overlooking the bay. It was a damp, dreary, and intermittent rainy afternoon. The waves crashed along the rocks, sending sea-salt spray up to mix with the already-chilled air. It had drizzled all during the prayers at the gravesite of the internment of Mark's father. Originally, Zac and Mark were going to spend a couple of days in San Francisco in between scheduled meetings Zac had, just hanging out. But when Zac got the call of the death of Mark's father, everything was canceled. The meetings were changed to web conference calls. Zac wanted to support his friend as best he could, so the plans to arrive in San Francisco remained. Zac rented a car and drove to Santa Cruz instead.

"Can I get you a plate of food? It won't be as good as your cooking, though," Mark called to Zac as he stood at the door to the balcony.

"How come you didn't tell me how bad your father was? I would have flown in sooner, you know that?" Zac asked.

"He didn't let on to anyone just how sick he was. He actually had a camping trip planned down in Big Sur next month," Mark said sadly. "So tell me about this mysterious cruise you are taking to Alaska."

Despite the circumstance of Zac's visit, the two friends spent their time hashing over old times and antics to the amusement of Mark's wife. Some of the stories included Mark's parents and Zac's parents and the close family friends they all had been. Zac regretted Lacey couldn't have come to the funeral with him. She would have loved some of the bittersweet stories that included her mother in part of the later years of the family friendship. But university class absenteeism policy didn't include family friends.

Later, after Mark's children were tucked in bed and his wife had bid them a good night. Mark again questioned how someone finally got Zac to take an impromptu vacation. Zac knew his friend would chew on the topic like a dog with a bone. He wouldn't stop until he got the answers out of him. Zac finally talked about keeping "the edge" at The Mermaid Isle with constant upgrades needed for his menu. He had the opportunity to take a cruise where cuisine was cutting edge and top-notch. Zac was fully aware that Mark was treading carefully when he asked questions about Kristianna. He had downplayed Kristi's involvement completely. Zac had already been scrutinized by one friend; he didn't need Mark to add to it. Besides, although it had been almost two years since Sara's passing, Zac had been very touchy about friends encouraging him to "move on."

Kristi's early morning trek across the sky to Vancouver, British Columbia, was uneventful. The first flight from the international airport in Tampa to Dallas was only two and a half hours long. Kristi spent her air time, like most people, mentally thinking: Her passport, money, and credit cards were in the side pocket of her backpack, check. The cat sitter was given the house key code and would come in every other day to play with Lucy, check. The cruise and land itinerary paperwork were in her backpack, yep. Maps and list of things to do were on her cell phone. The cell phone charger, Nikon camera, and extra battery were all at the bottom of the backpack, check. She got to the point of—oh good grief, it was too late to worry about any of it. Whatever, she didn't have, she could buy in the shops on board the ship or in any of the ports.

The flight from Dallas to Vancouver, although it was considered a four-and-a-half-hour-long flight, with time zone changes, was really six and a half hours long. Kristi was hoping to get a few hours of sleep; however, her conversation with her son the night before was heavy on her heart.

"Mom, please I'm begging you. Let me take off school and come on vacation with you," Elijah pleaded.

"Eli, the cruise is booked solid. There is no way I can get you on at the last minute," Kristi had said. She told him about how Alana Weeks had gotten her a last-minute booking when some couple canceled. "Besides you would miss senior prom, and I am pretty sure your girlfriend, Kimmy, already has her dress."

"I'm not serious about her, Mom. Besides, she's going to some college in Ohio. I'll never see her again."

"Look, you have finals week coming up. You need to study for them. And then there is graduation," Kristi pointed out.

"Okay, I could fly to Fairbanks. We could spend a couple of extra days there and then fly home together. Please, Mom."

"I promise we will fly somewhere for your graduation vacation once you get to Florida for summer. You decide where we should go," Kristi bargained.

Finally, she resorted to something she vowed never to do. Kristi never ever talked Eli's father down. No matter how much he caused her pain and embarrassment by having an affair with his secretary, she never said anything bad about him. After all, he was Elijah's father, and she respected her son and his love for his father. However, when Eli kept pursuing his vacation request; Kristi resorted to telling him, his father would have a complete meltdown if she took him out of his last days of high school. His father had spent a large amount of money on his grandeur Atlanta graduation party, and they would blame her for everything. Elijah had laughed and said that was exactly why he wanted to come on her vacation. He told her he didn't want a huge stupid "showy" party. In the end, she felt like she left him down once again.

Kristi closed her eyes as the intercom came on and the captain pointed out, they were passing Denver on the right side of the plane. She really didn't want to spoil the rest of her flight thinking about her ex-husband and his ex-secretary/wife. Their selfish behavior caused her son so much pain. It was understandable that he could fall out of love with her. It happens; that's life. But to flounce his love affair in front of his teenage son was hurtful.

Every few weeks, Eli would call wanting to vent all the stunts Dom's wife had pulled. Kristi would listen and give input on ways around the dilemma of the day without showing anger. She hoped she was teaching her son constructive ways in dealing with the "crap" situations rather than focusing on the "crap." Some days she just wanted to fly up to Atlanta and bring her son to Florida. Eli's life was more important than any educational opportunities the Atlanta private school he attended had to offer. But she could not move Eli, who was still a minor out of Atlanta without his father's consent. The only way was—*Stop!* Kristi yelled to herself in her head. *Enjoy the flight. Think about Ketchikan, Juneau, Skagway, and seeing Mount Denali.*

Zac had hated to say farewell to his best friend's father at the funeral. Now he had to say goodbye to Mark and head to Vancouver. The flight from San Francisco was only two hours; however, Zac was sitting on edge, knowing he was cutting it close to sailing time. One mechanical break delay before his flight left, and he would miss the ship. Sitting back in the plush leather seat of first class, Zac looked into last-minute flights from Vancouver, British Columbia, to Ketchikan, Alaska, just to be on the safe side. Finding there were still seats available on the last evening flight to Ketchikan, Zac relaxed a little bit. After the whirlwind of events in the last couple of days, he realized a vacation was just what he needed.

The death of Mark's father had been a shock. And the changes to his meeting plans Zac had to make at the last minute so he could be at the funeral were somewhat difficult. But the most unexpected was the information that Frank, his longtime private investigator friend had given him.

"Sir, would you like a glass of wine once we are in the air?" the flight attendant asked Zac.

"Yes, white please," Zac said and settled back in his seat. Thinking back, he had invited Frank to the penthouse for dinner one night right before he left for Santa Cruz. During the huge rib-eye steaks, jalapeno-and-bacon cheddar scalloped potatoes, and grilled asparagus meal Zac prepared, Frank had told him Kristianna Romanoff had requested a background and security check on him. Zac had not expected to hear that.

"When I asked her what her reasoning was for a check on you, she was fearful you might have ulterior motives for the cruise," Frank said sincerely.

"Are you kidding me?" Zac remembered asking incredulously. "What kind of ulterior motives?"

"I didn't have to look far to uncover her reasoning for looking into your background. You see, my friend, she had been married to and divorced from a snobby Atlanta stockbroker who was senior management with a well to do wealth and financial management company."

"Okay. Her ex-husband was a jerk."

"Wait, there's more. Her jerk of a husband had a very public affair with his secretary. The newspapers made Kristi look like a frigid gold digger. It wasn't until after the divorce, and his subsequent marriage to his secretary did the news stop. Kristianna dropped out of site from Atlanta. Even friends who were close to her didn't know what happened to her. She just disappeared. The jerk got their son, Elijah, in the divorce."

Zac remembered walking to the refrigerator to grab another cold beer for Frank, giving himself time to register the hurt Kristi must have felt.

"I think you better sit down, there is more. When Kristi dropped out of site in Atlanta, what she actually did was went to Gainesville and quietly got her law degree. Now it gets better, Kristi Romanoff is the only daughter, along with three sons of Jefferson Bradlow, of Bradlows and Gresheim."

It took a minute for Frank's latest facts to sink in before Zac realized why Kristi had been so cautious in her inquiry about him. "Oh my God, her father was a very high-profile attorney before he died. There were even rumors he was murdered. And weren't the Bradlow brothers just part of the murder trial in all the papers up in Tampa a couple of months ago?" Zac had asked, staring at Frank.

"Sir, sir, here is your wine," the first-class cabin hostess said.

"Oh, sorry, thank you."

"My name is Carlie, and just let me know if there is anything else I can get you."

Zac knew the cabin attendant was trying to be casual but flirt at the same time. She was probably hoping for an invite for drinks or dinner when they arrived in Vancouver. She made a point of making eye contact with him while she talked to the couple in the seats in front of him. Zac didn't want anything. He didn't want a casual cat-and-mouse conversation with Carlie. He wanted two hours to relax. Period.

Kristi's flight arrived in Vancouver, British Columbia, on time. She gathered all her luggage at the downstairs baggage claim and hurried to hail a cab out front of the terminal.

She actually felt sorry for the poor cabdriver who stopped to pick her up. "I would like to book you for the next four hours so I can see the sights of Vancouver before my cruise ship leaves," Kristi said to the cabdriver as she got in the cab.

Carlos, according to his identification name badge on the cab's sun visor, said, "No, no, missy, you cannot tie up the company cab for that long of time."

"Please, I just want to see some of Vancouver. You know, take some tourist pictures, check out some shops, maybe a museum," Kristi said.

"No, lady. I cannot do it."

"But, sir, it would take me longer to fill out the paperwork to rent a car than it would to just drive me around the city for a couple of hours."

"No, lady…"

But after begging and pleading, Carlos finally gave in after Kristi promised him a hundred-dollar tip plus her cab fare.

Kristi wanted to take the city bus tour, but it was five hours in length, and the tour had started before her flight landed at the airport. She had heard the Vancouver gardens were beautiful, but Carlos told her to walk the gardens took all day. He did take her to the Granville Island Markets. While she browsed through some of the quaint shops, Carlos trailed the cab on the street behind her with the meter ticking.

Carlos then took her to a beautiful marina and yacht club. It was full of sailboats and large pleasure cruisers. Since it was the middle of the week, there was very little boating activity around the docks. He showed her the water taxis. They looked like miniature blue and white tugboats about fifteen feet long. For the fun of it, Kristi wanted to ride in one. So she bargained with Carlos to pick her up at the Maritime Museum in two hours on the other side of False Creek, which of course he agreed to.

The little tug water taxi ride was so much fun. It was nothing like the large car ferries. It was small. The inside had very hard stark-white fiberglass seats all along the side walls. But since the ride only took fifteen minutes to cross the boat-lined creek to the museum dock, Kristi didn't care. It was fun.

She was amazed at the Northwest Territory history and information she learned at the Maritime Museum. Eli would have found it boring just like any other teenage kid. But she found it fascinating. She took several pictures of the turn-of-the-century anchors and pictures of the ice-crushing boats that navigated the Northwest Passage. She stood and read a story across an entire wall about how a ship crew was unsure about crossing the ice-over Prince of Wales Strait on course to the Bering Strait during a very cold winter. The Inuit people guided them without the use of charts. They had lived on top of the ship decks in small tents and never froze. It was an amazing read.

And then it was time to leave. Kristi took one last look at the small beach from the huge windows off the main entrance foyer. She noticed traffic on English Bay had picked up. There were huge freighters, fishing trawlers, pleasure cruising boats, sailing yachts, and two eight-manned kayaks all on the same waterway. It was such a spectacular scene, Kristi really felt blessed to have been given the opportunity to see all of it.

Carlos, the cabbie, was parked outside the museum as promised, missing his front teeth and all. After Kristi climbed in the front seat beside Carlos, he handed her a bag with a hamburger in it.

"Eat, you gotta be hungry, missy," Carlos said, shaking his head up and down, looking at the familiar fast-food restaurant bag.

"Oh, thank you, Carlos. How much do I owe you?"

"No, missy, you are good tipper. It's, how you say, on the house." Carlos grinned, showing the large empty space where teeth once were.

When Carlos dropped Kristi off at the cruise line port entrance, Kristi hugged and took one last picture of her cabby. She laughed when Carlos bobbed his head up and down, smiling. She had so much fun touring and taking pictures of Vancouver. She hoped the rest of her vacation could and would be this much fun.

CHAPTER 4

Zac was one of the last to board the ship. He felt torn, leaving San Francisco while his lifelong friend was still grieving. Yet he was grateful for the time he was able to spend with Mark, rehashing the past and reflecting on the good times. There had been nights when Mark had talked Zac through his darkest hours after Sara had died. There was no way Zac could ever repay Mark for that time.

When Zac left for the airport earlier in the day, Mark told him, "You haven't lost your mojo. Just find what makes it happen."

As Zac rode the elevator up to his cabin floor, he was impressed with the spaciousness of the ship. There were people milling around, but it still didn't seem crowded. There were open balconies looking down on marble floors and beautiful very impressive sculptures in showcases. After searching across the US and Europe for the perfect mermaids, he knew expensive sculptures when he saw them. There were staircases with polished brass railings and wall-to-ceiling glass windows looking out to sea. He wondered if Kristi had found the suite and, if she was, already settled in. He thought it was interesting she had contacted Frank inquiring about him. He knew Frank gave her the basics about him that she could have found out herself with a little internet searching. It was funny that Kristi had chosen Frank of all people to do a background check for her. He was actually glad she had inquired about who he was. Although her brothers were powerful attorneys like her father was, she kept a low profile. It was smart for her to be cautious. Of course, he grinned to himself, it was also good to know she wasn't a card-carrying nutcase.

Zac stopped and looked out the window across the Vancouver skyline. He realized he was actually excited about taking this trip. There were a lot of obstacles he had to maneuver around this past week, but stepping on board, he suddenly felt free. What was it Mark had said, something about he hadn't lost his mojo. Well, maybe this cruise would fix that too. He just had to keep a lookout for new menu ideas for his restaurant. Once that happened, he would claim this cruise a total success.

Zac slid his key card and opened the door to the posh signature suite. The main room was large with a beige sofa and coffee table, a couple of comfy-looking royal-blue chairs, and a credenza chest of drawers. He noticed the bottle of champagne compliments of A Weeks Adventure Travel Agency sitting in a bucket of ice on the credenza. The fruit basket, as part of the premier suite package he had purchased from the cruise line when searching for culinary excursions, was sitting on the coffee table. And then he saw it. The very large king-size bed with a beautiful satin comforter and royal-blue plush pillows. It never crossed his mind there would be only one bed. Most hotels with any class had two queen- or one king-size bed. They offered a choice. Of course, he hadn't been on a cruise in fifteen years. So things may have changed, but he hadn't slept with anyone other than his wife, in over twenty years. What was he thinking? He knew Kristi had seen it as her suitcase, and a backpack sat on the sofa. He could see her standing on the balcony through the sliding glass doors, watching the harbor activity. He wondered what she had thought. Was she mad? Was she going to scream and throw a tantrum? Judging by her stance at the balcony railing, she was taking pictures.

Taking a deep breath, Zac decided he better confront the situation immediately before the cruise ship pulled anchor or whatever they did to leave port. He may have to walk away from this vacation, after all. He walked through the open slider door and said, "Kristianna."

"Zac, you made it," Kristi said breathlessly as she lowered her camera. Jeans, a white shirt, and black sports jacket—dang, he looked good.

"Yes. So how are you doing? Was your flight good?" Zac asked, walking out onto the veranda, feeling the cool fresh air on his face.

"The flights were great, long, but hey, what can I expect flying across country? And yours?" Kristi said, knowing she was making nervous small chat.

"I've spent the last couple of days in Santa Cruz at a friend of my family's funeral," Zac said, looking beyond the harbor at the tree line of the mountainside.

"I'm so sorry for your loss. I thought…" Kristi hesitated. "I assumed you were going to San Francisco on business. You must be exhausted."

"Kristi," Zac said. "I saw the king-size bed. I better go to the information desk and see if I can get things changed."

"Don't bother. I already tried. The cruise ship is totally booked. There is not an extra suite anywhere. And no, they can't change out the bed in this suite to two double beds because the bed is actually bolted to the floor. They said due to the size of this suite, there is nothing they can do," Kristi said in frustration.

There it was again, Zac thought. He had seen the quick change in Kristi's expression once again. It was there and then gone like she briefly showed a side of her personality she usually kept hidden. It was something that triggered him into his badge-carrying scout role as Frank once called it. It baffled him because he didn't know her that well.

He questioned, "What do you want me to do?"

"I guess there is only one thing we can do. What side of the bed do you sleep on?" Kristi asked, looking directly at Zac.

"I sleep on my left side. Why?"

"Good, I will take the right side of the bed looking toward the balcony. And you sleep on your left side on the left side of the bed. It's a king-size bed. It will work," Kristi said, hoping her logic sounded reasonable.

"No, I'll sleep on the sofa."

"I sat on the sofa before you got here. You can't sleep on it. It's uncomfortable to sit on for more than five minutes. Sleeping on it every night, you wouldn't snore that's for sure. I'm afraid you would go after me with a butcher knife or Alana Weeks for setting this whole thing up when you get home," Kristi said with a shake of her head.

Zac walked over to the chilling bottle of champagne. He was trying to think of any other solution but couldn't. So he popped the cork and poured the pale frothy liquid into two flutes. He handed Kristi one and made a toast. He said with a wicked smile, "Here's to a very interesting cruise. May you not snore."

Kristi was so shocked by Zac's hilarious statement, she almost sneezed champagne out her nose. Any other time, she would have been embarrassed by her uncouth response to the toast, but that was the last thing she expected Zac to say. *Yes, Mr. Karas, I have no doubt this is going to be an interesting cruise,* Kristi thought as she grinned at the very sexy-looking guy standing in front of her.

As the cruise liner set sail north along the famous inside passage, Kristi and Zac decided upon eating in the main dining room. It was the last serving of dinner for the evening. Many travelers had already either retired to their rooms for the night or decided upon trying their luck in the casino.

Kristi chose the Chilean sea bass with creamy ricotta scalloped potatoes and asparagus while Zac ordered the French roasted duck with orange sauce, baby carrots, and jasmine rice. Another couple sat across from them studying the menu.

"We aren't used to such fancy foods. I'm Elsie and my husband, Ralph. This is our first cruise to Alaska," said the round-faced lady with blue eyes.

"Is there something special you would like to eat?" Kristi asked.

"Well, now, I was just hoping for a burger," Ralph said, looking up and down the menu board.

When the server whom Zac had motioned over asked if there was anything else he could help him with, Zac said, "Yes, Mr. Ralph would like a burger with cheese on it."

The server, whose name tag indicated he was "Alberto from Argentina," answered, "I'm sorry."

"It's not on the menu, but you will get it for Mr. Ralph right away, right, Alberto?" Zac stated as if that was exactly what Alberto was about to say. Zac grinned at Kristi.

"Your meals are being prepared as we speak. May I get you more bread?" Alberto said to no one in particular.

Elsie said they were from Kansas and were celebrating their fiftieth anniversary. She mentioned a couple of times, that their children had given them the cruise as a gift. She asked Kristi and Zac how long they had been married, in which Kristi put food in her mouth, and Zac took a sip of wine. After that, Kristi decided it was better to ask the questions than try to explain her and Zac's arrangement with someone who had been married for fifty years.

With dessert, Kristi asked Ralph what their plans were for Ketchikan. She could tell by the puzzled look on his face, they probably hadn't made any plans other than taking the cruise. So she said, "Ralph, why don't you and Elsie go to the excursion desk in the morning and see what there is available in each port to see and do?"

"Is there anything you would suggest, my dear?" Elsie asked.

"Each port has an entire list of things you can explore," Kristi explained.

"What are some of the excursions you picked?" Ralph asked.

"I am taking a tram ride into the rain forest of Icy Strait Point. Also, I booked the White Pass and Yukon train ride into Canada in Skagway. I am taking a helicopter trip up to the Mendenhall Glacier, and I'm going on a whale-watching trip. Oh, and I am taking an evening flight to the Arctic Circle when we reach Fairbanks. I have several more things planned. But anyway, there are huge lists to choose from," Kristi said, looking forward to her upcoming adventures.

Elsie turned to Zac and said, "Are you as excited about doing all those things as your wife?"

"I'm taking a boat to haul crabs to a food festival. I'm also going salmon fishing. I'm a chef, so I'm into food," Zac said with a shrug, ignoring the wife comment.

Elsie was about to say something when Ralph stood from his chair. He said, "It's time for me and the missus to head to our room. It was nice meeting you folks. Thank you for the information. You all have a nice night."

After Ralph and Elsie left the table, Zac turned to Kristi and said, "I didn't realize you were such an adventurous person. You really are taking an evening flight to the Arctic Circle?"

"Yes, the flight leaves from Fairbanks at 7:00 p.m. and returns at midnight. Sorry, but it sounds a lot more fun than salmon fishing," Kristi said.

Zac set his napkin on the table and offered his hand to Kristi. He said, "Ready to try your luck in the casino?"

Browsing past the noisy coin machines and all the filled poker game tables, Zac took a chair at the blackjack table. He soon had a drink by his arm and was focused on the cards he was dealt. Kristi watched for a while. It amazed her how absorbed he became in the hand he was dealt. After a while Kristi got tired of watching and decided to walk around the slot machines and quarter games. Nothing seemed to interest her. She finally settled back at the bar overlooking the poker and blackjack tables. She took her time sipping a rum and soda and watching Zac play cards. Every once in a while, he would scan the bar area until he saw her. His dark eyes and wicked grin were such a turn-on, Kristi thought. She wondered if he realized how sexy he was.

Kristi was getting tired. Maybe if she played some slots, she would wake up a bit. She decided to exchange a twenty-dollar bill for some quarters. A few of the slot machines were boring looking, and some were kind of complex; the odds of winning were not so good. She finally found a slot machine available that was middle of the line. She won some quarters, then lost some quarters then won some more.

"I see you are winning some cash there," a blond curly-haired guy said to her as he sat down next to her chair. He dropped a quarter in the machine and won nothing.

"Yeah, but a few more quarters, and I can lose it all," Kristi said flatly.

"That's true. Can I buy you a drink?"

"No. But thanks, I'm good," Kristi said, trying not to encourage the guy. He looked like he could be a sloppy, drunk kind of guy.

"Are you one of the bridesmaids here for the big wedding this weekend?"

"No. There is a wedding this weekend on board?" Kristi asked. She had never thought of getting married on a cruise ship. She wasn't sure if sea captains could marry people at sea. If she remembered correctly their license did not include marrying people. Besides, ships were owned by different countries, and the laws of some countries were tricky about such things.

"Yes. At dinner, there were about twenty people all talking about it. It sounded like it will be in one of the banquet halls. I think it would be fun to crash that wedding," the guy said.

"If you were flipping the bill for a huge wedding and someone crashed your party, wouldn't you be mad?" Kristi asked. She felt like she was once again speaking the voice of reason to someone her son's age, not an adult.

"Oh, hell yeah, I would beat the crap out of them."

"Well, there you are." Kristi grinned. Just then a voucher for $98 slid out of the machine. She quickly put it in the bucket with her quarters. She was hoping the guy didn't see it. Actually, she wished he would just go away. Kristi picked up her bucket and started to move to another machine. She changed her mind and walked to the desk to cash out the several vouchers she picked up over the past hour playing. Unfortunately the guy followed.

"So are you done playing for the night?" the guy asked.

"Yes, I have lots planned for tomorrow," Kristi said as she walked out of the casino. The guy trailed behind her.

"Are you going to buy me a drink with your winnings?"

"No, but I am going to buy my husband something from the gift shop," Kristi said and kept on walking.

Thank goodness the guy didn't follow her after that. Kristi glanced down at her watch as she continued to walk back to her suite. She realized although it was only eleven in the evening, it was actually two in the morning back home. No wonder she was tired.

Back in the suite, the cabin steward had turned back the bed quilt, and mints had been placed on the pillows. The empty bottle of champagne and glasses had been removed from the room. There was a fresh bowl of ice and bottled water waiting on the table. The fruit basket hadn't been touched yet. Kristi showered and readied her side of the bed. She opened the sliding glass door and walked out onto the balcony. The night was cool but not cold. She heard quiet talk from one of the verandas below. Kristi longed for that special something in the late-night hours between lovers. To be held close while standing on the balcony. Kristi knew better than to dwell on silly romantic stuff like that. She picked the wrong kind of guys. And the only way to break that cycle was to not look. Kristi started to laugh as her thoughts drifted to Zac. He was absolutely beautiful to look at but only interested in prime cuts of meat. Leaning on the balcony railing, Kristi grinned and decided she would never make it as a standup comic.

She looked at the silhouette of the mountains leading down to the dark water. It was such a calming sight. Leaving the slider open, Kristi thought about exploring the ship tomorrow as she climbed between the sheets. And in keeping her bargain with Zac, she lay on her right side, watching the water as she slowly drifted asleep.

It was near midnight when Zac finally called it an evening. He knew his luck would run out if he stayed any longer. After cashing in his winnings, he slowly walked back to the room. Kristi surprised him at dinner. The excursions she had chosen were bold, not quite what he expected of her. Her adventuresome nature was fascinating. However, he had seen that sleazy guy talking to Kristi while she was playing the slots. She had the right to talk to anyone she wanted to. He wasn't about to interfere with her vacation, but guys like that came into the restaurant looking for classy chicks to prey on. And that bothered him. He wondered if Kristi had a nightcap with the dirtbag. It was none of his business, he decided and continued to walk the long hall in search of their room.

The suite was quiet when Zac walked in. Only the sound of water rushing against the side of the ship was heard from the open slider door. A shell-shaped wall sconce dimly illuminated the room.

Zac was going to check if Kristi was sitting out on one of the deck chairs. But no, as he walked toward the veranda, he could see she was asleep on *her* side of the bed. He slid the slider closed and locked the door.

The fragrance of Kristi's body lotion lingered in the steamy air when Zac turned off the shower in the bathroom. It was a soft but rich buttery scent of shea and something else. Unable and too tired to differentiate the other fragrance, Zac toweled off and climbed into bed. He hated when his mind wouldn't shut down, but tonight…

CHAPTER 5

Kristi never needed an alarm clock to wake up. At six in the morning, day one of her vacation, Kristi tiptoed into the bathroom, not to disturb Zac. She exchanged her nightgown for comfortable exercise wear and running shoes. She closed the suite door and made her way to the jogging track and fitness center. Kristi loved the early morning hours of the day. Everything looked fresh, even today when the sky was cloudy, and mist hung over the mountain range in the distance. There were only a few people walking around the halls or even in the main corridors, probably because it was their first day of vacation. Kristi smelled the aroma of freshly brewed coffee as she passed the not-yet-open dining area. It was a good time to get in some exercises because if breakfast was as good as the delicious scent in the air, she would be in workout hell forever!

By eight fifteen, Kristi had burned off enough energy; she was sweaty and starving. She sprinted back to the suite with a towel around her neck in hopes of a quick shower before breakfast. Zac was standing at the bathroom sink in a pair of jeans and nothing more. Dang, he was even sexy while shaving.

"Morning," Kristi said, smiling as she walked to the bed and flopped down spread eagle. She didn't mind having to wait for the shower; however, she realized she needed to get a grip on her emotions, or it would be a really long one-sided frustrating vacation!

"Already hit the fitness center? Um, you know you are on vacation, right?" Zac said as he pulled on a T-shirt with his Mermaid Isle logo on it.

Looking at Zac's chest, grinning and nodding at his front, she said, "You're on vacation, right?"

"I like this shirt."

"Yeah, it's pretty cool looking." As Kristi rolled over on her side to study the shirt, she said, "I want one."

"I'll have my secretary send one to you. Or you can come down again for dinner, and I'll give you one then," Zac said, sitting down on the sofa. "So what do you have planned for today?"

"I'm going to take a quick shower, then breakfast," Kristi said as she got up to rummage through the outfits she brought along.

"I can wait for you, and we can eat together."

"Okay, give me ten minutes."

While Zac was waiting for Kristi to get ready, he grabbed the list of last-minute excursions still available. Kristi's plans for each port sounded fun. Lacey was right; he had gotten so caught up with the running of the restaurant; he had forgotten how to enjoy the moment. And Kristi was right; salmon fishing did sound boring.

Fifteen minutes later, Kristi emerged from the bathroom in black jeans and a black-and-white printed sweatshirt. She slipped into black shorty boots. She figured a day at sea, she could dress casually. Grabbing her camera, she turned to Zac and said, "I'm starving, ready to eat?" She lifted her camera and started clicking pictures of Zac.

"Wait a minute, you can't take my picture!"

Kristi, opening the door, almost ran into the cabin steward. So again she lifted her camera and took his picture also. "Thanks," Kristi called and walked quickly to the elevator, giggling all the way.

Zac decided to take the stairs two at a time. When the elevator opened and Kristi walked out, Zac pulled her close and said, "Give me the camera or you're whale chum, understand?"

"Never!" Kristi giggled.

Then out of the corner of her eye, Kristi saw the creepy blond guy from the casino last night leaning against the railing watching her and Zac. She tried to ignore him, but he came over and in front of Zac said, "Did your wife tell you how much she won last night? I thought she was pretty rude when she wouldn't buy me a drink."

"I think you should stay away from my wife, or I will call security," Zac said, taking Kristi's hand, and walked toward the dining room.

"Thank you," Kristi whispered. "Saying I was married, I thought he would leave me alone."

Once seated and breakfast ordered, Kristi started scanning through the pictures she had taken of Zac. One was blurry, delete. Another was so fantastic; she quickly clicked to the next picture, knowing she would review it again later, privately. Another picture caught his sexy grin. She thought she was going to melt and slip under the table. The picture she took of the steward caught the surprised look on his face when she snapped the photo. It was really cute.

"So, wife of mine, how much did you win last night?" Zac said, grinning.

"About $240," Kristi said, pretending to go along with his wife comment, but continued to look at the pictures on her camera.

"That much on quarter slots. I should have played the slots instead of blackjack," Zac said. He didn't want to lecture or insult Kristi on her choice of guys when she clearly hadn't encouraged the guy. All he could do was keep an eye out and make sure she had fun on her vacation.

"So how much did you win?" Kristi asked.

"Only $190, but that was actually good for me, I usually lose."

"I was playing the quarter machines last night, minding my own business as usual," Kristi said, dramatically putting her hand on her heart.

"Of course," Zac said, grinning.

"I was. Stop teasing me. Anyway, that guy sat down at the slot next to me and offered me a drink. I said no thank you."

"I have noticed that about you, very polite."

"Quit it! You are interrupting my story."

"Sorry."

"Hey, this is important. If I get murdered, you need to know the prequel to the story. So he just kept talking. I was tired. It was late. I decided to leave, hoping he would get the hint and move on. Well, he thought I should have bought him a drink with the money I won. I told him I was going to spend my winnings on my husband at the gift shop and walked away. He gave me the creeps."

"It was probably a good thing you mentioned a husband. And then he saw you with me this morning," Zac said, no longer teasing.

"Are you going to let me see the pictures?" Zac asked, leaning toward the camera. He figured changing the subject was a good thing right about now.

"Sure." Kristi pulled up the first pictures she had taken yesterday of Vancouver, and there were some photos from the balcony of the harbor when they were leaving. She showed Zac how to arrow over to each picture. It was a total enjoyment to watch him so focused on the pictures she had taken.

"These are really good. How did you get to all these places? How long were you in Vancouver before you boarded the ship?"

"Thank you. I hired a cabdriver named Carlos. He drove me around Vancouver for about four hours."

"Are you kidding me, four hours? Wow, where is this?" Zac asked as he studied one photo.

"That is Granville Island. There was a cool little pub by some of the shops."

"Wait a minute, you can't keep these. I look like a wide mouth bass about to be cooked," Zac pleaded.

"Not everything is about food, Zac!" Kristi said, grabbing the camera from him, just as their breakfast arrived.

Looking at their plates set before them, Zac said, "Kristi, did you really order everything on the menu?"

"Yeah, I guess I did. I was hungry, but how am I going to go rock wall climbing after eating all this?"

"You are going rock wall climbing?" Zac questioned.

"Yeah, at ten thirty, why?"

"I'm just surprised. Have you done it before?" Zac asked.

"I have paid big bucks for my son to do it. It looked like fun. But I didn't want to embarrass him, if I wasn't any good at it, so I never tried it. However, I am going to give it a try now, and he will never know if I get stuck on the beginners' wall," Kristi said in frustration.

"He will if I take pictures of you!"

"You wouldn't dare," Kristi said as she picked up a piece of bacon and pressed it to his lips.

Zac realized that their teasing had become the center of attention at the table of six. He grinned at Kristi and began eating his shrimp omelet.

It was almost 10:00 a.m. when they walked out of the dining room. Since Kristi had eaten so much, she decided to see if she could reschedule her rock climbing until closer to noon. While they were checking on time reschedule availability, Zac signed up to test his adventure side.

"I thought you have a fruit and vegetable carving demo you are going to attend," Kristi said, trying to sound sarcastic.

"I do, at two thirty," Zac said, regally pretending to straighten a tie at his neck.

"Oh my gosh." Kristi burst out laughing. "I'm going shopping. You're crazy."

While Kristi browsed the designer boutiques, Zac slipped into one of the men's exclusive shops and bought sportswear. He didn't want Kristi to know until this vacation he hadn't thought about much but food preparation. He returned to the suite, pulled the tags off the shirt and sport pants, and put them in his side of the closet. He left the suite shortly afterward and walked to the excursion desk.

A few minutes before noon, Kristi stopped at the information desk. There were several people in line before her, but she waited.

"Yes, may I help you?" said the man behind the counter.

"I want to report an incident both last night and this morning. It may be nothing, but it scared me," Kristi said.

"Your vacation enjoyment is very important to us. If you are feeling unsafe about something, we are here to help."

"Thank you." Kristi retold the story to the guest relations man and his supervisor. She described the blond-haired guy as best she could. She was told there were security cameras throughout the ship for the safety of the passengers. They would look into it. Kristi really felt like she was being patted on the top of her head and sent out to play. The security cameras wouldn't show anything other than a blond guy talking to Kristi and the same guy standing casually at the wall by the elevator the next day.

As Kristi had always believed, she would just have to make sure she protected herself by staying in well-lit areas and around other people.

Kristi returned to the room to change back into her sports clothes. Zac had also returned earlier though and said, "All that shopping and you didn't buy anything? Should I call for the ship's doctor?"

"Very funny," Kristi said from the bathroom where she changed quickly. "Actually, everything was made in other countries, and I only want to buy things made in Alaska."

"Oh, that's a good idea," Zac said. "Do you want a water to take with?"

"Yeah, thanks," Kristi said, grabbing her camera bag, key card, the water Zac handed her, and a towel.

"Oh, on the way back to the room, I stopped by the information desk and talked to the guest relations person about the creepy guy."

"He didn't bother you while you were shopping, did he?" Zac said, staring at her.

"No, I just figured they should be aware, so if someone else complains about him, they have documentation," Kristi said casually so Zac wouldn't get all testosterone on her. "Come on, I'm going to go take out my frustrations climbing a fake mountain."

An hour later, after instructions and getting strapped into the harness to prevent falls, Kristi was inching her way stone by stone up the rock wall. Zac slipped the camera out of her bag. He was in awe of Kristi's agility. He took picture after picture of difficult reaches Kristi made. She was limber and fearless of the fact she was scaling a wall on board a ship that was almost twenty stories above the sea. That took guts.

When Kristi reached the top, she yelled, "It's beautiful up here!"

"Okay, now hold the clamp like I showed you and rappel slowly down the wall. Hold the rope with your left hand, release, and clamp…There you go. You are doing great," the instructor yelled to Kristi as he talked her down the wall. "For a first-timer, you are doing great."

Zac could tell Kristi was on an adrenaline rush from the climb. Her face was flushed, and she was grinning from ear to ear. Zac had slipped her camera back in her bag and walked over to hug her. He whispered, "Your son would be proud. You did great."

"Yes! I did it!" Kristi said, fisting the air.

And then it was Zac's turn. He had studied Kristi's moves. And although she had made it look easy, it wasn't. He could feel his muscles burn as he gripped outcrop rocks during the climb. When he stopped to take a quick break, he realized the view of the horizon was breathtaking. He understood Kristi's excitement over the spectacular sight. The clouds from the morning had burned off. The sky was a vivid blue, and the temperature was cool but great for the workout. It was the perfect day for cruising along the Canadian border. He slowly continued to the top.

After Zac rappelled down, Kristi with camera in hand told him she got some excellent photos of him and of course his backside. He had laughed and hugged her.

While Zac headed off to the carving demonstration, Kristi decided to spend a little time being pampered in the steam room. She was hoping to relax a bit. The rock climb had been so much fun. But she already noticed her muscles were tightening up. Still, she couldn't wait to tell Eli about her climb when she got home. She thought about how much she enjoyed touring around Vancouver. It was a place she could see herself flying back to. There was so much more to see than she was able to cram into the four short hours she had.

The warm mist circled around Kristi. She could feel the strained muscles in her calves start to relax. The humid air felt like home, but without the salty tinge, Kristi thought. Her mind drifted to Zac's spontaneous hug at the wall. His embrace felt so good. He seemed genuinely happy she had accomplished her goal. And the comment about Eli even made it more special. It wasn't the first time she had noticed Zac had picked up on the small fine details of their conversations.

Kristi's thoughts slammed against a brick wall, and her relaxation was interrupted by three women who sat down on the steamy bench across from her. They laughed and snickered about their male scoring in one of the bars. They seemed proud of their achievement their first night out.

Why wasn't the creepy blond guy hitting on them instead of bothering her last night? Listening to the conversation of the three across from her, they would have devoured him like a midnight snack. Oh my gosh, Kristi thought, why was every thought related to food?

With regret, Kristi pulled her now very relaxed body off the bench. She wondered if Zac was back from his demonstration.

"Don't leave on our account," said one from the cackling trio.

"No, my muscles have turned to mush. It's time for me to go," Kristi mumbled and then thought, *food again.*

A towel animal sat on the bed with Kristi's sunglass on its head when she returned to the suite. It was so cute. Kristi grabbed her camera and took a couple of pictures. Still smiling, she walked out onto the balcony. The clouds had returned, and a chill was in the air. Kristi pulled the quilt off the bed. Funny how within a few short minutes, she had trashed the room as she surveyed the now rumpled bed. Sitting on the deck chair, though, curled up in the blanket, seemed like a perfect way to spend the afternoon: napping. And so she did.

Zac had seen Kristi sleeping in one of the balcony chairs after he had returned from the carving demonstration. She looked so relaxed. He figured since they had been rock climbing during the lunch service hours, Kristi probably hadn't eaten. So he ordered a lite lunch from room service.

He realized sitting across from Kristi watching her sleep was a luxury he would never have dreamed he would be doing, a week ago. There was always something that needed to be taken care of at the restaurant. Someone wanted a vacation or needed a day off, leaving the crew short-staffed. He hated when his team members were spread short or the fear that quality might slip. So he didn't mind filling in since creating beautiful meals for people was his love. When the room service order arrived, he took the foods and wine out and set it on the little round table next to Kristi's chair. She looked so comfortable and snug sleeping there. He hated to wake her.

Kristi dreamed of walking through a wooded area full of lots of moss. It was beautiful and so green. She took pictures of the thickness, the texture, how it grew up the sides of trees and along the path. Time was passing, and she knew she should head back. But she was drawn to the detailed structure of the moss-draped across a downed tree.

It was misty and almost dark. The fog had started rolling in off the inlet below the trail. It was silvery white and smelled of salt. She tried to turn around and walk the way she came, but the trail had vanished. Moss had carpeted where the path once was. It seemed like it was harder and harder to navigate between the exposed tree roots and the slippery wet dirt. She didn't want to panic when she heard a rustling deep in the forest. From which way the sound came, she didn't know. With a snap behind her, Kristi sat up.

"Zac!"

"Kristi, what happened?"

Taking a few deep breaths, she said, "I got lost. I was walking. There was the most beautiful moss. I was taking pictures of it. But the fog rolled in. I don't know. I got turned around somehow. It was so real." Feeling so disoriented, she looked around and tried to stand, but her legs were tangled in the quilt.

Zac grabbed Kristi before she fell. He pulled her into his lap. "Here, take a sip of wine."

Kristi was surprised how quickly Zac had prevented her from tripping on the quilt. She kind of liked the feel of Zac's arm around her waist. It felt safe. "I never have nightmares," she said as she felt the cool liquid slip smoothly down her throat.

"Well, look at all you have done in the last two days. You jetted across the continent; traipsed all over Vancouver, British Columbia, in four hours, no less, with a sweet, toothless cabdriver; and climbed twenty stories above sea level on plastic rocks. And now, you fear getting lost?" Zac questioned.

"You're right. Where did the food come from?" Kristi asked, noticing the tray of hors d'oeuvres sitting on the little table. She didn't want to think about the damp darkness closing in on her anymore.

"While you were sleeping, I ordered room service. I figured you hadn't eaten."

Kristi stood and examined the array of foods sitting on the little table. She took a sample of cheese and a piece of cured meat and placed them on a round cracker. She sat down on the chair opposite of Zac and said, "Thank you. This was very thoughtful of you. I'm actually starving. Oh, how was the carving demonstration?"

"There were four guys and twenty-something women, so they chose me to assist in carving, to prove how easy it was. Go figure."

"So how was it?"

"There were a couple of tricks I had never thought of. But the end results were pretty impressive. And not all that time-consuming. I think creating interesting carvings out of melons or gourds for special occasion table decor would be striking in the right setting," Zac said, taking a sip of his wine.

"I'm glad you were able to take some ideas away from the demo. This prosciutto is fantastic," Kristi said, examining the thinly sliced piece of Italian ham.

"Yes, its flavor is top quality. Oh, I forgot to tell you. I hope you don't mind. I booked us at the Brazilian grill for dinner tonight," Zac said, placing a black olive in his mouth.

"Isn't that one of the specialty dining areas?" Kristi asked.

"Yes, but I thought it would be interesting. Have you eaten Brazilian cuisine before? I mean, if you don't want to go, I can cancel," Zac said, looking directly at Kristi for an answer.

"Isn't there a Brazilian restaurant in Sarasota and also one in St. Pete?" Kristi asked, trying hard not to look outclassed.

"Yes, there are. I really like them both. Have you been to either one of them?" Zac asked.

"No. So yes, I would like to go to the Brazilian grill tonight. However…" Kristi paused as she watched Zac roll his eyes. "I will pay for my dinner."

"Too late, I have already put the meals on my tab. No big deal, I want you to experience the different cultural flavors."

Kristi and Zac spent the rest of the afternoon lounging on the balcony sipping wine and talking about nothing in particular. Kristi brought out her camera and used the four-hundred-millimeter lens to look across the water. She stood at the railing and watched dolphins riding the surf from the ship. She handed Zac the camera so he too could get a closer look. It was really quite interesting how Zac wanted her to experience his culinary world. Maybe that enthusiasm was part of his charm. Taking a deep breath, Kristi kept reminding herself, every time she gazed at him, in two weeks, life would return to normal. He and his fantastic looks would go on with his life, which didn't include her.

"Kristi? Earth to Kristi, Kristianna!"

"What? Sorry," Kristi said.

"You are thinking too hard."

"Oh, I was just wondering if we would get to see whales breaching or if it is too early in the season." Kristi dodged the truth, not wanting him to realize she was thinking of him.

Zac had to swallow twice when Kristi emerged from the bathroom ready for dinner later that evening. She wore a long, almost-to-the-knee black sweater, several gold chain necklaces, black nylons, and short boots. He didn't know how he was going to get through dinner sitting next to her without drooling, not over the food but about her. Funny thing was, he didn't think she was aware just how strikingly pretty she was.

The Brazilian Grill was in the stern area of deck II. Most of the guests were still not quite familiar with the whereabouts of many of the specialty diners were held. But since Kristi had made her share of wrong turns early in the morning on the way to the fitness center, she was feeling more confident navigating the decks. Zac had explained on the way to the Brazilian Grill that it was all about churrasco a rodizio or rotisserie barbeque meats, slowly cooked over wood. When he opened the door for Kristi, the aroma of grilling vegetables and smoking meats teased the salty sea air. A few couples were chatting at green-and-yellow linen-covered tables. Kristi assumed the colors were representative of the Brazilian flag.

"Right this way, please," the host said as he guided Kristi and Zac to a table near the glass windows looking out over the stern of the ship.

Another person came set a drinks menu in front of them and a stone platter. "Take a moment to look over the beverage menu. Please enjoy your pao de queijo. It is Brazilian cheese bread made with yucca flour and blended cheeses."

A drinks steward stepped in front of the table momentarily and asked if they had decided on their beverage. Kristi ordered the tucanos, which was mango, passion fruit, pineapple, papaya, lemon-lime, ice cream, and rum. Zac ordered a scotch and water.

Kristi looked across the water and remarked, "What a beautiful evening. I wonder if sea captains get tired of looking at the oceans their whole career."

"No, I loved it my entire life," said a man sitting across from Zac and Kristi. "I am retired Navy. I had command of my own ship for the last eight years of my career."

"What an honor. Were you out of Norfolk?" Kristi asked.

"Actually, I was in the Persian Gulf, the Gulf of Oman, and the Arabian Sea."

"Those are some dangerous waters," Zac said. "And you are still sailing the seas after you retired."

"My wife books cruises to keep me happy," the man said, grinning at his wife.

Drinks were placed in front of them. Zac ordered calamari for their appetizer. But raised his brows to Kristi for confirmation in which she nodded yes. Other guests ordered hors d'oeuvres some exotic and some guests not as risky. Someone farther down the table asked a few more questions of the retired Navy commander. It was obvious; he had a very interesting career filled with many unique tales.

The calamari appetizer arrived. It was served with a sweet but zesty carnival sauce. One man ordered the feijoada, which was a black-bean-and-meat stew served over rice. Kristi was glad she didn't order that. The serving size was more like a complete meal. The naval commander's wife asked Zac if the calamari was cooked correctly. Zac inspected the squid a little bit more closely and said, "I believe the strips have been tossed in manioc flour before frying. Some use a tempura batter, which is a bit heavier. But these have a tender texture and a sweet taste."

Kristi stared at Zac while he was describing the calamari. He said, "What? She asked. And I told her."

Kristi just shook her head and reached for her drink. She realized that Zac knew his craft well. He appreciated fine culinary skills. And that was probably the reason for his restaurants' success. It was all about the details.

The main course was decided upon by each of the guests at the table. While they nibbled on their appetizers, conversations again flowed. Drinks were replenished while they waited. One lady pulled out a huge diamond pendant necklace from its resting place on her breasts. She whispered that she bought it in the diamond gift shop on the way to dinner. A man at the end of the table broke into the conversation and said he spent the afternoon in the casino. He acted rather proud of the fact; however, he then complained about the exorbitant amount he had lost. Kristi looked at the commander's wife; her mouth had fallen open. She looked at Kristi and raised her hand to her chin and pushed up. Zac elbowed Kristi as she turned her head to the window to keep from laughing.

"Kristi, how did you spend your day?" the naval commander asked, steering the conversation away from the complaining man.

Kristi said sheepishly, "I went rock climbing."

"Good God, to the top?"

"Yes."

The commander seemed somewhat amazed that Kristi would try rock climbing.

Finally, the Brazilian gauchos brought skewers of meat to the tables. Zac had ordered the contra file, which was the New York strip, while Kristi ordered the alcatra, the center-cut sirloin steak. The gauchos carved and plated the meats in front of the guests. Each meal was served with tomato wedges, slices of yucca, onions, and broccoli. The gauchos beautifully showcased their skills as meat carvers.

"Oh my, this meat is tender," the commander said.

"The yucca tastes like a potato cooked in walnut oil. What do you think, Chef Zac?" the commander's wife asked Zac.

"Yes, yuccas do have a somewhat nutty potato flavor. I do not ever recall using it in French cuisine though," Zac said, grinning at the commander's wife.

"Our cooks never cooked with yuccas aboard ship in all my years either," stated the commander as he inspected the yucca on his fork.

Zac asked, "Kris, are you enjoying your meal?"

"Yes. Thank you for inviting me. The atmosphere here is not as great as Mermaid Isle, but it is pretty terrific," Kristi whispered back. She was rather shocked that Zac had shortened her name. No one had called her Kris except her father.

"Just wait till you try the dessert. If it is anything like what the Brazilian restaurant in Sarasota offers, you are in for a treat."

"But I'm so full now. I'm going to have to be in the fitness center most of the vacation if I keep this up," Kristi complained.

The commander's wife said, "I agree, Kristi. Did you go to the fitness center this morning, or was the rock wall your exercise for the day?"

"I worked out early this morning before the center got crowded. But the rock wall was a workout in itself. Zac did the wall also. I got some great pictures of his climb."

"I'm sure you captured some great photo memories that will be with you two for many years to come," the commander's wife said.

The kind woman's words hit a tender spot in Kristi's heart. She knew there would be a time when all the photos she was taking of Zac, the landscape, coming port stops, and the beauty she was seeing all around her would probably feel like a knife slicing through her heart.

Zac put his hand over Kristi's hand. He didn't have to look in her eyes to know she already knew their time together was limited and her photos would be the reminder. She deserved so much more, he thought.

The dessert menu was handed out. A photo of each item made selections more enticing than just words and descriptions. A great marketing idea, Zac thought. Maybe he could get Kristi to photograph each of the dessert selections at his restaurant. He wondered if it would increase revenue on that part of his menu. He could also design a late evening dessert and champagne menu. It could bring in the after-theater and other venue clientele. It was something to think about.

"Zac? the commander just asked what you were planning for dessert," Kristi said with concern in her voice.

"I was just thinking about asking you to photograph our desserts at the restaurant. If I designed a dessert and champagne menu, it would bring in an entirely different customer base," Zac confessed.

"Just like my husband, always thinking about work," one of the ladies down the table said, shaking her head.

"No, what do you think you want to order for dessert?" Kristi said slowly.

"Oh, sorry, I'm going to have the a'mazon."

"That is what I was considering having also. Tell me about your restaurant," the commander said to Zac.

While most at the table ordered the fudge brownie, Kristi had chosen the banana flambada. Fried spiced bananas with ice cream didn't sound as rich and filling as the a'mazon.

It was interesting to see everyone listening while Zac described his restaurant to the commander.

"Did you create the recipes for your dinner entrées?" one lady asked.

"Did you get your culinary degree in the states or in Europe?"

"Where did you come up with the name Mermaid Isle and where are you located?"

"Kristi, are you Zac's tester?"

It was fun to see the people at the table all interested in Zac's restaurant, Kristi thought. He described dishes from the menu. He told some funny tales that had occurred during a couple of important events. He had everyone laughing. Zac was in his element. With conversations flowing, their table was the last to leave at closing time.

Kristi and Zac slowly walked back down the hall from the way they came earlier in the evening. They wandered past the walls of art gallery quality paintings for sale, none of which caught Kristi's eye. She had expected Zac to suggest going to the casino for a while. She knew, if he did, she would have begged off. She had her fill of the creepy guy last night. She figured he was harassing someone else tonight. Maybe if she would have played the poker tables, he wouldn't have bothered her. He was probably the kind of sleazy guy who hit on women who were sitting at the slot machines, easy prey.

"Kris, would you like to stop here at the piano bar for a drink?" Zac asked Kristi.

"Yes, sure, that sounds nice," Kristi said as she looked around for a seat.

"What can I get you?"

"Amaretto and grapefruit juice, please."

A woman was singing a blues ballad so slowly, so seductively; a large number of people had stopped to listen. Her voice was low and raspy as she sang the story of a lost love. Even the pained look on her face reflected the sadness of the song. The piano man somehow echoed the heartbroken tale, note by note.

The bartender handed Zac his Jack and Cola and Kristi's favorite drink. Zac took a quick sip and nodded his appreciation to the mixologist before taking a seat next to Kristi. He leaned over and set her drink on the small table between them. With the woodsy taste of the liquor on his tongue, the sultry song being sung, and the scent of Kristi's body lotion so close to him, the combination definitely interrupted his thought process.

The next song was a familiar song Norah Jones had sung many times. Several couples swayed together on the dimly lit dance floor. Kristi sipped her drink. Its mellow flavor and the bittersweet words of the song crept into Kristi's soul. The lyrics unlocked a chamber of her heart. One, until this moment, she had kept buried deep to prevent feelings she couldn't handle. She wanted so much to be loved, really loved. Not the kind where she was only good enough until someone, not necessarily better, just sexier, came along.

Zac's hand reached down and slowly pulled Kris to her feet. He held her close as the music washed over them. Zac knew he would always love Sara; she gave him Lacey, his witty and beautiful daughter. But Sara was gone over two years now. He didn't want to be disloyal to her, but Kris brought warmth to his soul. She was someone he actually wanted to get to know, to be with. His heart ached, and his head hurt from thinking. But he realized the scent of Kris, touching her, holding her close, dancing slowly with her to the seductive music somehow felt like a soothing balm to his heart.

One song led into another and another. Time drifted by without notice until finally it was time to go. Zac kept hold of Kris's hand as they slowly walked to the elevator. Once inside the glass-walled lift, they stood staring out into the darkness of the ocean, in the late hour of the evening. Too exhausted from emotion, neither needed to talk as they walked the final passageway back to their suite.

Zac could see their cabin was dimly lit as he held the door open for Kristi to walk through. Not saying a word, Kristi stepped into the bathroom. After closing the door, she changed into her nightgown. Standing in front of the mirror, she looked at her reflection. She thought she looked haggard and old at that moment, so she quickly scrubbed her face and turned off the light.

Zac was already in bed, resting on his left side as promised. Smiling at the remembered rules she had set, Kristi crawled in between the sheets. Instead of curling up on her right side though, she lay on her back blankly looking at the ceiling. She was frustrated and angry at her raw emotions. After all this was her vacation. She didn't want to waste it analyzing the past.

After a while, Zac rolled over. He reached down between them and raised her hand to his lips.

"I enjoyed climbing the wall today. I wish I would have thought to ask you to take some pictures of my climb. Lacey will never believe I went rock wall climbing when I tell her," Zac said.

"Ah, I got a couple of great shots of your buns heading up the wall." Kristi laughed, one part out of the confession and the other part because his backside was dang good-looking.

"Oh." Zac laughed as he rolled toward Kristi. "I want to get to know you," he said quietly. He rested his lips on Kristi's forehead momentarily. He didn't give Kristi a chance to protest or deny his statement. He pulled her gently against his chest and whispered, "Good night, bunkmate!" and closed his eyes.

CHAPTER 6

Four thirty in the morning, a silvery mist covered the mountains of the inside passage as the ship sailed closer to Ketchikan. The sky was turning a pale gray. Kristi tried to keep her eyes closed, but they wouldn't stay shut. It was too early to get up; besides, she didn't want to disturb Zac. Last night was fantastic. The meal was great. The food was superb. She and Zac had been seated next to some really nice individuals. The conversations were an odd mixture of getting to know the people at the table, their quirky behaviors, and some very diverse personalities. The naval commander and his very quiet wife stood out in Kristi's mind. His wife was such a kind soul. Kristi thought she would have enjoyed getting to know them. But with the average cruise ship, there were about five thousand passengers, so they might never meet again.

The music at the piano bar brought back all the sadness of a marriage thrown away by her ex-husband's infidelity. Kristi's mind drifted back to that sad part of her life. At first, he had been fun; he loved, cherished, and lavished her with expensive gifts. He luxuriated in the glittery money empire he was building. It had been expected of her to host lavish dinner parties for the elite of Atlanta, at a moment's notice, which she did without any qualms. He had promised her the world. And she had naively believed in him. It was after Elijah was born that he lost interest. He looked at her differently, as if he was embarrassed she was a mother. Like a page out of a novel, he started working late and was always on the phone, whispering. That was the beginning of the end. A tear slipped onto Kristi's pillow. It was at that point in her life, she decided she would never trust a man with her heart again.

Kristi vowed she would not waste any more of her vacation thinking of her past. It was over long ago. In fact, if it wasn't for the piano blues, the memories and the sadness probably wouldn't have even surfaced. She slipped out of bed to get ready for her adventures in Ketchikan. She dressed for a day of being out in the damp, cool weather. When she walked out of the bathroom, she noticed Zac was dressed standing at the balcony drinking a cup of coffee. Kristi knew it would do no good to ignore the emotions that were left hanging from last night.

"Have you seen any whales breaching this morning?" Kristi asked as she walked out to the railing of the balcony.

"No. I would have gotten you a cup of coffee, but I know you don't drink the stuff," Zac said, raising his cup to his lips.

"Thanks for the thought. Hey, I'm really sorry I was a downer last night," Kristi said, watching the water go by.

"No, it was me. The lyrics to some of the songs last night took me to places in my mind that probably should have been kept under lock and key. You know?"

"Yeah," Kristi agreed. "How did she die?"

"Some kids in a stolen car, out for a joy ride, slammed into her car as she drove home from work one evening. She died on impact," Zac said quietly.

Wow, Kristi thought. Here she had been wallowing in self-pity when Zac had his heart ripped out in a matter of moments. How did one live after that?

"Your loss, I'm so sorry," Kristi whispered. It was all she could think at the moment to say.

"Hey, give me ten minutes to shower and shave. I'll walk to breakfast with you, or..." Zac smiled.

"No, I'll wait."

Everyone must have had the same idea. The dining areas were full of people milling around the buffet tables of piping hot foods. Zac told Kristi to grab her food while he secured a table. Rainwater trickled down the floor-to-ceiling windows on both sides of the large dining room. Zac could see an occasional seaside house built along the tree-lined mountain range. Granite jutted out into the water, with spruce and pine trees clinging to the sides of the cliffs. The territory looked extremely rugged. He watched fishing trawlers pulling their lines through the cold water. Zac smiled. He thought seafood lovers never appreciated the extreme temperatures and risks involved in obtaining their favorite fish dinners.

"Wow, everything looked scrumptious," Kristi said, setting her loaded plate down.

"Oh my gosh, you got a little bit of everything," Zac said, surveying Kristi's plate. "Start eating, I'll be right back," he added as he headed for the hot serving trays.

Watching the dock workers secure the ship at the port in Ketchikan was fascinating. The rain had stopped, but dark clouds and dreary gray skies seemed like the norm in this area of the world. Kristi read in a travel brochure, the average rain for Ketchikan was 163 inches a year. She didn't think she could handle that much time without her Florida sunshine.

"You're frowning," Zac said. He set his plate down and started to cut into his hot spinach, ham, and cheese omelet.

Some people from Ketchikan said they can always spot tourists because they are the only ones using umbrellas," Kristi stated incredibly.

"You are probably right. I don't see anyone with an umbrella out there." Zac grinned, looking out the window.

"It's difficult to hold hundred-pound ropes and an umbrella at the same time."

"You think?" Zac laughed.

"What are your plans for today?" Kristi asked.

"I'm going to visit Salmon Falls Resort, north of here. Their brochure offered a wide variety of outdoor activities, but what actually caught my eye was their menu. It looked really high end, you know, for a resort in the middle of the deep woods. So I'm going to check it out. Then as I make my way back to Ketchikan, I'm stopping at roadside restaurants, just to sample the local flair. At noon, I am taking the rain forest crab feast excursion. Do you want to come with?"

"Crab feast excursion, yum, I love Dungeness crab and Alaskan king crab, but no. Thanks anyway. I reserved today for shopping and scouting out totem poles. There are three different areas here in Ketchikan with a large number of totem poles: Totem Bight State Historical Park, which is on the north side of Ketchikan. I have read that Saxman Native Village has a large number of totem poles, but it is on the south side of Ketchikan. And then there is the Totem Heritage Center in the middle. So I will see how many I can get to without missing last boarding call this evening. I am trying to figure out how I can take a totem pole home," Kristi said, grinning in triumph, knowing she took Zac by surprise.

"As long as you keep it on your side of the suite," Zac replied with a grin. "Are you ready to hit the docks?"

Fifteen minutes later, Zac hugged Kristi goodbye and told her to be safe. He stepped into a cab and was gone. Kristi stood on the curb for a second or two, totally caught off guard by the hug.

"Hey, lady, you need a ride?"

"Yes, please." Kristi decided she really didn't want to walk in the mist this morning. She opened the cab's passenger door just as a hand grabbed her arm.

"Do you mind sharing a cab with me?"

Kristi turned her head to the voice and saw the creepy blond guy, with his hand on her arm. "Yes, I do mind. Stay away from me." She pulled her arm from his grasp. She jumped into the cab and slammed the door closed behind her.

To the driver, she said, "Drive, and as soon as we are up the street, I will tell you where I want to go."

"Gotcha, lady."

Kristi was shocked to see the creepy guy at the curb. She felt like her arm was burned where he grabbed her. She had been so preoccupied with Zac and when he hugged her.

"Lady, are you okay? You are really pale," the cabdriver said as he looked at her from his visor mirror. He had pulled alongside the street, two blocks from where he had picked her up.

"Yes, thank you for being understanding," Kristi said.

"Was that guy harassing you? Because if he was, we can find a cop."

"No, I already reported him to the ship's authorities. But thank you, I just would like to enjoy seeing some totems," Kristi said.

The taxi trip up the hilly road to the Totem Heritage Center was quick. Kristi would have spent much more precious time walking the streets trying to find the place. The thirty-foot totem standing proudly outside the building was very impressive. A sign explained the commemoration of the totem. It was created by a master carver born into the Sockeye Clan of the Raven side of the Chilkoot-Tlingit tribe. Most totems honored the identity and lineage of a clan or tribe. They also explained events, stories, and legends of the culture of the native peoples of the Northwest Coast. Kristi marveled at the beauty and workmanship of the giant totem. The intensive labor involved in creating these works of art out of cedar trees was so impressive.

Inside the heritage center, there were many totems excavated from villages such as Old Cape Fox village, on the Tongass Island, Prince of Wales Island, and many other small islands. They were carved in the nineteenth century. Many were weathered and in poor shape. But Kristi could still see the details and traces of paint used to prove the skills of the carvers of that era. She wandered through the center reading signs explaining the history of many of the different carvings on the poles. The Tlingit and Haida were two different groups of Native Americans: the Eagles, or Ch'aak', and the Ravens, or Yeil. The carvings also showed subclans symbolized by bears, salmons, beavers, or whales. Kristi's head was swimming with the amount of knowledge each of the totems shared. Just when she thought she understood, she realized that the totems also honored important events in individuals' lives or things like land ownership and lineages of the clan. The workmanship involved in carving these totems was amazing, to say the least. She also learned about mask carvings and basket weaving from other parts of the cedar tree's inner fibers. The masks were worn in ritual ceremonies and dances. They represented animals, spirits, and mythological creatures. It was all so interesting to see how the Tlingit and Haidas told their stories of life through their carvings and weaving techniques. Kristi was so glad she visited the Totem Heritage Center.

Rather than calling and waiting on another taxi, Kristi decided to walk down the hilly streets. Sooner or later, she would hit the cross street where the shops were or the cruise ship dock, whichever came first. Along the way, she stopped and took pictures of huge gardens of flowers growing along the sidewalk. One proud homeowner explained the twenty hours of light during the spring and continuous light during summer encouraged the blooms of his flowers.

Kristi chose to walk the historic Creek Street. She had read somewhere that it was built on wooden pilings over the water because of the rocky hills surrounding the creek. It was the old red-light district during the 1920s, where fishermen and businessmen went to find a working woman and some booze at the same stop. Backroom saloons during Prohibition were supplied by bootleggers with Canadian whiskey. They would bring the booze in during high tide through trapdoors under the houses.

The first stop was at Dolly's House Museum. Kristi took a picture of the sign on the side of the building that said,

Dolly's House
Where Both Men & Salmon
Came Upstream to Spawn

She browsed the shops looking at handmade and souvenir-type items. There were wool blankets and sweaters, beautifully made in some shops, and leather goods and sweet treats in others. She took a picture of a beautifully carved totem of two bears along the wooden planked street. She saw a beautiful calico cat sitting on a doorstep, which she took a picture of. She wandered into art galleries and candle and soap shops. Kristi could imagine the laughter and piano music of an era gone by as she continued to walk. She had heard the history of the Married Man's Trail, but now she understood it. Here was a wooden street full of houses of working women. The men didn't want to be caught walking along Creek Street and going into any of the houses. So there was a dirt path, probably mud since this was Ketchikan, leading from the woods along the creek to the back of the working girls' places of business. Thinking of her own ex-husband, obviously things hadn't changed much.

Kristi wandered into a gift shop full of fossilized walrus, woolly mammoth, and whalebone carved statues. Each one was ivory in color and beautifully designed. Some depicted natives in kayaks spearfishing. The local artists had caught the hardship the men endured while catching food for survival. Some were carved bears holding salmons and whales about to breach. Another display case featured women carrying bundles and smaller single-manned boats. Kristi chose a whalebone base with two natives spearfishing from a kayak. The description card said the two natives were carved from woolly mammoth bones and the kayak was carved from walrus tusk bones. She loved the intricate workmanship. Kristi also noticed a magnificent statue of two humpback whales. They were carved out of fossilized walrus bones balanced on a whale vertebra. The artist had captured the symmetry of the two beasts perfectly.

The shop owner confirmed the statues could be shipped anywhere after they were well wrapped in air-bubble blankets. Kristi gave her address for the natives' spearfishing carving. She also chose the statue of two humpback whales, but she gave Zac's restaurant's address. It was quite pricey but would fit in well with his mermaid decor. For some reason, she had to buy the whales carving for him. Maybe she was overstepping her boundary lines with the purchase of the sculpture of two whales for Zac, but they were so beautiful. She hoped he would appreciate the elegance in the carving. Kristi was smiling when she left the shop. Although she was empty-handed, she had left a lot of money at that shop. She had taken a couple of pictures of the carvings, so she could look at them during the remainder of her vacation time.

Kristi visited a couple of more souvenir shops along the docks, where she bought a T-shirt for Eli and a T-shirt for herself. She bought some packaged salmon jerky for Eli, George, and the postman and, as a joke, some for Zac. She was having fun shopping. But the hours had slipped away. The end-time of the port stay was four o'clock in the afternoon. The baggage search line, on return to the ship, could take more time closer to departure. Although it was a hassle, there were some really bad people around the world who would sabotage a vacation for their cause, so security checks were a necessary evil. Besides, in her shopping expedition, Kristi had forgotten to eat. She was starving and actually couldn't wait for dinner.

Zac had a very productive day. He had spent time at the Salmon Falls Resort. The chef was very helpful in the questions Zac had asked on menu item preparations. In turn, the chef had questioned Zac on foods the Mermaid Isle had served. From there he had stopped at the galleys and restaurants along Tongass Highway heading back toward the ship's dock. Many of the menu boards served burgers of all kinds and lots of comfort fried foods. The clientele were sport fishermen and tourists needing to fill their hungry spot after a day on the waterways. Zac was surprised to find on many of the menus, smoked Alaskan salmon, Creole style. It was made with Cajun spices, brown sugar, pepper, garlic, and other spices. The salmon was brined for about twenty hours, then spiced and dried for another five hours before being placed in a smoker for eight hours. Although it was a time-consuming process, the flavor of the salmon was sinful. It was smoky with a kick of heat.

By the time he got back to the ship, it was time for his noon excursion aboard a seaplane which would take him to a hauling and crab feast. He was looking forward to the seaplane ride which would be his first. He actually wished Kristi would have signed on for this excursion. He was sure she had never been on a seaplane. He grabbed his heavier coat since it was starting to mist again. He noticed that Kristi had not been back to the suite since morning. He hoped she was enjoying her totem hunting and shopping.

The pontoons on the seaplane made taking off and landing sort of a bumpy ride. But the view from the sky of Ketchikan heading south along the coast was a mixture of granite rock and thick with pine, cedar, and fir trees. The rugged territory looked dense and forbidden. Kristi's camera with its long lens would have captured the harsh and jagged terrain.

Hauling crab traps was a craft Zac really didn't care to add to his resume, so to speak. Out on the water, in this part of the country, the weather conditions were mostly cold and damp. Trying to keep his footing when the flooring was slippery and wet was a challenge. Hauling the traps out of the water was muscle-burning, bone-chilling, and hard work. He could see how it would be easy to lose a finger, and he hadn't even tried banding the crab's claws yet. There was very little leg room when all the traps were on board. But finally the trawler headed back to land.

The feast that followed was worth all the work getting the crabs. In a sandy clearing in the woods along the shore, there were black kettles hanging above firepits full of corn on the cob and potatoes. There were also huge pots waiting for the crabs. The picnic tables, under roof of a gazebo, were ready with everything needed to crack the crabs and devour all the side trimmings. The aroma of crabs and sweet corn wafted through the air as platters were set in front of the hungry diners. It was apparent everyone had worked up an appetite because there was very little conversation during the feast. The mist had turned into a full downpour, but no one seemed to notice as the food piled high on the serving trays disappeared. It was a well-planned feast and great excursion, Zac was glad he had signed up for it.

The last course of forest picked strawberry and blueberry made into pies and layered chocolate cakes followed. The groans of appreciation could be heard even though Zac didn't think he could eat another bite. He wasn't sure if it was from the fresh salty sea air or the hard work, but he was amazed at how much food had been eaten by everyone.

The rain had stopped just as quickly as it had started. It looked like the sun would maybe come out between the clouds as everyone hiked the path back to the seaplane dock. Only there appeared to be a problem with one of the engines of the two planes waiting to take the feast goers back to the ship. A guy working on the engine said they were waiting on a hose that had looked weakened to be flown in from town. The man said the hose was on its way. He explained the hose was not damaged, it just had a soft spot on it, and he was not about to take any chances with it. No matter how many checks they did prior to flying, things like this sometimes happened; he said salty air and dampness were usually to blame. Everyone seemed happy it was being taken care of before something major happened except for one lady. She was clearly beginning to panic. She expressed her worry about the ship leaving without them. But the pilot assured everyone that the ship was aware of the problem and was not going to leave without them. The reassurance didn't seem to quiet the lady down. She continued to voice her opinion that the cruise ship should refund their money. She ranted she was going to write letters to the cruise line. Her diatribe continued until finally her husband pulled her away from the group. Whatever he said, Zac was sure everyone wanted to thank him. She returned to the waiting group and said nothing.

Kristi was sitting in the main dining room eating a light dinner since she had only snacked earlier in the day in town. She kept watching the dock. Everyone had been instructed to be back aboard ship prior to the four o'clock deadline. She looked at her watch and realized it was after five. The dockmen were standing around talking, but no ropes had been pulled. She wondered if another ship was docking, and they were just waiting for their turn to release the ship from its moorings.

Kristi hadn't seen Zac since morning on the dock after the hug. That hug had been a surprise and thinking back, Kristi kind of liked it. Okay, she liked it a lot. The creepy guy had put a damper on her excitement for a moment, but shopping and the totems had pushed him from her mind. She pulled out her camera and looked back at the photos of totems she had taken. They were fantastic. And shopping had been so much fun, but Kristi was tired and hungry when she finally returned and dropped off her bags in the suite. She hadn't notice Zac's coat in the closet. However, he was probably talking to one of the special featured chefs somewhere. She wondered how the feast went. She remembered when she was little and the family went camping during the summer, food always tasted great out in the fresh air, no matter how bad it really was.

It was almost five thirty in the afternoon when Kristi saw Zac and a group of people walking up the gangplank. Something must have happened during the excursion to be this late. She could hear mumblings from others who had watched the fourteen or so people disappear into the side door of the ship. No one seemed to know anything about the reason for the lateness of the passengers. However, as soon as the last person cleared the dock, the ropes were being untied by the dockworkers and the ship's horn blew.

Zac was already in the suite when Kristi returned. Before she could ask what happened, Zac asked, "Do you mind if I take a quick shower? It was really cold and damp out there."

"No, sure."

"Have you eaten yet?" Zac asked as he gathered fresh clothes from the closet.

"Yes, I saw you walking up the dock, from the dining room windows."

"Okay, give me a few minutes. Then let's grab a drink somewhere, and I will tell you all about the crab feast," Zac said, heading to the shower.

Later Zac and Kristi were served cocktails and bacon-wrapped scallops in the club lounge as the ship distanced itself from Ketchikan. Kristi listened as Zac described his day. The resort sounded more like a romantic getaway than a fishing lodge. Zac was in his glory explaining the cuisine techniques he had learned throughout the morning trek along the Tongass Highway eateries. Then Zac filled Kristi in on his crab-hauling time. It didn't sound fun, but Zac seemed to enjoy it. He recounted the amount of food presented at the feast. He tried to describe the sinful amount of ice cream that had been heaped on the strawberry and blueberry pies. He told Kristi, it was a meal in itself.

Finally, he related the scene at the dock when the maintenance guy was trying to fix the almost broken hose on the plane. Kristi couldn't quit laughing as Zac in falsetto complained about the wait time on the dock by the lady. Unfortunately, he had to admit it was probably the most entertaining part of the day. Everyone was stuffed from the crab picnic. They were starting to have a carbohydrate crash from all the food they had consumed. Then out of the blue, a lady stuffed with crabs started crabbing. Zac laughed as he admitted it really was an interesting and fun day.

As Zac and Kristi made their way back to the suite, Zac decided he was out of shape. His muscles ached, and even his hands, from pulling the traps, hurt. He thought maybe he should join a fitness center when they get home. But for now, all he wanted to do was sleep.

"Kristi, have you noticed how long this ship is? I think I just hit a wall. I'm totally exhausted."

"Do you want me to call Uber for you?"

"Funny, very funny."

When they finally reached their suite, Zac walked out to the balcony, giving Kristi privacy to get ready for bed. She noticed the clothing he had worn crab trap hauling was in a heap on the floor of the bathroom. They were damp and smelled of crab and saltwater. She gingerly draped them over the shower stall curtain rod to dry. When Kristi came out of the bathroom, Zac was in bed, sound asleep. She sat down on the edge of the sofa and took a moment to enjoy looking at him. His face was relaxed and turned toward her pillow. She noticed his face was pink probably from being out in the fresh air all day. She would have loved to run her fingers through his dark hair lying against the white of the pillowcase. His chest was tanned. Lord, he was beautiful, she thought.

Kristi walked over and picked up Zac's black jeans and shirt he had dropped on the floor by his side of the bed. After draping them over the chair by the sofa, she walked out on the balcony. The breeze stirred her dressing coat of her long nightgown. Although the air was cool, she loved the smell of the salty sea and the sound of the water. She returned to the room, leaving the door open a bit, then climbed into her side of the bed. She was smiling, thinking of the fantastic day she had in Ketchikan. She thought about the package on its way to Zac's restaurant and hoped he would love it as much as she did.

Kristi had gingerly, so as not to disturb Zac, repositioned her pillow and settled on her side looking out to sea. She could feel the ship's slight sway like drifting on a cloud as she closed her eyes. The sounds from other decks became faint. The night breeze, which had earlier caressed her face while standing at the balcony rail, now calmed. Zac, in his sleep, slipped his arm across her middle. He pulled her to him and whispered, "Good night."

CHAPTER 7

After a couple of days aboard ship, it's easy to lose track of time. Is it Tuesday or Wednesday? What island, what port are we at? Dancing all evening by moonlight on deck 13. Watching the latest movie on the large screen, poolside, deck 11. Bridge tournament starting at 9:00 a.m. in the library, deck 5. Casino slots and tables open one hour after port departure until late, deck 6. The list goes on and on for every type of activity and entertainment for every hour of the day aboard ship.

On each elevator, there are brass plates on the floor telling the day in bold letters. A cruise paper is delivered to each cabin highlighting the need to know happenings for the day.

Day 3
Icy Strait Point, Alaska

Today's Forecast
Sky: Partly cloudy
Temperature: 59°F/15°C
Sunrise: 6:15 a.m.
Sunset: 8:01 p.m.

Ships Arrival in Port: 6:30 a.m.
Approximate Ship Clearance: 7:00 a.m.
All Aboard: 4:00 p.m.

The Tlingit people settled their village of Hoonah back in the 1700s after having to relocate from Glacier Bay because of glacial advancement. After much trial and hardship, these people have continued to survive and thrive. They are proud of their heritage and have blended their culture and traditions with the modern world.

As Kristi was getting ready for another early breakfast, she remembered the salmon jerky she bought Zac the day before. She waited for him to return to the suite from getting a cup of coffee.

"While you were out hauling crab traps yesterday for your meal, I was afraid you might go hungry. I bought you this in town," Kristi said to Zac as she handed him a small plastic bag.

"What is it?" Zac asked, peeking inside the bag; "Oh, my, gosh, how funny, salmon jerky."

"I figured if you quit your day job, you wouldn't starve right away," Kristi said, shrugging.

"That is pretty cool. I wonder what it tastes like. Thanks for thinking of me," Zac said, grinning.

"What do you have planned for today?" Kristi asked.

"I am talking with a couple of the chefs this morning. How about you meet me at noon and we can grab some lunch at one of the three restaurants on Icy Strait Point? You decide. After lunch, maybe you can check out the warehouse shops at the cannery," Zac asked.

"Hey, that sounds good. I should be back from the tram ride through the rain forest around that time. But I think we end up at the cultural center. Why don't you meet me there?" Kristi suggested.

And so the day began. The two-mile tram ride through the rain forest was beautiful. When one thinks of a rain forest, it is always somewhere in the tropics with large overgrown ferns, macaws, and toucans. This rainforest was made up of cedars, hemlock, and spruce. The animals ranged from black bears, deer, and mountain goats to humpback whales, orcas, and several types of migrant birds. The tram followed a path deep into the forest, where the sunlight was blocked by tall trees. The air was cool with the scent of pines and saltwater. Kristi took picture after picture of the beautiful thick moss. It grew on stumps and toppled trees lying on their sides. There were streams trickling between rocks making its way toward the waterway. Kristi recognized the ferns and the densely wooded forest from her nightmare she had on their first day at sea. The only thing missing was the fog rolling in off the water, Kristi thought with a shudder. She was so thankful to be on the tram rather than walking the path alone.

The host of this excursion was one of the elders from the Hoonah village. Not only was he very knowledgeable of Alaskan history, he spoke from his heart. He expressed his love of the land and respect for the sea, which fed his people. It wasn't a boring sympathy grabbing diatribe about cruise ships polluting their fishing water or the destruction of the rain forest. His narration during the tram ride highlighted his part of paradise.

The elder host announced the tram driver would stop at the stone shore for a few minutes of stretch break. Many passengers walked down to the water's edge, took group pictures, worked the kinks out of their legs, and examined the dark-colored rocks along the small beach. The elder pointed out a small island across the inlet. It didn't seem far until fishing trawlers motored by. The distance was actually much farther in relation to the vastness of the sea. He told a story about a group of brothers who had gone to the island for mussels for a feast. Everyone, after eating the mollusks, became ill and died. Now, no one gathered mussels, or anything else for that matter, from that island. It was forbidden. Red tide was strong there, the elder said. Kristi found it very interesting since she thought red tide was only a Florida thing. It caused every fish, eel, and crab to die. It caused beachgoers to cough, choke, and have respiratory difficulties. She didn't realize it was found also in the cold waters in Alaska. It made her sad that harmful algal blooms would also damage the marine life living in the pristine-looking waters of Alaska.

After everyone returned to the tram, the elder pointed out bald eagle nests high up in the fir trees. Kristi took picture after picture hoping some of them would catch the beauty of the proud birds. She was glad the elder continued to call attention to different animals throughout their journey. Sea otters played along the rocky shore. The elder mentioned a certain type of woodpecker banging away on one of the pine trees and turtles resting on a fallen tree sticking out of the water. There was a calm to the misty woodland, so different from Kristi's dream. Maybe it was the reverence the elder had shown regarding the forest and all the land he spoke of.

At the end of the tour, the tram stopped at the cultural center. A group of high school teens put on a spectacular show wearing ceremonial attire. The capes were hand sewn. The masks and drums were all hand-carved. The dance told the story of their Tlingit ancestors and the trials they endured. The teenagers stepped with the rhythms of the drum. Their hands gestured sadness, fear, anger, and the endless task of searching for food. The performance was flawless; it demonstrated their ability to tie their history and culture with modern times. Pride shone in the eyes of each of the kids as their production ended. They received a standing ovation from the large audience who had attended. Many stayed, taking pictures and talking with the performers. It was another successful excursion.

Zac was waiting by a tree outside the cultural center when Kristi walked out. The sun came out for the first time in days and shown on her blond hair. He greeted her with a hug. His arm around her waist, pulling her to him, felt good. Kristi told Zac all about the tram ride as they walked to the Crab Station Restaurant on one of the docks jutting out into the quiet inlet. Alaskan king crab was the featured item on the menu board. Kristi laughed and pointed out the price of the Alaskan king crab was the same market price at home.

Zac grinned and said, "And about 3,250 miles between fresh out of the water and kept cool for transport to Florida."

They took a seat and waited for their platter of crabs and coleslaw to arrive. Zac waved to the Navy commander and his wife, who were clearly debating whether to go to The Cookhouse Restaurant or the crab place. They ended up walking over and took seats at the picnic table next to Kristi and Zac.

"It's nice to see you again," the commander's wife said, looking first at Kristi, then to Zac. "Are you enjoying your trip?"

"Yes, it has been great. And you?" Kristi asked.

"We were adventurous today. We took the ATVs around the island," said the commander.

"That sounds like you had fun. Ahhh, here's our food," Zac said.

"Kristi, have you been to the shops in the warehouse?" the commander's wife asked.

"No, we are going to explore them after lunch."

"Then we will let you eat," the commander said, eyeing his wife.

The Alaskan king crab proved to be as tasty as they had hoped. Zac was sure the "fresh from the sea" made all the difference. He could see Kristi enjoyed digging the meat from the leg shells and drowning each piece in butter. She grabbed extra napkins as the sauce dripped down her chin. Even the commander loosened up and was enjoying cracking the shells with more vigor than needed. They all laughed and enjoyed each other's company and the meal.

Zac reminded Kristi they needed to go to the Cannery Warehouse soon. The end port time was 4:00 p.m. So after excusing themselves, they bid the commander and his wife a great afternoon.

The Cannery Warehouse of Icy Strait Point was originally a salmon cannery back in 1912. Over the years, it changed ownership many times; however, as a packing and canning company, it was very important to the residents of Hoonah. Not only were many employed by the cannery, it hosted many residents after a fire destroyed the town in 1944 while the rebuilding of the city occurred. In the late 1990s, the cannery was once again sold. Changes were made to Icy Strait Point, many of which Zac pointed out to Kristi as they toured.

"How do you know all this stuff about Icy Strait Point?" Kristi asked as they walked along the side of the warehouse.

"I'm just smart like that," Zac said with a smug grin.

"Really," Kristi said, giving him the "I don't believe you for a minute" look.

"No, I actually read it in a pamphlet while I was waiting for you at the community center," Zac confessed.

The warehouse was partitioned off into stores. Some had wood carvings. Some were strictly clothing shops. Others had canned goods and jellies made in Alaska. Kristi urged Zac to buy Lacey, his daughter, a T-shirt, while she bought Eli a pair of boxer shorts with moose walking across the back side. Zac bought his secretary a box of chocolates shaped like salmons. Kristi selected some postcards she thought maybe she would send to a couple of friends of hers and to Eli.

As end port time drew near, Zac and Kristi walked along the beach trail back to the ship. Past The Cookhouse Restaurant was an old cemetery. Kristi pulled Zac through the opening in the white picket fence.

"I love cemeteries. They have so much history. Just five minutes," Kristi pleaded.

Zac walked up to a black granite headstone. It read, "Captain Paul E. Dybdahl Sr. Born 1893, Trondheim, Norway. Died 1978. A Pioneer Alaskan." There was a nautical knotted cross next to the grave. Kristi walked past another small stone in the far corner: "Frank Norton, 1900–1996." A lone pine tree must have been planted at least two hundred years ago graced the middle of the cemetery. It was partially uprooted, probably from a strong winter storm. A wooden swing swayed in the slight breeze off the inlet, from one of its branches. It seemed odd that a swing was hanging from the tree, but then maybe not. Children of family members, who came to plant flowers, or the caretaker's kids while tending the graves, might have played on it. Kristi wandered over to a tall slim headstone. Wind and weather had made it hard to read the engraved words. Her fingers traced the etched granite. Zac walked up to Kristi as she read the name: "Harry Wonk. Died Nov. 19, 1907. 26 years."

"It is so important to remember those who have passed before us," Kristi said, searching Zac's eyes. "I'm sure it was hard for you to walk in here. But if we don't visit their resting place, who will remember them?"

Zac put his arm around Kristi's shoulders. He pulled her close against his chest and kissed the top of her head. They stood there for a while. Zac had to admit it was difficult for him to walk into the small cemetery. Yet he realized, Kristi was actually honoring people she never met, not wanting them to be forgotten. She was showing a side of herself very few people probably ever saw in her. After one last look, they left.

Kristi and Zac walked past three small wooden-framed houses. They didn't look fake or like tourist attractions. There was an ATV beside one of the homes. A calico cat sat in the rocking chair of another. They were the only private residential properties they had seen. But this was just Icy Strait Point of the Hoonah Village. The town must have been inland or on a different part of the island. As they continued to walk along a bend in the trail, they came upon several people from the cruise ship standing around a firepit. A couple of the people were holding sticks roasting marshmallows.

"That smells really good," Zac said, squeezing Kristi's hand.

Someone must have heard him because a little boy asked Zac if he wanted his nearly burnt marshmallow. Zac thanked him, smiled at his parents, but kept walking.

For a minute, Kristi stopped to watch some people coming down the longest zip line she had ever seen.

"I'm surprised you didn't sign up for that excursion."

Kristi looked longingly at the zip rider line. She said, "I would have, but I couldn't fit it all in. I really wanted to take the tram ride more."

"I should have known."

Walking up the wooden planked dock toward the ship, Zac asked if Kristi wanted to take in a show after dinner with him. She put her hand around his arm and teasingly said, "Are you asking me out on a date?"

"Yeah, I guess I am."

There it was again, Kristi thought. The grin on Zac's face could melt all the ice on Glacier Bay. She didn't think Zac realized just how sexy he really was. She was glad her hand was on Zac's arm or she would have lost her balance.

CHAPTER 8

Dinner at the specialty Granite Grill was superb. Kristi ordered the swordfish and filet mignon. The wine steward suggested a pinot noir. He explained how it would not only bring out the flavor of the filet; it would enhance the swordfish. Zac, on the other hand, ordered the Frenched and denuded rack of lamb. The wine steward suggested either a Châteauneuf-du-Pape or a Gigondas. He stated the Gigondas was more powerful and would intensify the flavor of the lamb, while the Châteauneuf-du-Pape had a refined elegant flavor. Zac discussed the merit of each wine in detail with the sommelier. Kristi was impressed how Zac was able to hold his own in the discussion with the wine expert. The couples next to them were following Zac's conversation closely. The topic of subtle wine flavors based on technique, timing of grape harvest, dry year, cool year, rocky soil, and barrels used seemed like a mixture of complexed hard work and a very expensive gamble. Kristi slowly folded and refolded the napkin lying on her lap until Zac gently took her hand in his and raised it to his lips.

Zac realized, he once again got carried away in his conversation with the wine steward. He whispered to Kristi, "Sorry."

When dinner arrived, each guest was stunned at how beautifully the meals were plated. Kristi wished for her camera; the presentations were that artistic. And then, the first bite. A hush came over the group. A tsunami could have hit the ship, and no one at the dinner table would have noticed. Each morsel was more succulent than the bite before. The wine steward was correct. The reds served with the meal brought out the flavor of each piece of meat.

The evening meal was a pampering of the senses—the way the food was plated, the tastes, the aroma of flavors wafting through the air. The essences of grape whirled as the wine touched and teased the taste buds. Soft murmurs of pleasure created by each of the dinner companions could be heard. The rhythm of the quiet violin music in the background caressed the soul of each guest while they had been treated to a bit of paradise on a plate.

Later that evening, the movie, the latest spy thriller, was shown on the huge open-air screen by the pool. There were people sitting on chairs and benches, sipping drinks. Kids were in the heated pool watching the movie and splashing each other. Lounge chairs in the bar area were filled with moviegoers also. Zac offered to get some drinks and popcorn, but Kristi was still full from dinner. It really did feel like a "date," Kristi thought. Before she left Florida, she had thought, once on the cruise, Zac would go his way and she would go hers. She figured they would seldom see each other on a ship that carried three to four thousand passengers. Kristi remembered when she first met Zac, he wasn't standoffish but he had an invisible wall around himself. After her talk with the private eye guy, she understood why he protected himself. But now, she was amazed at how easy it was to be around him.

Thank goodness Kristi had read the spy thriller book a couple of months ago. Zac wouldn't realize she might have watched the movie, but she really hadn't seen any part of it. Her mind had drifted to the sexy guy sitting next to her, holding her hand. She had stored bits of their adventures in a part of her heart, to be brought out when their time together passed. At the end of the movie, she clapped along with everyone else. She asked Zac if he liked it.

"Na, I'm a cooking show kind of guy." He laughed and said he was kidding.

"No, you're not."

"Actually, I am usually at the restaurant making sure everything runs smoothly. It's what I do, but my daughter said I needed to get a real life. So here I am," Zac said as he guided Kristi up the stairs to the upper deck to look out over the water.

"A real life?" Kristi said teasingly. "Floating on ice-cold water in the north Pacific, being catered to and pampered 24-7, is a real life?"

"I could get used to this," Zac said as he pulled Kristi against him. He slid his hands to the sides of Kristi's face and slowly lowered his lips to hers. Her mouth was warm and soft against his. The kiss lasted only a moment, but it seemed longer. Kristi looked into Zac's eyes and slowly kissed him back. She kissed him again. And then, Zac returned her kiss only deeper and a lot longer.

Neither Zac nor Kristi saw the creepy blond guy standing in the shadows, a glass of scotch and water in hand, watching them.

Once back in the suite, Zac continued to kiss Kristi as he lifted her sweater over her head. He unzipped her trousers and let them slip from her hips. Kristi fumbled with Zac's belt. So he placed her hands on his chest and unzipped his own pants. He continued to touch his lips to Kristi's with light, short kisses. He ran his hand along her satiny smooth back to unclasp her bra. Once their clothes were piles on the floor, Zac poured Kristi a glass of white wine from the bottle he had picked up on the way back to the room.

Kristi had thought Zac's grin was sexy. His naked body was way beyond sexy, even in the very dim light of the wall sconces. He slowly kissed her again, his lips tasting of wine. He kissed her neck and her shoulder, and slowly backing her up, she slid down on the bed.

"Kris, I want you."

He called Kristi by her shortened name for the second time since he met her. It sounded foreign to her ears. She had never let anyone except her father call her Kris. But the way Zac said her name, it felt right. She laced her fingers through his thick black head of hair. She had wanted to do that since seeing him asleep the night before.

Zac slowly kissed his way from Kristi's knees up the inside of her leg. His hands caressed her body like no one had in a long time. His mouth continued to stroke her with light kisses. The sensation of his lips sent electric currents through her body. She ran her hands up and down his back urging his body over hers. She couldn't think of anything other than wanting this moment to last forever. Since she had met Zac, she hadn't let herself think of what kind of lover he would be, for fear it would only be a dream, never to come true. She took a breath through her teeth fearing she might wake alone in the dark. *Stop thinking*, Kristi commanded herself, *just enjoy him.*

Zac loved seeing the pleasure he was giving Kris, in her eyes, in the way she arched her back, in the way she fisted his back muscles. Lying on top of her, he took a sip of wine from the bottle. He felt her hands move to the sides of his face so lightly. She caressed his cheeks with her thumbs. Her mouth was open as if she wanted to say something.

"I will stop if you say no."

"No, no, don't stop…I want you." Kristi wasn't sure if she said the words to Zac or if she was chanting them in her mind. She said it again, "I want you. Make love to me."

Zac crushed her mouth with his, running his tongue along the inside of her lip. He felt her tense for a moment as he slowly entered her. But he knew she felt the waves of pleasure as he filled her with each thrust. Her hands gripped his sides and back as he continued to move inside her and over her. He kissed her neck, her shoulder again and again. His muscles beneath her palms were slick with sweat as he urged her higher and higher. She called out his name when her body spasmed and then climaxed a second time. Zac felt her muscles clench and followed with his own release as she wrapped her legs around him.

"Kris," Zac whispered as his head dropped to her neck. He inhaled the scent of her hair, her skin, the fragrance that he had come to associate with Kris.

Kristi could feel Zac's warm breath against her ear as his breathing slowed down. It was crazy how comfortable she felt with him still inside her and lying on top of her. She ran her hands down the length of his back, trying to memorize the touch of his skin beneath her palms.

Afterward, Kristi's head rested on Zac's chest. She listened to his heart beating. Its rhythm began lulling her to sleep. But Zac turned on his side rolling Kristi to her back. His hand caressed her arm. It felt like silk touching her skin. He kissed her forehead, her lips, her shoulder trailing kisses down to her breast. His tongue teased first one nipple, then the other. She didn't want him to stop. Yet her mind felt foggy and her limbs too limp to move. He lay back against the mound of pillows behind his head. He reached for the bottle of wine sitting on the bedside table. The clear liquid, no longer chilled, slid down his throat. He wanted her again but instead drew her sleeping body to him. He gently pulled the quilted blanket over her shoulders. He listened to her quiet breathing. The moon had come out and shown through the sliding glass door, illuminating her blond hair. Kristianna Romanoff, her name fit her personality, he thought, but Kris was his name for her. He slowly drank the rest of the wine. And as he laid his lips to her hair, he whispered, "Sleep well, my beauty."

CHAPTER 9

Kristi didn't want to wake up. What if making love with Zac last night really was a dream? What if the passion they shared was her one and only fantastic moment with him? Or worse, what if he never touches her, as a lover, again? Lying on her side, Kristi stretched and slowly opened her eyes. Ahhh, seeing Zac first thing in the morning made waking up a pleasure.

"Do you know, you frown in your sleep?"

"I do not."

"Yep, you do, but that's okay. If we argue, I'm going to claim makeup sex in a few minutes," Zac said, grinning at her.

Kristi leaned into Zac's pillow laughing. Once again, Zac had taken her completely by surprise. And it was in a good way. She felt his lips on her upper back, his hand caressing her hip. Her entire body still tingled from last night, and now, her worries were forgotten. She wanted him again.

Zac nudged Kris onto her back. He knew he could save his "makeup sex" option for another time when she trailed a lone fingernail down his shaft. With touches like that, this early in the morning, his staying power wouldn't, couldn't last long. He pulled Kris's hand away.

"See, you're frowning again."

"But I'm not asleep."

"I can see that." Zac grinned as his lips met Kristi's. He raised her arms above her head as he slowly kissed her again. He wanted to take his time feeling how soft she was beneath him.

"Oh, my, gosh, what time is it?"

"Are you timing how long we make love?"

"No, I have to be on the docks at 8:00 a.m. I'm taking the train up to White Pass Summit into the Yukon."

"It's four thirty, the same time you wake up every morning," Zac said, realizing making love to her this morning wasn't going to happen.

"You know when I wake up?"

"Yeah, your breathing changes, and you bury your head in your pillow. I need a cup of coffee," Zac said, getting out of bed. Finding his jeans, after pulling on a sweatshirt and shoes, he walked out the door.

Kristi's mouth fell open. She stared at the door as it clicked shut. What just happened? Did he really prefer coffee over making love with her? Shaking her head, she decided to grab a quick shower before he got back.

Once in the shower, Kristi's mind wouldn't stop analyzing what had just happened. As she lathered the shampoo in her hair, she thought about the entire situation. First, she was in disbelief; Zac was upset because she was worried about what time it was. She only asked because she had a schedule already in place that she couldn't change. Well, she could, but she had been looking forward to the train trip to the Yukon since she booked the excursion. As she rinsed the soap from her hair, she realized the real problem was her insecurities with Zac. He was beautiful. He was thoughtful and sweet. He was successful. He was… And that was when her tears mingled with the warm water of the shower. She ruined the moment with her own fears. All he wanted was to make love with her, and her fears pushed him away. This trip was supposed to be an adventure. If she kept it up, there would be no fun memories to look back on.

Zac spent the next hour walking along the upper deck of the ship sipping coffee. Kristi needed to keep it light. Her ex caused her to have trust issues; he got that. But for the first time in a long time, he actually wanted someone. Shaking his head, he smiled; her soft body next to his all night long sure encouraged his want.

When Zac returned, the steam from the shower and Kris's body lotion wafted through the air. It was like balm to his senses. In the short time, they had shared the suite; he had come to rely on the soft fragrance to carry him through the day. Kris was placing her camera and other items in her backpack for the train excursion. "Hey, if you give me ten minutes to shower, we can grab a quick breakfast before you head to Canada," Zac said as he closed the bathroom door.

"That sounds great."

Skagway

From everything Kristi had read about Skagway, it was considered the Garden City of Alaska. Summers were cool, between forty-five degrees and sixty-five degrees Fahrenheit, which was cold by Sarasota, Florida, standards. And winter temperatures ranged from eighteen to thirty-seven degrees Fahrenheit. She had envisioned all of Alaska cold and buried in snow from early fall till June. But as she and Zac walked along the dock toward the waiting train cars, the only snow she saw was high on the upper levels of the mountain range.

She had stood in the shower after Zac left for coffee earlier that morning and cried. Her tears couldn't wash away how bad her words probably hurt Zac. He must have thought she was more worried about missing the train than making love to him. It pained her deeply. Yes, she could apologize, but the damage was done, and she didn't know how to fix that.

Breakfast had been a very "polite" meal. The conversation between Zac and herself was safe and neutral. He had remarked how amazing the granite mountain range was, right at the water's edge. How Skagway, viewed from the ship, was just a small parcel of flat land between the mountains. Kristi read from the ship's paper, the native Tlingit name "Skaque" originally translated meant "the place where the north wind blows." Kristi thought that was just how her heart felt, hit by a cold north wind.

Just before 8:00 a.m., just like many others getting off the cruise ship, they made their way toward the train platform. "Do you want me to grab you a bottle of water to take with, on the train?" Zac asked as he walked up the steps to a red building called The Caboose On The Dock. It advertised espresso, memorabilia, and gifts.

"Thanks, that might be a good idea," Kristi said as she followed Zac into the imitation-box-car-looking building. She couldn't remember seeing anything on the excursion website about food and drinks offered or provided on the train trip.

Beyond The Caboose On The Dock were huge signs that detailed Skagway's Historic Waterfront, Captain William Moore, the visionary who discovered the White Pass Route and the White Pass Yukon Route challenges. The black-and-white photos really drew attention to the difficulties the Alaskan territory dished out to the pioneers, in the late 1880s. It showed grim photos of the wharf, early stampeders, and the animals jammed into ships. And to think, America purchased Alaska from the Russians in the 1860s for seven million dollars. The stampeders needed to find a lot of gold for the government to recoup that sort of money back then.

Walking toward the boarding platform, Kristi turned to Zac and said, "Thank you for walking me to the train. I really appreciate it. What are you going to do today?"

"Probably hold on to you, so when you are taking pictures, you don't fall out of the train window."

"Oh, thank you, Zac. What a wonderful surprise! I'm so sorry. I didn't mean to hurt your feelings this morning," Kristi said, wrapping her arms around Zac's neck. She kissed his earlobe and whispered, "I was praying you would come with me. Thank you."

Zac just grinned. It felt good to surprise Kristi.

Once the passengers were seated, the guide stood, welcoming everyone to the vintage narrow-gauge train to White Pass and the Yukon Territory. She said they would be traveling the same steep Chilkoot Trail as the gold rush stampeders followed. But first, she detailed safety measures for the train. Things like not leaving one compartment to go to another while the train was in motion. There are no platforms over the antique couplers and slipping, falling through the tracks would damage them and death to you. Everyone laughed but understood the hazard. There was no smoking on the train because it was made of wood. She explained she would be pointing out different flora along the way, many of which would be in bloom this time of year. Also, the conductor and she would point out any moose, bears, or other wild animals as they saw them. She let everyone know that she would highlight the history of some of the landmarks as they passed them along the trail. Lastly, she asked that people would not seat-hop to get a better view. She explained, once at the top of the trail, the train turned around and they would see it all again on the other side of the car. With that, the train started its slow journey to the Yukon.

Zac rested his arm on top of the old leather bench. He watched Kristi pull her camera from her backpack and inspected the lens. She leaned back against his arm as the train moved past the back buildings of the town. He was glad she didn't know before boarding, he was going with her. It was fun to surprise her. He had seen her docket of excursions the first evening it was delivered to their suite. She was one adventurous person. Yet she seemed bummed at times, like when she couldn't zip line the longest one in Alaska yesterday. It was quite obvious she was eager to try new things. His mind drifted to earlier that morning. It was probably good they didn't have sex; they would have never made it on time to the train. He had to smile at that thought.

"You're smiling."

"We would have missed the train."

Kristi started laughing until Zac covered her mouth with his hand. "Shhh, we are passing the Gold Rush Cemetery."

Sure enough, to the right of the train was the final resting place of some of the early members of the Skagway community. The guide mentioned gangster Jefferson Randolph "Soapy" Smith and Frank Reid, who died in a shootout. It sounded like this was the far north territory's version of the Wild West.

Kristi had put her long lens on her camera, so she was able to zoom in on the cluster of graves in the woods. She loved taking pictures. Sometimes, it was so hard to get the perfect picture when there were people milling around. Someone would, many times, photo-bomb a winning photo, usually accidentally. However, between her son and some of her friends acting silly, there were some fantastic shots turned totally laughable. After the train passed the cemetery, Kristi clicked on the playback to quickly view and edit the photos. Zac leaned in to take a look. She could smell his aftershave lotion. It reminded her of fresh sea air and some unique herb or spice. She didn't know what it was, but it gave her a yummy warm feeling all over. She gave Zac a quick kiss on his cheek, then turned back to clicking through the pictures.

The train followed along the Skagway River. According to the guide, when they passed the Denver Glacier, they were already 402 feet above sea level and climbing. She pointed out the White Pass and Yukon Route red caboose "cabin" could be rented through the US Forest Service. It was a real caboose that had been converted into lodging for hikers. As the train curved around one of the mountains of the Tongass National Forest, Kristi turned around in her seat to one of the most beautiful views she had ever seen. Through the view-finder, Kristi could see the valley behind them. The cruise ship was about an inch in length anchored in the Lynn Canal. There were spectacular tree-lined mountain ranges on both sides of the valley. It was breathtaking. She grabbed Zac's arm to point out the view before she went back for more photos.

"Was that beautiful or what?"

"Yes, it was," Zac said smiling.

"What?"

"I am enjoying watching how everything is exciting to you," Zac whispered to her.

"I'm sorry. When I was growing up, I would sit in the front seat of the car with my dad. I would follow the maps and point out all the scenic stops on our trips out west or to Canada. My brothers and mom would play cards and read books in the back seat. They didn't notice half of the cool stuff I saw. There is so much beauty to see. You just have to search for it sometime. But it's there," Kristi said, looking out the window.

Zac thought maybe Kristi's enthusiasm was about being on the trip, her thrill of the adventure. But it was more of an appreciation for the pleasure the trip brought. He had noticed the same joy when she had visited The Mermaid Isle. She was actually finding happiness in everything she saw. He realized he was seeing the depth of her beauty, a layer at a time.

The train slowed a bit as the guide urged the passengers to look to the left of the train. She explained back in the summer of 1898, two men working for the railroad were killed after a blasting accident. They were crushed under a one-hundred-ton boulder. The black cross marked the site where they were buried. The guide actually paused from talking, showing respect for the men who had labored and died on the mountain. Zac put his hand on Kristi's shoulder. He knew she was probably feeling sadness for their loss.

"Again, to the left of the train, on the other side of the gorge, this is truly a photo opportunity," the guide gushed. She was proud to present Bridal Veil Falls. The spring melting of snow on the glaciers of Mount Cleveland and Mount Clifford was the cause of the six thousand feet of spectacular cascading falls.

As Kristi raised her camera to take a couple of photos of the falls, she got to thinking. In her past travels, she had seen Bridal Veil Falls in California, Washington State, Idaho, and North Carolina. She was sure there were several other states that had mountains and the same type of picturesque falls. So much for a blushing bride. Obviously that bridal veil got around. Thinking that was funny, she started chuckling.

"Kris, oh, babe, look at that," Zac said in total awe, pointing at the view out of the other side window. "Look at that wooden trestle bridge. Now, that is beautiful." He couldn't wait to see how Kristi would capture photos of the trestles.

As the train followed the curve in the tracks, toward Tunnel Mountain, the wooden trestle bridge over Glacier Gorge, was jaw-dropping beautiful and scary at the same time. The lattice works of wooden beams were bolted together, one thousand feet above the floor of the gulch. There were at least twenty coaches attached to the engine. As the engine started to enter the tunnel, the perfect picture came into view. From several coaches behind the engine, Kristi could see the tunnel, the train, and the trestle bridge. She turned to Zac excited about the pictures she had just gotten. His lips met hers, warm, soft, and so inviting. *What pictures*, she thought. She hoped the tunnel would last until they got to Canada or the Yukon or Alaska—no, wait, they were in Alaska. He tasted so good.

The guide obviously didn't get the opportunity to kiss anyone. She wasn't breathless. She wasn't holding on to the hand railing for dear life. Instead, she pointed out, if everyone would turn in their seats and look back, they could see Skagway and Lynn Canal. She said the train was now seventeen miles up the mountain, and the view of the Chilkat Range and Mount Harding was how this sight became known as Inspiration Point. There was a rugged beauty to the wilderness. The rock face of the mountainside scattered with spruce growing straight and tall, reaching for the sky. The railroad track followed the curve alongside the mountain. In other words, looking out from the window, Kristi could see straight down the mountainside. There were no guard rails. There wasn't a shoulder alongside the track. It was a mixture of rock and granite gravel, cluttered with underbrush, too steep to attempt to climb down by foot.

Further up the mountain was an area known as Dead Horse Gulch. As the story goes, some three thousand packhorses were used to carry supplies by the stampeders on the trail to the Yukon. They were starved and overworked to the point of total exhaustion. Either their legs snapped from the pack weight on their backs, or some fell down into the mud water, drowning. Some horses were shot when they couldn't keep up. In the stampeders' lust and rush to get to the goldfields, they didn't care about their horses. More would be brought in from Seattle and the rush to find gold would continue on. The remains, the bones of those horses can still be seen, at the bottom of the gulch, just like the gravel trail of '98.

"That is so sad," Kristi whispered to Zac.

"I remember learning about gold fever when I was in grade school, same with the trail of '98 where many people died on their quest for gold. We just never heard the really gory details," Zac said, looking down at the gulch as they continued on their way. "Look, I bet that path is part of the trail of '98."

"I thought the gold rush was in California."

"The California gold rush was in the 1850s, I believe. Both of which were before my time," Zac said, trying to lighten the mood.

When the stampeders reached the US-Canadian border at White Pass Summit all those years ago, they were waved on by the mounted police. When the train came through, the coaches were motioned on, by the train switchman. The five flags swaying in the breeze were the only evidence of the crossing.

"I know the American flag, the Alaskan flag, the Canadian flag, I think one is British Columbia, but what is the other?" Kristi asked.

"Yukon Territory."

"Wow, who knew the Yukon Territory had a flag. I mean, I'm not trying to be disrespectful, but I didn't know. How did you know?" Kristi asked Zac.

"I read about it in a pamphlet at The Caboose On The Dock," Zac said, acting all superior.

"Snob."

All of a sudden, the train stopped. The guide explained that it was now time to head down the mountain. She instructed everyone to stand and pull the back of the bench seats forward so that the seating was now facing down the mountain. Almost everyone on the coach started laughing and did what they were told. Once that task was completed, the guide explained the engine was going to uncouple from the front cars, go to the last coach, and recouple, pulling the cars back down the mountain. Sure enough, a few minutes later, the engine on another track passed the coaches. It was now also time for everyone on the right side of the cars to move to the left, and the people on the left were now given the opportunity to view the Skagway River and gorges on the way back down the mountain.

Since Kristi had gotten some very pretty photos on the way up, she set her camera inside her backpack. She gave Zac his bottle of water and drank from her own. Once again, Zac had put his arm on the back of the bench. Kristi settled against him, and rubbed her cheek across his arm. She liked the feel of him beside her.

The guide continued to give information all the way down the mountain. Some of the history was interesting, some not so much. One thing that did stick out was that in 1994, the White Pass and Yukon Route became part of the International Historic Civil Engineering Landmark. Just like the Eiffel Tower, the Statue of Liberty, and the Panama Canal, it had met the criteria because of the unimaginable weather conditions, steep grade, granite stone mountains, and cliff-hanging turns. Many of the trip and auto clubs had recommended the vintage locomotive trip as a must-see while in Alaska.

As Kristi was watching the rock side of the mountain go by, she looked across the coach out the window. It was a sheer drop off down the gulch. So she turned back to her window and looked down. The tracks were actually staked to the side of the mountain with cable and huge fasteners and bolts. Let that sink in, she thought, when they were 2,500 feet up the side of the mountain. No wonder one of the passengers was sitting on the floor of the coach, not looking out the window. And others stayed on the mountainside of the train. It didn't seem to bother Zac. She actually liked looking out the window down the side of the mountain.

"What do you want to do when we get back to town?" Kristi whispered, not wanting to disturb the guides and those who continued to listen to the highlights along the route.

"That is a loaded question. Do you really want the answer?"

Kristi placed the palm of her hand on Zac's chest. She could tell he hadn't expected her teasing touch when he sucked in his breath. "Okay, I guess we are going to eat lunch and then do a little bit of shopping.

"Only a little bit?"

"Well," Kristi stammered. "I have a horseback riding excursion this afternoon. Would you...by any chance...be going with me?"

"I think that could be arranged. That is, if you really want me to go with you."

"Yes," Kristi announced, then grabbed Zac's sweatshirt front and kissed him while the guide once again was talking about inspiration point.

Everyone sitting near Zac and Kristi started laughing and clapping because the noticed kissed was scripted perfectly with the inspiration point viewing. It was great timing. One lady turned around and asked, "Sweetie, did your young man just propose to you?"

"Oh no, nothing like that, he's going to go horseback riding with me," Kristi said, smiling at her.

The lady turned back around in her seat with the strangest, puzzled look on her face. Kristi started laughing again, but this time, she put her hand over her mouth to keep her giggles to herself. Zac just hugged her to him, smiling.

The guide, even as the train slowed to return to the station, continued to give information. She informed everyone the coaches they had sat on were actually restored from the 1890s and that each coach was named after a lake or river of the north. When the train finally came to a stop, the guide thanked everyone for taking the White Pass and Yukon Route Vintage train trip with her.

Once again, some of the passengers stayed behind and discussed certain scenic areas along the way while most filed off the train. They had traveled 2,865 feet up the mountain from Skagway to the border of British Columbia in a few hours. It took the stampeders several grueling months, if not longer, to travel the same distance. There was not much comfort, only a dream of gold and a year's worth of supplies. Another excellent excursion checked off Kristi's list.

Zac took Kristi's hand as they walked the two blocks to the Bonanza Bar and Grill for lunch. The building itself was rustic barn boards on the outside and varnished wood on the inside with brass railings around the bar. When they entered the rustic saloon, they were told to grab any available seats. Since many of the other people from the train had the same idea as Zac and Kristi, there were only a few booths left. People were boasting about their own adventures, some laughing. There were families talking about their shopping purchases. The music was really loud. So some customers were actually hand gesturing for more beers or shouting their orders to the servers. The multiple types of beer on tap were being poured and hustled off to waiting customers at a rapid rate. Everyone seemed to be enjoying themselves.

When it came time to order, Zac ordered the Alaskan chowder and the crab and spinach quesadilla.

"Kris what are you ordering?" Zac asked.

"I was going to order the fish tacos, but…I changed my mind. I feel like a big fat juicy bacon cheeseburger and fries!"

"Oh my gosh, are you turning into a mountain woman?"

"Maybe," Kristi said shyly.

The chowder was placed in front of Zac. The aroma was heavenly. He picked up his spoon, scooped some of the thick broth up, and served himself. Zac closed his eyes; it was that good.

"Zac, you looked like you died and went to heaven."

Zac smiled. He thought the thickness of the soup and the flavor was right up there next to sex. But he didn't want to sound crude even if it was a culinary compliment. "It's a cheesy chicken broth base with chunks of salmon, halibut, clams, and bacon. Kris, you have to try it." He held a spoon full to Kristi's lips.

Kristi never liked when people ate off each other's plates. She didn't know why, but it was never done in her parent's household. So when Zac put the heaping spoon of food in front of her, she was kind of taken back. Yet she didn't want to be rude. If Zac wanted to share something that gave him pleasure, who was she to stick her nose up at the gesture?

"Zac, you're right. It's really good. I bet you could make this. Maybe add celery and some chives, and call it mermaid's treasure," Kristi said.

"Mermaid's treasure, I like that. Can you take a picture of it so I won't forget?"

"Sure."

Soon after that, Zac's crab and spinach quesadilla and Kristi's whopping bacon cheeseburger platter were set in front of them. Kristi's mouth fell open. Yes, she was hungry, but the burger was huge. It looked like they had used at least two pounds of meat, and the mound of fries was enough for at least four people.

Zac started laughing. "When are we horseback riding? Giddyap, missy, you have some eatin' to do!"

Kristi had been able to eat most of the burger but passed on the fries. Although she had been starving, she thought she probably waddled out of the bar. Zac said the crab in the quesadilla had a Mexican salsa kind of kick to it. It was really good. They both decided they hadn't had one bad meal in their adventures. The food everywhere they had gone was really tasty.

They walked past the ever-present diamond stores associated with cruise ship dock shops. They browsed a strictly northwestern apparel shop. Kristi teased Zac, telling him he wasn't the Paul Bunion type of guy. When Zac faked having hurt feelings; she held a heavy flannel plaid shirt against his chest. "Um no," they both said in unison. Kristi bought Eli a bag of chocolate candy called Bear Poop. She thought it was funny, and she was sure Eli would too. Zac found a jade beaded gemstone bracelet for Lacey. The shop owner explained that jade was the state gemstone. To which, Zac had said, it was something he had not known. Kristi found a pair of chandelier earrings she couldn't live without. They were cream-colored fossilized wooly mammoth tusk carved and polished into round disc with inset abalone in the middle. There were more cream-colored carved rods hanging from the rounds. Zac insisted on buying them for Kristi. She tried to convince him not to buy them for her, saying the earrings were too expensive. She told him he had been paying for all their specialty meals. But he insisted. The shopkeeper quickly charged Zac's credit card before either of them changed their minds. Kristi wanted to wear them out of the store but decided against it. She explained she didn't want to lose them while horseback riding.

"Speaking of horseback riding, we need to get back to the ship's dock," Zac said.

When excursions were purchased through the cruise ship, it was the ship's responsibility to provide transportation to and from the outing. A tour purchased on the passengers' own and not from the cruise ship's approved list was risky. If the expedition got delayed somehow and the passenger missed the return time, it was their own financial responsibility to get to the next port of call to get back on board. Did the self-purchased day trip meet high-quality safety standard? Was it one of those scary-movie types in which the vacationers were left stranded in some infested nightmarish place? Kristi remembered how the ship waited in Ketchikan two hours after final port call until all fourteen guests of the crab festival trip returned to the ship.

The riding trip turned out to be fun. The horses were not the tired nag kind of horses found in a lot of horseback riding outfits. These horses were healthy, alert and liked being headstrong. Once on the trail, some of the horses actually pranced their way through the woods. Kristi had her camera around her neck for easy access. She clicked photos of two horses sidestepping and nodding. She got a couple of great shots of Zac and the horse who chose Zac for the trip. The guide was somewhat stunned at the behavior of Jet, Zac's horse. He had told Kristi, Jet was temperamental and loved to give some riders a hard time. Kristi laughed and told the guide, Jet had probably smelled Zac's fish lunch and realized he wasn't a predator. The guide looked at Kristi sideways and told her that was an interesting philosophy and in Jet's case could be true.

The trail not only took the riders into the forest, but it skirted along a shallow creek filled with Salmon. Kristi could have let her horse stand there while she gazed at her surroundings; it was such a beautiful spot. But she kept her horse, Maggie, moving.

"There is no way I could have been a stampeder," Kristi announced sometime later. Her buns were getting sore. A couple of the other riders agreed with her.

The guide must have taken Kristi's statement as a reason to take a break. After dismounting, he put stakes into the ground and asked everyone to tether their horses for a quick break. While the horses munched on sweet grass and wildflowers, the guide handed out granola bars and water. The sun was high in the sky. The snow-covered mountains. The grassy meadow with a creek full of salmon. What could be better? Kristi thought.

"Are you enjoying the ride?" Zac asked, standing next to her.

"Yes, it's really beautiful here, how about you?"

"Jet hasn't bucked me out of my saddle yet, so I guess I'm good."

"You're not having fun. I'm sorry this is boring for you. Think of it this way, I could have taking the musher camp."

"The musher camp, what's that?"

"It is the excursion where you meet the sled dogs and puppies. You go on a dog sled mini trip through the woods."

"Oh. But there's no snow."

"I think they pull you on a wagon. But its' cute puppies and barking dogs."

"Thank you for not."

Kristi walked back to where the horses were tethered. She stroked Maggie's mane. The horse responded with a shake of its head. Jet booted his head toward Zac's back.

"Um, someone isn't paying attention to Jet."

"I can see that," Zac said, running his fingers through Jet's mane. He smiled and patted Jet's neck. The horse responded by nuzzling Zac's shirt front and shaking his head up and down.

"You know, it's hard to believe the stampeders loaded beautiful animals like them, with a year's worth of supplies," Zac said as he continued to stroke Jet's neck.

"Yeah, Jack London wrote in one of his books about the horrid treatment the packhorses received. Their legs physically snapped from the weight. I can't imagine," said another person, whom Zac remembered seeing on the train.

"Total disregard for the health and safety of these creatures. They just let them die and then got more brought in from, I think, Seattle," someone else piped in.

A lady, looking through binoculars, pointed to a moose grazing between some bushes and tall grasses a distance from where the group was standing. The guide said that they needed to mount up. The moose cow probably had a calf nearby. He let the riders know, they never wanted to mess with wildlife and their young; it would cause probable health issues.

By the time the group got back and dropped off at the dock, it was almost 5:00 p.m. Kristi felt tired, and all she wanted was a shower.

"Why don't we walk back to town? Do a little shopping. Then have dinner at the Skagway Fish Company," Zac said, looking toward town.

Kristi knew Zac wanted to scout out the restaurant. He had been a great sport on the horseback ride, which he really didn't have to even sign up for. "Okay."

They walked along the docks, past a couple of smaller cruise ships. Kristi took pictures of the cleat tethering the ship. She took a picture of a tug guiding another ship out of Lynn Canal. They laughed as they recalled Jet, trying to follow Zac back to the bus when they were leaving. As promised, Zac started walking past the restaurant to do a little shopping before dinner.

"You know, I really don't feel like shopping."

"Oh my God, are you okay? Do you have a temperature? I didn't see your horse buck you off. Are you hurt somewhere?" Zac said dramatically.

"Stop it, no. I'm fine."

"Women love to shop. What's the catch?" Zac asked skeptically.

"We did shop. It was fun. You bought me those earrings. I love them. I just don't feel like shopping."

Zac opened the restaurant door for Kristi. He was secretly happy she wasn't going to drag him through any more tourist shops. He had fun surprising Kristi when he bought her the earrings. But some of the shops were chock-full of touristy stuff. He remembered all those things Lace had insisted she had to have at Mickey's house in Orlando. Yet when she got home, she only played with them for a couple of days. He realized he hadn't thought of that part of his life in a while. He missed his little Lacey girl.

"Zac, Carman just asked you what you wanted to drink."

"Oh, sorry, what beers do you have on tap?"

When Carman, their hostess, brought back a beer for Zac and a soft drink for Kristi, she asked for their orders. Zac ordered the peel and eat shrimp cocktail to share, if that was all right with Kristi. She shook her head, that it was fine. Then he ordered the king crab leg dinner. That sounded so good. Kristi ordered the clams in garlic and chili sauce and crab cakes.

As they ate the clams and peeled their shrimp, Kristi remarked how fresh seafood was always so much better in flavor. Zac agreed. But Kristi noticed he was quiet tonight. When their main course came, she noticed he was even quieter. He didn't talk about the crab legs or the quality of food like he normally did.

"Zac, are you okay? You haven't said ten words tonight."

"I'm fine. I realized when we were walking in here a while ago. I hadn't talked to Lacey in a week. I miss her," Zac said, looking into Kristi's eyes for some sort of answers.

"When we get back to the suite, why don't you give her a call? No college kid goes to bed before midnight. She will still be up," Kristi said, touching Zac's cheek with her hand.

"Thanks, baby."

After they boarded the ship, Zac said he was going to pick up a bottle of wine. Kristi continued on toward the suite. It wasn't even 11:00 p.m. in Atlanta. She knew that Eli was probably playing computer games with his friends. As she walked into the suite, she speed-dialed her son, so anxious to hear his voice.

"Hi, Mom."

"What are you up to?"

"Studying for finals."

"I miss you." Kristi could hear muffled voices in the background. And then it sounded as if Eli put his hand over the phone.

"You have a lot of nerve calling Eli at this time of night. You are a self-centered, selfish bitch. Don't you ever call this late at night." The phone went dead.

Kristi walked to the balcony railing. She stared at her silent phone, then looked up at the granite mountain on the other side of the dock. All she wanted to say to Eli was hi. There was nothing wrong with that. He never went to bed early. He had called her at midnight, sometimes, just to say good night. If she had been self-centered and selfish, Eli would be living in Florida with her rather than Atlanta. Her heart felt like a knife had sliced it open. She tried taking deep breaths to keep the tears from falling, but it didn't help. Hot salty ones slid down her face in silence.

As Zac walked to the bar to order a bottle of wine, Lacey picked up the phone.

"Hi, Dad."

"What are you up to? Studying?"

"No. Me and Lee are playing some lame computer game."

"I thought your roommate's name was Monica."

"It is. Lee is a guy. We are working on a political science project and needed a break."

"Just be safe. You know what I mean?" Zac said. He could hear Lacey walk out of a room and shutting a door.

"Dad, he is just a friend. I have met a lot of guys around campus here since fall. Some are nice, some are just okay, but I want what you and Mom had. So far, none of them have come close. I gotta go. I love you, Dad."

"I love you too."

Zac walked toward the suite. Lacey's words had taken his breath away. He kept hearing the words "I want what you and Mom had." His heart hurt. He had been angry at the senselessness of Sara's death. He would have sold his soul to bring her back. He sat for days looking out the window at nothing. Mark had stood by being as supportive as a lifelong friend could ever be. For the most part he hid his pain by making The Mermaid Isle the best it could be. But Lacey, she moved past her grief. She had used her mother's love to grow into a better person. She had actually called him out on it a couple of times, pretending to give him a hard time about working 24-7. She was trying to get him to return to who he really was and get back into life. And then one day, he walked into A Weeks Adventure Travel Agency, and he took a cruise to help out a beautiful blonde.

As he opened the suite door, he remembered he forgot the bottle of wine. It was just as well. His motto had become "If you think you need a drink, that is the time you don't drink." He sat down on the sofa and put his head in his hands. He had come to terms with life and death one day at a time. But it was Lacey who wanted what he and Sara had. She wasn't willing to shut herself off from love. The words echoed again in his head: "I want what you and Mom had." She was stronger because of her mother's death. Sara taught him to love. He needed to live what she taught him and continue that legacy, for his daughter's sake. His head was spinning. *Life didn't have to be this difficult, so don't let it*, he thought.

He stood from the sofa and walked to the balcony. "I forgot to pick up a bottle of wine."

"It's okay. I think I'm going to shower and go to bed," Kristi said, walking back into the suite. She kept her eyes focused on stepping, one step at a time to the bathroom. Her heart hurt too much to try and explain what happened. And what good would it do anyway?

Zac noticed the tears on her face as she walked past him. He watched as she grabbed her nightshirt, not her usual lace nightgown, walked into the bathroom and shut the door. A minute or two later, he could hear the shower water running. He walked to the door, dropped his clothes, and stepped into the stall. He turned Kris around and saw the tears had continued to fall. He pulled her to him, letting the hot water cascade down their bodies. It was a while before the water had washed the sadness from them. Kris stood in his embrace, not moving, not lifting her head from his chest.

Zac pulled some shampoo from the dispenser and massaged the soap into her hair. He hoped what he was doing was relieving Kris of whatever caused her to cry. Finally, he knew caressing her head had helped as she opened her eyes and looked at his chest. He rinsed the soap bubbles from her hair and turned off the water. He toweled her dry and then himself, never taking his eyes off her.

Kristi walked out of the bathroom, tripping over Zac's clothes on the floor. It was the second time she had picked up his jeans and shirt. She smiled at that but continued to her side of the bed and slid between the covers. She knew Zac had climbed in on his side of the bed as the mattress shifted with his weight.

Zac pulled Kris against him until her back was up against his chest. He slid his leg over her hip and held her close. He knew for some reason her heart was in need of time and repair as much as his. He kissed her shoulder and again on her neck. She laced her fingers with his and whispered, "Thank you."

Kristi woke to the scent of pine. It was a soft musky, earthy forest smell. She frowned, not wanting to dream the nightmare of walking through the moss rain forest, like she did before. She rolled over and instead of seeing tall firs and spruce; she saw the soft silhouette of Zac's face. His eyes were closed, and his dark hair fanned out on the white pillow. She traced her finger along his forehead to move a few strands of hair from his eyes. Her finger trailed down his face, and as it skimmed across his lower lip, he kissed it and smiled.

"Hi," Zac whispered.

Kristi rose up on her elbow and softly kissed his lips. The scent of pine was the lingering body wash on Zac's body. Kissing Zac in the middle of the night was like a dream effortless and slowly floating across her mind's eye. She felt his hand slowly caressing her arm. It eased its way down her body. She wanted him to touch her, to bring her to life. And softly he was granting her every wish. He brushed his palm over her sensitive breast and drifted down to rest on her warm moist area between her legs.

"Let me make love to you."

Kristi touched Zac's face with her hands and ran her tongue across his lips. She deepened the kiss and whispered a yes to him.

His lovemaking was gentle and dreamlike. Nothing rushed, just soft, slow strokes that slid deep deeper deepest into her only to ease almost completely out, only to return deep again. His touch, with his hands to her sides, was butterfly like. She could feel her muscles tingling with each thrust as her skin became slick with perspiration. She welcomed Zac's warm breath against her shoulder as he increased his passion for her. She wrapped her legs around his back when her body climaxed against him, taking her breath away. His heart pounded against her chest after he too climaxed and relaxed against her. Kristi was too satisfied to move.

Zac was so comfortable; however, he realized he was too heavy for Kris's slight frame. He reluctantly rolled off her body, but when he did, he carried her with him. Smiling, he snuggled next to Kris, with his head on her pillow and her head on his shoulder they both drifted off to sleep.

CHAPTER 10

Why did I set the alarm this morning? It's too early to get up, Kristi thought. She didn't want to go to the workout room. She wanted to stay warm, cuddled up against Zac. Kristi's eyes flew open. That wasn't her alarm, that's the phone. She quickly untangled her legs from Zac's protesting body and slid out of bed. Grabbing her phone, she quietly slipped into the bathroom, closing the door behind her.

"Hello?"

"What took you so long to answer?"

"Dominic, it is 4:00 a.m. here in Juneau," Kristi stated slowly between gritted teeth. "Why are you calling me?" How could she forget the heated phone call and the hang-up from his "lovely" wife?

"I had an argument with Eli. You need to fix it."

"You're a big boy, you fix it. I'm tired of covering for you, when it was you, who destroyed our marriage, my life with my son, and now you want me to 'fix' it? *No.*"

"I made a mistake, I want you back. I want Eli, I mean. I want us to be together for his graduation."

"Whatever you and Eli argued about, you need to fix. I am four thousand miles from Atlanta. I can't help you." Kristi ignored Dominic's little play-on words blunder in hopes to weaken her resistance. She saw through his manipulative behavior long ago and wasn't about to get suckered in again.

"But I want you back—"

Kristi turned off her phone. She stared at her reflection in the mirror. Moose poop looked better than she did, she thought. She brushed her teeth and added a little blush to her cheeks. She smeared some lotion on her arms and legs. *Sorry, mirror, that's as good as it's going to get this early in the morning.*

Kristi tiptoed back to bed. Zac looked peaceful, sleeping on his side. She crawled in next to him and kissed his chest. She could feel his hands suddenly move down her back.

"It must be four thirty," Zac whispered, rolling onto his back, pulling her on top of him.

"How'd you guess?" Giggling, Kristi kissed him and wiggled her hips.

"Oh, don't do that. You will miss Mendenhall Glacier."

"The flight isn't till 10:00 a.m. Besides, I can fit you in."

Zac started laughing and then sighed as Kristi sat up and flexed her hips just enough for him to slide into her. Between her sexy body sitting on top of him and her body lotion scent on her skin, teasing his senses, he couldn't resist anything she did to him. The strokes she gave him were giving her as much pleasure as he was feeling. He put his hands on her waist, gently lifting her until he felt her muscles climaxing around him. He thought he needed more time, but when she came down hard, pushing him deeper inside her, he felt like he had exploded. Making love to her a few hours ago and now again, he decided life couldn't get any better than this.

Kristi was extremely comfortable lying on top of Zac. His hands were caressing her back and bottom side. His touch was so relaxed. She listened to the rhythmic cadence of his heartbeat. It was strong, steady and with its calming effect lulling her slowly back to sleep. Her eyes were heavy and moving seemed like such an effort. She didn't have to think, just drift along on a silvery fluff of a cloud for a couple of more hours.

But then, Dominic's words started to crowd space inside her comfort zone. His voice grated against the velvety smooth sensation she was feeling. She wanted to yell for him to stop hurting her, leave her to find some real happiness. Ignoring the words, she turned her head and kissed Zac's neck once, twice…

Zac shift and lifted Kris so he could see her face. "Babe, I don't know what hurt you, or who hurt you last night. I hope you will tell me when you are ready and feel you can trust me. Shhh, let me finish. I think this vacation is the therapy we both needed. Let's go see the Mendenhall Glacier and everything else you have planned for today." He kissed the tip of Kris's nose and smiled at her.

Juneau

Sunglasses, check; ID and excursion vouchers, check; room key card, check; credit card for lunch and shopping in Juneau afterward, check; camera, check; lip balm, check; gloves, check; scarf, check; coat, check; thick socks, on; wooly sweater and jeans, on; backpack, yep. Kristi decided she had everything she needed.

"I'm ready to go."

"Me too, where are we supposed to meet?"

"The excursion document says lower deck port side exit. Let's go," Zac said, opening the suite door for Kristi.

Once inside the helicopter terminal for the Mendenhall Glacier walk excursion, a woman handed out a clipboard with forms to be filled out by everyone.

"Good morning, everyone, as soon as you return the paperwork, we can calculate for seating and proper weight distribution in the helicopters. After your information is returned to us, you will see two rows of black rubber boots along the wall. Please take the size close to your shoe size and put them on. All backpacks and nonessential items, please stow them in the lockers along with personal shoes and boots. The storage units will be locked while you are exploring the glacier. Thank you."

While the helicopter passengers waited their seating placement, they wandered around the waiting area. There were huge black-and-white prints hanging on some of the very cheery yellow walls. They showed the Mendenhall Glacier in 1770 when the thawing from the Little Ice Age started and of the present-day glacier field. It was amazing to see how the glacier had changed the land in almost three hundred years. The elder of the Tlingit Nation at Icy Strait Point had told how his people had to leave Glacier Bay because of the destructive movement from the Grand Pacific Glacier. It had cleared the land, wiped out the streams, and destroyed their villages of the early 1700s. These photos were damaging proof.

The lady returned with another clipboard. She said, "When I call your name, I will be giving you a numbered decal. Please place the sticker on the left upper side of your coat. It will let our flight crew know which helicopter you will fly up the glacier and return in. Thank you and enjoy your visit to our glacier."

Twenty minutes later, with the heavy insulated black rubber boots on; they were seated in the helicopters. Zac got to sit in the front across from the pilot, which was pretty cool. He had a bird's eye view of the world. Kristi was behind the pilot's seat, which was just as neat as the door was all glass. She had a perfect view of the icy landscape and down to the landing skids. Everyone was instructed to put headphones on, so they were able to hear the pilot. Also, it cut down on the really noisy sound of the blades rotating and the engine right behind their seats.

Zac looked back at Kris as they were lifting off from the helipad. Naturally, she had her camera butted up against the window taking pictures. She had explained, if she didn't press the lens against the glass, she would get a flash glare. She had told him, once she had gotten a reflection picture of the camera taking a photo of the camera. She said even though it sounded funny, it wasn't when she flubbed the fantastic shot.

The two helicopters weaved back and forth in between the mountain ranges. It reminded Zac of that old Vietnam movie where the helicopters flew low along the Mekong River. The pilot pointed to different mountains and named each one of them. The air was clear, and the view was fantastic. There was a grassy path along one of the ridges; Zac could see three mountain goats walking in a single file. He hoped Kristi got a picture of it. Then he wondered if she even saw it. The pilot instructed everyone to remain seated when he landed. He told them someone would help them out of the helicopter since it had been sleeting, the ice would be slippery.

Standing on the white frozen ice, Kristi could see the vastness of the glacier. They were miniscule compared to the glacial field that seemed to go on as far as her eyes could see. The groups from both helicopters gathered together around the three glacier guides. They first identified themselves and told a little bit about themselves. All three were each born and raised in Juneau. They stayed up on the glacier in a tent at a slightly protected area from the breeze coming down the mountain, in between tour group visits.

Leon, guide 1, let it be known that the guide job was paying their tuition at the University of Alaska Southeast main campus in Juneau. Kerri, guide 2, talked a little bit about the three-thousand-year-old glacier and the initial melt of the Little Ice Age starting in the late 1760s through 1909.

Danny, guide 3, led the group over to an eighteen-inch-wide crevasse filled with the most vivid blue color of water, in the ice. Danny, the cutest of the guys, explained the long wavelengths of light are absorbed by the dense ice of the glacier, where blue light, which is short wavelengths, are scattered, hence the brilliant blue color. He explained there was very little taste to the water due to the lack of or very small amount of minerals in the ice. He then gave everyone the opportunity to kneel down and sample the water. Zac, being who he was, tried it along with several others.

"It was ice-cold but had very little taste, just like he said. That was really neat," Zac said to Kristi. Another guy agreed with him and quickly put his hands in his pockets.

Kerri pointed to the exposed granite mountainside. "There is a couple of Dall sheep on the side of the mountain. See the dark bush halfway up, then there are some trees growing out of the crack in the rocks. Right above the tree to the left. See them?"

Zac pointed his arm in the direction while Kristi followed his line of sight to the mountain. She followed the directions the guide had given, looking left of the bush. She raised her camera. The autofocus pulled in the Dall sheep in the viewfinder as she snapped off several pictures. "Thanks, Zac."

Kerri continued to explain, "Dall sheep are smaller and lighter in color than mountain goats. They usually can be seen on steep slopes and extremely rugged mountain terrain. They use the ridges and the meadows in the high country to feed and rest. But we have seen them here below the timberline."

"That was cool," Kristi said to Zac as she leaned against him. She was starting to get cold but loved every second of being up on the glacier. Not only was Kristi standing on three-thousand-year-old ice, she felt a silent reverence for the sweeping beauty before her. She reached for Zac's hand and knew when she looked in his eyes; he felt the same emotion toward the vast icescape.

Leon pointed to the blue flag gently waving in the breeze. "If you notice our state flag, it has a very unique history behind it," he said. And so he told the story. "Back in the late 1920s, the territorial governor decided if Alaska had a flag, it would help them become one of the states of the union. So a contest was held for all the Alaskan children grades 7 through 12 to use their creativity to design a flag. There were 142 submissions. A boy named Benny Benson, a thirteen-year-old who had been through much heartache in his short life was the winner. When Benny was interviewed, he said, 'The blue field is for the Alaska sky and the forget-me-not, an Alaskan flower. The North Star is for the future state of Alaska, the most northerly in the union. The Dipper is for the Great Bear—symbolizing strength.' And there you have it."

"Oh, that was a great story," some lady said, holding her gloved hands to her face.

"Thank you, that was nice," Kristi said in agreement with the lady. She smiled at the male guide.

"What kind of tragedy did Benny Benson have before creating the flag?" another lady inquired.

"His mother died when he was three. His father was poor, a fur trader who couldn't support his kids. He sent Benny and his brother to an orphanage on Unalaska, an island in the Aleutian Islands chain. Their sister was sent to Oregon," said Leon. "And now we will give you a few minutes to take pictures before you all freeze to death, I mean the helicopters take you back to Juneau," the guide said, laughing at some of the red faces and blue lips in the group.

Sure enough, many in the people exchanged phones and camera to take pictures of each other. One of the guides came up to Kristi and said, "Nice camera, do you want me to take a picture of you two?"

"Sure, thanks," Kristi said as she adjusted the lens and handed the camera to Danny. She instructed him which button to push.

Zac pulled Kristi to him and draped his arm on her shoulder. He said something funny, so as Kristi was looking at him laughing, the guide took a picture. When Kristi and Zac turned and looked into the camera, not realizing the guide had already taken one picture, he took another. And another as Zac said something to Kristi, and she poked him in the ribs. Danny, the guide, was clearly having fun with the expensive camera.

"Thank you for taking the pictures," Kristi said, reaching for the camera.

"No, thank you for letting me play with your camera," the guide said before walking off.

Kristi took several more pictures of the flag, a long-range view of the glacial field with large boulders and mud in the rivers of melting ice, the dirty snow and ice down from the glacier field, and the waiting helicopters.

As they were climbing back into the assigned helicopters, Zac looked at his watch and realized they had spent only twenty minutes on the glacier. It seemed like so much more time had passed. He knew that Kristi was cold even though she layered her clothing and had gloves on. Of course, he also knew she would never admit she was cold.

On the way back down the mountain, the pilot said he would take them over some of the lesser glaciers. But to the untrained eye, they all looked the same, ice and snow in a river type pattern between the mountains. There was nothing lesser about the glaciers. They were all huge.

Kristi took several more pictures. She was happy when she got a great picture of the long-range view of Juneau and the creeks flowing down from the mountain ranges. It had been a great trip to the glacier. How many people could say they had walked on a glacier? Well, probably a lot, but she thought it was special.

After the group had returned their very clunky, heavy boots, which probably saved their feet from frostbite standing on the glacier, they all gathered their belongings. They were returned to the dock by the ship, as promised. They each bid each other goodbyes before setting off to tour Juneau. Kristi asked if Zac would like to walk down the street to the Red Dog Saloon for lunch. She had read up on its colorful history and really wanted to see it.

Zac and Kristi sat down at one of the wooden tables once inside the old-time saloon. There were sawdust and wood shavings all over the wood-planked floor. Kristi pointed to the stuffed bear leaning against the main support column holding the ceiling trusses up. Higher up the post, there was a plastic man with mining attire on, holding on to one of the trusses for dear life. It was really cute. There was a guy with a bowler hat on, sitting in the corner playing a piano like in an 1880s saloon. There was a stuffed elk on the wall and a bear rug tacked to another wall. The hanging chandeliers were made out of old wagon wheels with hurricane globes for light. Everywhere they looked; there was some type of cool memorabilia on the walls. Zac mentioned to Kristi that he thought the stuff wasn't reproductions, but the real turn of the century relics.

"Kris, look at the sign over the bar. It said Wyatt Earp had checked his weapon at the US marshal's office in Juneau, June 27, 1900. He left for Nome on June 29 but never claimed his gun. Wonder if that's true?" Zac asked just as their waiter came to take their order.

"I'll have the BBQ sandwich and a soda," Kristi said.

"I'll have the same but make mine a beer instead of the soda, thanks." Once the waiter left, Zac asked, "What time is your whale watch trip?"

"The voucher says I have to be at the dock at one thirty. I take it, you aren't going with," Kristi said quietly.

"No. I had set up the Juneau food tour right after we booked the cruise. I was looking forward to it. I'm sorry."

"No. Don't be sorry. I wish I would have known. I could have canceled the whale watching boat tour and come with you. I mean, you did go horseback riding with me."

"I didn't think about it until yesterday afternoon. We got back too late to change it, and then this morning left early," Zac said, taking a sip of his beer.

"You know, we shouldn't have ordered food here. You are going to be too full to enjoy sample tastings."

"But, Kris, you have to eat. How long is your trip?"

"Three hours."

The waiter set their BBQ sandwiches and bags of potato chips in front of them. He asked if there was anything else, he could get them.

"Just the check, we have another excursion. Sorry," Zac said.

The BBQ was a basic vinegar, brown sugar, and Worcestershire sauce recipe, but the pork was tender. It was piled high on a regular bun with a French onion ring. It was tasty and filling but nothing spectacular. They hurried through the meal. Zac left some money and a generous tip.

When they walked out, Kristi pulled Zac next door to the Red Dog Saloon souvenir and gift shop for a quick look. She ended up buying a Red Dog Saloon T-shirt for Eli and one for herself and three Red Dog Saloon logo etched beer steins for her brothers. She also had taken six menus that were so cool. She asked if it could be shipped to her address and handed her credit card to the cashier.

"I have never heard of a woman shopping as fast as you." Zac laughed as they were in and out of the shop in ten minutes flat.

"I really don't like to shop. I mean I do, but I get overwhelmed by the amount of merchandise jammed in these places. Did you buy anything?"

"Yeah, I bought myself a Red Dog Saloon T-shirt. But it's blue, not red."

As they walked back to the dock to head out for their excursions, Kristi said she wanted to take the tram up the mountain when she got back.

"Of course you would. I mean, it's only 1,800 feet up the side of a mountain. Listen, I will meet you right here when you get back. My food tour is over before your boat trip." He hugged Kristi and walked to his waiting area.

"Have fun!" Kristi yelled to Zac, but he never looked back.

Kristi climbed aboard the sixty-foot cruiser along with thirty other people. They were all bundled in coats and scarves as the weather had turned cloudy and misty. The captain instructed everyone, it would be a twenty-minute trip to the cove where humpbacks were feeding earlier in the day. As people settled in the bench-type seating area, the talk was focused on how many whales would be seen. Some people were drinking the hot coffee being served in the galley. The ship was actually very spacious inside. The seating was comfortable and warm. There were large windows, so the passengers didn't actually have to go outside on the viewing decks to see the whales. Not only did the galley serve coffee, but they bragged of freshly baked blueberry and raspberry muffins. The aroma would have made Zac drool.

Kristi kept her eyes on the water, hoping to see a fin or breaching. It would be great to get some action shots of orcas or humpbacks. There were no guarantees of seeing the larger sea life. Nothing was predictable or scripted in nature. She had read somewhere that orcas actually hunted and killed baby humpbacks. Yes, she had heard a pod or pack of animals would be stronger if the weak were thinned at times. It seemed so sad but a necessary evil. Kristi wondered if the local fishing trawlers when, out in the open waters, actually saw orcas breaching like on the National Geographic channel showed on TV.

While the cutter rode the waves in search of whales, it gave Kristi the time to think about Eli. She wondered if the so-called fight between him and his father was over Dom's mean-spirited wife. She felt sorry for Eli. Her hands had been tied at the time of the divorce. All because the private schools of Atlanta were better and had more to offer than any place Kristi could suggest at the time. All she could do was pick up the pieces after the fall. As far as Dom was concerned, he had played her, tried to pit Eli against her, lied—okay, maybe not totally lied but stretched and twisted stories to let people believe he had always "been wronged" somehow. She wasn't about to be a part of his latest escapade. She pulled her phone out of her pocket and looked at the time. She couldn't call Eli yet; they were probably sitting down to dinner. So she would wait.

Kristi did some people watching until she felt the boat slow.

"I am going to idle for a short time to see if there are any fin sightings," the captain announced.

Kristi decided to wander out on deck. The air was cold and damp. She was glad her layers of clothing kept her snug for the time being. She wished Zac was with her. His presence alone made her feel warm. She loved and hated the fact that she was falling hard for him. She loved being around him. He was easygoing, very easy on the eyes and easy to love. There, she said it. He was easy to love. She hated the fact that when they got home, she really didn't have any connection with him and his world. Sure, she could go down to his Sarasota restaurant for dinner. But they didn't share friends other than Alana Weeks. She was a neighbor, not a true and close friend. And Kristi had seen neighborhood parties when the booze was flowing, and the skeletons were popping out of the closets, so to speak. She stayed clear of them.

Kristi shook her head to clear the downward spiral of thoughts. She had six more days left of fun with Zac. She would spend every moment she could creating memories to tuck away in her heart. And when it was time to say goodbye, well, she would have to deal with her heart when the time came.

Kristi scanned the horizon just as a humpback breached. It was beautiful. The creature's power and strength were magnificent. She raised her camera, and when a second one lifted itself out of the water, she got picture after picture. It was so exciting. The seagulls were flying around the humpbacks. They were diving into the sea, searching for food scraps left over from whatever the whales had eaten. She leaned her hip against the railing to steady herself against the waves hitting the side of the boat.

Just as quickly as the humpbacks came, they were gone. The seagulls circled high in the sky, watching the dark shadows below.

The sea calmed a bit, but the ship continued to bob. Finally, the captain said he was going to move to a different area. Someone thought they saw a dolphin in the ship's wake, but another passenger thought it was rather a sea lion or otter. Kristi wasn't sure what marine life lived in the sea in this area. After all, she lived in Florida with stingrays, dolphins, manatees, and sometimes sharks.

Kristi continued to stand at the railing, looking out to sea. She loved the feel of the salty air on her face. The solitude of the ocean was somehow comforting. It was like having some time alone in church with God.

"Here, I bought you some hot coffee. You looked like you could use it," said a man as he handed Kristi the Styrofoam cup.

"Thank you. I was just enjoying the ocean. But this will really help," Kristi said, pretending to take a sip of the much-disliked drink.

"Where are you from?"

"Florida. I would say saltwater is saltwater, but this is much colder," Kristi said, looking out to sea.

"Wow, you are a far ways from home. My wife and I are here from Arizona. She hates water so she's shopping," the man said with a grin.

"Sir, you should be worried. With all the diamond and expensive shops on Franklin Street, you may have to wash dishes at the Red Dog Saloon to be able to financially leave Juneau!"

"Now you are scaring me."

"Sorry. Oh, look, fins…over there," Kristi said, setting the cup on the deck and raised her camera.

Once again, the captain slowed the ship down. A lot of the passengers again scurried on deck to get a closer view of the humpbacks. But only this time, they were orcas. Kristi couldn't decide if they were showing off for the passengers or in a feeding frenzy. They breached one after another. They acted like they enjoyed being watched by the tourists on board. The black-and-white mammals were mesmerizing to watch. The pod must have been about six or eight. Kristi got a lot of great action shots. Again she noticed the abundance of seagulls coming out of nowhere, looking for scraps.

The captain turned the ship around. It seemed he was keeping his distance from the orcas but following them all the same. Kristi wondered how close to Juneau the orcas would get. She wondered if people who lived on the waterfront homes got to see orcas breaching every day. She knew that hanging out at Bradenton Beach in Florida; she saw dolphins all the time and never grew tired of them. Looking at her watch, Kristi realized they had been out to sea for more than two hours. It was time to head back to port.

Zac had been looking forward to the food tour since he signed up for it. He thought it would be something Sarasota restaurant owners could do to draw in possible customers to their area. Once the Juneau food walking tour got started, the host and guide explained due to the gold rush, Juneau was rich in history. Downtown Juneau had about thirty saloons. Some of the first bars were built in the 1890s and still had much of the original features of that era. They walked to their first sampling at the Imperial Bar, one that was built in that era and actually still had original pressed tin ceilings. Zac walked from one restaurant to the next bar and grill to the next inn, sampling the best each place had to offer. The higher-end restaurants such as the Bubble Room at the Westmark Baranof had a more contemporary Northwest cuisine. The halibut, king crab, and salmon samples at Hangar on the Wharf were actually the local's favorites. And as Zac knew well, the local clientele could make or break a restaurant. Tracy's King Crab Shack was also proof of that.

The guide had told them about free tours of Alaska's capital during the summer months. She pointed out the State Office Building which the locals referred to as the SOB; that got a laugh out of the group. By the end of the tour Zac was thankful it was a walking tour because he was stuffed. Of course, if he hadn't eaten the huge BBQ sandwich with Kris at the Red Dog Saloon, maybe he wouldn't have felt so uncomfortable in his middle. But Kris had wanted to visit the notorious bar. She knew how many owners the saloon had had. She said the place started out as a tent on the dock. She also had told him how many times the place had changed locations but preserved the integrity and memorabilia of the saloon. He had to laugh; she must have worn her search engine out on her computer. She had researched everything about the trip that she wanted to see. She was totally organized. She was actually a great person to go on a vacation with. She didn't spend hours in the bathroom getting ready. She hadn't said anything about his clothes on the floor, even though she almost fell on her face when she tripped over the heap last night. She definitely was not vain. He had noticed she did not have a clue how many heads had turned when she walked past people.

Yes, Zac thought. He would have enjoyed the food walking tour a lot more if Kris had been with him. He loved sharing his food with her. There was something very intimate about sitting close to her, placing morsels of succulent foods in her mouth. It gave him pleasure when she tasted something with superb flavor. She would close her eyes as if she was drifting away. Zac walked back to the dock where he told Kris he would be waiting for her. He wondered how her whale watching excursion had gone. He hoped there had been a lot of whales to see.

Zac had gone deep-sea fishing off Monterey Bay California with Mark a couple of times a while back. The weather was cold and rainy, and it had been brutal. Thank goodness they had at least caught enough fish for dinner. If it hadn't been for the abundance of fish caught that day, he would not have enjoyed his time at sea. But Zac had realized that Kris enjoyed life where ever she went. She was just that type of person.

At last, Zac saw the small ship Kris was on, coming into another docking port in the harbor. She opted to walk rather than wait for the shuttle to bring them back to the cruise ship dock. He saw her stop. She raised her camera to take some pictures of something. He started walking toward her for fear she would keep stopping to take pictures. She had to be cold from being out on the water for a couple of hours. Living in Florida, their blood was thinner; they got cold easier.

Kristi saw Zac walking toward her. She could have melted right there on the spot. He was so gorgeous, and he was walking to her. She stopped and took a couple of pictures of him walking and laughing. Lordy, he was beautiful, she thought. When he reached her, he stopped and kissed her on the lips. Yep, she thought, melted on the cold damp dock in Juneau after being kissed by Zac Karas. Life was good.

"I thought you would be waddling after spending all afternoon eating," Kristi said, laughing as he pulled her into a bear hug.

"What?"

"Just kidding, so how was eating your way around Juneau?"

"We can talk about it in a bit. Do you want to get back on board ship to get warm? "Zac asked as they walked toward the main dock.

"Actually, while we are out, do you want to take the tram up the mountain?"

"Okay, I just wasn't sure if you still wanted to venture up the side of the mountain or go back to the ship."

At almost 6:00 p.m., it wasn't difficult to get tickets for the tram. Nor was there a line to ride the tram up the mountain, like Kristi had seen earlier in the day. She thought she would fall asleep if she would have had to wait for any length of time. The sign said the aerial tram rises 1,800 feet from the cruise ship dock through the rain forest. It also stated it was the highest in Alaska.

"Oh, look, Zac, there are painted bear footprints in the cement. I have to have a picture of that. And look at that sign," Kristi said.

Attention:
Dogs, snowboards, skis,
firearms, and bears are
not allowed on the tram.

Zac and Kristi stepped into the gondola with four other couples. The man who had given her the coffee and his wife also stepped in. Kristi said, "I see you haven't started looking for that job yet?"

The man laughed and said, "The night is young."

Zac had put his hand on Kristi's hip as the tram started its upward journey. The sun had broken through the clouds and created a fantastic scenic view of the shrinking cruise ship docked in Gastineau Channel. Kristi tried to take some pictures, but the angle of the sun was hitting the glass wrong. The glare bounced off the glass-framed cable car. She hoped she could get better shots on the way down. When the tram finally stopped at the Mountain House, they walked to the open patio to look down the mountain at Juneau and the channel.

"Why did you ask that guy on the tram about looking for a job?" Zac asked Kristi.

"Oh, he was on the whaling tour. He said his wife didn't like water, so she was shopping. I had joked with him, saying he might need to get a job to pay for everything his wife probably buy on Franklin Street. You know, all the cruise ship diamond stores are right there. And most women love to shop. Come on, the Raven Eagle Gift and Gallery is calling my name," Kristi said as she pulled Zac's arm to follow her into the shop.

Zac took her hand and noticed how cold it was. "Kris, your hand is like ice."

"I didn't just bring you along to spend your money. I will let you keep me warm too." Kristi laughed.

"Oh really," Zac said, laughing. But he let go of her hand as people turned to look at them when they walked in the door.

Zac found a couple of cookbooks published by the Tlingit natives and also by some Alaskans pioneer women. As he looked through one of them, he noticed some interesting recipes with seasonings he would never have thought to use together. He found a silver bracelet he thought Lacey would like. And Kris pointed out a whale fin charm to add to the bracelet. As he wandered around the tables and cases of gifts and crafted items for sale, he noticed Kris in conversation with a salesperson. As he got closer, he saw she had a jade sculpture in her hand. "What is that?" he asked.

"It is an Inuksuk. In the Arctic region of North America, the Inuit, Inupiat, and other people who live up there placed stones together to look like humans. It is their way of communicating directions in the harsh conditions of the Arctic. It is like a signpost to show which way to go for better fishing or the way home. This one is made of Jade. And I need it. What do you have? Are those cookbooks?"

"Yes, this one is really interesting. It is full of Tlingit recipes, and here is an Alaskan cookbook. As you said, I need it," Zac joked.

Kristi took the books from Zac and pretended to look through the recipes on the pages. She handed them to the saleslady waiting on her.

"Would you ship the Inuksuk, oh, and that carved mask to my home and I also want these two books, but I will take them with me. Thank you," Kristi instructed the lady as she handed over her credit card.

"You aren't buying those cookbooks."

"I already have. No debate. I bought them for you. Is there anything else you want to look at?"

"No. Are you ready to go already?"

"Yeah, I am getting tired," Kristi said as she turned toward the exit.

Kristi was able to get the photos on the way down the mountain that she couldn't have gotten earlier. The sun glare on the glass-enclosed tram was not as noticeable. She didn't know why since the tram was actually facing west and the sun was starting to set. Maybe it was just her. But again, the views of Juneau and the bridge to Douglas Island were impressive.

Kristi turned around to Zac. She slid her arms around his waist and kissed him lightly on the lips. She said "Just because" and turned back around.

Zac was surprised by Kris's spontaneous public display of affection. But then there was only one other couple in the tram, and they were distracted by the view going down the mountain. Zac wondered if when they got home, she would flirt kiss him if they were walking along the beach at sunset. He slid his arm around Kris's waist and pulled her backward to him. He kissed her neck and watched her smile in the light of the fading sun.

After going through the security check and baggage and backpack check, Zac and Kristi headed for their suite.

"Wait, Kris, you haven't eaten since lunch. You need to eat."

"I really would need to clean up before they would let me into the main dining room. It's already 8:30 p.m., and I think the main dining room closes at 9:00 p.m. I'll eat a granola bar," Kristi said as she continued to walk toward their door.

Kristi dropped her backpack and coat on the sofa. She kicked off her boots and said, "Oh no, I'm turning into Zac Karas. Boots here, coat there, next there will be toothpaste in the sink."

"I didn't bring boots. Hey babe, I'm going to order you room service. What would you like to eat? How about shrimp cocktail?"

"Shrimp cocktail sounds great, a bottle of water and two cans of Pepsi also. I'm going to take a quick shower while you order. I'm freezing," Kristi said as she grabbed a pair of jeans and her new Red Dog T-shirt.

Kristi was just drying off and putting on clean clothes when Zac came into the little bathroom for his shower.

"You want to take another shower?" he asked as he unzipped his jeans and stepped out of them.

"I think there is still some hot water left…maybe," Kristi answered as she watched his reflection in the mirror, as he finished undressing and climbed into the small shower stall. She waited till Zac turned the water on and pulled the curtain closed. Then she filled a glass with water from the faucet and poured it over the top of the drape.

"Hey, you better run. You know about paybacks!"

Yep, she did, but seeing Zac laugh and having some fun was becoming a top priority.

Kristi walked out on the balcony as the ship's horn blew to signal goodbye to Juneau. Leaving port was a big deal. Most passengers were counting down the minutes until the casinos opened. They couldn't have cared less how the ship got out to sea—just get a move on! But Kristi was fascinated with the maneuvering of the ship out of some of the small but deep canals. What was also interesting was how much control was given to the pilot boat. They knew their waterways, the currents, and the hazards of their ports. Once the ship was in safe or open waters, the ship captain was given back control.

Zac walked up behind Kristi and put his arms around her. "I'm sorry, I didn't mean to startle you. I guess you were in deep thought, not hearing me talking to you while I was getting dressed," Zac said, kissing her neck.

"I was just watching the ship leaving port and watching the pilot boat. I wonder if I was a ship captain in a past life. I love every minute of being on water and boats."

"You were probably a Greek shipping company owner like Onassis. You could have been his father." Zac grinned.

"Right, with blond hair and blue eyes, I don't think so."

"You got tired of having black curly hair and dark eyes. Oh wait, will you get tired of me?"

But before Kristi could answer and show her feelings, there was a knock at the door. One of the stewards dressed in white came through the door pushing a small cart with covered white china plates.

"Wow, that's a lot of food."

"Well, I ordered you shrimp cocktail. I thought about it and figured you might not want to share. I ordered me some too. Then I ordered a bottle of wine and two cans of Pepsi, and you said you also wanted a bottle of water. I figured cheese, crackers, and grapes would add to the presentation of the platter...just kidding," Zac said as he took the tray of food from the room steward. "Where do you want to eat, on the balcony?"

"No, set it on the bed."

Zac decided he liked that idea a whole lot better. Funny though, he knew if he would have suggested dinner in bed, she would have probably said on the balcony. *Why is it*, Zac thought, *men could never be right?*

Zac and Kristi sat cross-legged on the bed. Zac had opened the bottle of wine when Kristi reached for and popped open the Pepsi. "You don't want any wine?" Zac asked.

"I like wine, but the tannins give me a headache. And I'm too tired to have a headache on top of it," Kristi said as she popped a grape in her mouth. She handed Zac the two cookbooks she bought at the mountaintop gift shop. "So tell me about your walking tour."

"I can't remember eating so much food. Thank goodness it was a walking tour. Each saloon gave a sampling of their best bar food. The Inns and restaurants had samples of stuffed halibut, smoked salmon, and crab dishes you would have loved. I so wish you would have been there," Zac said, dipping his shrimp in the cocktail sauce. "I can't believe I am eating again."

"So did you get to see price listings of these samples? I mean would it be feasible to create some of the dishes at your restaurant?" Kristi asked, taking a sip of her Pepsi out of one of the wine goblets.

"You are drinking Pepsi out of a wine goblet?" Zac asked.

"Do you have a problem with that?"

"No. Guess not. I needed you on the tour so you could have taken pictures. I won't remember all the dishes when I get home. And yes, we either use local fish or get a lot of our fish fresh from the Northwest. They are overnight expressed shipped and kept cool but never frozen," Zac told Kris just like he had told many customers who worried the fish dinners they created were from frozen fish rather than fresh.

Kristi got up, rummaged through her backpack, and pulled out her electronic pad. "Okay, what were some of the items?"

Fifteen minutes later, she had gotten every sampling Zac could remember and described to her on her pad. She asked for his email address and sent it to him. She looked down and was amazed she had eaten her entire shrimp cocktail and some of the grapes. She fluffed the pillows on her side of the bed. She grabbed her camera and settled back, looking through the pictures she had taken over the past several days. "Wow, Zac, look at this."

Zac had also stretched out on his side of the bed and was looking through the cookbooks Kristi had bought for him earlier that day. He leaned over to see what Kristi was looking at.

"You got some great pictures of the orcas today. What other marine life did you take pictures of? Oh, I like that picture. The gulls were that close?

"Well, no, I zoomed in. But I must say, it would have been a better photo if the dang gull would have just smiled."

Grinning, Zac leaned over and kissed Kris on the lips. "You taste like Pepsi."

"Oh no, you knocked the plate of grapes and cheese all over the bed." Kristi laughed, picking up grapes and putting them either in her mouth or back in the bowl on the tray. Zac put the small plate of cheese in the minibar frig. He took the dirty cocktail dishes and tray and placed it outside the door on the floor. He poured some more wine in his glass and settled back on his side of the bed. "Kris, what do you think of this recipe?"

Kristi stood up and took her jeans off. She slipped between the sheets and brought her pillow close to Zac's shoulder. She laid her head on the pillow and looked at the recipe. "Yuck, that doesn't sound good. Who would put those spices together?"

"Some women here in Alaska, I guess," Zac said and turned the page. He took a drink of his wine and looked at more recipes. He was about to ask Kris about a recipe from some Tlingit women from Huna, when he noticed she was asleep. Obviously, the caffeine in the Pepsi didn't keep Kris awake like some people. Zac closed the book and set it on the bedside table. Who would have thought he would have read recipes to a blonde beauty, in bed, on a cruise ship. Shaking his head and thinking Mark was right, he must have buried his mojo under kitchen scraps and dirty plates.

As Zac turned off the lights for the night, he decided to leave the wall sconces on dim. It gave the room a warm glow during the darkest hours. Funny thing was, Zac grinned to himself, he would have never thought about leaving lights on or room ambience at home: he would have flipped the switch off. Here, those details seemed to matter. Kris loved to smell the salty air and listening to the water against the side of the ship, so Zac opted to leave the slider door halfway open. Besides, he liked the coolness of the nights; it gave him a good excuse to cuddle up with Kris. He got back into bed, drank the rest of his wine, and then pulled her closer to him.

It might only be 10:00 p.m., and most passengers on the ship were partying the night away, but for the first time in a long time, Zac was right where he wanted to be, holding Kris in the darkness, listening to the night sounds on the ship.

Kristi woke up sometime near one in the morning. Zac had rolled over, and the blanket had gone with him. Her backside was cold; actually she was freezing. She crawled out of bed and closed the slider. She found Zac's sweatshirt lying on the sofa, so she took her T-shirt off and pulled his shirt on. It was big, but the smell of

Zac's aftershave gave her a warm feeling all over. When she turned to get back in bed, Zac was holding the blanket open for her to climb under.

Kristi wanted Zac to make love to her. Actually, she didn't want to wait for him to slowly touch her, to caress her. She loved that he wanted to prove it wasn't just sex. He gave her time to trust that he wouldn't hurt her. He took his time exploring her. She knew he was opening his heart to her slowly especially knowing he wasn't and probably never would be over the sudden and unexpected death of his wife. She understood that. She appreciated all the care he had given her. But she wanted him now. He excited her like no other, in a very long time. She wanted him to touch her, and right now she was impatient. She wanted to hold every part of him to her for as long as she had with him. She wanted to feel the magic that he gave her when he pushed her to her limits.

She leaned over Zac and kissed him as he pulled the blanket over her. As the kiss deepened, she put her hand over his heart. He tried to warm her icy fingers by putting his warm hand over hers. But she slipped her hand away only to trail her fingers down his abdomen. She ran her thumb over the tip of his shaft. She wanted to touch him, to tease him, to ignite a fire in him. Kristi wanted Zac to realize how much passion she was capable of giving.

Zac groaned when Kris touched him. Her hands might be cold, but they felt good against the heat of his body. He felt her nipping at his tongue as her fingers kept stroking him. He didn't want her to stop. He turned, lifted his shirt from her body, and ran his tongue, hot and wet over her breast. He slid his fingers between her legs. He wanted to give her the same pleasure as she was giving him. Her skin was incredibly soft, and when he stroked her, she inhaled suddenly, arching her back. She was so wonderfully moist. He had wanted her when she was walking toward him on the dock this evening, but it was nothing compared to this moment.

Kristi was way past ready for Zac. She welcomed his body on top of her, nudging her legs apart. Kristi curled her lower abdomen, so when he entered her, she slammed her pelvis against his. The shock wave triggered a furiously fast pace. But she kept demanding more of Zac, pushing him deeper and harder. He dug his fingers into her hips bringing her to him. Kristi couldn't believe Zac's staying power. She saw him bite his lip. She knew he was waiting for her. It wasn't all about him and his needs. It was for her. He was fantastic. And then, the electrical current hit her. She screamed his name and held onto him as he slammed into her for one last time. His body never felt so good lying on top of her.

Zac thought his muscled had gone to jelly. He could feel Kris's heart pounding. She was breathing as heavy as he was. His body might be spent, but he wanted to explore this new layer of Kris that she just revealed to him. She was wild in her pursue of giving him pleasure. She was wickedly sexy. And he couldn't wait to make love with her again and again. But at this moment, he just wanted to enjoy holding her. He wanted to spend what was left of the night, looking at her. He raised his head from Kris's neck and brushed her hair away from her eyes. He ran his thumb over her bruised lips. She took his thumb in her mouth and sucked. He felt a jolt run through his lower body.

"My God, Kris, I don't think you know how incredible you are. I want to make love with you again," Zac said, never taking his eyes off her as he kissed her hand.

"I think it is more like we were incredible together. And right now, I just want to curl up next to you. I want to listen to your heart-beat," Kristi said sleepily. "Just hold me."

"I won't let you go, babe," Zac whispered. He rested his chin on her head. Her body fit so comfortable against his. He realized as he reassured Kris, his words meant more than just for tonight. He wanted more.

CHAPTER 11

Kristi woke to the sun sparkling on the snow-covered mountaintops. She didn't remember it being this sunny since she left Florida. She turned to see Zac resting his head on his hand, watching her. "What time is it?"

"It's not 4:30 a.m."

"I'm on vacation. I'm sleeping in this morning," Kristi said as she pulled the blanket over her head.

"I beg to differ, my lady. I have booked you with a personal workout trainer at 9:00 a.m. Ken texted me and asked if you wanted to do the advanced rock wall at 11:30 a.m., followed by a spin workout with Gretchen at 3:00 p.m. I heard she is brutal," Zac said, pretending to be serious.

"Say what? Nope, no way, I worked out yesterday," Kristi mumbled from under the blanket. Kristi wondered if making love to Zac in the middle of last night would count for exercise yesterday or today.

"Standing on a glacier is not working out. Standing on a whale tour boat is not a workout. Riding a tram up a mountain is not a workout," Zac said, lying against a bunch of pillows, counting off on his fingers one by one, the many ways Kristi did not workout yesterday.

"I went shopping, and I carried my souvenirs back to the ship." Kristi giggled.

"No, you didn't. You had your stuff shipped home."

Kristi folded the blanket down from her face with her arms and said, "Excuse me? One, I lifted my credit card, and two, I carried your two cookbooks," Kristi said, finding it really difficult not to laugh.

"I'm sorry, you're correct. And I thank you for those books," Zac said, once again trying to act humble.

"I might as well get up. I can't get any sleep around here," Kristi said as she grabbed a pair of jeans and sweatshirt from the closet on her way to take a shower.

"You weren't worried too much about sleep in the wee small hours of this morning," Zac said, throwing a pillow at her.

Kristi dropped her clothes on one of the sofa chairs. She turned around and walked, swaying her hips as sexy as she could, back to Zac, lying in bed. She dramatically kissed him, running her tongue along his teeth, and then dueling with his tongue while running her fingers up and down his chest. When she knew he was aroused by her tongue and caressing hands, she wickedly ended the kiss, turned around, and walked back into the bathroom laughing.

While showering, Kristi knew there would be paybacks for that very hot kiss. After all, there were always consequences for her actions; she had three brothers, so she knew. She remembered how her brothers gave her Barbie doll a Mohawk hairstyle for Halloween one year because she laughed at Kevin's haircut. Or the time, Kevin and Keith had been watching a monster movie. She crawled into the family room and jumped out from behind the sofa, scaring the twins. In retaliation, they put their hamster in a shoebox and slid it under her bed. They knew that the rodent was nocturnal and would scratch at the side of the box all night. Kristi had thought it was a monster trying to get her. As she thought back, she couldn't remember any time when KC was mean to her. He actually slept under her bed one night to prove there were no monsters. And if she remembered correctly, their mother thought someone stole KC and called the police. Kristi sighed; she missed KC.

Just as Kristi turned around in the dinky shower to rinse the suds out of her hair, the water turned ice-cold. She shrieked from the blast of frigid water until she saw Zac behind the curtain, laughing. "That is so not funny," she said, grabbing a towel.

"I thought you needed a little something to cool your hot body down a bit. As I recall, you said something about expecting me to make love to you in a couple of hours," Zac said as he leaned his "muscled in all the right places" body against the counter.

"You must have dreamed that last night."

"No, no, Counselor, you said, you were giving me, Zachariah Phellepe Karas, fair notice that you wanted me, Zachariah, to make love to you, Kristianna. What is your middle name?" Zac asked.

"Grace."

"Kristianna Grace Romanoff in a few hours. Its been a few hours. Actually, it's past a few hours, so you might have to handcuff me for contempt of court and send me to bed," Zac said, folding his hands together in prayer formation.

"As the prosecuting attorney for this case, I advise the courts to seek a psych evaluation before proceeding any further," Kristi said as she wrapped the towel around her head and marched out of the bathroom.

"What? Seriously, I'm not crazy."

"That's what they all say," Kristi hollered over the noise of her hair dryer.

"Good morning, everyone, I am Captain Augustinovich of this ship, and I would like to announce we will be entering Disenchantment Bay around 11:00 a.m. this morning. I have been notified there are some large icebergs floating in the bay, so we will be taking it quite slow. Once we get to Hubbard Glacier, if you so choose you may stay on your balcony suites as we will be maneuvering the ship 360 degrees so everyone may have the opportunity to view the glacier. Thank you."

As Kristi and Zac were on their way to breakfast, Zac said, "Since this is our last day at sea, I scheduled myself a massage after breakfast."

"Oh, that sounds really nice. Maybe I will wander through the gift shops. There is a sale going on this morning. You know, they are trying to get as much money out of the tourist before the end of the cruise as they can." Kristi grinned as they stood, waiting for the elevator to arrive on their floor. She was kind of hurt Zac didn't ask her if she wanted to get a massage also. But it was his vacation, and she had gotten to spend much more time with him than she had ever expected.

After Zac and Kristi had crammed into the elevator along with eight others, Zac whispered, "Oh, did I forget to tell you, I booked you a massage at the same time."

"You are so mean," Kristi whispered.

"Yeah, I know, but you love it," Zac whispered back.

Yes, Kristi thought, she did love it. She loved last night when he read recipes to her. Who does that? She loved that he had booked excursions at the last minute so she wouldn't be alone. She even had learned to love when he fed her food from his plate.

There was no rain-streaked windows this morning. The sun was out. The dining room was bright, and it seemed everyone milling around the food stations was in a happy mood. It looked like it was going to be a beautiful day. Kristi decided on a bowl of cantaloupe, watermelon, strawberries, and grapes. She added two slices of French toast and a mound of bacon. She was quite proud her plate wasn't heaping like some of the other days. Her excuse had been, what if they got stuck somewhere in the wilderness, she wouldn't get hungry and become a cannibal like in the movies. For some reason, Zac had found that seriously funny.

"What, are you on a diet?" Zac asked as he sat down at the table with his plate of waffles and bacon.

"Very funny, I'm going to get some orange juice. Do you want some coffee?" Kristi asked.

"Thanks, black, please," Zac said, then changed his mind. "Wait up, I will come with you." He had spotted the stalking jerk talking to the beverage attendant and didn't want the creep within ten feet of Kris. He didn't know what the guy's agenda was, but hopefully the guy only took the cruise and not extended his trip with the land tour.

Kristi was thankful Zac had come with her to pick up his coffee. She couldn't have carried two orange juice and two cups of coffee for Zac. After she had gotten the juice, she noticed the creepy blond guy leaning on the counter, talking to the man brewing coffee and setting up breakfast drinks. It was easy for her to ignore him since he was closer to the coffee and cappuccino service area. She would have waited for Zac and walked back to the table with him, but the creep scared her. And she wanted to keep as much distance from him as possible.

Once seated at their table by the window, Kristi watched Zac carrying his coffee back toward her. Even in a sweatshirt and jeans, he radiated confidence, success, and a sex appeal that turned many heads.

"Thanks for not letting me get your coffee. I appreciate it," Kristi told Zac when he sat down. "That guy is a persistent stalker, isn't he? Try this cantaloupe, it is so sweet," Kristi said as she held a piece of cantaloupe on her fork for him to taste."

Zac let Kristi place the piece of fruit in his mouth. He was surprised she was exposing a little bit more of her personality day by day. And today, she trusted him with her food. He had to agree with her the cantaloupe was very flavorful.

"Didn't you like it?" Kristi asked.

"Yes, it was really good. I was just wondering if it was shipped from Chile or Argentina. And I just want you to know, no one has ever served me breakfast fruit like you just did," Zac said quietly.

Kristi didn't know what to say. She noticed lately, out of the blue, Zac made little statements or said things that touched her soul. She loved every time he surprised her like that. Kissing her hand during dinner, for no reason. Calling her Kris and trying to protect her from that creepy guy. She wanted to enjoy every moment she had with him this week, remembering every personal gesture he made. But at the same time, she was so fearful his words were seeping into the deepest part of her heart. She didn't know what she would do when she had to say goodbye to him.

"Sir, would you like more coffee?" asked one of the dining staff.

"No thank you, Kris do you want more juice or a glass of water?" Zac asked before the staff person could get away.

"No thanks," Kristi said and smiled. "Zac, help me eat some of this bacon. The French toast was too filling. I am full, but it would be wasteful to just leave it."

"Would you want to fly in and stay at one of the resorts by Glacier Bay? You know do some hiking or skiing?" Zac asked as he was looking out the window at the snowcapped mountains.

"I never thought about skiing Alaska. I have skied most of Colorado and Lake Tahoe. What about you?"

"When I lived in France, I went skiing in Val d'Isere, Tignes, and Courchevel. And I may have skied Val Thorens, I can't remember, but I know for sure they know how to party there. Don't even think about mentioning that place to Mark. It is like taboo. When I came back stateside, I needed to take my French cuisine background and establish myself here, so after that, there was no time to ski," Zac said.

"So you and Mark used to do some hard partying, huh?"

"Oh, look at the time. Let's go get the kinks worked out of our backs," Zac said, pulling Kristi to her feet. He wondered how obvious it was to Kristi that he really didn't want to talk about the partying days of his life. Why did he even bring it up? It was a fun time in his carefree life back then, but culinary excellence and this lifestyle were more important to him.

They walked past the gift shops, the photo salon, the gallery walls full of auction artwork, and down the hall toward the spa area. There had been signs everywhere explaining the cruise-ship artwork auction later that evening. As Kris had said, it was just one more way of the shipping line getting the last hundred bucks out of the tourist. Right before they entered the spa's wooden doors. Zac stopped Kris by a porthole window looking out over the sea. He turned her to him and kissed her. It was one of those sensuous kisses that could last forever, and Kris wouldn't have minded.

"I couldn't remember what you tasted like, and now I know—strawberries and bacon," Zac said, hugging her to him.

Twenty minutes later, Kristi was on her stomach naked except for her lace thong and a towel over her bottom, on a mattress massage table across from Zac. She had never gotten a massage with a guy getting a massage at the same time. It felt awkward. But Zac had signed them up for a couple's massage, so here they were. The massage therapist drizzled very warm oil down Kristi's back and began to rub and massage the oils into her skin. It reminded Kristi of those baking shows where the contestants were kneading bread. Oh no, she was once again thinking of food.

Kristi had asked not to have a deep massage. Every time she had gotten one, she had spent the next day with muscle aches to her shoulders and back. It didn't matter she had drunk the recommended gallon of water to "remove the toxins" from the muscles; they still ached. She wanted a massage that made her purr, not one that beat up her muscles. She didn't care about the toxins at this moment; she wanted a pleasurable vacation-type massage.

Kristi looked over at Zac. His eyes were closed. She noticed his dark hair was starting to curl in his neck. It made his Greek heritage more noticeable, not that Kristi was complaining. She watched as the massage therapist worked on Zac's lower back. She would have loved for her hands to caress and massage his muscles. She wondered what he was thinking about—it was probably food. Oh, oh, the therapist massaged a knot between her shoulders; it was so tight. *Just give up*, Kristi thought. The soft music was so soothing; it was like a trickling brook—no, wind chimes in a breeze, soft and rhythmic. The coconut-scented mister reminded Kristi of suntan lotion on a hot day at the beach. The beach, she missed the white sand and the white sand and the—she was feeling no pain. Oh yeah, the beach, as she drifted while the therapist kneading her back, circles within circles within circles.

Kristi opened her eyes, which she thought was just moments from when she last looked at Zac, but the massage to her back and legs had stopped, and the massage therapist was gone. Zac was sitting on the edge of his table with a towel over his privates.

"How do you feel? Personally, I now know how a wet noodle feels," Zac said with a lazy-looking grin on his face like he could fall asleep if a breeze hit him.

"Did you hear me purring?" Kristi joked. She really didn't want to move; she was so comfortable. But also, she really didn't know how to get up off the table gracefully while almost naked with only a towel as cover. So she rolled on her side away from Zac and grabbed the thick fluffy robe lying on a stool next to the bench.

After they were dressed, they walked back the way they came. Zac asked if Kristi wanted to go shopping or if she wanted to stop at the juice bar. He saw her shake her head and just kept on walking.

Once back in the suite. Kristi flopped down on the freshly made bed. The massage had been great. Her skin felt soft, and the scented oil continued to lull her senses into such a calm state. She was so relaxed she could take a nap, one that she decided she desperately needed. Zac sat down on the side of the bed; he pulled off her boots and slid her jeans down her legs. The sweatshirt came next and was added to the pile of clothes once again on the floor. Zac ran his tongue along the lace cup of her bra. Kristi smiled thinking it felt like an extension of the massage they just had. She tried to pull Zac's sweatshirt over his head, but again her muscles wouldn't cooperate. So she watched as he stood and removed his shirt and jeans along with his shoes. He settled back down on his side and ran his thumb over Kristi's sensitive nipples. Kristi was surprised; she would have easily been subservient to Zac's lovemaking. But he instead, chose to pull the blanket from the side of the bed over them. He rested his head on her breast and slid his leg over her hips. Kristi slowly drifted off to sleep.

CHAPTER 12

"Come on, sleeping beauty. Wake up. The captain just announced the ship just entered Disenchantment Bay. Kris, it's time to take pictures. Yes, I should have said grab your camera, first. You would have been out the door." Zac laughed. He felt so much better after the quick nap. The massage had worked wonders on his tight muscles, but a nap and waking up with Kris had complimented the entire morning perfectly.

"Once again, I am putting on clothes from a heap on the floor. I am beginning to think you are a slob, Zac." Kristi grinned.

Zac had walked out on the balcony. Large chunks of ice were floating by, then he realized they were stationary in the bay, the ship was maneuvering past them. "Kris, grab your camera."

Kristi leaned up against Zac; she slid her arms around his waist and kissed him. "Just because." She smiled at him. "Why don't we go up to the top deck overlooking the pool? I bet the glacier will be beautiful from up there," Kristi stated as she then lifted her camera and took a few more pictures of the floating ice before they left.

It seemed there were a lot of people who had decided to stand along the railings of the ship, like Zac and Kristi. As the ship sailed deeper into the bay, Kristi could see the whitish-blue mountain of ice that once cascaded down the mountainside, in front of the ship. Although it was still miles away, the glacier was massive in size. The air was cool and crisp with a touch of sea salt.

A forest ranger from the Glacier Bay National Park service stood on the deck above the pool area, next to the twenty-foot totem pole. He picked up a microphone and said, "Welcome to Disenchantment Bay. We will soon be approaching the Hubbard Glacier. It is the largest tidewater glacier in North America. What that means is, it is a glacier that flows into the ocean. Hubbard Glacier is about seven miles wide. It is about seventy-six miles in length with its cirques or source from Mount Logan in Canada. Hubbard Glacier, like I said before, is a tidewater glacier. It continues to grow and move forward, calving into the bay. Calving is the huge chunks of ice that break away from the glacier and splash into the bay. The Tlingit people call it White Thunder.

"When we get closer to the glacier, you will see a channel in the bay that leads to Russell Fjord. Several years ago, the glacier was on a rapid move and completely iced off the fjord and almost flooded the village of Yakutat. No, the flooding was not due to global warming. A tidewater glacier constantly is forming and growing and moving, pushing ice and water from the bay into the surrounding landmasses."

Zac and Kristi watched as an orange inflatable motorboat with three crew members aboard motored away from the ship. They were so tiny in comparison the vastness of the bay.

"I wonder where they are heading," Kristi stated as she looked through the viewfinder of the camera. "Here look, Zac." She handed him her camera.

"You really can't tell how big the icebergs are, standing on the ship. But when you see that little boat near them, the bergs are huge," Zac said.

The mountainside surrounding the bay was different from the canals leading into Juneau, Icy Strait Point, and Skagway. There were gray-black stone-covered beaches here instead of the granite mountain jutting up from the sea. Kristi guessed it was from the submarine glacial sediments pushed up by the moving glacier settling along the shore over time. Since the sun was out, the water seemed such a vivid bright blue. The bay was actually mesmerizing to Kristi; the color was so pretty to watch.

It was very quiet out. There was a hush about the sea today, sounds were muffled, or the people on board were in awe of the beauty in front of them. She could hear the three crew members on the small vessel talking, even though they were quite a ways from the ship, above the hum of their small boat motor. She still couldn't figure out what they were doing out in the middle of the bay. Maybe they were getting water samples for some research project at the University of Alaska or something.

"Can you feel that? The ship slowed their engines down. Look at the size of Hubbard Glacier," Zac said to Kris just as a loud thunder echoed across the bay. A large chunk of ice fell into the bay, sending waves across the water. The ship, as large as it was, was dwarfed in comparison to the massive glacier field.

"Zac, look, the little boat just hauled an iceberg on board. Do you think it is for research on the glacier?" Kristi questioned.

"I don't know, but with the waves coming off the calving of the glacier and the weight of the iceberg on that little blowup boat, they better be careful of capsizing," Zac said, watching the little orange boat. "Kris, do you have video capacity on your camera?"

"Yes, I do, but it does take up a large chunk of memory space on the video card. Of course, I do have two cards in this camera," Kristi said, clicking through the options in the viewer's box.

"That camera has two different memory cards in it?" Zac looked at Kristi. "It might be cool to sit on your deck at home in the ninety-five-plus-degree days of summer watching a video of Hubbard Glacier calving. Your son might like seeing it also," Zac suggested.

"That was a really good oxymoron, you know, cool sitting in ninety-five-degree weather watching a glacier calve." Kristi laughed. "The nap was good for you."

Zac pulled Kristi to him and whispered in her ear, "Maybe, it's you. The nap had nothing to do with it."

Kristi's heart did another flip-flop. She turned and kissed Zac's cool lips.

Kristi held her camera, with her elbows on the railing to prevent lots of movement and readied the camera for video filming of the glacier when it calved again. She didn't have to wait long as another huge bluish-white sheet of ice let go from the glacier and thundered into the bay. The sound was loud, and of course many of the people standing next to the railings along the deck clapped and whistled. The latest calving opened a cave-like tunnel into a part of the 350-foot-high glacier. Kristi wished the ship could go closer. She would love to see how far the cave extended in; however, she knew how dangerous that was; the ice was unstable and already calving into the sea without notice. She took picture after picture of the blue ice. Then she spotted some really dirty ice floating close to the channel into Russell Fjord. "Zac, look how dirty that big hunk of iceberg is, wonder where on the glacier that slid from," Kristi asked.

"Yeah, that is really dirty. Wait, Kris check your camera. I don't think that is dirt," Zac said, and he squinted his eyes to try and see the iceberg better.

"Here, look."

"Hey, those are seals and a lot of them actually. How cool is that? Can you get a picture of them?" Zac asked.

As the captain had promised, the ship practically stood still, slowly rotating 360 degrees in place. It didn't go around in circles, but with one engine in forward and one engine in reverse, the engines' propellers moved the ship in a slow lumbering stationery circular rotation. Most anyone sitting in their balcony suites could see every aspect of the glacier, surrounding mountain ranges and open waters of the bay leading back out to the open waters of the northern Pacific Ocean. The rotation of the ship in the bay was a treat the navigation team probably dreamed up when the seas were calm, and radar showed nothing on the horizon but open water.

Kristi wondered what the retired commander was thinking about the 360-degree rotation of the ship. He probably saw all kinds of tricks his navigation team devised to combat boredom on slow time.

Clouds were starting to drift in, and although the air was fresh, it was turning chilly. Zac asked, "Kris, do you want to go to one of the café pubs for either a drink or a bite to eat?

"Sure, that sounds good."

Zac led Kristi to an elevator she had never been on. She actually hadn't been to this part of the ship. The elevator doors had been locked down, or maybe she didn't have the right key card. The inside compartment was a polished bronze color with black leather-textured doors. It had a fresh sea and leather smell to it. When the doors closed, Zac kissed Kristi with an urgency that almost melted her legs into a pool of goo on the gold-veined marble floor.

As many times as Zac had kissed her, each time was so very different. He had kissed her lightly, which urged her to want more. There was the kiss when she could see the teasing in his eyes, and he was pushing her to laugh and enjoy it for just what it was. There also was the surprise kiss in the tunnel, which was more like a secret-rendezvous kind of kiss. He had spontaneous kisses, which Kristi hoped meant he needed to touch her, but they were in public. And now, his urgent elevator kiss, as if he couldn't wait to be alone with her or at least that is what she wanted to think the kiss meant.

The elevator doors open onto a spacious sitting room surrounded by a wall of floor-to-ceiling windows. There were overstuffed chairs and small cocktail tables with bowls of fresh roses and carnations on each. And in the middle of the room was a circular bar fitted with everything in brass and black leather. It had the most impressive stock of liquor Kristi had ever seen. The entire room was designed to impress. And it did just that.

"Welcome, Mr. Karas, madam, to the Eagle's Nest. I will give you a moment to decide what you would like to snack on. But first, is there something special you would like to drink?" the bartender asked.

"Scotch and water for me. Kris, what would you like?"

"Cranberry vodka martini please," Kristi stated.

After the bartender left, Kristi whispered to Zac, "Is the key card programmed with your name on it, so when you unlocked the elevator, your name appears on his computer screen?"

"Yes, you are right. It probably tells him everything about me, including shoe size and the secret fact that I hit Billy Marshall in the butt with a rotten apple back in third grade," Zac said with a laugh.

The ship continued on its 360-degree turning as promised by the captain. Hubbard Glacier slipped out of view as the channel deeper up into Disenchantment Bay came into view. Zac sat in a very comfortable chair that he decided was probably used to encourage more lounging and drinking. He reached for Kris's hand. He loved the surprised look on her face when he did something she was not expecting. As he rubbed his thumb over the visible veins on Kristi's hand, he said, "I talked to my daughter, Lacey, the other night when we came back from dinner. She was working on a project and playing video war games. It is always interesting to talk with her. She usually has a perspective on things I would never have thought of," Zac said, looking out the window.

"What university is she attending?" Kristi asked.

"She's at Yale. Here comes our drink, do you know what you would like to eat?"

"You decide."

"Here is your cranberry Martini, madam, and, sir, your scotch and water. I would like you to know at 5:00 p.m. we start our happy hour with Glaciertinis, martinis made with genuine glacier ice. Have you decided what you would like from the grill?" the bartender asked.

"An order of crab bombs and garlic butter escargot. Thank you," Zac said.

"Are you going to try a Glaciertini with dinner this evening?" Kristi laughed.

"No, I don't think so, but it's a cute idea. And now we know why they were out trying to snag an iceberg," Zac said, taking a sip of his drink. He set it aside.

"Yale is a tough school. And far away from her dad, it must be hard on you," Kristi said, taking a sip of her martini.

"After Sara died, I didn't want Lacey out of my sight. But I realized it was selfish on my behalf and unhealthy for her. I had to let her go and grow into who she needs to be. It was so hard. First, I lost my wife, and then, I'm sending my daughter out on her own. I had a hard time with that. Anyway, when I talked to her the other night, she said something that was so deep and from the heart, it kind of blew me away," Zac said quietly.

"It's good she trusts you enough to speak her mind without repercussions," Kristi said.

"I never asked, were you able to get in touch with Eli?" Zac asked, knowing he was pushing Kris out of her comfort zone. He hoped the trust she just spoke about would apply to their relationship also.

Kristi watched as the glacier was coming back into view. She wondered how many times the ship had turned a complete circle already. Trust, did she have enough faith in Zac to explain what caused her so much pain the other night, or should she ignore it? Should she take the easy, less complicated road on this, or should she, for once, take the pothole-riddled nasty path. Maybe if she talked about it with him, she would get a different perspective and could blow the entire thing off.

Taking a deep breath and a gulp from her drink, she said, "Yes, I called him. All I wanted to say was hi. And tell him I loved him. But his father's not so nice wife got on the phone. She called me a couple of very nasty nouns, yelled I called too late, and clicked the phone off. I'm not looking for sympathy, I'm really not. I have done everything I could possibly do to keep Eli's life as normal as possible. I walked away so he wouldn't have to deal with the publicity of lies. It was just too much to handle that evening when all I wanted was to say hi."

There, Kristi thought, she said it. It was out in the open. And although she hated when people aired their dirty laundry, so to speak, on social media, she was not doing that. She just wanted to understand why she was considered an evil person when she had done nothing but call her son at 11:00 p.m. to say hi. He had done it to her so many nights in the past.

"Excuse me, can I refresh your drinks?" the bartender asked.

"Can I have a dram of water for my scotch? Kris, is your drink okay?" Zac asked.

"I'm fine, thanks."

"She actually interrupted a conversation between you and your son. She called you names and then hung up the phone?" Zac asked.

"Yes."

"Oh, babe, I'm sorry. Where was Eli's dad? Sorry, it's none of my business. But I do feel bad. You had to deal with that by yourself," Zac said. He picked up his drink and then set it back down.

"Actually, you stayed close to me that entire night. Every time I woke up, you were caressing my arm or tucking the blanket tighter around me. And I thank you for that. When I thought to call Eli or had a chance to call him, it has always been too late at night with the time difference, or I knew they were probably sitting down for dinner. Of course, I have been having very poor reception here. So that hasn't helped. Anyway, thank you for listening.

The bartender brought the crab bombs and escargot in garlic butter and set them on the coffee table in front of the glass windows. He added china salad plates, forks, and napkins on the side. He left and returned with the dram of water for Zac's drink. He said, "I'm sorry your scotch wasn't to your liking. Is there anything else I can get you?"

"No, thank you," Zac said. He wanted the bartender to go away. Yes, he knew the guy was just doing his job. But with Kris and the conversation he was having with her, timing was everything. He had wanted Kris to tell him about her tearful night. Now that he knew, there wasn't much he could do to help her. So he scooped out some escargot from the garlic butter and placed it on one of the plates. After one of the escargot was balanced on the fork, he turned to Kris. "Here taste this." He placed the tender morsel on her tongue, never taking his eyes off her.

"As my culinary expert would say, it's tender with the right amount of garlic to butter ratio. By the way, you might know him, his name is Zachariah Phellepe Karas," Kristi said.

"I've heard of him. Yes, I think he is arrogant, rather fat and bald," Zac said. As he picked up a crab bomb by its skewer, he added a little sauce to it and handed it to Kris.

"No, I don't think he's bald," Kristi said, holding her crab bomb in just the right angle for Zac to take a bite from it. "Hey, mister, maybe you should find your own woman, to buy you some crab bombs."

"The one in front of me is just fine. So you think I'm arrogant and fat?" Zac said, patting his hands on his stomach.

"Fat, no. Arrogant, hmm, well," Kristi said. "No, you aren't arrogant, but I had to tease you a bit. You did turn the water to cold in my shower this morning."

"Yes, I did and proud of it," Zac said, puffing his chest out the best he could.

While they ate the crab and escargot, Zac asked different questions about Eli trying to find out how damaged he was from being the pawn in an ugly divorce. Finally, when the last of the crab was gone, Zac said, "Thank you for telling me about the tears. I'm sure it was hard sharing that information with me. I understand how difficult it is to trust when faith in someone has been shattered. However, sometimes an outsider doesn't have a vested interest in the situation and can give a better perspective."

"Go on."

"It sounds like you are doing the best you can with Eli living there. Until he is out of that environment, you have to keep the peace for his sake," Zac said, thinking about the different possibilities.

"Thanks. I appreciate it. Eli will spend the summer with me before going off to Northwestern in fall," Kristi said.

"Northwestern, good school. What is he leaning toward career-wise?"

"Bioengineering, he wants to work on robotics and prosthetics but needs the biology degree first. What about Lacey, what is her field of interest?"

"She started with a major in political science but realized she really hated it. So it cost me about thirty-five thousand for her to change to physics and philosophy. I told her if she went into business management, she could intern at the Mermaid. I don't think she liked that idea, but you never know," Zac said.

Zac and Kristi sat and watched from their comfortable chairs as the ship completed its visit to Hubbard Glacier. The ship's horn blew as it set sail from Disenchantment Bay. Kristi watched as others came into the lounge; some took seats along the windows, and others hung out at the bar. Conversation with Zac was fun. There always seemed to be something to talk about or topics to explore. When they weren't talking it was a comfortable quiet time also. Like right now, when he seemed to be content to hold her hand. There didn't seem to be a need to say anything.

"You know we should probably get back and start packing our suitcases. We have to have them ready for pick up at 6:00 a.m. tomorrow morning," Zac said, pulling Kristi to her feet.

"I think the paperwork says we meet our land guide at 9:00 a.m.? So it will be an early breakfast. Oh, we need to split the room tab. Was the bill in the paperwork because I didn't see it?" Kristi said.

"I took care of it already," Zac said.

Once they stepped into the elevator, Kristi said, "Zac, that's not fair, you paid for all of those meals and the rock climbing and massages. I owe you half."

As the doors closed, Zac kissed Kristi once again. "You just paid your half of the bill." He smiled and kissed her again. "And that's for the fee for using my credit card."

"Thank you," Kristi said as her lips met his the third time.

CHAPTER 13

"Thank goodness most of my souvenirs were shipped," Kristi said as she packed her suitcase for the next part of her journey. Also, thank goodness for the laundry service the ship offered, she thought. Everything was clean and packed. All she had to do was put the last-minute things in her suitcase and have it at the door for the room steward to pick up at six in the morning. She placed the identification tags on her suitcase so it would be on the motor coach that she and Zac would be boarding at Seward tomorrow morning.

"I don't remember you buying all that much stuff in the port shops," Zac said while he folded his shirts and placed them in his leather duffle type suitcase.

"I got Eli a bunch of T-shirts and a couple of other things," Kristi said, thinking of the statue she had bought in Ketchikan for Zac. She looked at the pictures of it every once in a while. She still thought it was a great choice and idea. She hoped Zac would think the same when he opens the box. "Actually, Alaskan decor doesn't really fit well with flamingos and palm trees," Kristi joked.

"Don't tell me you have those pink plastic flamingos in your front yard," Zac said, putting a hand to his heart.

"Well, of course I do, it is the only way to spot my house from the street." Kristi laughed.

"Please tell me you are joking."

"I am. There are some in my neighborhood who would not approve of plastic lawn clutter. Do you want to eat at the main dining room this evening? It would be nice if we ran into the commander and his wife so we can say goodbye," Kristi asked.

"I thought about reserving a table at Carla's Crab Shack tonight. I was told it had top-of-the-line seafood. But we haven't eaten in the main dining room since our first night aboard ship. We can do that," Zac said.

It was the last evening of watching the sun go down out over the open water. Unfortunately, the fiery beauty setting in the west was diminished by the white shears draped over the massive windows of the main dining room. Kristi and Zac were guided to their seats at a table set for eight. As they sat down, Zac recognized the couple already at the table. They had been on the other helicopter on the Mendenhall Glacier excursion.

"Aren't you the couple from Florida?" asked the lady sitting next to Kristi.

"Yes. How did you like Mendenhall?" Kristi asked.

"We loved it. We went to lunch after the excursion with the other people from our helicopter. When we mentioned you were from the other side of the country, someone laughed and said you probably wouldn't thaw out until you got home."

"Oh, that's funny," Kristi said.

"Actually, I expected it to be far colder than it was. Of course, we weren't up there long enough to freeze," Zac said.

Another couple with a pouting teenager was given the seats next to Zac. Kristi watched as the mother asked her daughter to sit up straight in her chair rather than sloughing in an almost prone position. It was interesting, Kristi thought. There was a simple eloquence about the main dining room. The white damask table linens, the gold rimmed china, and the crystal stemware created the perfect table setting. And one unhappy child could dash the ambience of the place in a matter of moments.

The beverage steward made his way around the table pouring ice water as a last guest took the one remaining empty chair. Kristi turned from talking to the lady next to her and saw the creepy blond guy had taken that seat. Thank goodness there was water in her glass as she reached for it and took a gulp. *Put on your professional face and tolerate him*, Kristi thought. She looked at Zac and smiled.

"Baby, have you decided what you are having for dinner?" Zac asked Kris quietly.

"I think I am going to have the stuffed chicken marsala. And please do not let on any of our plans for the next week," Kristi said very quietly. She had turned her head so the creepy guy sitting across from her could not read her lips as she spoke to Zac. Thank goodness the table was large and round and not one of the rectangle tables like down the center of the room.

"I think I might have the beef wellington with asparagus, and I have a better plan," Zac said in a low voice.

"Are you going to the last stage show after dinner?" the lady next to Kristi asked.

"What is the show?" Zac asked.

"*The Phantom of the Sea*," the lady said excitedly. "It is like *The Phantom of the Opera* but a sea version, I guess. It starts at 8:00 p.m., but we are going right after dinner to get good seats."

"I think that is an excellent idea to do after dinner. We may just follow your idea," Kristi replied to the lady.

Once the meals were all ordered, Zac asked the couple's daughter what she was doing after dinner.

"I wanted to go to the pool and watch the *Star Wars* movie from when my parents were my age, with my friends. But I have to pack. It's not fair. I'm not going to get to say bye to them," she said with a scowl on her face.

Zac said to her, "They probably won't be there either; their parents will make them pack also."

Kristi stole a glance at the creepy blond guy. He was on his second drink and not really following any of the conversations at the table. She knew it was not nice to stereotype someone, especially in her profession, but her instincts were usually right. He had that shady character look to him. His eyes kind of darted around the table, not really tracking any one thing. It was weird. He was weird. And she just hoped he would eat and leave without a scene.

The meals arrived, and conversation slowed down between mouthfuls. The beverage server brought the creepy guy another drink. Zac had ordered a glass of red wine with his beef wellington and still had half a goblet remaining. Kristi was drinking ice water. She didn't feel like having a headache from wine later in the evening. And she really wanted to stay focused on not letting the creepy guy get any information. So far, he wasn't doing anything but eating.

Sure enough, the man next to Zac asked him if they were going to Denali tomorrow.

"Actually, an important business matter came up, and I am trying to make arrangements for us to fly home in the morning," Zac said.

"Oh, that is a shame. I heard Denali is awesome," the man said.

"What about you, what are your plans?" the man asked the creepy blond guy.

"I'm not sure. I haven't looked at my schedule in a while," He said.

Zac looked at Kristi, and she looked at him. Well, that was odd, Kristi thought. She wondered how fast she could inhale her dessert. She just wanted to be away from here. And she was sure Zac felt the same way.

The dessert for the evening was either brownies with ice cream or cheesecake with raspberry sauce over the top. Zac ordered the brownie, and Kristi ordered the cheesecake. Kristi had to laugh because the couple next to her was eating fast so they could get those "perfect" seats.

"Are we ready?" Zac asked Kris and took her hand. "Good night, everyone."

Kristi was behind Zac as they started to walk between their table and the next when the creepy guy's hand grabbed Kristi's arm.

"I need to talk to you."

"No, you don't. Leave me alone."

"Get your hand off her arm," Zac hissed quietly.

"You are making a mistake. I need to talk to you."

"Zac, please let's go," Kristi said to Zac and pulled her arm free from the creepy guy's grasp on her.

"Wait."

"Either you leave her alone, or I will get security," Zac said as he started to guide Kristi out of the dining area.

But the guy followed them.

The lobby leading to the dining room was full of people waiting their turn for dinner service. Kristi could see maneuvering through the double doors would be a slow process. The hungry guests wanting to get into the dining room were passing the time, describing their adventures in different ports. They were ignoring anything other than their conversations. Kristi pointed out two either guest relations or security at the dining entrance doors to Zac.

"Please help us," Zac said as they neared the personal by the doors. "That man has been following and harassing us." He pulled Kris close and continued to move through the doors into the main concourse of the ship.

Kristi turned and thankfully saw security rush to block the creepy guy from advancing any further toward them. She felt Zac's arm around her shoulder, moving her away from the line of hungry guests.

"You are making a mistake. I was hired by your ex-husband to bring you back to him. He doesn't want you with that loser!" the creepy guy yelled as he motioned toward Zac.

Kristi stopped in her tracks. She turned around slowly and said, "What did you say?"

Security had slackened their grip on the creepy guy's arm.

"I was hired by Mr. Romanoff to watch over you. And report to him if you were serious about him."

"I have filed a complaint with guest relations earlier in the week. Now, I demand that you keep him away from me," Kristi said to the security guard. She was shocked that Dominick would pull such a low-down trashy stunt. She realized she was no longer scared but angry as all hell. How dare he continue to think he had ownership of her life?

"What country or jurisdiction do we have to contact to file a harassment suit against this man?" Zac asked the security.

By this time, several people were milling around trying not to watch the scene unfold, but since there wasn't any other drama on board, it seemed like the only action going on. Kristi wanted no part of it. She let Zac guide her away but not before Zac said, "Keep him away from us."

Instead of going to *The Phantom of the Sea* stage area, Zac lead Kristi back to their suite. Once inside, the door locked, they both walked to the balcony and fresh air.

"I didn't see that coming," Zac said, leaning against the rail with his back to the sea.

"No, me either. However, it's all starting to make sense," Kristi said, staring out over the water. "Remember the night of tears?"

"Yes, go on," Zac said, putting his arm around Kristi's shoulders.

"Well, the morning after, I thought I was dreaming the alarm was going off, but it was really my phone ringing. It was my ex-husband. He said that he and Eli had gotten in a fight and Eli stormed out. He said I needed to fix things. As if I was there. Then he said he wanted me back, as in a family for Eli. I turned off my phone on him. We have been divorced for five years."

"So you are saying your ex hired this guy to check up on our relationship because he wants you back?" Zac stated.

"It makes sense to me," Kristi reasoned. And maybe that was the same reason she wasn't more upset about the entire situation. She now knew the guy wasn't a stalker, just a pawn in her ex's never-ending ways to get an edge on things not going his way. Well, she still wasn't going to buy into Dominick's game.

"Gee, I wonder how much your ex will pay me to stay away from you. I could pay off my restaurant mortgage," Zac teased, grinning to lighten the tension.

"You are so mean to me," Kristi whined but threw her arms around his neck, pulled him to her, and kissed him. She loved the feel of Zac's arms as they slid around her middle. "You know they aren't going to do anything with him," Kristi said between kisses.

"Yes. But I wasn't sure you wanted to hear that." Zac kissed Kristi's neck.

"I am not an expert on maritime law. It's a cool field of interest though." Kristi's brain was turning to mush as Zac continued to kiss her neck. "Cruise ships determine punishment of crimes based on the country the ships are registered in. They can detain or confine a person to their quarters. And they may report issues to the port authorities when they dock. But since the creepy guy didn't actually harm me, they won't do anything," Kristi said.

"Are you okay with that?"

"The guy is a hired thug for Dominick. That makes me angry, but I am also doing a happy dance because I know how much it cost Dominick to pay for that's guy's working vacation," Kristi laughed.

"Two things don't add up. One, how did Dominick know which ship you were taking, and two, didn't Alana tell us the cruise was totally booked?"

"Eli probably told Dom. I don't remember giving Eli the specifics though. And someone else might have canceled their cruise at the last minute, and that's how Dom got the creep on. There isn't anything I will do until Eli is out of Atlanta for good," Kristi said, lost in thought as she stared out across the dark water.

Zac turned and stood behind Kristi with his arms around her and his chin resting on the top of her head. Neither spoke. It was a peaceful last night at sea. The water quietly rushed the side of the ship; the moon shone on the flat sea as Zac swayed back and forth on his feet.

"Come on, I want to take you somewhere," Zac said, grabbing Kristi's hand, and headed for the door.

CHAPTER 14

There were very few people in the hallways after the late serving of dinner. Many guests went to the evening performance of *The Phantom of the Sea* musical. Some guests headed back to the casino to try their luck one last time. Hopefully, the little girl at dinner got her packing done and was granted privilege to visit her friends at the pool. He had learned through experience, those childhood friendships were a kid's entire world, which most adults dismissed.

As he and Kristi headed to the elevator, they were the only ones who needed it at the moment. So naturally, when the door closed, Zac kissed Kristi. Zac decided it had become a new policy to kiss Kris in all elevators. When the door opened, he stared at her for a second, grinned, and said, "Just because."

They walked hand in hand to the piano bar. A man sat at the baby grand playing a song Dionne Warwick had once sung from the sixties. It was one of those slow-moving love songs Kristi remembered her parents had danced around the living room to. She and Kai, her brother, closest to her in age, sat on the stairs, out of sight but still able to watch them. Kristi smiled at the memory. She walked over to one of the high-top table and chairs and took a seat. There weren't many people this evening listening to the music which suited Kristi just fine.

"I got you an amaretto and soda," Zac said, setting the glass down on the table. "The bartender said the singer should be back from his break any time now."

Kristi swirled her drink around the sides of the glass. There was something special about the fragrance of almonds and vanilla that gave her a warm feeling of remembrance of something from long ago. She didn't know what it was, she had searched her memory every time she drank amaretto, but nothing came to mind. It was there like a soft cloud drifting in the corner of her mind, just out of reach.

"Kris, you are far away. But wherever it was, sure must be a pleasurable place," Zac said with a sad smile on his face.

Kristi handed him her drink. "There is something about amaretto, I can't put my finger on it, but it is a very soothing aroma to me. Like you said, it is a pleasurable place I just can't remember."

"Maybe you were Bernardino Luini's lover in a past life," Zac said, smiling.

"I don't understand. Who was Bernardino Luini?" Kristi asked, continuing to swirl the liquor around in the glass.

"You love the scent of the amaretto. Aromas trigger memories, and in your case, maybe with the amaretto *il y a un amour secret*, there is a secret love," Zac said, thinking of the story and how it was told to him in French. "I was sitting at a small outdoor café in Paris one night, drinking, when an elderly lady came to me. She was very refined. She sat and with a hand, jewelry on every finger, motioned for *bouteille de vin*. The bottle of wine she shared was a lot more expensive than I could afford back then. Anyway, she spoke only in French but told me a very romantic story. It was a *légende*, a legend about a painter. He was looking for a model for a painting he was commissioned to create. This Bernardino Luini met a lonely young innkeeper who became his model and quite possibly his lover. As the story goes, she gave him a gift of apricot kernels soaked in brandy. And that is how, some say, amaretto originated. Who knows, but when you had that faraway look in your eyes and I mentioned you must be at a pleasurable place, it reminded me of that story."

"That is so interesting and, of course, romantic," Kristi said. She was fascinated by the story, or maybe it was how Zac retold the legend. She could see in her mind a secret romantic love affair between a painter the odor of turpentine and paint surrounding him and a lonely overworked innkeeper. Oh, good grief, Kristi thought, she was fantasizing about a possible legend because she was sniffing amaretto. But then she watched as a tall man with a dark beard and dark eyes picked up the mic and started singing a familiar ballad about two hearts missing love in the night.

"Kris, I would like to dance with you," Zac said, placing his hands on Kris's arms. "I don't want your ex-husband to ruin our dance," Zac explained, touching his finger to her temple. "It's time he stopped trying to take everything away from you that you enjoy in life. And I don't want that creepy guy messing with your mind, either." Zac paused, never taking his eyes off Kris. "My wife, I will always love her, but she will never come back. The things that she taught me will be forever in my heart. But tonight, I want to dance with you," Zac said, holding his hand open for her.

The singer's voice was clear and sometimes full of pain as he sang love song after love song while the ship sailed through the icy waters of the northern Pacific Ocean. Kristi floated in Zac's embrace as they danced, never taking her eyes off his. Some danced to songs remembered. Other guests danced unnoticed. The bartender swirled potions to enhance some dancer's rhythm. And yet, some danced who shouldn't. But tonight, for Kris and Zac, there were no injured toes or awkward twists, just an easy-fitting continuous waltz around the marbled floor.

Zac lightened his hold on Kris as the last notes on the piano faded into the night. The other dancers slowly drifted off the dance floor. One couple discussed with another, their plans to spend a few more hours rolling the dice in the casino. One last walk along the top deck in the moonlight sounded romantic to one couple, dashed away by the reminder of the chill off the icy dark water.

Their drinks now watered down and forgotten, Zac asked, "May I walk you back to your suite?"

"Thank you, that would be nice. Did you enjoy your evening dancing, sir?" Kristi asked as they slowly walked back along the long narrow hall to their suite. It was a rather boring hall with door after door on either side. There was nothing on the walls to look at, no pictures, just gold color wallpaper or textured paint maybe. Kristi couldn't tell which it was in the dim light. But she couldn't remember thinking about it any other time they walked the walk. Actually, she decided she didn't care because after tomorrow morning she would never see it again.

"Ah, here is your suite, miss," Zac said and bowed as he inserted his key card into the lock slot.

"Would you like to come in for to see my artwork, or maybe a cup of coffee?" Kristi said, grinning.

"Since this hall is rather boring, yes, I would like to come in. I didn't know your suite has a coffee machine," Zac stated.

"It doesn't, but it was a great way to lure you into my room." Kristi giggled as she slammed the door shut and kicked off her boots.

Zac pulled Kristi's sweater over her head while she fumbled with his trouser belt buckle and zipper. Zac's sweater landed on the sofa along with Kristi's black pants. He undid the clasp on her bra and slipped his thumb under her tiny wasp of lacy underwear, sliding it down her legs. Every time Zac touched Kristi's skin, he marveled how soft and silky it was. Tonight was no exception. But this evening, he not only wanted to caress her body; he wanted to explore every inch of her slowly, oh so slowly. Kissing her neck, then her shoulder, Zac gradually guided her to the bed. Thank goodness the room steward had pulled back the quilt and folded it neatly at the foot of the bed because Zac knew it would not have that professional look to it if he tried it.

Kristi scooped up the mints the room steward had placed on the pillows and set them on the bedside table. "Remember our pact, Zac. I sleep on the right side of the bed on my right side and you on your left," Kristi said, grinning.

"Not going to happen, my lady. If I have it my way, you are going to get very little sleep tonight whether you are on the right side or the left side of the bed," Zac said quietly. With the sliding glass door open, the cool crisp air, and the sound of the water rushing the side of the ship, Zac felt like they were removed from the rest of the world. It was just him and Kris. He wanted nothing more than to slide into her warm moist body. But it was their last night aboard ship, and while it drifted northward through the night, he wanted to take his time making love to her.

Kristi put her arms around Zac's neck and pulled him down with her onto the bed. "So it is the middle of the bed for us, right?" Kristi giggled, but loving the feeling of his entire body stretched out alongside hers. It was unbelievably sensuous Kristi thought when Zac started caressing her hips, pulling her even closer to him. She could feel how aroused he already was. So when she rubbed her breasts against his chest and heard his moan, it excited her even more.

Kristi wanted this evening and her time with Zac to last as long as possible, but she couldn't stop her hands from wanting to touch and explore every part of his body. She ran her tongue along the curve of his mouth and then slowly sucked on his bottom lip while her hands pressed ever so lightly against the side of his face.

Zac urged Kris onto her back and began to inch his way kiss by kiss down her body. He stopped to explore her very tender breasts. Rolling his tongue around her right nipple, he decided he enjoyed Kris's hands massaging and running her fingers through his hair. It reminded him of the kneading paws of a very content kitten. And that was his main desire for Kris; he wanted to see total contentment in her eyes and body after making love to her.

Kristi enjoyed the feel of Zac's warm tongue playing with her nipple. He sucked it into his mouth. His tongue teased and rolled around it until she knew it was rock hard. She wanted Zac to feel the same pleasure as he was giving her. She rubbed the palm of her hand over his breast as she felt the tingle of his sucking on her nipple deep in her abdomen. She instinctively drew her knees up only to have Zac lower his head and run his late evening facial stubble across her stomach.

Kristi ran her fingernails up and down Zac's back. She wanted to caress her way down his body the same as he was doing to her. She thought about how the massage therapist had pressed her hands along Zac's lower back earlier today. She wanted to trail her hands down the column of his spine and caress his taunt bottom side, pulling him against her pelvis.

"Zac," Kristi called out as she felt his tongue tease the inside of her leg inching closer to the very spot she couldn't wait for him to explore deeper. She loved the sensations Zac was creating in her. She tilted her hips and arched her back; his tongue was provoking every sensual nerve in her body. She knew she was way past being ready for him. *So much for taking it slow*, she thought. She pulled her fingernails up the inner part of Zac's thigh, knowing for sure it aroused him as he pulled his leg in toward her hand and groaned. She moved her thumb over the tip of his firm shaft. The texture was so hard but velvety smooth.

Zac wanted to continue to explore and pleasure every inch of Kris's body. But when her thumb slid over his shaft and she ran her fingers up and down its sensitive sides, he didn't know how much more staying power he had left. Yet he thought of all the ways he had wanted to excite Kris's body. He loved hearing her call his name. But for one selfish moment, he thought how great it would feel to stop his exploration of her and enjoy what she was doing to him. Her fingers made him so hard; he ached to sink himself in her very moist and soft body. He wanted to feel her muscles around him and caress him. He wanted to dance with her and inside her until she arched her back. He wanted to feel her climax, gripping him from within and hear her calling out his name. He wanted her to push him to his own threshold and then beyond, where he could not hold back any longer. He wanted everything Kris was willing to give him. He realized he was being greedy in his want of everything from her.

Kristi couldn't wait any longer. She needed Zac deep inside her. She wanted him to fill her empty body with his. She pleaded with him, "Zac, I need you now. Please, Zac." She had never begged or craved anything as much as she wanted him to satisfy her body's hunger. She wanted him inside her at that very moment. His fingers had teased and circled her, but it wasn't enough; she wanted to feel him all the way to her very core.

But Zac continued to tease her very wet spot. He slid the tip of his shaft to the edge but would not dip into her. She cried out, begging him, but he continued to deny her what she wanted. She pleaded with him, raking her fingernails down his back. Zac felt her nip at his shoulder, her breathing deep and rapid. He knew she was almost to the very edge. Her skin was damp and her muscles tight. She moved against him trying to obtain the satisfaction her body was demanding.

"Zac, I want you. I want you now." Kris knew that the words were like a double-edged sword. By admitting she chose him, she was admitting her weakness for him. It both excited her and scared her. She knew from experience that by exposing her heart, it could be broken in pieces. But she was also finally telling Zac she chose him and not just for sex.

Zac plunged into Kris as deep as her body would take him. He knew when she said she needed him, she was seeking pleasure, but when she said she wanted him, she had chosen him. She finally opened her heart.

Kristi thought she was going to die from relief when Zac finally slid into her. His pelvis rocked against hers, stretching her muscles until they too cried out in a frenzy of spasms. She held onto Zac for fear she was free falling into an abyss.

As much as Zac enjoyed Kris's muscles climaxing against him, he continued to stroke her. His hair felt damp on his neck, and Kris's fingers slipping on his skin. He shifted his weight and pushed deep again and again. He felt Kris's muscles tighten a second time against him, finally pushing his own body to climax in wave after wave deep inside her.

Kristi wrapped her legs around Zac and held him to her. It took a while for his muscles to finally relax, and his breathing slowed down. Kristi kept her hands on the back of his neck, running her thumbs in slow circles across his shoulders. She ran her fingers through his hair; his scalp was damp. His skin smelled of citrus and almonds, or was that the fragrance of her body lotion on him? Her mind felt fuzzy, and she just wanted to rest her eyes. She had gotten used to the sound of his heartbeat in her ear; it was soothing, so comforting. *Stop thinking so hard*, she thought.

Zac finally raised his head from Kris's neck. In a slow sensual kiss, Zac explored her mouth with his tongue. She tasted good. It wasn't the word he ever wanted to hear in the culinary world. He demanded superb. He demanded excellence. But at this very moment, he was content to hold her and savor every part of her. Zac realized whatever energy he had left in reserve, that kiss took it. So much for his plan to make love to her all night, maybe he would call this their practice for tomorrow night. Amazing, he thought, he was already thinking about making love to her again.

Kristi was pulled from her tranquility when Zac started to roll off her. "No, stay, I love the feel of your body on top of me." She heard herself whisper to Zac.

"Oh, you are so beautiful," Zac said, easing Kris's hair away from her face. "Are you falling asleep on me?"

"No, I think I'm under you. I'm not complaining, though. I could stay this way all night," Kris murmured as she raised her head to kiss Zac's lips.

"Baby, I need a shower. If you come with me, I'll wash your hair," Zac tried to joke. All he wanted to do was curl next to Kris, but his skin and hair were damp and salty from their sexcapade. He didn't want to spend all tomorrow, make that later today, sitting in a leisure traveling coach feeling grungy. So he did in fact slide off Kris and ambled into the shower not bothering to turn on the light.

The warm water felt good, slushing down Zac's body. He soaped up his body and then just stood under the spray letting the water wash over him. The suds sliding down his back reminded him of Kris's fingers tracing his spine just a while ago. And then Zac realized Kris's fingers were really sliding down his back; he wasn't imagining it. As she pressed herself against his back, he smiled because he wanted her again. There was enough room to barely turn around in the tiny shower stall. He realized the tight quarters of the shower stall, the last time he tried to wash Kris's hair. Yet he still would have loved to slide into her wet body and make love to her again. Grinning, he wondered if he was really asleep and dreaming he was in his twenties, hot and bothered by the thought of wanting this sexy woman, again and again. He turned the sprayer to cool.

"Hey, turn the water back to warm," Kris complained, hugging Zac's back. "That's cold."

"You should have gotten in here earlier. I think we ran out of hot water," Zac teased. He knew they had to get some sleep. It was only a couple of hours until they had to set their suitcases out for the steward and leave the ship.

"No, we didn't," Kris said as she ran her tongue along Zac's shoulder. She could feel him shudder from the unsuspecting sensation of her mouth on him.

"Baby, as much as I want to make love to you right here, the shower is too small and we have to get some sleep."

"Yes, father dearest. I hate your logic. But I guess you're right." Kris pouted, running a soapy cloth over Zac's back and then down her own body before rinsing and grabbing a towel.

Before heading back to bed, Kris tucked the remnants of her discarded clothes scatter across the room into her suitcase. She closed the slider door to the balcony and climbed back into bed. She welcomed the heat of Zac's warm body as she snuggled next to him and closed her eyes. Her lips curved into a smile as she thought how great it would feel to always fall asleep in Zac's arms.

CHAPTER 15

Zac woke when Kristi snuggled her head deeper into his pillow. The dim glow from the wall sconces, they let on every night, cast enough light for him to see Kris's velvety smooth shoulders. He pulled the blanket over her exposed skin and listened to her quiet breathing. It had amazed him at how easily Kris had touched his heart. She was not only beautiful to look at, her personality was consistently sweet. Even when she was upset, she was still kind. Zac sighed and reached for his phone to check on the time. He realized he could rest a little longer, but sleep would not come to him. So slipping out of bed, he reached for his jeans and the denim shirt he had laid out before going to bed.

Zac tiptoed to the door of the suite. He needed to set their suitcases in the hall for the cabin steward to pick up. He and Kris had put the travel destination tags on their luggage the night before, as instructed on their final destination departure papers. It said they needed to be set out before 6:00 a.m.; an hour or so wouldn't matter. As Zac set them out in the hall, the steward who had turned their beds down, removed their room service trays, and made all sorts of creative animals out of their towels came by to pick up the early cases.

"Ah, thank you, Mr. Karas," whispered the steward.

"Hector, I know we prepaid our gratuities, but here is a little something extra for the exceptional service you provided for us," Zac said, handing him an envelope.

"Thank you, Mr. Karas, I appreciate it," said Hector as he bowed his head.

"You told Kris you were from Brazil. When will you get to return home to see your family?" Zac asked.

"I am with the cruise ship until the last voyage late in October. Then I return home for a bit of time. But I would like to try to sign for some South America cruises. You see, that is will be our spring vacation season and then Christmas holidays," Hector explained.

"Wow, that would be fantastic. I hope it works out for you. I won't keep you. But again, thank you for all your service," Zac said and stepped back into the suite.

"Zac, who were you talking to?" Kristi slurred, half-asleep.

"I just put our suitcases out for the steward to pick up, babe. You can sleep a little longer," Zac said as he sat down on the side of the bed and brushed Kris's hair away from her eyes. "I'm going to go get a cup of coffee. I'll be back."

"Okay, I'll get dressed while you're gone."

As Zac clicked the door shut, Kristi still hadn't moved from her comfy position in bed. Zac smiled.

Getting to breakfast early must have been on everyone's mind, not only Zac's and Kristi's. The main breakfast buffet area was busy with people standing in line to select their food. The chefs were busy fulfilling orders for omelets and eggs benedict. The help crew was replenishing the hot food pans as fast as they could. Tables were filling up fast. Zac grabbed the last table by the window while Kristi went for some sustenance. She returned with fruit and yogurt dip and some scrambled eggs and bacon. When Zac returned, he had pancakes, a veggie omelet, and some smoked salmon.

"Babe, did I leave my toothbrush on the bathroom counter or did I put it in my backpack?" Zac asked Kristi looking at his food with a puzzled look on his face.

"You did."

"Counter or backpack?"

"Huh?" Kris asked as she pushed the scrambled eggs around her plate.

"What's wrong?"

"Nothing, I just had so much fun on the cruise and island hopping, I hate for this part to end," Kristi said with a grin, not reaching her eyes.

Kristi was watching Zac as he cut into his hotcakes when all of a sudden, in front of their table, there was a large crash. Two people in their hurry had bumped into each other. A huge blob of scrambled eggs landed inches from Kristi's booted foot. Shards of china plates and bits of golden-brown French toast were scattered all over the floor. Both victims of the collision had food down the fronts of their shirts. The chatter in the dining room stopped, conversations ceased, heads turned to stare, and bites of food on forks stopped midway to mouths. The two slimed in the process, burst out laughing at the sight, and apologized to each other, then life resumed.

"I didn't do it," Kristi said to Zac, shrugging.

"I think you did."

"Nope, did not." Kristi watched stewards rushed to clean the broken china and goo from the carpets.

"I saw you," Zac said.

Just then, the commander with his wife walked up behind Kristi and said, "Kristi, why did you throw your food at those people?"

Zac looked at Kristi as she looked at him. They both erupted in laughter.

"We just wanted to stop and say goodbye before we leave ship. I hope I'm not breaking in on something really funny," said the commander, grinning.

"No, we were just laughing about how close we were to getting splattered with eggs and French toast. Commander, it has been a pleasure meeting you and your wife," Zac said as he stood and extended his hand.

"Are you traveling onto Fairbanks?" Kristi asked the commander's wife.

"No. We are taking the train to Anchorage, where we will catch our flight home this evening. It was so nice to meet you, Kristi, and you too, Zac," she said bending down to hug Kristi. She whispered in Kristi's ear, "Take care of your hunk of a man. He loves you dearly, I can tell."

"Thank you. I will." Kristi smiled. "You have a safe trip home."

After the commander and his wife left, Kristi pushed her half-eaten plate of food aside. She was happy they had gotten to know the commander and his wife, but the deception she and Zac were a couple made her sad. It just seemed easier than trying to explain the whole thing out.

"Babe, you're not going to finish eating?"

"I'm not really hungry. Oh, it's in your backpack." Kristi sighed.

Zac laughed when he realized what Kris meant. "Let's go find our coach." He extended his hand to help her up.

Once again, there was a long line waiting at the elevators to descend to the portside lower level, to leave the ship. Zac grabbed Kristi's hand and led her to the stairs. People were orderly, but still not everyone could maneuver the stairs as rapidly as others. Once off the wide staircase, the trek down the narrow, winding halls were slow and crowded. The air seemed thick and warm. It had a slight salty brine smell to it, so they must be almost to the hatch doors, Zac thought.

Thank goodness the ship had the foresight to understand that the luggage would be cumbersome to many of the passengers as they bumped and pulled their cases down the gangways. It would slow the time of walking the halls even more. All personal baggage had been picked up at or around six o'clock that morning. It was sorted and placed on the docks, steering each passenger leaving the ship toward their transportation zone. Some passengers disembarking the ship were traveling to Anchorage by train to fly home. Some were leaving by rental cars touring Seward and the surrounding areas. Kristi and Zac were among the many traveling by coach toward Anchorage for the afternoon and then onto Denali National Park for the night.

Zac continued to hold Kristi's hand; however, walking side by side was, at times, difficult. People jostled and banged into each other, apologizing along the way. Once outside the ship on the gangplank leading to the dock was no better. Everyone seemed to be in a hurry to find their luggage and be on their way. Thank goodness it wasn't raining or bitter cold as Zac and Kristi stood in line on the descending wooden ramp.

Kristi, although she was looking forward to the land part of their journey, was sad to leave their cabin and the ship. She had enjoyed getting to know Zac's personality. He made her feel warm and secure, like she hadn't felt in a long time. He gave her reason to smile and laugh. Yet she was sad; they only had a few more days before their time together ended. At the thought of going back to her normal life, life without Zac, her stomach knotted, and she felt nauseated.

Someone accidentally stepped on Kristi's booted foot. The lady gave an apologetic smile and complained how crowded the walkway leaving the ship was. Kristi grinned and agreed as she glanced past the lady for one last look up at the balcony suites on the upper deck side of the ship. Making love to Zac these last couple of nights had been so amazing. If someone would have told her when she signed the papers at Alana Week's travel agency that she would fall in love with Zac, she would have laughed. But it was true; he had charmed his way into her heart. He may not have realized it or even planned it, but he had romantically selected foods to share with her. He had chosen to forgo many of his culinary ventures to spend time with her on her excursions. Thinking about their evenings together warmed her heart. It gave her hope.

Kristi felt a tug on her arm. She thought the sleeve of her jacket had gotten caught on part of the steel guard railing. She had gotten jostled against it a couple of times. When she turned around, there stood the creepy blond guy with a grasp on her arm.

"Let go of my arm," Kristi said through clenched teeth, glaring at him.

"You need to come with me. I will take you back to Atlanta."

"No, let go!" Kristi screamed.

Zac turned to see the creepy blond guy's hold on Kris. He gave the guy a shove backward to get him away from her. The guy lost his grip on Kris's arm, flung his hands up in the air, hitting the gentleman behind him in the face. At that point, everything seemed to move in slow motion. The gentleman reacted by shoving the creepy blond guy to the side toward the protective guard railing. At the same moment, a little boy had stopped to tie his shoe. The creepy blond guy tripped over the little kid, which in turn made the child's parents really angry. The mom bent down to comfort her now howling youngster. The furious father stoked by his anger, grabbed the creepy blond guy by the shoulders, and shoved him back into the railing, hard. The creepy blond guy tangled around and lost his footing once again, tripping over the child and now the kneeling mother. He rammed with such force against the railing, he somehow fell over it and into the dark-blueish-green ice-cold water. Everyone around the scuffle had seemed to have paused and watched the entire scene play out. Some were shocked with mouths open forming a large O, while others clapped their faces or hid their snickers and laughs at the well-deserved misfortune of the creepy blond guy.

One of the ship guards sounded a horn and hollered man overboard. Several of the dock workers ran for life preservers and ways to assist in retrieving the creepy blond guy from the water. Another guard attempted to climb down the steel rungs of the ladder on the outside of the ship. A ship steward blew a whistle, trying to keep the passengers from gawking and encouraged them to move forward. The father of the once wailing child was cuddling him and kept slowly stepping toward the dock the same as Zac and Kristi.

Finally standing on the cement port dock, Kristi looked back to see the wet very water-logged creepy blond guy grabbing hold of the top rung of the steel ladder. She squeezed Zac's hand as they walked toward the line where people were taking their luggage off trolleys and walking toward assigned coaches. She heard fragments of conversations and viewpoints of how and why the creepy blond guy fell in the frigid water.

Zac pulled Kristi out of line and hugged her to him. "Are you okay?"

"Zac, I can't believe he grabbed my arm. After all, we have done to try and get him to leave me alone. And still, he tried again," Kristi said into the warm fabric of Zac's shirt.

"You tried to warn the ship security of the creep's persistent harassing behavior. He continued to stalk you. I'm glad he didn't drown, but he also didn't listen when you asked him to leave you alone. Let's get our luggage and enjoy our bus ride to Anchorage," Zac said, rolling his eyes at the thought of spending hours on a travel bus even though Alana made it sound like a luxurious and plush way to travel. It was still just a bus.

Kristi giggled at Zac's remark about the "bus" and realized he wasn't looking forward to sitting for hours seeing pine tree after pine tree. She had had more fun climbing the rock wall, devouring plates of food, not just one but a couple of plates of food at each meal, and even getting lost trying to find the exercise room the first day aboard ship.

"There is our luggage," Kristi said, holding the paper tags for the steward to read.

"And there is our coach," Zac said, pointing across the parking lot.

Kristi didn't know how she felt about the creepy blond guy as she set her suitcase down by the luggage compartment on the side of the charter bus. In the back of her mind, she was angrier at her ex-husband and the stupid stunt he pulled by hiring the creepy blond guy in the first place. She figured she would have plenty of time to think once on the coach. She felt Zac's hand on her hip as she walked to the two men standing with clipboards greeting people before they climbed up the steps.

"Welcome, I'm Jonathan, your shore excursion director and tour guide for the next several days. And you are…"

"Hi, I'm Kristianna Romanoff."

"And I'm Zachariah Karas."

"Ah yes, there you are," said the man as he skimmed an ink pen down a list of names on a paper clipped to a brown board. He put a checkmark next to Kristi's and Zac's names. "This is Willard. He will be driving our coach." He paused. "I'm Jonathan."

Zac understood the dazed look on the tour guide Jonathan's face. He had the look of total awe looking at Kris. She had a way of turning heads even though she wasn't aware of her beauty. Zac knew the feeling, but still he was irked and felt territorial toward Kris. He was irritated that it took the guy a moment to remember what he was saying before he mumbled, "Watch your step. Have a seat anywhere. We will be underway once everyone is on board."

Unaware of the awkward moment by the director, tour guide, whatever he was, Kristi walked down the aisle and chose two royal-blue cushioned seats midway down on the left side of the chartered bus. She looked out the window across the black-topped parking lot, not really seeing the people milling around. She kept trying to figure out how she felt toward the creepy blond guy and his falling overboard, while Zac settled into his seat.

"You know, you should probably call your lawyer. I'm not trying to tell you what to do, but maybe you should keep him informed. Your ex-husband did hire the blond creepy guy. And the guy did harass you while you were on board ship. Plus the incident on the gangway," Zac said logically.

"Yes, you are right. I know this sounds dumb, but as creepy as that guy was, I really did feel sorry for him when he fell in the water."

"Kris, he was a hired thug. His job was to badger you and return you to your ex," Zac whispered.

"You're right. I will call my attorney when I get to Denali."

"Babe, Atlanta is four hours ahead of us. You better do it now. It will be about eight in the evening in Atlanta when we get to Denali. Besides, you have a few minutes before we leave."

Kristi grudgingly had to admit, Zac was, of course, correct and only trying to help. Enough with the denial bit, she thought. It was time to end this entire situation with her ex-husband. She was tired of feeling guilty when she didn't do anything wrong. The creepy blond guy, although she didn't wish him harm when he fell overboard, was just a pawn used by her ex. She stood up and walked toward the front of the coach.

As Kristi climbed back down the steps off the bus, Zac could see she told the Jonathan guy she had to make a cell call. He almost smiled at how tongue-tied the guy was, just staring at her. He could have sworn a red flush was spreading from the neck of his white shirt across his face, poor guy.

Kristi knew it would only take a few moments. She walked a bit of a distance, out of earshot from the tourist getting on the bus.

She hated hearing people whine on their cell phones in public. It was annoying and grated on her nerves to listen to the rants. Everyone had problems, but they didn't need to shout it out for the world to hear.

Zac watched Kris from the window. He could tell she was in full attorney mode as she talked on the phone. She was standing very straight, the look of determination on her face and pacing as she talked. He noticed, every once in a while, she would glance around like she was keeping an eye out just in case the creepy blond guy had dried off and was searching for her. He could see when she ended the call, made another call, and took a deep breath. He was sure it was hard for her to continue having to deal with the drama of her ex-husband.

When Kristi returned to the coach and sat down next to Zac, she said, "I talked to my attorney. I told him about the creepy blond guy and his admitting Dominic hired him to follow me around and bring me back to Atlanta. He said he would draft up a letter to Dominic to cease the continuing harassment, including the use of the creepy blond guy, or we will file suit against him. I am not sure what repercussions this will have on Eli, though. I made it clear to my attorney to be mindful of wording so as to not cause harm to Eli. What do you think?"

"Is your attorney going to send you a copy of the letter before he sends it to your ex," Zac asked, looking into Kris's eyes.

"Yes. He said he would work on it immediately before the creepy blond guy returns to Atlanta. Do you think I did the right thing?"

"Babe, for your sake, this has to stop. You don't have a life. You walk in fear constantly. It sounds as if Dominic holds Eli like a pawn in his bullying tactics."

"You know until this vacation, I didn't want to admit he was holding so much leverage over me, with Eli. It was so gradual. It just became part of life for me. But just a few more months and Eli will be off to university and away from Dominic's clutches," Kris said as she sat back in her seat and relaxed a bit. "Oh, I also called my brother, KC. He said he would keep in touch with my attorney in Atlanta. He said he hopes I lose phone service up here and to have some fun," she said with a grin. She was actually feeling excited about the land part of their adventure vacation now. She leaned over, slipped her hands on both sides of Zac's face, and kissed him on his lips. They were soft, oh so soft. She thought and would have liked to continue exploring his mouth, but Jonathan, the land director, cleared his throat while looking at her.

CHAPTER 16

"Good morning, everyone, my name is Jonathan, and I will be your guide for the next several days. A little bit about myself, I have been a land tour guide for the last four years. I hope I will be able to answer all your questions you may have about Alaska. But if I can't, I would like to introduce Willard. He is not only our driver, but he has lived in Alaska his entire life.

"In a few minutes, once everyone is settled into their seats, we will be leaving Seward. I will point out things to see on both sides of the coach. If you have any questions, feel free to ask at any time. If you need a cold bottle of water, I have some in a cooler here at the front of the coach. The trip from here to Anchorage is approximately two and a half hours long. We will be driving north on the Seward Highway."

Kristi stared out of the coach window, looking across the glistening water of Resurrection Bay. The words of Jonathan, their host, drifted away. She thought of how much fun it would be to explore the area. Maybe she could bring Eli back for a vacation getaway. She would have liked to visit the Alaska SeaLife Center. From what she had read it was full of sea lions, octopuses, and puffins. Of course, Eli would love to rent mountain bikes and hit the trails. She had read about the Tonsina Creek Trail and camping along the Exit Glacier Road. She smiled and thought she wasn't really a camping-type person, but there were enough day trails to get Eli's wilderness fix in. She turned her head and saw that Zac was also looking out the window. He squeezed her hand.

Kristi whispered, "Have you ever thought about renting mountain bikes and hitting the trails?"

Zac smiled. "Here in Alaska? Nope, never thought about it, but obviously you are thinking about it."

"I had searched and researched all the stuff to do in all the places we would travel through, and there just seemed like so many cool things to explore along the way," Kristi again whispered, looking into Zac's eyes.

"Okay, if no one has any objection, Willard, if you please, start your engine and let's get started," Jonathan chanted from the front of the bus, sounding like the starter voice for the Indianapolis 500 race.

"Where did you get this adventure streak in you?" Zac asked, ignoring Jonathan's voice.

"When KC and I were little, we would go across the street from my father's office to the library. We would look up information on stuff like the Florida Cracker Trail. We were going to ride horses across Florida and then up the east coast to that island where the wild ponies were," Kristi whispered.

"KC is one of your brothers, right? What does KC stand for?" Zac asked.

"Yes, KC is the youngest of my brothers. His name is Kai Christopher. My mother's maiden name was Christoff. And my mother used to tease that KC was conceived on Kailua Beach in Hawaii so that is why he is named Kai. But yes, KC and I planned all kinds of adventures around the world from that library." Kristi smiled as Zac kissed her lightly on the lips.

Kristi noticed that Jonathan was slowly making his way down the aisle, talking to each person as he went. That seemed like a nice way to get to know the people on the bus. It was a very personable gesture, she thought. But she really didn't care, at this point, to have idle chitchat with him or anyone else. She felt kind of paranoid that her ex could have plotted people throughout her vacation to keep track of her. So she turned her head back to looking out the window as the bus started its journey north along the Seward Highway. As the coach left the port, Kristi noticed the businesses along the highway had a more rural look, and homes were modest homes with gravel driveways. She had read somewhere that commercial fishing was the number one occupation of Seward. Tourism from the major cruise ship lines from May to late September was just as important.

Zac noticed that while Jonathan was talking to each of the individuals on the bus, he kept glancing at Kris while he talked. It wasn't as if he had any claim on Kris, but it somehow irked him that Jonathan had zeroed in on her from the moment he saw her. Zac thought it was really rude of Jonathan to practically drool over her publicly while she was clearly with him.

"Kristianna, Zachariah, did you have the opportunity to take any excursions while on the cruise?" Jonathan said, directing his question to Kristi.

"Yes," Zac and Kristi said in union.

"Where did you all go?" Jonathan asked, again directing his question to Kristi.

"Whale watching, train to the Yukon, horseback riding, Mendenhall Glacier, crab bake festival, food tour, and a bunch of other stuff," Kristi said just to see his reaction.

"Wow, it sounds like you had an amazing cruise. I heard some guy fell from the exit ramp coming off the ship this morning. Did you see it happen?" Jonathan asked.

"The guy was behind us. He tripped over a child," Zac said.

"Oh my gosh, I hope he is okay."

One of the ladies sitting behind Kristi and Zac said, "I saw him, he insulted some man, the man pushed him away, and he tripped over a little kid tying his shoe. And then he went over the railing. I saw the guy one night hitting on three women at the bar by the pool. The jerk deserved to go for a swim."

"Oh my," was all Jonathan could say.

Kristi squeezed Zac's hand as she turned her head and looked out the window. Jonathan sounded just like a couple of her catty neighbors, wanting to know all the details of some drama. Luckily, the lady behind them decided it was her duty to fill him in. Thank goodness Jonathan moved on to hear more ship gossip.

There were few cars on the road as the coach drove north along the pine-tree-lined highway. There were small lakes glimmering through the trees and sometimes small homes were along the road with dirt-covered cars parked next to them. Every once in a while, there was a small store or what looked like a bait shop.

"On the left, you will notice the very scenic Kenai Lake. Willard said that there are times when the water looks turquoise in color. It is great for kayaking and fishing. You fishermen may want to put Kenai Lake on your list of places to fish," Jonathan said.

Once again, Zac noticed Jonathan was directing his tour information toward Kris. Only the funny thing was, Kris wasn't paying attention to him. She had her camera to the window and was taking pictures. Zac ran the palm of his hand over her back. He had gotten comfortable touching her, playing with her hair and reaching for her hand. He started thinking of ways to keep her in his life once they were home. She wasn't clingy like some of the women who came into the restaurant looking for a man who could support their spending habits. She had her own career, and when she wasn't busy with that, she had an amazing adventure streak in her that was hard to keep up with.

"Hey, babe, do you need some water?"

"Sure, I think I have two bottles in my backpack," Kristi said, sitting back in her cushioned seat. "I'm sorry. I was hogging the window."

"No, I'm fine. I was able to pick up reception and actually tried to get emails caught up. Here you go. The water is still nice and cold," Zac said, handing a bottle to Kris.

"Thank you." After Kristi took a drink of water, she leaned against Zac's left chest as he wrapped his arm around her shoulder. He kissed her hair.

"You will be seeing the Upper Trail Lake on the right side of the coach for a while as the highway follows along the southern tip of the lake. After we leave the lake behind, we will be traveling through the gorge between the mountains. There is still snow on the upper peaks as you will be able to see. Summit Lake will be on the right side—again, it is great for fishing. There is a Summit Lake Lodge and also campgrounds in the Chugach National Forest on the right, off the side of the road."

"I wonder if the air smells like pines or just fresh air," Kris asked Zac. It seemed like a silly question, but there had been times when they were riding horses, the meadow smelled like freshwater and wild flowers even though there were forests of pines nearby.

Someone excitedly pointed out the window, chanting that there was a bear in the distant meadow. One person in the second row stood leaning toward the window, searching frantically only to plop down in her seat, complaining it was a fallen tree stump. Zac did notice that everyone kind of perked up and started searching for any type of wildlife. Well, almost everyone, except the three couples in the back of the bus who had started drinking about a half hour ago. The more they drank, the louder they got. Everything seemed funny to them. And now it was all about bear poop. If a bear pooped in the woods and no one was around, did it still smell? Zac didn't find anything remotely funny about that, but booze made all the difference in what was kinda funny in a twisted way and what was really funny. Of course, hearing it from a drunk's mouth, it was entertaining for the moment. Zac looked to the front of the bus and noticed that Jonathan was talking quietly with some folks in the first seats. He must have run out of trivia to tell everyone, for now.

Kris turned to Zac and said, "Do you know why it is taking us so long to get to Anchorage?"

Zac wasn't sure if he should wait for the punch line or if she was being serious. "No, why?"

"Because we just passed a sign that said fifty-five miles per hour, seriously the state is too large to go that slow in!"

"Oh look, there is a sign that says Alaska Wildlife Conservation Center, so maybe that is where the moose, elk, bears, and other wildlife are hanging out," Zac pointed out grinning because he too was tired of sitting. However, he did notice, there seemed like a lot of large rivers that they were passing over. The sign they just had passed stated the river was called the twenty-mile river. "Oh, look, that sign says that Anchorage is only forty-six miles. Do you realize we aren't counting blue cars, we are reading posted information signs?"

One of the ladies sitting behind Kris's seat sat up and said, "Forty-six miles, huh? I wonder how long we get to shop in Anchorage."

Another traveler who was also getting restless, he said, "Yeah, I'm getting hungry."

"See what you started?" Zac teased Kristi.

Sensing the shift in conversations, Jonathan walked halfway down the aisle and said, "If you have noticed, we have just come around a large curve in the highway and are now on the final forty-minute drive to Anchorage. On the left, the body of water is called Turnagain Arm. It is a large. I guess you could call it a tributary of the Cook Inlet."

"There must be good salmon fishing in there," someone said.

"King salmon fishing is not permitted here in the Portage Creek area at all. However, wild silver salmon is best in July and August. Most fishing here is tide sensitive," Jonathan said.

"What do you mean tide sensitive?" one of the drunks asked and mumbled. "Like only on laundry day?"

Smiling since Jonathan had heard the sarcasm, he said, "When the tide comes in, the fishing is good. The water on this end of the Turnagain Arm is otherwise really shallow, full of silt and few fish. A couple of years ago, some men were fishing quite a ways out. The tide started coming in. One of the guys got stuck in the silt and drowned."

"No way," said one of the drinking guys, in the back of the coach.

"Actually, it's called a Bore Tide," Kris said.

"I have never heard of that," Jonathan said. "Can you tell us what that is?"

"A tidal bore is when the tide is coming in, a wave is created. It is usually in shallow inlets like Turnagain Arm. This bore tide here probably is quite unique since it has a mountain border on both sides. The water is pushing into the inlet about ten miles per hour and the wave is about six to ten feet tall. People have been known to surf them all the way to shore. But this was probably how the man drowned. He couldn't get out of the silt fast enough, and the tide wall of water came over him," Kristi explained, feeling uncomfortable with all eyes turned to her.

The lady sitting behind Kristi and Zac leaned over the seat and said, "Wow, thanks, that was really weird." Others sitting around them agreed.

"Way to go, brainiac," Zac whispered into Kristi's ear, grinning, as he watched Jonathan turn and retreat to the front of the bus. "Shut down the tour guide with a wave of water."

"Zac, do you think I hurt his feelings?"

"Just his ego."

After a while, Kristi sat up straight in her seat. "You know, we must be getting a lot closer to Anchorage. I am seeing more cars and traffic on the road."

"Yes, I think you are right. Are you getting hungry? Where do you want to eat?" Zac asked as he pulled out his phone.

Kristi lifted her camera and watched for potential photos to snap. It was a little after eleven in the morning. The sun was shining, and the sky was a beautiful color of blue. She had thought of Anchorage as a gray, dreary, cold city, but with the snowcapped mountains touching the sky, the buildings coming into view looked clean and white. There was a huge sign across a parking lot welcoming everyone to Anchorage Market and Festival. Too bad it was set for the weekend; it would be fun to browse the market. She wondered if there would be local bands and music at the festival. Her stomach started rumbling. Since she had pushed her eggs around her plate at breakfast earlier; her stomach was definitely running on empty, she thought. "Yes, I am actually starving."

Jonathan once again stood up, and holding onto the pole behind the driver's seat, he said, "We will be stopping in Anchorage for two hours. Willard is planning on parking the coach on Fourth Avenue, if there are enough spaces open. That way you will be close to many of the pubs and restaurants. Also there are quite a few shops to visit. Once we park, I will need you to be back to the coach at one thirty. It is a four-hour drive from Anchorage to Denali. Please, I will need you to be prompt. I'm sorry we couldn't give you more time to shop."

Once off the coach, it seemed everyone scattered immediately, to see as much as possible in the short amount of time given. Zac had found a cool-looking pizza place on the food app on his phone called Fat Ptarmigan. It was only two blocks from where the bus had parked. They walked down the street, looking in storefront windows. Kristi paused in front of a fur gallery. She wasn't expecting to see a fur gallery with so many animal cruelty protesters in America; however, this was the land of very cold winters, so survival was kind of top priority. Besides harvesting the entire animal not only for their pelts but for the meat they provided wasn't vicious it was ensuring life during harsh winters. There was a touristy souvenir shop on the other side of Fourth Avenue with a huge grizzly bear out front. Anchorage streets were like walking down any large city filled with quaint shops, trendy restaurants, department stores right next to old-world pubs with scarred wooden floors. They passed a nationwide trendy café, when the lady who sat behind them called out asking if they wanted to dine with her and her husband at the restaurant at the corner of the street?

"Thank you, but we are heading down the street to a pizza place called Fat Ptarmigan," Zac said when he and Kristi had turned to talk to the lady. "I'm sorry, I don't know your names, I'm Zac and this is Kristi."

The man extended his hand and introduced himself as Fred and his wife as MaryAnn. He asked, "Is the pizza place any good?"

"We don't know, but their menu looked great on the app," Zac informed them.

"Do you mind if we tag along? I would rather have pizza than go to another noisy franchised restaurant. Do you mind?" MaryAnn asked.

"No, we just don't know if it is any good." Zac laughed and turned to continue walking down the street toward the restaurant sign.

Once inside the pizza shop, Zac liked the seating arrangement. There were barstools along the bar, tables in the middle, and row seating along the large windows. The hostess seated them promptly. She listed the types of beers and other beverages offered.

Zac ordered some Alaskan beer; Fred and MaryAnn ordered a name-brand beer on tap while Kristi ordered a glass of pinot noir.

"Honey, don't you like beer with pizza?" MaryAnn questioned Kristi.

"No, I never acquired a taste for beer. I hope you don't mind me drinking wine," Kristi said, not wanting them to think she was a snob.

"No problem. So where are you all from? We are from Omaha, Nebraska," MaryAnn said.

"Sarasota, Florida, south of Tampa," Zac said. "Have you decided what you would like to eat?"

"I think we will get our usual pepperoni pizza. We haven't had a good one since we left home," Fred said, closing his menu.

"That sounds good. Babe, would you like to split a smoked salmon pizza with me?" Zac asked Kristi.

"Yes, but I think I am also going to order a half Caesar salad. That sounds so good," Kristi said and smiled.

"So did you really go on all the excursions that you told Jonathan?" MaryAnn asked Kristi.

"Yes, we actually did. I have pictures on my camera. Would you like to see some of them while we wait for the pizzas?"

It was no time before the pepperoni pizza was set in front of Fred and MaryAnn and the smoked salmon pizza with a side Caesar salad in front of Zac and Kristi. Fred held up his beer to make a toast. "May we all enjoy the rest of our stay in Alaska? More than the last two hours!" Everyone toasted and laughed at that.

Zac tasted and inspected the dill sauce beneath the smoked salmon and leeks. He smiled and continued eating.

MaryAnn was quiet for quite a while, happily savoring the pepperoni pizza, but then she said, "Kristi, I have to ask. Please tell me if I am out of line, but didn't it bug the heck out of you that Jonathan was practically drooling all over you? I mean, give me a break. Have some respect."

Kristi, not expecting to hear that, started choking on her salad. Zac patted her on the back and asked the waiter for a glass of water. She was only able to take a shallow breath. Tears came to her eyes.

She put her napkin to her face and continues to try and take small gulps of air. Finally, she was able to cough deep enough to move the lettuce from her upper airway. Zac handed her the glass of ice-cold water to sip. The color came back to her face. She sat back in her chair, taking small shallow breaths.

"I'm so sorry. I didn't mean to cause you to choke," MaryAnn said, biting her lip.

Kristi held up her hand. "No, no, it's okay. I just wasn't expecting you to say that."

"Was I the only one who felt he was inappropriate?"

"No, I think we all noticed it," Zac said quietly.

"Oh my gosh, where was I?"

"Well, I think we are going to get our check and go see some sights before our two hours are up. Thanks for sharing lunch space with us," Fred said, grabbing his wife's arm and abruptly walking to the counter to pay the bill.

"What just happened?" Kristi asked, staring at Fred and MaryAnn leaving the restaurant.

"I think Fred thought MaryAnn overstepped her boundaries by mentioning Jonathan ogling you on the bus, and the fact that you were unaware of it," Zac said, motioning for the waitress to bring the check.

"Sir, the other couple paid the bill. Is there anything else I can get you?"

Zac and Kristi drifted in and out of the quaint boutiques and souvenir shops. Kristi took pictures of huge orca murals painted on the side of buildings and the statue of a bear on the street corner. The weather was unseasonably warm, so there were many people walking the sidewalks and sitting on park benches in shorts and flip-flops. Zac bought a newspaper and a couple of magazines for Kristi to read on the four-hour trip to Denali. Kristi bought a navy-blue Alaska T-shirt for Zac just because. And then they headed back to the bus.

"Do you really think Jonathan was gawking at me?" Kristi asked.

"Yes."

"Why didn't you say anything?" Kris asked as they neared the parked charter bus.

"Kris, since you got off the ship, you have been stressed. You weren't aware, nor were you concerned with Jonathan's attitude toward you. I didn't want to add to your tension. You were indirectly taking care of the situation by ignoring him. What better way to deescalate the problem?" Zac said as he pulled her to him and kissed her accidentally on purpose in front of Jonathan and the few already seated on the coach.

Laughing at him, Kris climbed the steps onto the bus to clapping and chants to get a room. Laughing even harder, she and Zac found their seat in front of MaryAnn and Fred. Several more people boarded the coach and quickly sat down. Kris watched Jonathan climb the stairs and grab onto the pole. Willard once again started the engine and slowly eased into the early afternoon traffic.

Zac turned in his seat and thanked Fred for paying for their lunch. He said, "That was unexpected and very nice of you. Thank you."

"My pleasure, the pizza was great."

"Thank you all for returning to the coach on time. I hope you enjoyed your visit to Anchorage. I would like to recognize a couple of individuals as we get started on our northward trek. Martha and Joe were the first on the coach. Here is a gold token of appreciation," Jonathan said as he handed Martha the token with an orca stamped on it. She laughed as everyone applauded.

"Nancy returned with the most souvenirs, Anchorage thanks you and here is a key of appreciation, but I am not sure to what city." Jonathan handed Nancy a small silver key.

"Jean and Carl returned without one souvenir bag. Here is a touristy key chain to remember Anchorage by. What? You had them shipped home? Sneaky!" Jonathan laughed.

"Zac and Kristianna had the grandest and most romantic return, a rose for our special couple." Jonathan walked down the aisle and handed Kristi a red plastic rose and winked at her. Most everyone clapped. The still drunk couples in the back hooted and whistled.

"And the last to return, but on time, thank you very much, Casper and Renee, a watch to help you remain on time." As Jonathan handed Renee a cheap plastic child's watch, everyone laughed and joked.

"Thank you all for being good sports, while we had a little fun. And now I hope you will take one last look at Anchorage, a beautiful city with snowcapped mountains in the background as we head north. It will take us approximately four hours to get to Denali," Jonathan said before he settled back in his seat and quietly talked with the travelers sitting in the second row of seats.

Kristi watched as several people pulled out books, tablets, and newspapers to pass the time. Zac was reading some article in the Anchorage paper he had picked up before getting on the coach. One lady pulled out some multicolored yarn and knitting needles. Kristi studied the lady's wrists as she weaved the needles in and out of the fibers. She wondered if the lady's mom had taught her how to knit.

Zac leaned over and asked, "Do you know how to knit?"

"No, my mom was always busy running my father's business or driving us kids to baseball practice or soccer practice or music lessons or some summer program…and then she died."

"I'm sorry. What happened?"

"I went to senior prom after my mom and I picked out the coolest dress ever. Spent the weekend with KC and a bunch of both our friends at a beach resort, drove home on Sunday, and found out my mom had taken a nap that afternoon and never woke up. My father didn't want to ruin our weekend, so he waited until we got home. It was sad, but she didn't suffer, and that is all that matters." Kristi shrugged. She didn't want to think about it or talk about it. For some reason, Zac had learned more about her, in such a short time span, than any other guy ever.

"Thanks for sharing," Zac said as he put his arms around her and hugged.

"If you look out the left side of the coach, you will see a large body of water. This is the Knik Arm. It is 192-mile branch off the Cook Inlet. As we travel north you will see larger homes along the water. You will notice if you look closely, you will see boathouses. Some actually house seaplanes. Because Alaska is so large, there are areas that are only accessible by plane. I know, wouldn't it be great to fly your seaplane to work and back? You know, like honey, I'm taking the plane for groceries," Jonathan said dramatically.

Kristi turned around in her seat and grinned at MaryAnn. "You're right." She laughed.

"Men," MaryAnn said and shook her head.

As they passed a forest of what looked like half-dead pine trees, someone asked about them. Zac saw Jonathan lean over and talk with Willard. He then said, "Last summer there was a house fire. Everyone in the area pitched in to help put out the fire as best they could. The fire department had to travel a great distance to get to the fire. Anyway, the fire demolished the house and most of the forest around the area. As unfortunate as it was, it did make the forest stronger and clean out the underbrush.

Kristi took a couple of pictures of the beauty she saw through the coach window, then leaned back against Zac. She was so tired. It must have been all the carbs in the pizza they had eaten in Anchorage. She inhaled the scent of pine and vanilla aftershave that she associated with Zac when he put his arm around her. She snuggled closer and closed her eyes. She didn't want to think about how fast her vacation days were slipping away. She still wasn't certain how she would cope once they got home. Zac was so easygoing, so considerate, so much fun to be around. She was convinced Eli would even like him. She felt the slight pressure when Zac rested his chin on top of her head. She was sure he had closed his eyes. She too slowly drifted off to sleep.

CHAPTER 17

Zac woke with a start. He had been dreaming of floating on top of a very-warm-water bore tide. Kris was laughing, telling him he was supposed to surf the wave not float; he remembered thinking. He could feel Willard changing gears on the motor coach. Out of the side window, Zac saw a parking lot come into view as Willard turned off the main road. Shifting in his seat, Zac felt bad because he had accidentally awakened Kris in the process.

As the coach came to a stop in the parking lot surrounded by pines, Jonathan said, "Traffic was light, and Willard has been making good time. We figured everyone needed a fifteen-minute stretch and restroom break. We are stopping at the Denali State Park Alaska Veterans Memorial. I am sure you will enjoy it. Plus you are getting the perfect opportunity to see Mount Denali. Only 20 percent of all tourists visiting this area get this rare sighting. Due to Denali being so high, it has its own weather conditions. It is usually shrouded in clouds or blizzard-type climate most of the time. Okay, enough for now. Remember, please be back on the coach in fifteen minutes. Thanks."

It was a beautiful sunny and warm afternoon. While most people walked the footpath toward the restrooms or the monuments, Zac and Kristi wandered the granite gravel trail along the pines. There was a quiet hush, not even a rustle of tree branches as they walked. Zac turned, pulled Kris into his arms, and kissed her. He said, "I have wanted to do that for a couple of hundred miles."

"Hmmm, then maybe you should do it again." Kris grinned and tasted his lips one more time before they heard the crunch of gravel as a couple started walking up the narrow path.

Kristi stopped several times to take pictures of Mount Denali. The snowcapped mountain stood out proudly, some eighty miles away, with the backdrop of royal-blue sky. There was something mesmerizing about the mountain. She couldn't understand what it was, but the beauty held her captive. Even when Zac came up behind her and put his arm around her waist, she continued to take picture after picture.

Willard walked up the path. He was also carrying his camera. However, when Kristi glanced his way, she practically melted.

"You have an eight-hundred-millimeter lens?" Kristi questioned.

"You want to change lenses and see the difference between the eight hundred and your four hundred millimeters is?" Willard said while he removed the lens from his camera body.

"This is fantastic. Zac, you have to see the mountain with this lens. It is awesome," Kristi almost squealed, and she handed the camera for Zac to see the mountain with.

"The closer detail is fantastic," he said, handing the camera back to Kris.

"Thank you for letting me try out your lens, Willard," Kristi said appreciatively.

After they followed the gravel path, they came to the stone memorial plaques that honored Alaskan veterans who had served their country at home and throughout the world. The quiet breeze whispered through the pines. Zac felt the same reverence and calm he had felt when he had visited the memorial grounds in Normandy, France. He saw people walking from the Marine memorial to the Navy, Army, Air Force, and Coast Guard. And also, the bush pilots who helped the Air Force. There was a plaque honoring the little-known men and women who were part of the battle of Attu. There was a huge granite boulder with three black onyx tablets on it honoring three men who were awarded the Congressional Medal of Honor for Conspicuous Gallantry in action above and beyond the call of duty.

"Look, there's even a plaque showing how Alaska and the Bering Sea were part of the American Civil War, amazing," Zac whispered to Kris, hugging her to him and kissing her forehead.

"Alaska did a beautiful job creating this memorial," Kristi whispered as they slowly walked between the monuments of remembrance.

After everyone had returned to their seats on the coach, Willard had the coach back on the highway heading north toward Denali.

"I hope everyone was able to stretch and visit the stone tributes. We have about an hour and a half before we get to Denali. Did everyone get to see Mount Denali? It's beautiful, huh? The summit is 20,310 feet, and most of you know it's the highest peak in North America. But what is more fascinating is, from the footpath to Mount Denali was like only eighty miles."

"It's kind of hard to miss, don't you think?" Zac whispered to Kris.

"Shhh." Kris giggled. "He is just doing his job."

"I have to tell you a really funny story. You saw me check everyone's name off as you got on the coach. Plus I did a headcount as a double-check. Well, a couple of years ago and not on our cruise tour line but a different one, the tour guide decided to let everyone have a few minutes of stretch time along the road. There was a pull-off by this huge meadow of wildflowers," Jonathan said, raising his arms in a grand gesture. "Some of the people got off the bus and took pictures. Some stretched by the side of the road but slowly drifted back to the bus. The guide asked if everyone was on, if everyone was ready to leave, and they were off. Well, about twenty-five miles down the road, the driver got a call to check their passenger list. One of the ladies decided she had to go to the bathroom, so she had walked down in the small incline to go. The bus left without her. She had her phone with her. She called her husband on the bus. I guess he said, 'Oh, I thought you were sitting somewhere else.' But he didn't do anything about it. He didn't notify the tour guide, nothing. She called the police. The police went and checked the situation out, then called the tour company. I guess a special car was sent for her, and she was taken to the cruise ship port. Bet that was a very long cruise or very expensive souvenir excursions for the husband."

Some chuckled and elbowed husbands, but most of the laughs came from the drunken guys in the back of the bus. Kristi pulled out one of her magazines and started paging through while Zac worked on something on his phone. Kristi noticed after she finished reading a couple of articles that there seemed to be more snow on the mountain range. The sky was a vivid blue with tiny wisps of white clouds here and there. The road had more curves and dips, and there were signs warning of moose and deer crossings. She grabbed her camera as the coach drove around a bend in the road and then crossed a bridge over a quite pretty body of water called the Nenana River.

Once again, Jonathan stood up and announced they were almost to the park entrance. He said, "You will be spending the night at the Denali Park Village. When you get off the coach, you will have this evening to explore the area. Many of the shops are open late.

"Tomorrow, there are two different tours through the park. The history tour is approximately four hours long that was included in the land part of your vacation package. You will be picked up in front of the lodge, at 8:00 a.m. tomorrow morning. There is also a nature tour. It is six hours in length. You travel farther into the park with the possibility of seeing more wildlife. You will be picked up at 6:00 a.m. in front of the lodge, but this tour includes a boxed breakfast. There is an increased fare for the nature tour. If you would like to be included in the nature tour rather than the history tour, see me after we get off the coach and I will sign you up.

"For both tours, please bring your luggage to the coach before you leave for your adventure through the National Park. Make sure you have your pills or immediate items you may need with you, as you will not be returning to the resort after the tour. You will not have access to your luggage until you reach Fairbanks tomorrow evening. It will be stored and locked on this coach, taken to the lodge in Fairbanks, where you will stay tomorrow night. All the instructions I just gave you are on this paper I will hand you as you leave the coach."

"Where do we go after the tour," asked a man, midway down the aisle.

"When you get off the green buses, after your tours, we will take you to the train depot for a fantastic four-hour train ride to Fairbanks."

Kristi looked at Zac; she thought she would love to take the nature tour. "Zac, what do you think?"

"Kris, this is your adventure. You may never come to Denali again, so you decide."

"I really can't see sitting on a school bus for six hours. I don't want to take the extended tour, even though I would love to see some grizzly bears. Do you?" Kris whispered to Zac.

"No."

Five minutes later, the motor coach pulled into the Denali Park Village parking lot. The resort looked like a huge two-story wood lodge hidden by pine and spruce trees. Huge rock boulders were scattered along the parking area. As Kristi and Zac stepped down from the coach, she could smell the smoky fragrance from the firepit across the parking lot. There were couples sitting around the fire with children roasting marshmallows. It looked like fun.

"Zac, here is your room key card. You two are on the first floor. The dining area is off the main entrance to the left," Jonathan said and handed the envelope to Zac. "Remember, everyone, if you would like to sign up for the nature tour, I will sign you up in five minutes. Your luggage will be delivered to your rooms in ten minutes or as soon as we can unload it. Remember, you have to bring your luggage here to the coach when you leave for the park in the morning."

Zac took Kris's hand as they walked into the lodge. A beautiful stone fireplace with a sitting area and a gift shop were to the left. Zac located a wide brightly lit hall leading to their suite. They walked past several rooms, a condiment area with soda machines, an ice machine, and a chip and candy machine next to it. There was a huge coffee station with the scent of freshly brewing Java beans. Their room was located right beyond the double doors leading to a wooded area. Kristi walked into the room and turned on the light. The suite was decorated in cream-colored walls and mocha chocolate-colored blankets draped on the end of two queen-size beds. Zac dropped his backpack on one of the beds. He opened the drapes covering the sliding glass doors leading to a deck while Kris flicked the light on in the bathroom.

"Kris, you have to see this view of the river."

"Zac, you have to see this bathroom," Kris said. She decided the bathroom could wait. Zac sounded too excited. She walked to the balcony to where he was standing. Tall pine trees lined paths to the river. There were a couple of benches facing the water, and once again, huge boulders and pieces of driftwood scattered along the trails. The water rushing past the gravel walkway was the only sound they heard as they stood at the balcony railing. Zac turned toward her, pulling her to him. His lips slowly kissed her neck, her jaw, her chin, and finally her lips. Kris loved the soft hold Zac had on her as his tongue slowly explored her mouth. Kris wanted to memorize every moment Zac kissed her. He tasted so good, and the fact that he pulled her to him and was kissing her felt great."

"Do you want to go for a walk along the river?" Zac asked as he kissed the tip of Kris's nose.

"Do you want to find the dining room and get something to eat?" Zac asked as he kissed Kris's top lip.

"Do you want to decide which bed you would like me to make love to you on?" Zac asked as he again kissed Kris's top lip.

"That one," Kris pointed to the one closest to the balcony. She didn't think she could make it to the other bed.

"That was a quick decision. Are you sure you don't need more time to decide?" Zac grinned as he slowly backed Kris into the room to the bed while continuing to kiss her.

"Nope, I'm good."

"Oh, you sure are," Zac said as he pulled Kris's sweater over her head. All he wanted to do was to bury himself in her lovely body. He wanted to drift on the scent of her skin, the fragrance of the pines wafting in through the open slider doors and the sound of the river.

Kris unzipped Zac's jeans and pulled his shirt down and off his arms. She couldn't wait to feel his skin against hers. The sun shone between the branches of the spruce trees onto their bodies as they made love in the late afternoon.

The sun was still shining when Kris and Zac walked into the dining room for dinner later that evening. Kris almost said that the sun would be sinking into the Gulf of Mexico at home at this time of night but didn't want to be reminded of time slipping away. So she said, "It amazes me how late the sun remains high in the sky here. It is eight o'clock, and you can still see the beautiful view of the river."

"What would you like to drink while your food is being prepared?" asked the server dressed in a white shirt and black slacks.

"I would like a sauvignon blanc and a glass of ice water, please."

"I will have the same," Zac said.

"Would you like to order the bottle or just the glass?"

"I think just the glass tonight," Zac said with a smile.

"Are you ready to order, or do you need a moment yet?"

"I think I will have the pan-seared Alaskan halibut," Kristi said as she set her menu on the table.

"And you, sir?"

"I was going to have the honey glazed Alaskan salmon, but the halibut sounds really good. I will have the pan-seared Alaskan halibut also," Zac said.

"Kris, did you want to upgrade to the nature tour tomorrow instead of the history one?" Zac asked once the server had walked away.

"No, the cross-country drive from Seward to here, with the stops along the way, was enough nature for me. We still have the ride through the park and the four-hour train ride tomorrow," Kris said, looking out the window. "Don't get me wrong. I think we have seen some beautiful country so far. But..."

A different server brought a tray with two glistening goblets of pale-yellow wine and two glasses of sparkling ice water with lemon. "Your meal will be here shortly."

The server who took their order brought a small carved wood bowl full of dinner rolls and butter sculpted like a salmon. She also brought crystal bowls of Alaskan Crab salad and placed them in front of Zac and Kristi. "Is there anything else I can get for you?"

"No, thank you," Zac said, impressed with the classy service they were receiving.

Kristi took a bite of her crab salad and closed her eyes. "Oh, this is so good. I didn't realize how hungry I was."

"Yes, you kind of worked up an appetite this afternoon." Zac grinned, and then he inspected the pink morsels of meat. "The crab is cooked perfectly."

While they were finishing the last of their salads and sipping on the chilled wine, the server returned with their meals. She said, "The chef prepared for you pan-seared Alaskan halibut with blistered tomatoes grown locally, Reggiano and herb basmati rice, and truffle butter. Please let me know if there is anything else I can get for you."

"Thank you," Kristi said.

Later, completely full, Kris pushed her plate away. She grabbed the bill before Zac could get his hands on it. She had explained to Zac, he had paid for all of the excursion meals on board and at the different seaports for her. She said it was only fair and whipped out her credit card. In which case, Zac gracefully said, "Thank you."

The sun had dipped behind the mountain range when Zac asked if Kris would like to take a walk along the path behind the resort. There were others who had decided to do the same. Hand in hand they walked, talking very little but enjoying each other's company. Finally, Kris said, "Have you ever felt uncomfortable when someone you are with doesn't talk much?"

"Are you saying you feel uncomfortable because we aren't talking right now?"

"No, just the opposite."

"Then, shh." Stopping, Zac turned and kissed her quickly on the lips.

They walked over to one of the park benches near the river and sat down. The sound of the water was so soothing. Kris put her head on Zac's shoulder and just listened.

Zac thought about Kris's comment. Yep, he enjoyed talking with her. He had been fascinated when she was totally focused on taking pictures or just sitting quietly watching the world go by, like on the bus earlier in the day. She didn't need to be entertained, and he liked that.

All of a sudden, Kris sat up. "Oh my gosh, oh my gosh, oh my gosh, is that a bear? Look, Zac, across the water on the other side. That's a bear." Kris pointed across the river on the other side of the bank where the underbrush and trees were thickest.

Zac stood, and with squinted eyes, he said, "Yes, you are right. That's a bear or a very furry guy. No, it looks like a bear."

Several of the other couples had stopped and looked across the water, pointing and exclaiming, "That's a bear."

One of the resort night patrol guards walked along the river's edge turned and confirmed that it was a bear and her cubs were not far behind her. He said they come out every evening to fish for dinner. He then warned to keep a far distance from any bear, to not leave food out, and to stay on the lighted paths.

It was dusk when they headed back to the lodge. Zac realized it was almost eleven in the evening. The days grew longer as spring turned to summer. They had a lot scheduled for tomorrow. So when they got back in the suite, Zac said, "To save time, don't you think we should take a shower together? I mean, the shower is huge, it would save water too?"

Trying not to laugh, Kris said, "You are absolutely right. Besides, corporation liability policies are always looking for ways to prevent slips, trips, and falls."

The shower was huge. It was triple the size of their little shower on the cruise ship. There was probably enough room to fit three people in comfortably, not that Kris was into that sort of thing. The granite tiles on the walls and floor were color coordinated and quite beautiful, she thought. The counter had double sinks and was at least eight feet in length. There was a basket of shampoos, soaps, lotions, toothbrushes, and pastes of boutique brand names. The towels were top quality fluffy bath sheets; there was nothing cheap about the suite. The water was hot immediately when Kris turned the shower sprayer on and stepped under. Zac stepped in behind her. He massaged shampoo into her hair. As the lather slid down her neck, she realized she loved the feel of his hands in her hair. She scooped some of the suds and dropped them on Zac's shoulders and chest. There was something erotic about the white foam on Zac's tanned and buffed upper body. She slid her thumbs over his button nipples and watched as he unexpectedly inhaled deeply. Stepping closer to him, he slid his hands down her back and pressed her bottom against him.

Although Kris wanted to make love with Zac in the shower, it wasn't as easy as it looked in the movies. The floor and walls were slippery. Kissing Zac's body parts tasted like soap. She started giggling, and the passion slipped down the drain. But one good thing, they were both very clean, super clean to be exact.

Zac turned the water off and grabbed one of the bath sheets. He bundled it around Kris and kissed her lips. Wrapping another towel around his waist, he turned out the light and followed Kris to the queen-size bed close to the bathroom door. He watched as she dropped the towel on the floor and crawled into bed. Normally she folded everything neatly before going to bed, so he knew she was exhausted. He lay down on the bed and pulled her to him. Once again, she said nothing but curled up against him, kissed his chest, and fell asleep.

CHAPTER 18

Kristi sat up in bed. The room was cast in a pink glow, and the air was cold. She couldn't remember where she was. She looked toward the light coming through the open sliding glass door. Oh yeah, they were in Denali National Park, at a resort for the night. Zac must have left the slider open last night, she thought. The sounds of feet crunching on the gravel paths outside the balcony and voices of kids complaining about being tired could be heard through the open doors. She could smell spruce trees and freshly brewed coffee. It was almost five thirty in the morning, according to her phone by the bed. She looked at Zac, still asleep on his side. She really should let him sleep while she took a hot shower to get warm. But her resistance was low; all she wanted to do was run her fingers along the side of his face.

She leaned over and lightly kissed his exposed shoulder. She could feel his soft, warm skin against her lips. Her hair brushed his neck as he reached around and pulled her on top of him.

"I woke you up, I'm sorry," Kris said, looking down into his beautiful chocolate-brown eyes.

"No, you're not. Babe, you slept late this morning." Zac grinned, running his hands up and down her naked back.

"After being out in the cool fresh air last night, I guess it hit me, I was so tired."

"I know, your towel is in a heap on the floor and your clothes are thrown on the other bed."

"So what are you going to do about it?" Kris sassed back.

Zac quickly rolled Kris onto her back, nudged her legs apart with his knee, and slid his manhood inside her. He could hear Kris sigh as he entered her, and she wrapped her legs around him. He smiled thinking her bottom might have been cold but not for long. The way she slid her hands up and down his back, the way she sometimes licked her lips while he rocked into her or the enchanted look of her eyes, made it difficult to maintain staying power. He wanted her again and again and again. He rested his head in her now damp neck. "I'm going to need another shower," he said between deep breaths.

"Me too," Kris whispered but didn't move. She could feel Zac's heart pounding against her breast. His back was damp beneath the palm of her hands. She closed her eyes and listened to his breathing. It was soothing.

"Baby, don't fall asleep. We have to get ready to leave for our 'adventure' into the wilderness," Zac said as he slid off Kris and offered his hand to help her out of bed. "A quick shower and off we go."

"You are way too happy this morning."

Thirty minutes later, Zac and Kristi pulled their suitcases out of the suite and headed for the Trolley Café off the main foyer. There wasn't time to order breakfast before dropping off their suitcases at the coach and leaving for their history tour of the park. So Kristi decided upon a huge blueberry muffin and a banana nut muffin for Zac, while Zac picked up four granola bars, two bottles of water, and a cup of coffee to take with on their journey. It seemed several other couples had the same idea and walked out to the coach, also carrying brown paper bags of fresh baked goods.

Zac noticed that Jonathan stared at Kris while they handed over their suitcases.

"Good morning, I hope you enjoyed your accommodations last night," Jonathan said to Kristi.

"Oh yes, the view of the Nenana River from the balcony was beautiful, and so was the bear on the other side," Kris said, holding her camera in one hand and the bag of baked goods in the other.

"You got to see a bear last night?" Jonathan said in amazement.

"Oh yeah, and her little cubs too," Kris said as if it was no big deal. She climbed the steps into the coach.

Zac knew that Kris was being a smart ass this morning to Jonathan. He grinned all the way to his seat. "I loved the look on Jonathan's face just now. Kris, you got him good."

"I know, right?"

The first part of their journey into the wilds of Denali National Park was a stop at the Wilderness Access Center. It was a beautiful huge convention center type building surrounded by tall fragrant spruce trees. The welcome area was staffed with park rangers ready to answer any questions and offer booklets, pamphlets, and information needed to enter the park. A map of the park hung on another wall. A large statue of a menacing grayish-black Toklat wolf with amber eyes guarded the entrance into a larger room full of lifelike animals in their element. Dall sheep on granite rocks, a life-size moose with a full rack of horns, and a realistic eagle with a small animal in its talons midair to its nest of young near the second floor were some of the very impressive animals around the room. There was another room off to the left filled with the kind of souvenirs you would never see in a regular tourist shop. There were handmade baskets, books written by local residents describing their adventures in Denali and surrounding areas, and homemade jams, jellies, syrups, and baked goods from the berries grown locally. Kris purchased a sealed small glass pitcher of blueberry syrup for Zac. She was able to place it in her backpack before he saw what she bought. She also picked up a postcard for Eli.

Once back outside, Zac and Kris headed for the old school bus painted green. Jonathan stood with his clipboard in hand.

"You didn't buy anything?"

"No room to carry it," Zac said as he climbed the stairs.

"Right. Good morning, Peggy, here, let me help you up the steps."

"Good morning, everyone, my name is Jessica I am your host and Denali National Park Naturalist. We are about to start our journey into the park as part of your natural history tour. This area was first inhabited by the Koyukon Athabaskan natives. The word *Denali* in Athabaskan means 'the Great One' or 'the High One.' So let's get started, and I hope you find out just how great our national park is. If you have questions, feel free to ask at any time. If you see any wildlife along the way, please point it out by saying 'bear at three o'clock,' which would be on the right side of the bus, or 'nine o'clock on the left side,' so everyone can see. I ask that you not stand while the bus is in motion. George our chauffeur is excellent at maneuvering through the turns. However, the road is uneven, and I wouldn't want any of you to spend time in the hospital on your vacation.

"There are many things to do in Denali and the surrounding areas. As we drive through the park, you may see hikers with backpacks and mountain bikes, and there are rafting trips down the Nenana River and helicopter rides through the mountain ridges. Private cars are only permitted up to mile 15."

"Why can't you drive beyond that?" asked a man in the second row.

"There are several reasons for cars not being permitted past the Savage River checkpoint—falling rocks on the road, mudslides, rough gravel road conditions are the obvious reasons. There are six million acres in Denali National Park. There are very few established trails. No rivers have been altered, and if you have noticed, there are very few accommodations in the park. You see, there is a delicate balance between wildlife and nature. We here in the park strive to keep the ecosystem healthy and intact and the human footprint small. Sometimes humans get excited when seeing wildlife and think it's okay to go 'off roading' for a better view. Or vehicles break down contaminating the soil and flora. Great question, sir.

"On the right, you will see the railroad trestle over Riley Creek, which, if you came to Denali by train from Fairbanks, you passed right there.

"As we ride along Park Road, the pines and bushes are dense, but as we head up in elevation, the trees thin out. The aspens, paper birch, poplar, and spruce you will soon notice are stunted in growth unlike the same trees in the lower forty-eight, and that is due to the wind and severe cold."

"Zac, would you like the blueberry muffin or the banana nut?" Kris leaned over and whispered into Zac's ear.

"Blueberry please, unless you want it."

Jessica introduced the name Charles Sheldon as an early conservationist who fought to preserve Denali back in 1907 as Kristi handed Zac the blueberry muffin. She noticed others had pulled out fried egg sandwiches or granola bars from their brown paper bags or were sipping coffee. She was glad they had purchased the baked goods before leaving the resort.

"On the left side of the bus, I would like to bring your attention to our sled dog kennels. While you are here in the park you may want to visit Denali's sled dogs. They are used to clear paths for winter hikers. They patrol the boundaries or assist in reaching remote research stations. Hauling and pulling sleds of equipment are part of their tasks. Stop by the headquarters, the rangers will explain in more detail the purpose of the dogs. And the dogs are eager to give demonstrations of all they can do."

The green bus lumbered along the park road as more and more people were unwrapping breakfast food. Zac whispered to Kris, "How's the banana nut bread muffin?"

"I'm not sure if it is really good or I was just very hungry," Kris whispered back. She reached down into the backpack and grabbed a bottle of water.

"There is a trash box up front here, for your wrappers and bags when you are done eating. Also, if anyone is in need of a bottle of water, I have a cooler full of bottled ice water behind George's seat. Thanks," said Jessica as she turned and sat down on the hard leather bench seat behind George, the driver.

"If you notice on the right, that ridge in the distance is called Healy Ridge. It reaches the elevation of six thousand feet. Notice how the spruces are already showing signs of being stunted in growth. We will be stopping in a few minutes at the Savage Cabin. It originally was a cookhouse for road workers in summer. It was used by early settlers for decades and, in fact, is still in use today during the winter by the rangers on patrol. I would like to point out that the front and only door of the cabin opens out rather than in so that bears cannot push the door in and cause harm. The Savage Alpine Trail and Savage River Campground are nearby. We will spend about thirty minutes at the cabin, so everyone gets a chance to see inside. Remember to stay on the gravel walkway areas as there may be bears in the nearby woods. It is spring, and they are waking up and hungry."

Zac and Kris walked along the path to the cabin. The air smelled of spruce; it kind of reminded Kris of Zac's aftershave lotion. The cabin had the basic single bed in one corner, a table, and a cook area. There were shelves built into the wall for canned goods and supplies. There were a couple of windows that could be shuttered during the winter months. After looking inside the primitive cabin, Zac grabbed Kris's hand as they walked along the winding path back to the bus. He joked that Kris didn't seem like the camping-hiking-type person and pulled her to him for a hug.

"So what does a camping-hiking-type person look like?" Kris asked.

"Rugged hiking boots, maybe a Thinsulate jacket, that sort of thing."

"Na, I'm more of a beach girl. Don't you think?"

"Most definitely. I would hang out with you on the beach any day," Zac said as he continued holding Kris to his chest.

Back again on the park road, the bus continued to climb in elevation until finally coming to a stop at the savage station checkpoint. Jessica explained this was mile 15 and private cars could not go beyond. The ranger inspected the bus, checked the number of passengers, and wished everyone on board a safe journey.

Kristi had her camera to the window taking pictures as Jessica pointed out highlights of the area. The river they were crossing was the Savage River. Kristi noticed two caribou downstream about a half mile. She adjusted her lens to pull them up close in her viewfinder. *Beautiful,* she thought and smiled. She could hear other camera's clicking the same wild beauty. Jessica said to keep an eye out on the sheer mountainsides to the right of the bus. Dall sheep with their curved antlers are only found in Alaska and Western Canada. They like to scale the rugged cliffs.

"Why do they climb along the steep cliffs?" asked a young boy sitting next to his dad.

"Excellent question, for those of you who couldn't hear this young man, he asked why Dall sheep climb along the steep cliffs. When wolves or other predators approach, they scale up the sheer rock ridges to escape. Also, it is a great resting place for them out of danger."

"Bear, three o'clock—no, I mean nine o'clock," a woman shouted pointing out the window.

The bus came to a stop. Jessica asked everyone to keep as quiet as possible. The bear was a mama bear and two wee little cubs. The cubs were trying to climb small sapling trees, which bent with their weight. The mama bear, although keeping an eye on her cubs, was foraging on some early spring berries. "Remember, I said there is a delicate balance between the wildlife and nature here in the park? The hares, squirrels, bears, and moose eat crowberries, which are black, and lingonberries, which are red. They inadvertently move leaves around which slowly regenerates the slow-growing forest and tundra. Caribou feast on the lichens, often called lacy reindeer moss, during the long winter months. Okay, here is a question for you. How do you tell the difference between a brown bear and a black bear? Anyone? A brown bear's fur is anywhere from dark brown to light blond in color. And they have a big hump on their backs. Black bears do not. Did you know polar bears and caribou stay warm in winter by having hollowed hair, which provides them with extra insulation?"

Everyone, including Zac, had their eyes on the open wilderness scouting for any sort of wildlife as the green-painted bus ambled around tight corners with loose gravel.

"Did you know that Congress passed a bill to establish Mount McKinley National Park in 1917? And in 1980, it was renamed Denali National Park and Preserve. When we turn the next bend, you will see a beautiful overlook clearing called Primrose Ridge. George will be stopping there. And a presentation will be given by an Athabaskan woman. Her clan has lived in Denali for generations. I hope you will enjoy it."

Kristi and Zac walked to the edge of the ridge and looked out over the meadow with the snowcapped Alaskan Mountain Range in the distance. Once again, Kristi was able to capture the beauty in pictures all that she saw. The yellow cinquefoil and pink fireweed growing wild down the ridge into the valley gave the vast openness a look of warmth. The quiet whisper of the breeze, gently caressing her face, felt so welcoming. Zac tugged at her arm. The pretty brown-haired lady had already been introduced and began her presentation. She was dressed in lavender and pale green cotton shift, wooly leggings, and leather shoe boots. She was describing the life of the Athabaskan people over the last eleven thousand years. Kristi tried to determine the woman's age. She couldn't have been more than twenty-five years old. She didn't have a wrinkle on her face. But the wisdom and knowledge she had as she spoke of her ancestors came from the deepest part of her soul. Even Zac was mesmerized by her voice and hand gestures. It was almost as if the slight breeze coming down the mountain removed all sound except for her quiet talk. Behind the woman, the sun broke through the gray clouds that had gathered over the valley. The rays touched a stream that braided through the meadow and sent a shimmering light across the tundra. The woman began singing a song she had learned as a child.

And then it was time to go.

The bus bumped along the gravel road, twisting and turning, but suddenly stopped. Everyone looked out the windows to see if there was wildlife in the thickets. But Jessica pointed out a huge moose meandering down the center of the road. Obviously, the bull knew he had the right of way and took his time.

Jessica said, "The moose is the largest of the deer family. This bull's antlers look a good five feet in length, don't you think, George? He is full grown and could be very dangerous if at all provoked. You see, here in the park, we are their guests in their land. We need to respect and protect it. If we do, it will remain as is for generations to come."

Soon the moose must have found something interesting to eat. He turned and quickly left the road but still could be seen wandering through the spindly spruce and shrubs. Zac looked at Kristi and smiled. "He was cool looking. Let see, did you get some good photos of him?"

As they crossed the railroad tracks leaving the park, Kristi happened to see a couple of caribou walking along the tracks. It was totally unexpected and a beautiful sight to see and photograph. As Zac gathered their backpacks, everyone was laughing and talking about the wonderful adventure they had and the number of wildlife they were able to see. There were many thanks to Jessica for the great information she gave. It was time now for the adventure to continue on toward Fairbanks.

CHAPTER 19

The Wilderness Express train on the Alaska Railroad was not just your ordinary tired-looking train and cars. Zac was surprised by the huge Alaskan bear murals painted on the side of the rail cars. The engine was painted in a medium blue with a bright yellow streak all along its side. From a business standpoint, it gave the engine a very inviting look to it, he was impressed. Zac had to smile as Kris had her camera up and was taking pictures of the train. Jonathan was standing with his brown clipboard, checking everyone on board. It was kind of becoming predictable.

"Please head up to the second-floor domed coach. Thank you."

As Kris and Zac climbed the narrow circular staircase to the upper level. The curved paneled wall was a soft brown color with chrome handrail and slate steps. Kris stopped and gasped. "Zac, look at that statue. It's beautiful. Look at the detail. He's fantastic. I wish I could find one like that. Oh my gosh."

"The plaque says the statue is called *The Fisherman*, hand-carved out of fossilized whale and walrus bones by native Alaskan carver Kent Heindel. Maybe we can find some carvings of his in Fairbanks," Zac said as he studied the beautifully carved piece of work.

"That is a great idea. Where do you want to sit?"

Once everyone was seated and the train slowly departed from the Denali depot, Jonathan walked to the front of the railcar. "How did you all like your stay in Denali National Park? Yes, I know it would have been nice to stay and explore a little longer, but there is still so much for you to see. Some of you were on the history tour, and some of you were on the longer nature tour. Did you all get to see a lot of wildlife in the park? Wow that's impressive," Jonathan said as he listened to someone as they named off all the animals they saw. "Our rail ride is about four hours in length, and we will be arriving at the Fairbanks train depot approximately at four this afternoon. I would like to introduce to you our host guide for the next four hours, Tina. She will be pointing out interesting scenery and landmarks along the way. I would also like to introduce to you our bartenders Becky and Roger to assist your thirst needs. Tina…"

"Thank you, Jonathan, for the introduction. As you have noticed the curved glass dome gives you a 360-degree view. Some of you have already taken advantage of the reclining seats. There is also a fold-down tray and pocket where you will find the drink list available from the bar. There is also a catalog of items you can purchase as souvenirs of your Wilderness Express experience. The train dining area is on the lower level. Menus for your viewing are available in your seat pocket."

Zac pulled out the drink list from the pocket and read over the available drinks. Kristi rested her head on his shoulder while she too looked over the list.

"Are you tired, babe?" Zac asked. He laid his hand on her knee.

"Sir, ma'am, would you like something from the bar?" Becky, the bartender, asked.

"Not right now, thank you. Kris, would you like anything?"

"No, thank you. What time does the dining room open?"

"In about thirty minutes, the dining hostess will come and offer seating. That way, no one is standing on the staircase waiting for a table."

Tina stood up and instructed everyone to look to the right of the train. She said, "You will see all the hotels, restaurants, and shops, this area is called Downtown Denali or as the locals call it Glitter Gulch. It is not run by the park service. As popular as it is in summer by visitors and cruise ship excursions, during the winter months it is completely shut down, even the stoplights."

Kristi took a couple of pictures of the very impressive lodges built along the hillside, looking down over the town. Traffic on the streets and people milling around shops; it was hard to believe in a couple of months' time, it would look like a ghost town. Kristi turned around and noticed several of the couples in the back two rows by the staircase were being ushered down to the dining car. Good, she thought as her stomach was beginning to protest with a growl.

"If you look to the left, you will see the Moody Bridge that crosses over the Nenana River. The winds that come down the canyon can be quite strong. See the windsock in the middle of the bridge? It is there to alert motorist when to drive with caution over the nine-hundred-foot long bridge," Tina pointed out.

Another set of guests was ushered down the stairs. Zac leaned over and whispered. Are you sure you don't want a granola bar? Your stomach is rumbling!" He was smiling, knowing how much Kris could eat.

"No, I can wait," Kris said in a hushed voice but wasn't all that sure.

"If you would like to get a great photo of the train engine, we will be traveling along the terraced canyon of the Nenana River. The curve in the tracks is the perfect moment to see the river down below, the mountains in the background, and the train engine and several boxcars."

"Sir, ma'am, would you like to have lunch in the dining area on the first floor with us?"

"Yes, thank you," Zac said as he and Kris stood to follow the hostess to be seated. It seemed strange to ask if they would like to have lunch. Wasn't everyone hungry by this time of day? Everyone on railcar had either been on the six-hour nature tour or the four-hour history tour of Denali. He feared Kris might bite someone's arm if she didn't eat soon. Yet he had seen some travelers decline. They were probably going to snack along the way and had plans for dinner in Fairbanks, he thought.

Kristi stopped on the spiral staircase to admire *The Fisherman* statue. She didn't want Zac to think she had an obsessive personality, but the fine detail of the almost two-foot statues touched something near her heart. It was crazy. It was like when she walked in Zac's restaurant, The Mermaid Isle. The beauty he had created was breathtaking. Maybe it was an appreciation for other people's vision or because she didn't have a talent for creating works of art? Oh well, the aroma of something delicious grabbed her and her stomach's attention as she continued down the steps.

Zac looked around the dining coach after they were seated. The booth had an antique look to it with wall sconces, tanned leather chairs, and large picture windows. The table was covered with white linens and starched folded napkins. Leather bound menus were handed out along with the inquiry for beverages to be served with lunch.

"I think I will have a lemon-lime, Zac?" Kristi said, closing her menu.

"I would like the pinot noir," Zac said with a smile and handed the hostess his menu.

"Would you like the glass or the bottle, sir?"

"Just the glass," Zac answered, turning his head to look out the window. He didn't want to laugh. He was sure there were many people who could and would polish off an entire bottle of wine during the four-hour trip north, watching trees and rivers whizzing by. Not everyone was as enthusiastic about the wilderness scenes as Kris. But he had found much pleasure in seeing her appreciation of everything from the ugliness of a moose to the fungi and moss growing on rocks and tree stumps. It wasn't as if she hadn't traveled much. She just wanted to preserve the beauty she witnessed in photos. He smiled because he had actually found someone who took the time to enjoy what was in front of her.

"Zac? You seem like you are a million miles away," Kris said, studying his face.

"No, just trying to figure out how I would drink an entire bottle of pinot noir. Wouldn't Jonathan be shocked if I took the bottle back to our seats? You know, keep taking a squig from the bottle along the way." Zac grinned.

"I'm sure someone has already tried that! I just can't see you chugging down a bottle of wine from the bottle."

"Really?"

"Well, you don't seem like the pinky up sort of person either." Kris laughed.

After the beverages were served, Zac ordered the halibut Caesar wrap and a side order of reindeer chili. Kristi ordered a shrimp Caesar salad. While they were waiting for their food to arrive, Zac asked Kris about her plans for the evening.

Kristi looked at Zac. He looked so calm and relaxed, sitting across from her as if he didn't have a care in the world. She wished she could relax, but right now she was really concerned. "Zac, I'm worried."

"What do you mean?"

"You know I booked an evening flight to the Arctic Circle. That is tonight, and I am stressing about the time frame between arriving at four this afternoon in Fairbanks and the preflight check-in time at the airport at six this evening."

"We could talk to Jonathan after lunch and see if he can help you. He is hosting this tour. But I was thinking maybe we should order food to take with us since we might not get the opportunity for dinner," Zac said quietly.

"Did I just hear you correctly? Are you going with me? Oh my gosh, seriously? You are going with me? Ohhh," Kris said excitedly as she rested her head against the leather back board and looked at Zac.

"Yeah, I don't want you to have all the fun. Besides, I just love watching you take pictures," Zac said, rolling his eyes and laughing.

The server brought a huge bowl of steamy hot reindeer chili and a crystal tray of crackers. She explained their meals would be out shortly.

Zac looked at the large portion, handed Kris a spoon, and said, "Help me eat this."

Kris was so hungry; she didn't need to be asked twice. But after one bite, she sat back and said, "Oh my gosh that is so good. The reindeer sausage has a bit of spice to it. Oh no, I am sounding like Chef Zac." The reindeer chili was so delicious; Kris couldn't put the spoon down. It didn't have a gamey taste, just a sausage-flavored chili. The Caesar salad was crisp, and the shrimp actually added flavor to the Caesar dressing on the salad. Even Zac complimented the flavor of the halibut Caesar wrap.

When the server came by to ask if they would like anything more, Zac asked if he could order two chicken wraps to go? He also asked if they could be packed in ice so they would not spoil. The server was more than happy to accommodate his wishes. She promised to have them made closer to the end of the journey so they would be fresh and deliver to them to their seats. Zac made sure she received a very generous gratuity. He even stopped the hostess on the way back to their seats and asked for a card to give compliment and recognition to their server.

Kristi was half dozing in her seat when she saw a huge moose walking in a field of what Tina called the Nenana Flats. It was a swampy land of low to the ground scrub bushes, dead trees, and mosquitos. Kris grabbed her camera and was once again rewarded with great photos of the beast. Then as the train traveled across a bridge, she looked down and saw two rubber boats with people rowing along the river. She was so pleased. But then she looked at Zac and remembered he mentioned her taking pictures, like she was overdoing a good thing. So she put down her camera.

"What," Zac said. "Don't stop taking pictures because I teased you earlier. It is what you enjoy. Think of it this way: we will enjoy looking at the pictures and memories made when we get home."

"How did you know what I was thinking?"

"You set your camera down, and the pleasure that it gave you left your face."

Kris leaned over and kissed him. "Thank you."

Tina pointed out the abandoned trapper cabin with a sod roof deep in the woods. The sod insulated the cabin in the harsh winters. She said it had been built back in the '40s. It looked dilapidated as if the next snowfall would cause the place to cave in. Soon the train slowed down. Tina explained they were traveling past the Nenana Depot. Any time the train came into a city of any size, the speed limit on the tracks was reduced. This town was special though; it was originally inhabited by Athabascans. It was located between the Tanana and the Nenana Rivers. The rivers had an abundance of fish for the natives' prosperity. Later, Russian fur trappers used this waterway and the gold rush in the early years of the twentieth century brought prospectors and supplies up and down the two rivers.

As one of the bartenders brought drinks to the couple behind Zac and Kristi, the man asked about one of the bridges the train was passing. Becky said, "That is the Alaska Native Veterans' Honor Bridge over the Tanana River."

Tina stood up and said, "I have a funny but true story for you. You all know how boring winters are with low temperatures and lots of snow, well, maybe not Kristianna and Zac, they are from Florida. Anyway, coming up on the right side of the train, you will see a green tower and a black-and-white-painted log tepee. Back in 1916, some of the workers from the railroad construction camp were bored or maybe anxious for the spring ice break of the Tanana River. So they started placing *wagers* to guess when the river would thaw. They wrote the dates they each thought the ice would start breaking up, on papers, and placed them in the log tepee. Even the town folks got involved. It is said the first winner received $800, which would have been a lot of money back in the day. I said the word *wager* because betting was against the law for many years in Alaska. The Ice Classic tradition has continued to this day with of course much larger jackpots."

While the travelers were laughing about the story and now talking between themselves, Zac stood and walked to the back of the coach. Jonathan was working on some paperwork, when Zac slipped into the seat next to him. He said, "Jonathan, I have a concern that I need to talk with you about."

Jonathan sat up straight and asked, "What can I help you with?"

"The train is due in Fairbanks at four this afternoon. Kristianna and I are booked on an excursion to the Arctic Circle at seven this evening. But we have to be at the airport at or before six. Will we have time to get to the lodge we are staying at, get checked in, and go back to the airport in the short time frame?" Zac asked. He wanted to laugh when Jonathan seemed to relax some as he heard the dilemma rather than a complaint.

"The excursion was made through the cruise excursion list. Therefore, it is our responsibility to make sure you get to your excursion. So let me make some calls, and I will let you know what I come up with. Thanks."

When Zac got back to his seat, Kris was holding a white bag. Kris said, "Our server brought our sandwiches in plastic bags, wrapped in ice placed in an insulated box. Is that cool or what?"

"Yes, it is. Now we won't die of salmonella from eating spoiled chicken in the Arctic Circle! I just got done talking with your bud, Jonathan. I explained the time frame between arrival at Fairbanks and the Arctic trip. He said he would look into it and get back with us," Zac said as he reclined his seat a bit and went back to working on his phone.

Kris turned her head toward the window and shut her eyes. *Great, what a way to die, salmonella, ew,* she thought. Everything would work out how it was supposed to be, she kept repeating in her head. Zac had done all he could. Time would tell. *Stop fretting, you are going to get worry lines. Relax, it is out of your control. None of the clichés are working.* She looked over at Zac and said, "What are you working on?"

"Since we are in the continental US, I have service. So I just got caught up on emails for work, payroll is done, and I paid several bills. My secretary said there was a package from Ketchikan, Alaska, on my desk at work. I didn't order anything from Alaska. But I told her I would deal with it when I got home."

"Maybe it is from one of your contacts on the city food walk you did?" Kristi suggested, knowing it was the whale carving she had shipped from Ketchikan.

"No, that was in Juneau. This is from Ketchikan."

"Oh, maybe it is something from one of the chefs at the fishing resorts you went to by cab, in Ketchikan."

"Yes, that is probably it."

"Zac, I think I have resolved the timing issue this evening," Jonathan said as he leaned in close in front of Zac and Kristi. "We don't usually do this. However, your excursion is through the cruise line. So when you get off the train, here is a voucher for a cab that will be waiting to take you to Pike's Waterfront Lodge. After you check in, the lodge will provide you with transportation to the airport. Here is a form to give them to expedite the travel time to the airport. Do you have your paperwork for the excursion and your passports with you? Make sure you get the lodge's after hour's phone number to call so they will come pick you up when you return at midnight. Your luggage will be placed in your suite for you along with the itinerary for the next two days. I hope this helps. Enjoy your excursion. I want to hear all about it so we can encourage others to be as adventurous as you."

"Thank you, Jonathan, for your assistance," Zac said and extended his hand.

"Yes, thank you so much, we really appreciate it," Kristi said and smiled.

After Jonathan walked away, Kristi turned to Zac. "Thank you for talking with Jonathan. I appreciate you getting it straightened out for me. Jonathan is still not my bud. But I am happy he pulled whatever strings he did, to make the transition from the train depot to the hotel to the airport work smoothly. Now, I can relax and be excited that you are going to the Arctic Circle with me. Thank you so much."

"Kris…"

CHAPTER 20

"Welcome to Fairbanks. We are about to pull into the station. First, I would like to give a big hand of applause to railway host Tina and to our favorite bartenders, Becky and Roger," Jonathan said encouraging everyone to clap. "Please, check under your seats. Make sure you have all your belongings. Once off the train, you will have a ten-minute restroom break at the train depot before getting on our coach. We will be traveling across town to Pike's Waterfront Lodge. As soon as we get there, take your luggage from the coach, get checked in, and enjoy your evening. I will see you in the dining room tomorrow morning at eight.

Zac found the cab without any difficulties. After giving the driver the voucher and letting him know they were going to Pike's Waterfront Lodge, he maneuvered the cab out of the congested Fairbanks train depot parking lot rapidly. It didn't take as long as Zac had inquired on his phone map to get to their destination, but then the cabbie might have known a shortcut. Either way, he was glad when they pulled into the very impressive-looking lodge. Both Zac and Kristi thanked the driver, while Zac handed him his tip.

"Oh my gosh, this place is beautiful," Kristi said, looking around the parking lot. The lodge was a massive two-story building with a ten-foot-tall moose statue standing guard under the porte cochere.

"Come on, let's go check in, and then get to the airport," Zac said as he walked to the front entrance and held the door for Kris.

The foyer opened into a huge room with a fireplace on one wall with cozy-looking sofas clustered around it. There was a gift shop to the left, which looked like a place easy to spend money in. At the reservation desk, a lady and a man stood by waiting to check them in. Zac handed their reservation paperwork with identification to the woman. As the lady was entering the information in the computer, she began to frown. She said, "I'm sorry, there is a problem with your room. There was a water leak. The carpets have not dried yet. We apologize for the inconvenience."

Zac looked at Kris, who was looking unbelievingly at the desk clerk.

"Let me see. Okay, I have placed you in the cabin suites by the bocce ball courts and river. I apologize. The cabins are a further distance from the dining room and activity center. But I hope you will enjoy the more rustic cabin. You go to the end of this hall, out the door, follow the paths beyond the second tier of rooms, you will see the cabins. Your cabin will be the end cabin near the river's edge. It has a lovely little balcony. But to get ice or refreshments from the soda machine, again, you will have to come back to the lodge. Here is your passkey. Oh yes, I spoke with Jonathan. I hope you will not mind, our steward will place your luggage in your room while you are out for the evening. Here is our card with phone numbers on it for your return ride back. I think that covers everything. Sign here and off you go."

Kris would have loved to see their cabin by the river, but there was no time. The shuttle driver was out front waiting to take them to the airport. After giving the address of the hangar they were to meet at, they were on their way. Although it was a quarter after five in the evening, the sun was still high in the sky. Kris's jacket was stuffed in her backpack along with her gloves and scarf. Their food was still in the wrapped container being held by Kris. Zac watched as they drove past the airport and turned onto University Avenue S. The driver passed several storage-type buildings before he pulled into the Northern Alaska Tour Company. The building was nothing to look at from the outside. It was a basic industrial warehouse building with a huge aluminum-sided airline hangar facing the backside of the airport. After thanking the driver, they walked into a room full of chairs with aircraft pictures on the walls. The reservation area was a bar-like counter with a man standing behind it working on a computer. Zac walked up to the desk with their paperwork in hand.

"Welcome to Northern Alaska Tour Company. Here are two clipboards, please fill out the forms and return them to me. We have several other clients coming for the evening flight to the Arctic Circle, but we will be leaving on time."

After the paperwork was completed, Zac and Kristi walked outside and leaned up against the railing in the early evening to eat their chicken wraps. Kristi couldn't believe how hungry she was again. She wondered if it was all the fresh air.

"This is really good. Glad you thought to buy them. And I am really happy that you changed whatever plans you had, to come with me," Kristi said.

"The first night at dinner, when you told that couple on their anniversary cruise, you were going to the Arctic Circle, it sounds interesting. My daughters' words kept echoing in my head: *Get away, explore life*. I guess the Arctic Circle is a little extreme, but it is 'getting away.'" Zac explained before taking another bite of his wrap. "What made you want to see the Arctic Circle?"

"You probably never saw the television program where the big rigs drove on the Dalton Highway in the middle of winter to Prudhoe Bay? I am not sure if it was the dangerous road conditions of winter or just the adventure of it all, but I secretly wanted to drive the Dalton," Kristi said after taking the last bite of her chicken wrap.

"Well, you are going to get your chance, and I'm going to witness it for posterity and all that!" Zac laughed and held up his bottle of water as a salute.

Kristi laughed. She watched a little Cessna take off across the airstrip. "Oh my gosh, look at that rainbow. It is huge."

The door opened, and the manager of the flight company came out. "We just got the weight distribution worked out. Radar shows there is a big storm coming in out of the west. So although it isn't nineteen hundred hours yet, I want to get your flight in the air. Please come with me."

Kristi, Zac, and two other couples followed the man with baggy work jeans and a white long-sleeved shirt around the building to where two Piper twin-engine planes sat. One looked like the pilot had just finishing his checklist and was preparing to head toward the runways.

"Watch your step climbing aboard. You can sit anywhere. Ma'am, ma'am, the rainbow is really pretty, but you need to get seated before the storm hits."

Kris looked at Zac as she sat down; she started laughing and said, "Thank goodness, it wasn't me he was talking to!"

"Good evening, my name is Ben. I am your captain this evening. Would anyone like to sit in the copilot seat on the way up to Coldfoot this evening? Great, sir, come on up and strap yourself in. There are headphones in the pocket of your seats. If you will put them on, it will be easier to hear me. If you have questions, pull your mic down and I will be able to hear and answer you. Let's get in the air, and then I will tell you more in a few minutes."

The sky was blue with some clouds forming over the mountains surrounding Fairbanks as Kristi and Zac bucked into their seats. One of the couples had chosen to sit in the back. Zac sat on one side of the plane so he could see out the window, and Kris has decided to sit in the seat in front of the wing. The lady whose husband was acting copilot sat behind Kristi. The small plane smoothly lifted off the ground and climbed into the heavens.

"Okay, if you can hear me, raise your hands. Good. If you look to the right of the plane, you will see Fairbanks in the background and the airport. The river right below us is the Chena River. As I said earlier, my name is Ben. I am retired Air Force. I flew with Delta for many years until my wife was stationed in Fairbanks. With our young children at home, my flights to the Arctic Circle and surrounding areas give me the perfect opportunity to do what I love, and that is being home with my family and flying. Our cruising altitude will be between three thousand and five thousand feet, depending on how bumpy it is. We will arrive at Coldfoot a little after eight this evening. I will point out highlights along the way."

Zac looked over at Kris and smiled. She had her camera against the window taking pictures. He was glad she was enjoying herself. But he decided she was going to have a real job sorting through all the pictures when they got home.

"The zigzag river below is the Yukon River. Just a bit of trivia, the Yukon River is about 1,982 miles long. Its start is in northwest British Columbia and travels through Alaska to the Bering Sea. Okay, okay, I know, just fly the plane."

The lady who was sitting behind Kristi tapped her on the shoulder. When Kristi turned around, the lady took off her headphones. She yelled above the noise of the aircraft, "Are you a professional photographer?"

"No!" Kristi yelled back, shaking her head, just in case the lady didn't hear her. "Why?"

"Because you have a real camera and a long lens. If I gave you some money and my address, will you mail some of your pictures to me?"

Kristi shook her head yes and smiled. She slid her headphones back on and turned back to the window. She got to thinking; most people did use their cell phones to take pictures. She loved the feel of the camera with the ability to zoom in for an up close photo. She could change to black and white or take up to eighty minutes of video. Of course, the video mode drained the battery, and that was the reason she had an extra battery in the bottom of her backpack, along with a second video card if needed for more photos taken.

"Folks, on the right of the plane is the Stevens village. The only way to get supplies to this Koyukon Athabascan village is by barge down the Yukon River. During the winter, long haul trucks can bring supplies in across the frozen Yukon River. But as you can see, they are a far ways from Fairbanks."

Zac could hear Ben, the pilot, every once in a while, talking to the pilot of the plane that took off about fifteen minutes before them. It sounded like they were discussing worsening weather conditions and altitude.

"For your inquiring minds, the mountains to the left of the plane are the Ray Mountains. The summit elevation, if I remember correctly, is about 5,500 feet. The road below us on the right side of the plane is the Dalton Highway. It is 414 miles long and extends through the Brooks Range, those mountains in the front of the plane, to Prudhoe Bay. You are probably wondering what runs alongside the highway. That is the famous Trans Alaska Pipeline."

Zac looked over at Kris when he noticed there seemed to be more turbulence as they flew north between the mountain ranges. She had rebuckled her seat belt. She might be adventuresome, yet she was cautious and appeared to know her limits. That was a good thing.

"I have been talking to the plane that took off before us. It is about forty-five miles ahead, the storm has moved over the Finger Mountains. Therefore, instead of going over them, we are going to have to go around. No worries, just a bit of a delay in getting to Coldfoot."

Kristi turned around when once again the lady behind her tapped on her shoulder. She handed Kristi a folded piece of paper. Kristi set her camera on her lap. She noticed, when she unfolded the parchment, the letterhead name of one of the prominent hotels they had passed on the way to the lodge earlier in the day. Six single-dollar bills slid out and landed on Kris's camera. The lady's home address was written on the paper. She folded the bills back up and stuffed the folded paper in the inside pocket of her coat. She gave the lady a thumbs-up gesture and smiled.

The small plane banked to the left. Kris could barely see the mountain they were going around. It was raining quite heavily. The plane rocked and turned as the stormy air currents stressed the plane. She turned and noticed the couple in the back row had moved up to the middle of the plane. They were not kissing and hugging like they had been right after the plane had taken off. Kris decided it would be difficult explaining to their dentist how their front teeth had gotten knocked out flying to the Arctic Circle. She wondered how the amateur copilot felt seeing the side of the mountain that close to his side of the plane. She was curious what Zac was thinking when she looked at him across the aisle, looking out the window. He probably thought this flight was another harebrained idea of hers. It was an adventure, right? Hmmm, she thought, she had confidence in their pilot!

"Ladies and gentlemen, you now have the bragging rights to say, you just crossed the Arctic Circle. Congratulations! And since we have gotten around the storm, the Alaskan sun will soon be gracing our flight. We will touch down in Coldfoot in a few minutes. The time will be eight thirty, and yes, there is almost four hours left of sunlight!"

Sure enough, a gravel landing strip came into view. It was large enough for a small plane, and that was about it. Kristi was impressed by Ben's smooth touch down landing. He slowed the plane down to a stop in front of a yellow pole barn, next to a small log-cabin-type building with a small single-engine plane tied down with anchors in the ground and a very dirty maybe navy-blue truck. The other plane that had taken off was parked to the side of the runway. If this was Coldfoot, Kristi thought, how much more was there to tell in a presentation?

After everyone had piled out of the plane and stretched, the man who had gotten to sit in the copilot's seat decided they all needed a group photo moment. Everyone handed their cell phones to the pilot of the other plane as they all stood together for the photo shoot. And then Kristi handed her camera to him. The pilot joked, she may not get the camera back; it was that cool.

Zac decided it was bitter cold out. Although the sun remained high in the sky and shining bright, it was frigid there. When they walked on the Mendenhall Glacier, it was a damp, raw, sinking-into-your-bones cold. This was a dry coldness that came down the mountain ranges to chill the valley they were standing in.

It wasn't long before a van came to a dusty stop a few feet away from the plane. A man in a red-and-black plaid shirt, with BRAD embroidered above the left chest pocket, hopped out and extended his hand to each of the members of the two flight groups. He said, "As you can see, my name is Brad," and pointed to his shirt. "I am your driver and tour guide to Wiseman. If you will climb aboard, we will get on the road. Beautiful evening, isn't it?"

Once all twelve people had squished into the back of the large van, Brad stepped on the gas. "We are now leaving Coldfoot, you shouldn't have blinked." Brad laughed at his own joke. "The population of Coldfoot is now up to twelve people. Back in the turn of last century, you know, 1900s, Coldfoot was a mining camp along the banks of the Slate Creek. The populations peaked at three hundred, but gold was discovered in 1906 to 1907 north and west. Rumor has it; prospectors heading up the Koyukuk River got cold feet and turned around. Hence, Coldfoot and that is how the town's name got changed from Slate Creek. In 1970, it became a pipeline camp, and in the 1980s, it became the northernmost truck stop. I just turned onto the Dalton Highway made famous by the television series. The road is narrow with a very soft gravel shoulder in some spots. This is a trucker industrial haul road to Prudhoe Bay. It always looks better in the movies with an eight-inch snowpack on it. Anyway, I would like you to notice the aspen, spruce, and mountain alder trees. As we drive north, their height diminishes, which is all due to the extremely cold temperatures and windy conditions. We are now going over the middle Koyukuk River. Chinook and chum salmon can be found in the river and tributaries. If you are lucky, you may see a moose or two along the river. Sometimes brown or black bears come searching for berries or fish at this time of the evening."

Kris leaned over and whispered in Zac's ear, "I don't think he has taken a breath since he started talking." Zac quietly chuckled after Kris's statement.

Brad continued to talk nonstop as he followed the curves and dips in the road without slowing down. Zac grabbed Kris's hand as he tuned Brad out and brought Kris's hand to his lips. His idea of an evening at the Arctic Circle would have been the scent of a freshly caught salmon on the grill with fresh herbs. He would be sipping a glass of white wine with Kris sitting on a fur pelt blanket against a granite boulder. The sound of the Yukon River rushing against its banks as background music would be the perfect late evening picnic in the sun. Kris placed her head on his shoulder until Brad made a sharp turn off the highway and followed a freshly grated gravel road with ratty-looking aspen and spruce trees at its edge.

The van came to a stop in a clearing overlooking the north fork of the Koyukuk River. Everyone took their turn climbing out of the cramped quarters and followed Brad to a cluster of several homes, some of which looked totally dilapidated. The cry of an eagle flew across the blue sky dotted with white puffy clouds. An American flag with the Alaskan state flag under it waved in the faint evening breeze. A man wearing a baseball cap that had seen better days, a faded jacket, and maybe black jeans stood next to a wooden stake. Zac studied the four racks of antler bolted to the sides of post with a sign in the middle that said,

Wiseman Alaska
63 miles north of the Arctic Circle

"Good evening, my name is Marvin Kveerik, and I would like to welcome you to Wiseman. In the next hour I will be telling you about life here in the settlement of Wiseman."

Kristi took pictures of the log cabin with a corrugated tin roof and sod packed up against its sides. Marvin explained the sod acted as insulation against the harsh cold and snowy weather conditions of the long winters. Someone interrupted Marvin's speech to ask why there was a smoker grill outside the front door. Marvin chuckled and said, "You know the aurora borealis that the upper forty-eight states see in winter? The northern night lights start here. On December 21, the longest night of the year, people actually come up here to see the burst of color light show. Since it is bitter cold, they stand in front of the cooker to keep warm. If you will follow me, I would like to show you inside the Carl Frank Log Cabin."

Kristi and Zac stepped into the dusty wood floor cabin. Two walls were lined with black-and-white photos of early nomadic Eskimos from the Kobuk River and Koyukon Athabaskan natives living along the river. A post under one of the pictures stated trapping and hunting provided essential food and materials for clothing. The residents of Wiseman trapped fox, lynx, mink, beaver, wolf, ground squirrel, and many other animals. Some of the pelts were traded at the roadhouse store or through the Seattle Fur Exchange. There were pictures and captions of achievements made while struggling to carve out a life in the rugged north Arctic land. In each photo that Kris studied, she noticed weathered but pure beauty in the humble faces. The women's smiles were radiant, while the men's were fierce but proud. She could not envision the life they lived with months of day-light when chores only stopped when the sun went down and then months of complete darkness or near darkness. The entire family lived in one room. In her mind's eye, Kristi could not imagine the isolation and boredom of total darkness blizzard conditions on the outside and family physically side by side inside.

The room also featured bench like rustic furniture and utensils used to cook and work the land. It was amazing. One of the guests again stopped Marvin's presentation to ask about the wood trapdoor in the floor.

"It is a fruit cellar. With the continuous light of summer, they were as we are able to grow and harvest crops that will sustain us through the winter. We grow carrots the size of baseball bats, hun-dred-pound squash, potatoes, turnips, cabbages, and beets. All of which are Alaska size, not like the small produce you buy in grocery stores in the lower forty-eight. We must dry fish, caribou, and other meats. The dirt space under the home, which was cool but not freez-ing cold, preserved their harvest."

Zac was fascinated with the size portions of crops. There was a sign that said in the summer of 1930, 26.5 tons of crops were har-vested. Zac shook his head; that was a lot of produce.

Time slipped away with the fascinating presentation that Marvin Kveerik gave. He was not boastful or arrogant while talking about the land he loved. At the end of his speech, he handed out information papers on how to reach him if any of the tour members had questions. Kristi scanned the color copy page and stated, "You have internet access."

Marvin smiled and said, "We may be off the grid, but we keep up with the times, we aren't complete backward up here."

"That explains the satellite dishes I saw on the mountaintops on the way up here," Kristi said in awe.

"Yes, great observation. It takes about fifteen minutes for our internet signals to bounce from one dish to another to Fairbanks. But we do keep up with the news of the day and our families not living in Alaska. Thank you all for your journey up here. Safe trip back and come see us again."

Before Brad turned onto the Dalton Highway, he pulled the van to the edge of the gravel road. He pointed to a huge pipe on steel poles driven into the ground. He said, "That is a close-up view of the Trans-Alaska Pipeline. The crude oil comes from Prudhoe Bay down the pipeline all the way to Fairbanks. The temperature is about 120 degrees Fahrenheit coming through the pipe. Up here you hear the word permafrost all the time. What that means is the ground is completely frozen. Yes, we do have mosses and vegetation that lies on top of the frozen ground, and yes, the ground may thaw two to five inches into the topsoil during the summer months, but that's about it. What you have to realize is the heat that radiates off the pipes when the crude flows can and will damage the permafrost. See those silver rods on top of the pilings?" Brad said, pointing to the pipeline. "Those tubes have chemicals in them to keep the pilings cold so the permafrost isn't damaged. The State of Alaska is trying to maintain the pristine beauty by being very environmentally conscious."

A lady from California interrupted Brad as he pulled onto the highway, informing him of the environmental laws of California and how they were far superior. Brad tried to graciously ignore her insulting statements, but she continued with her interrupting diatribe. Finally, as he curved around a bend in the road, he pulled over along the guard rail, stopped the van, and said, "I would like you all to look to the right of the van. See those tall peaks of those mountains over there? For as far as you can see, that range is called the Brooks Mountain Range. It is one hundred fifty miles wide from north to south and seven hundred miles in length across. That is only seventy miles short of the entire length of California. California with all its mountains and canyons is only one hundred miles wider." Brad put the van in gear and pulled back on the highway. The individuals sitting next to the outspoken lady watched as her open mouth clamped shut. Zac was amused at the silent laughter that seemed to fill the van.

On a lighter note, no pun intended, Brad started talking about the Alaskan land of the midnight sun. He described how the Earth's axis tilts toward the sun in summer. He said, "In the sky up here in the Arctic Circle, the sun can be seen physically going around in circles. The sky is light around the clock and the same with winter, only it is dark or dusk around the clock." He again turned off the Dalton highway and into a muddy and pothole-filled gravel parking lot. A plywood sign informed them they were at the Coldfoot Camp. Set back against the tree line was another parking lot filled with several mobile homes, pickup trucks that hadn't seen a car wash in like forever, and a couple of small buildings clad in weathered boards. In front of the now parked van, Brad had informed everyone they were at the Coldfoot diner and truck stop. He said they would spend twenty minutes stretching and maybe grabbing a bite to eat in the diner. He said the building next door was the post office. He suggested for the fun of it, to send a postcard home as a souvenir stamped with the postmark of Coldfoot. He also requested everyone to use the restroom before they leave stating there were no facilities until Fairbanks.

"Zac, I would like to take a couple of pictures out here while everyone rushes inside," Kristi said as she started walking toward the bright blue post office.

"Okay, I'll walk with you, but I do need a cup of coffee."

It wasn't long before an old coach bus backed into the open area next to the diner. A guy jumped out and hollered into the small restaurant that the supply truck had arrived. Every available and able body came out of the diner and helped to carry in cases of toilet paper, sodas, beer, snacks, foods, and produce. It was neat to see everyone working together for the survival of the small community.

It was ten thirty when the two groups returned to the lonely airstrip in the middle of nowhere. The sun was finally beginning to descend as Kris and Zac's group gathered around Ben, in front of the piper. He asked over the noise of the other plane as it taxied down the gravel strip, "Who would like to sit up front in the copilot's seat?"

Kris looked at Zac, stressed her lip with her teeth, and said, "I would."

Zac shook his head and laughed, happy that Kris was adding more to her adventure resume.

Kris excitedly climbed into the seat right of the pilot's. The seat was confining with very little leg room, but it didn't bother her. Ben climbed in and slipped his headphones on, and everyone followed suit. Ben explained the instrument panel to Kris as he checked all the gauges. He talked into his mic to the tower, and within minutes, the plane was in the air. There were very few clouds as they passed over the mountains that earlier in the day, due to rain, they had gone around. Kristi glanced at the satellite dishes, now understanding their use, helping to connect the very isolated areas. She smiled. She took pictures of scenes she didn't see on their trip north. She took pictures of the captain which made him laugh. She turned and took pictures of the passengers as they waved to her.

Ben pointed out different landmarks as they traveled south to Fairbanks. Kristi realized she was becoming tired, bone-tired. She didn't want the pilot to see her falling asleep. She turned her head to the right so Ben would not see her eyes close.

"Although we never use the word crash, it's kind of taboo. I think my copilot is out for the count," Ben said into the mic for everyone to hear.

Kris looked at him with a surprised look on her face as he started laughing. "Nooo," she said and also started laughing.

"Folks, we are almost to Fairbanks. We are passing the pump station for the pipeline on the left of the plane."

As they got closer to the airport, Kristi remarked about the lakes so near the airport. Ben explained that not only was the Fairbanks airport a commercial airport but many smaller planes flew in there. The waterway between the long runway and the shorter run was used for pontoon planes. He pointed to the left where the water planes could dock. It was such a different way of life. However, Kristi got to thinking about it. It would be such a cool way to fly up and down the coastline of Florida along the Gulf of Mexico.

Zac noted when they touched down in Fairbanks, the city lights were just coming on. It was twelve thirty in the morning. No wonder Kris was starting to doze, they had been up since early morning and had a full day of adventures, he thought. Everyone slipped off their headphones. They were talking to each other about the great experience they had. Kris talked to the lady who had given her money to send pictures of their trip. Kris told her it would be a week before she could mail them. The lady was fine with that and said she couldn't wait to see them.

The manager of the Northern Alaska Tour Company came out to the group standing together. Zac couldn't believe he was still there, but then it was his job to make sure everyone returned safely. He asked how the trip was, if everyone had a good time, if they saw any wildlife, if they were all exhausted. He thanked the pilots for their skills during the heavy rains through the mountain pass, and everyone clapped. Unexpectedly, he handed out sheets of thick paper. Zac thought it was probably a postflight survey.

"This is a certificate claiming that each of you has successfully crossed Alaska's Arctic Circle. Congratulations and have a wonderful rest of your evening," said the manager before he walked away.

"Wow, that was cool and very personable," Kris said, looking down at the recognition.

While they walked to the front of the office building, Zac was on his cell calling Pikes Waterfront Lodge for their pickup. He explained his location and said they would be waiting out front. Slowly he noticed while they stood waiting, everyone had gotten picked up. The office had closed down. He and Kris were alone standing on the isolated walkway. He was so glad that Kris hadn't taken the Arctic Circle excursion by herself. She would be standing here alone waiting.

A minivan with Pike's Waterfront Lodge logo on the door came to a stop on the gravel parking lot. "Here to pick you up."

Zac opened up the front seat door for Kris, but she asked him to sit up front, and she would sit in the back. She just wanted to get to the lodge and go to sleep.

"Thank you for picking us up," Zac said, trying to make conversation. But he noticed the guy didn't want to be bothered with customer relations. As long as he drove safely, Zac decided it didn't matter. Zac watched the road and debated on the amount to tip him.

When they pulled into the resort parking area, Zac asked where their cabin was located. The driver asked, "You don't know?"

"No, we went directly from the train station to the airport; so, no, we don't. It is late, and I don't want us to wander around in search of the cabins. I am sure your security guard doesn't want that either," Zac said, putting the tip money back in his pocket.

After the directions were practically pulled from the guy's memory bank, Zac and Kris slowly walked the stone path between two of the building and passed the bocce ball court. Zac pointed out to Kris, who was almost a sleep-walking zombie, their cabin. He hurried up the three steps and unlocked the door. As he walked in, he moved the suitcases that had been placed right inside the door as promised.

Kris followed Zac in and stopped. The room was bathed in soft lighting. The bed had been turned back and looked so inviting. The walls were real pine logs. A light breeze through the open screened window ruffled the white sheers. Kris was too tired to appreciate her first time staying in a log cabin; however, the large bed looked too enticing to pass up. She walked into the bathroom, pulled off her clothes, and dropped them in a heap on the floor. She asked Zac if she could borrow one of his sweatshirts.

Zac watched Kris go through the motion of getting ready for bed; he could tell she was almost beyond exhaustion. He put their two suitcases on the credenza, under the wall hung flat-screen television. After unzipping his case, he pulled out the requested shirt. He walked over to Kris and tugged the bulky, too-large-for-Kris sweatshirt down over her body. He leaned over past Kris and pulled the top sheet back from the bed. He watched as Kris climbed onto the firm mattress and rolled on her side. Zac smiled as he pulled the sheet and quilted comforter over Kris's shoulders and decided she was asleep before her head even hit the pillow.

CHAPTER 21

The shadows of trees danced across the wall of the log cabin. The early morning rays of pink light touched the window. Kristi stared at it in fascination. The call of a bird, the rush of the water against the riverbanks were the only sounds in the wee hours of the morning. The distinct smell of damp grass scented the air coming through the open screen. Zac's head was on her shoulder as he slept on missing the beauty she was looking at. She wished this moment would last for a while longer. As if in prayer, she slowly closed her eyes.

Zac kissed Kris's soft shoulder his head had rested against most of the night. There was a chill in the air probably because he forgot to close the screened window before they went to bed late last night. But as long as he kept beneath the heavy quilted comforter and next to Kris, all was well in his world or at least for the moment. Yet he was dying for a cup of coffee. He couldn't remember seeing a coffee maker on the counter over the small refrigerator next to the sink last night. It really hadn't been his top priority then, but now, heaven help him, he needed it.

Zac slid to the edge of his side of the bed, careful not to disturb Kris. Walking past the bathroom door, he noticed as big as you please sitting on the counter, a four-cup coffee maker. Ahhh, he thought as he ripped open the premeasured grounds and filter pack sitting in a wood basket on the counter. He plopped the mesh bag into the coffee maker's strainer basket, added water, and pushed the on button. He turned around to head back to bed and—

"Crap, you scared the hell out of me."

Kristi laughed so hard she stepped back and fell on the bed.

"Oh, you think that's funny, do you?" Zac flopped down on the mattress next to Kris and started tickling her sides. He felt her hands grab his arms. Wiggling and laughing, her one hand grazed his hip. It stopped when her palm came in contact with his shaft. He groaned. *Not fair*, he thought, but he loved her touch all the same. Slowly he silenced her laugh with his lips to her lips. *Oh so soft*, he thought. Kris responded by running her tongue across his teeth. When she did that, it was so hard to think, to remember when he last made love to her. It didn't matter, he decided. He wanted her now at this very moment. He kissed her jaw, her neck, her collarbone, but her hands pulled his face back to her lips. She held his cheeks with the palms of her hands as he kissed her again and again.

"Zac, I want you."

Zac didn't want to experiment with different positions. He lacked the need to play sex games. When Kris said she wanted him, all he wished to do was give her pleasure. His desire was to watch her eyes soften as he touched her. He wanted to arouse the fire in her. He enjoyed seeing the perspiration gather on her skin from the passion between them. He felt her hands slide down his back, urging him on top of her. She massaged his buns pushing him against her pelvis. He rose up on his elbows and brushed her damp hair from her face.

"You are so beautiful."

"Zac, please," Kris whispered. She wanted him deep inside her. She craved that feeling of utter abandonment of all reason when he pushed her body to the edge. She loved the feeling of her muscles when they contracted around him giving the pleasure back to him that he gave to her. She didn't have to wait long for her desire to be fulfilled. Zac slid into her again and again. She marveled at his lengthened stamina. His staying power was unbelievable. He was so fantastic, she thought. He pulled a pillow under her hips and gave her even deeper pleasure until she couldn't wait any longer. She felt like the stars were raining down from the sky as she climaxed.

Zac rolled Kris on top of him as he looked into her eyes. She had the same dazed look as he was sure he had in his. He enjoyed the incredible prolonged pleasure he willed his body to give her. He just wished his heart would stop racing. He pulled the sheet over their damp bodies and closed his eyes, if only for a moment.

"Zac, the coffee's ready," Kris whispered and then started giggling.

"I don't know if I could handle any more stimulants. But I do know I need a shower. You wanna join me?"

The next half hour was spent lathering each other with all the complimentary bottles of body wash. Soap bubbles were splashed and slowly slid down the walls of the large shower stall. Steam filled the entire bathroom. Zac laughed when Kris kept rinsing her hair as more foam drizzled down her body.

"I think we are clean," Kris said as she grabbed a towel and wrapped her hair. She felt Zac patting her back dry as she reached for another towel to wrap around her body. She walked back to the bedroom to get dressed.

The breakfast buffet at Pike's Waterfront Lodge was amazing. An entire area was set up with cheese and fruit-filled pastries. There was every type of bagel to select from and breakfast rolls, cereals, and waffles, enough to cause a carbohydrate crash within minutes. Another banquet table offered fresh fruits, salmon, bacon, ham, hard-boiled eggs, and scrambled eggs and a chef slicing reindeer sausage for the guests.

Zac selected an "everything" bagel and added cream cheese and salmon. He added a scoop of scrambled eggs, bacon, and some reindeer sausage to his plate. While Kristi also chose scrambled eggs, she couldn't wait for some reindeer sausage. She was amazed at the huge bowl of cut bananas, oranges, grapefruit, pineapple, and grapes available. She added a cup of the fruits along with a strawberry yogurt / sour cream drizzle over the top. They sat at one of the tables by the window. Every once in a while, a pleasure boat with fisherman casting their lines into the Chena River floated by.

"How was your flight to the Arctic Circle last night?" Jonathan said as he walked up to their table.

"It was an adventure with some very beautiful country," Zac said.

"Did you see a lot of wildlife?"

"No, actually we saw more in Denali. But the history of the Wiseman Settlement was very interesting," Kristi said as she set down her fork.

"I wanted to drop the itinerary for today and tomorrow off with you. I will see you in the main lobby at nine fifteen for the Gold Dredge 8 tour," Jonathan said as he handed a folded pamphlet to Kris and to Zac. "Maybe you could tell the group more about your flight on the coach this morning." He walked away.

"I kind of got the impression, he didn't care."

"Yep, me too, but he made sure we got to the airline company on time so, it's all good," Zac said as he continued to eat.

After they finished breakfast, Kristi wanted to walk through the gift shop really quick. Zac laughed and said he was going to step outside while she shopped; he needed to check in with his manager at the restaurant.

The gift shop was interesting to browse through. There were toiletries like toothbrushes and toothpaste. She guessed to replenish if the vacation was a long one, and personal items were running low or forgotten along the way. She was amazed to see two shelved dedicated to potato chips, crackers, and candy. Of course, there were the usual Alaska T-shirts and sweatshirts in a multitude of colors with moose, bears, the Alaskan flag, wolves, Iditarod Dog Sled Race, and fish stamped on the fronts. She found a beautiful wood salmon fish hand-carved by local Alaskans. She bought it for George, a very old family friend and the husband to KC's law firm's secretary. He loved fishing. Thinking of KC, she decided to head outside and make a call to her brother to see if he had any news from her attorney in Atlanta.

Kristi walked out and found a park bench by the huge wooden grizzly bear in front of the entrance canopy. She was able to get in touch with him on first try. It was amazing to her since she was 4,700 miles away. "KC, how's it going there? Have you heard from my attorney…yes, yes, oh really. Oh. Hope you win your case this afternoon. See you in a couple of days. Love you too. Bye," Kristi said and then shut her phone down hugging it to her. She continued to sit on the bench in the sun staring across the parking lot.

"Is everything okay?" Zac asked as he came and sat down next to her.

"I just talked to KC. He said the police picked up a guy nosing around my house. The guy confessed he had been hired by Dom. KC has spoken to my attorney pertaining to harassment charges. He couldn't talk any longer; he was in the middle of a case trial and lunch was over. Now Dom has hired a guy to snoop on me at home. I can't believe it. No, actually I can at this point." Kristi sighed.

"I am glad you were on the land part of our trip and not home. Who knows what would have happened if you had run into the snoop," Zac said, looking at the ground.

"You are right, I hadn't thought of that," Kristi whispered.

"Do you think your attorney could get the paperwork on the complaint you filed with the cruise line?" Zac asked. He decided he needed to get Kris's mind away from the new worry of someone invading her home space.

"The cruise line probably didn't file true paperwork. You know, 'just bobbed their head up and down to appease the client in front of them' sort of thing. Besides it would be very difficult and expensive trying to get documents from the ship's country probably, I'm not sure," Kris said, looking at a flower growing in a crack in the sidewalk. "I don't wish Dom harm, just leave me alone."

Kris looked up to see Jonathan walk out of the entrance doors while she and Zac were talking. He gave her an odd look. She wondered if he overheard part of her conversation. She hoped not. *Jeez, what a mess*, she thought. And she hated drama.

"Come on, babe, we have to get our backpacks. We are going to need them to lug back all the gold we'll find, panning," Zac joked. But once they walked out of earshot of people milling around the front entrance, Zac said, "When we get to Fairbanks later, you can give KC another call. Won't he be out of court by then?"

"Good thinking, glad I have you along," she said as she kissed Zac's cheek before climbing the steps of the cabin.

On the way to the place where they were going to pan for gold, Kristi noticed Jonathan looked at her with a puzzled look on his face. She thought back to the last words she said before she and Zac walked back to get their backpacks after breakfast. She remember it now; it was something like "Just leave me alone." Or did he hear when she told KC she loved him too? Did he think that she and Zac had a fight, that something happened on the way to the Arctic Circle? Maybe Zac was right. Jonathan had the hots for her. Was he someone who ogled women? But why? It didn't make sense at all. She was with someone else. Or was he one of those who liked a quickie vacation fling? He wasn't on vacation though. She had room to talk, she thought with a laugh. She went on a fantastic cruise and land holiday with a perfect stranger. It was so out of character for her. In fact, she was amazed that KC, her own brother, hadn't given her a hard time. But she had hired a private investigator to make sure Zac was who he said he was.

"What are you thinking about?" Zac whispered.

"You."

"That I am a fantastic lover?" Zac grinned.

"No, that you used up all the soap and shampoo this morning." Kristi glared at him. It was so hard to keep from smiling, thinking about all the bubbles in the shower.

"But you are clean."

They had spent almost an entire day on the white coach line riding from Seward to Denali. And now, here they were again sitting on the bus. Kristi never thought about how big Alaska was. Thank goodness it was just a twenty-minute jaunt up the highway this time. The coach came to a stop on a muddy gravel parking lot. It seemed to her most of the roads they had traveled on were grimy with mucky gravel emergency stopping lanes. This place, though, looked like an abandoned construction site. There were no cars parked or people milling around. Kristi grudgingly pulled her backpack off the seat and filed out of the bus. She really didn't want to pan for gold. Standing in a cold river with a metal pan didn't sound fun, just wet.

Jonathan acted like this was an interesting adventure. He had said many people in Fairbanks took mining seriously. All she could think about were the little yellow canaries dying in the poor air quality of coal mine shafts. She thought about how men risked their lives with cave-ins, and so many developed black lung disease.

A man in a plaid flannel work shirt and denim jacket walked over to the group who had climbed down the steps and had clustered together. "Welcome to the Gold Dredge 8 National Historic District. It is also a National Engineering Landmark. My name is Walter Sheridan. In the next few minutes I will give you a short presentation of the Alyeska Pipeline. But for now, I will let you look around and take some pictures."

Zac was about to take Kris's hand when he smiled and thought, *She can't take pictures and hold hands.* So he rested his hand on the small of her back and walked alongside her. They inspected the inside of a pipe sitting off to the side of the road. There was a billboard under the pipeline itself explaining the history, design and pipeline system, pump stations, and the recognition of wildlife protection the Trans-Alaska Pipeline focused on. And the awesome sight of the huge pipeline itself. Zac watched as Kris took pictures of the pipe, the billboards, and the people milling around the pipeline.

Walter again walked up and said, "Impressive, isn't it?" He waited for people to gather around. "Let me give you a bit of history. Petroleum was discovered in Prudhoe Bay. The Trans-Alaska Pipeline System was designed and constructed to move crude oil from Prudhoe Bay to Valdez Marine Terminal. There are eight hundred miles of pipeline and eleven pump stations, and as you can see, the pipes are forty-eight inches wide. On any given day 1.8 million barrels of 120-degree Fahrenheit crude oil is transported through this pipe. We supply 15 percent of the nation's oil production.

"After the gas shortage in the early '70s; the need for a pipeline was determined. There were 515 federal permits and 832 State of Alaska permits obtained before construction started in 1975 and completed in 1977. Seventy thousand people were employed during those construction years. The pipeline was built over three mountain ranges and thirty major rivers. Believe it or not, there are 550 elevated crossings for large animal herds such as caribou and moose to pass under. There was worry prior to construction that the pipeline would harm the animals, so that is why it is so high aboveground."

"He definitely is a numbers kinda guy," Kristi whispered to Zac.

"Four hundred and twenty miles of the pipeline are above the ground. The pipes couldn't be buried in permafrost. For those of you not familiar with the word permafrost, it means the ground is permanently frozen. However, there was a concern the super-heated oil would melt the soil. The wet soil could cause the pipes to sag and possibly cause oil leaks. See the rods sticking out of the tubes holding up the pipeline? Chemicals were placed inside the vertical tubes to prevent trapped water from freezing during winter. When the hot crude oil flows through the piles, it aids in the heat transfer from the rods up into the air. Are there any questions?"

"Why do you keep calling the pipeline the Trans-Alaska Pipeline when the sign says Alyeska Pipeline?" asked a man standing next to Jonathan and Willard, the coach driver.

"Alyeska Pipeline Service is a company of the seven major oil corporations that own and operate the Trans-Alaska Pipeline System or Taps as we call it. Excellent question any other questions? Okay, then, if you will follow me this way. You will now be climbing on board a replica of the original narrow-gauge Tanana Valley Train. I hope you now have a bit more understanding of the Trans-Alaska Pipeline, and you enjoyed this part of your journey."

"Oh my gosh, I was so worried there was going to be a test. My mind jammed when he said how many permits and hoops had to be jumped through to start construction," Zac said with a grin as he sat down on the very hard and cold wooden bench.

Kris and several others laughed and agreed.

"Good morning, and welcome to the Tanana Valley Railroad. This train is a replica of the original narrow-gauge train. I will be telling you all about the prospectors who arrived by the thousands during the gold rush days, here in Alaska. Gold was found in the Kenai River in 1848. Gold mining started in Juneau in 1870. How many of you were on one of the cruise ships that stopped in Juneau? Did you see the stampeder's billboards in Skagway? And how many of you rode on the train up to the Yukon and saw the trail of tears? So you have heard some of the tales and legends. I am here to tell you that gold was found right here, a little north of Fairbanks in 1902, by a man named Felix Pedro. It started the Fairbanks gold rush. Felix was actually an Italian immigrant who wanted to blend in, so he changed his name to a Mexican name. His real name was Felice Pedroni."

Kristi took a couple of pictures as the rail followed the tracks through the forest. They went past a replica miners camp with a wood-burning cookstove sitting near the tracks. She could feel the radiating heat; it actually felt warm on her chilled cheeks. Sitting on the wooden bench, Kris was feeling really cold. She snuggled against Zac as he put his arm around her. Although she had her coat on, she hadn't thought of bringing her gloves. The man kept talking and sometimes strumming a guitar, like he was reminiscing about the old days.

The train came to a stop in front of a huge gray barge sitting in a river. A lady walked to the side of the waterfront and introduced herself as Martha. She said, "The Gold Dredge 8 started mining in 1928. It played a major role in the economy of the Tanana Valley. During WWII, all gold mines were closed down by government demand. After the war, miners found better-paying jobs, so few mines were able to reopen. Gold Dredge 8 was one that did and was successful until it closed in 1959. Over the years, millions of ounces of gold were extracted."

Kristi started taking pictures as the lady's discussion continued on describing the breakdowns of the dredger over the years. She was sure it was interesting. But she didn't think she would ever have to work a workmen's comp case since the place had been shut down way before she was born. Kris looked over at Zac and noticed he too was having a hard time staying awake. Finally, the train jerked to life. Kristi looked to see if the lady had died or fallen in the murky brown water that the dredge was sitting in. Nope, she was waving and walking away as the train chugged along the tracks once again.

"Zac, you did a great job of sleeping with your eyes open," Kristi whispered into Zac's ear.

"Since it didn't have a cook station in the dredge that I could see, I wasn't interested in learning how to fix a rock jam on the conveyer," Zac whispered back.

The train stopped at what looked like a picnic pavilion. There was a gift shop and mini museum that advertised sandwiches and a snack bar inside. When everyone stepped off the train platform, a guy who couldn't have been more than twenty-one years of age, in jeans and again a plaid flannel work shirt, directed everyone to have a seat in front of six huge dingy-looking water troughs. He handed everyone a bag of gravel and an old galvanized pan. Once everyone was seated, the guy explained how to pan for gold. He demonstrated the technique of panning a river by dumping the gravel in the bottom of the shallow pan. He dipped the pan into the water from the trough, then tilted the pan just a little; he swished the gravel in the pan from side to side. As the gravel slid out, the gold bits would stick to the bottom of the pan.

Zac and Kristi followed the instructions. Zac couldn't believe that gold would stay in the pan as the gravel slid out, but as he slowly swished his pan back and forth, one of the instructors pointed out the gold already visible. Zac was shocked. Then he watched Kristi. She tipped her watered-down gravel pan back and forth while the gravel slowly slipped away into the trough. But there was no gold to be found. Zac could tell she was feeling disappointed.

"I will never make it as a gold-panning-type person. I didn't get any gold," Kris said.

One of the instructors, who was helping people get the hang of swishing and tilting their pans at the same time, walked over to Kris. She looked in Kris's pan and said, "Just like in the gold-panning mining days, it was hit-or-miss finding gold for long periods of time." She dumped another bag of gravel in Kris's water pan. And she watched as Kris tilted the watered-down gravel back and forth, she finally said, "Look, there is some starting to show up in the bottom of your pan. See?"

"Zac, I found gold," Kris said acting, all proud of herself.

Zac offered a hand to Kris, helping her from the bench. They walked into the gift shop to get their gold weighed. They found out

Zac had $84.00 worth and Kris had $18.00. He handed Kris his black plastic bottle of gold. "Here, combine it with yours, and you can buy a little bottle pendant with the gold in it."

"You should give yours to Lacey."

"No, I want you to have it," Zac said.

As Zac and Kris walked around the gift shop, instead of putting the gold toward a necklace pendant or a nugget of gold to wear on a chain around her neck, she found a water globe. It was of medium-size and inside it had a molded river. When her gold was poured into the water, she shook the globe. The gold swirled and glistened in the light, sparkling as it drifted to the bottom. It was perfect and just what she would rather have. She bought Zac a whiskey shot glass with the number 8 painted on the side, as a memento from visiting the Gold Dredge 8. It had a clear wax candle inside with gold flecks in the wax. She also slipped a cookbook called *Baking with Gold* to the cashier before Zac could see it.

They walked through the small museum of gold rush history. There were pictures of rugged bearded men panning for gold. Etchings of the original Gold Dredge 8 and pictures of safes with gold bars sitting inside. Again, Kristi noticed how there was muddy water or dirt in every picture.

"Kris, did you want something to eat from the dining area?"

"No, aren't we going to Fairbanks when we leave here?" Kris asked as she put her purchases in her backpack.

"Yes, so you want to eat there instead?"

"Yes."

According to the itinerary pamphlet Jonathan had handed out yesterday, after leaving the Gold Dredge 8, lunch would be in Fairbanks with an afternoon of touring the city.

"Babe, would you like to find a place to eat first or shop?" Zac asked as he helped Kris off the coach after it stopped at the Antler Arch Park.

"Oh, Zac, I need a couple of pictures of the arch first," Kris said as she walked toward the park along the Chena River. The plaque outside the entrance explained the arch was made up of over one hundred moose antlers collected from all over the interior of Alaska.

There was a pristine yet rugged look to the silvery bones attached to the arch. Kris thought it would be stunning to walk through the park in winter when the snow was deep, and the sky was pink behind the racks of antlers. "Okay, that was beautiful. Isn't that the culture center over there Jonathan said something about at breakfast?" Kris pointed up the street.

"Let's walk that way and find out," Zac said grabbing Kris's hand. "You aren't cold, are you?"

"Not anymore, your hands are so warm. How is it you never get cold?"

"I'm just a hot-blooded male," Zac said with a grin on his face. "Do you like my lecherous look?" He tried to raise his eyebrows and squinted his eyes.

Laughing, Kris said, "Don't quit your day job."

The landscaping leading up to the Morris Thompson Cultural and Visitor Center was a combination of huge boulders and paths leading through clusters of conifers and white birch trees. The building itself was a modern building with very-light-orange-colored walls and large glass windows. Once inside, Zac and Kris were greeted by two women who explained the layout of the center. Zac smiled and walked past a huge rack of pamphlets promoting anywhere someone would like to visit in Alaska. Kris stopped and took a picture of a bright yellow single-engine bush plane suspended from the ceiling. She then followed Zac as he walked into a darkened room with spotlights of glass cases full of native baby carriers, moccasins, and gloves made out of caribou, moose, and bear hides. There were wooden bowls carved from the wood of trees. They looked at exhibits telling life stories of natives at the turn of the century. A huge map hung on the wall delineating the five major groupings of natives across Alaska.

"Zac, look, we were in the Tlingit and Haida native land when we were in Icy Strait Point and Ketchikan. When we flew up to the Arctic Circle, we saw pictures of the Aleuts and Northern Eskimos. And at Denali the Athabascans. The only natives we have not gotten to visit is the Yuit of the St. Lawrence Island and Bering Sea."

"Yeah, look at these pictures of the land around the Bering Sea, it doesn't look very hospitable," Zac said as he waited for Kris to decide it was the next place she would like to visit. When she didn't say anything, they continued to walk past murals of grizzly bears in the tundra of Denali and bald eagles standing majestically on granite boulders. They decided against walking through the log cabin since they had viewed the Savage Cabin during their History tour in Denali National Park.

Once outside and back on the sidewalk, Kristi said, "I would like to get a picture of the Golden Heart Plaza. I think it is just down the street along the river."

"You know, as a tourist, you are supposed to be spending money here. Kris, you are not holding up your end of the bargain. Jonathan is not going to give you the keys to the city, you know that, don't you?" Zac teased as they walked up to the Golden Heart Plaza fountain. In the middle, a gray metal sculpted group of Eskimos stood together. They were wearing hooded winter hide coats. It was depicted to look like it was really cold with white flecks in the metal, not just because it was in the middle of the fountain. Kristi interpreted the sculpture to illustrate the strength and energy of the people who endured the fierceness of their land. The monument gave honor to the native Eskimos.

"That is a very powerful and spiritual statue. Whoever cast it understood and loved the native Eskimos," Zac said as he thought of the beautiful mermaids he had searched several continents for.

He watched as Kris turned and focused her camera lens on the Fairbanks clock tower and a white church steeple through the trees.

"The afternoon is young. Give me time, I am sure I will find something special or even maybe foolish to spend my souvenir money on," Kristi said. "Hey, look, do you want to tour the ice museum? I saw online pictures of really cool ice sculptures of polar bears, a man panning for gold, dog sleds, igloos, and grizzly bears. There were colored lights beneath the ice to highlight the details of the carvings." But when they walked across the street and up the sidewalk to the door, there was a sign saying it was closed for repairs.

"What, did all the ice melt?" Zac asked.

"No worries, let's find someplace to eat," Kristi said as she grabbed Zac's arm and kissed him teasingly on the cheek. It was fun to see him smile, she thought.

They continued along on the sidewalk past a financial advice business, a real estate office, a flower shop, and a couple of jewelry stores not owned by the cruise lines. Zac stopped in front of a door and stared at it.

"What's that matter?" Kristi asked.

"This building was subdivided."

It has one door, but on the right was a diner with several booths, and on the left was a tourist-type shop. Zac decided to explore the shop with Alaskan T-shirts, postcards, and hand-crafted jewelry in glass cases, first. There were knives with stone and intricately carved wood handles. Zac walked up to a case full of ulu knives. A man stood behind the counter and said, "The ulu knife was used by Inuit and Aleut women for the last five thousand years. They used them to fillet fish, to skin the meat away from hides, and to sew with." Holding up the ulu, the man pointed to the blade, he said, "This is a stainless-steel blade. You hold the handle and press the blade directly on top of a piece of meat. It may be frozen, but this blade will cut right through it. Using the chopping bowl, you can chop, mince, dice, and slice anything. If you want to skin a fish, you place it at an angle and lift the meat away from the skin and slide."

Kris looked around the store a little longer before she picked up three of the ulu knife and chopping bowl sets. "I think I am going to buy three, Zac. One for KC, one for an old family friend, and one for myself. Do you ship, sir?"

"Yes, I do for the post office express mail fee."

"I think I am going to get six but not with the chopping bowls. I would like to ship them home also," Zac said. "They would be great at the restaurant."

After giving all the shipping details and paying for their ulu knives, Kris pulled Zac across the hall into the diner. They sat down at one of the booths looking out over the city street. Although the sun was out, the sky was hazy, and the temperature was maybe in the high fifties. It was a perfect day to shop.

"What will you have, folks?"

Zac looked at the chalkboard menu leaning against the wall. He said, "I think I will have the BBQ caribou with the side of potato salad and your local brewed beer."

"And I will have the BLT with coleslaw and lemonade. Thank you," Kristi said to the server.

"I will get this order right out to you."

"So it's only two o'clock. Do you want to shop a little more, then take the coach back to the lodge with the rest of the group?"

"Well, actually."

"Oh, oh, here it comes."

"Zac," Kristi said in a whiney voice. "I was thinking, and if you don't want to do this, it's okay. But I would like to take the bus to North Pole. It isn't far on the map. And then I can say I went to the North Pole."

Zac started laughing. Kris was the only person who would rather get lost in the middle of Alaska than shop like most women. "What's there?"

"I don't know, probably nothing. But it would be fun to say, I went to the North Pole. Besides, I have never been on a city bus," Kris admitted.

"Never?" Zac asked.

The server placed their drinks in front of them. As she turned to walk away, Kristi asked, "Where is the bus station, please?"

"Two blocks down that street, then turn left, you can't miss it," she said.

The server returned with their food. "Let me know if there is anything else I can get you." The server walked away.

The scent of Zac's BBQ caribou was smoky. He had heard that caribou ribs were horribly tough. So he was interested to find out. After he bit into the rib meat, he rolled his eyes. The flavor was a cumin, garlicky, chili rub with the sweetness of brown sugar. It had been in a smoker for several hours by the way the meat practically fell off the bone. "Kris, you have to taste this. The flavor is so good," he said as he stabbed a piece of meat with his fork and handed it to Kris.

She had to smile. It had taken her a while to get used to Zac wanting her to sample foods from his plate. He thought it had exceptional flavor. So she tasted the morsel of meat. It really was good. "It doesn't have a gamey flavor. I like it. Look at this BLT. This isn't bacon. This is a half of pork tenderloin. Look how thick it is," Kris said picking up a slab of the bacon from the sandwich.

"But how does it taste, is it any good?"

"I am spoiled with the food we have eaten up here. This BLT cannot be replicated at home, I am sure of it," Kris said.

"Let me have a taste, I will see if I can make you one, as good if not better at home," Zac challenged.

Kris smiled when he said home and connected it with her name. "So are you going back to the lodge, or are you going to go on my adventure to see if I can find Santa at the North Pole?"

Thirty minutes later, they were on a bus traveling east out of Fairbanks. The only problem was it was a city bus with cracked seats, and a drunken guy sloughed against the dirty window. The bus stopped along the road to pick up some passengers carrying huge bags of groceries, then continued on. It happened several more times, the bus would stop, pick up or drop off a couple of people, and then be on its way. All of a sudden, the drunken guy stood up, surprising Zac. He stood by the stairs midway down the coach by the door. The driver must have known where the guy lived because he stopped at a long winding gravel road with weathered and tattered houses on either side. When the door opened, the man stumbled down the stairs and stepped out of the bus. He fell down on the gravel incline of the road shoulder. It must have been a regular occurrence since no one seemed to react. The door closed, and they were on their way.

Kris nudged Zac and pointed to a city information sign that said "Badger Road and Santa Claus Lane," indicating next right. She smiled until they pulled into a black-topped paved parking area in front of a huge two-story building. Her mouth fell open. On the front of the building was written "Santa Claus House." Murals of Santa with his sleigh and reindeer were painted on the white tiles on the entire side of the building. There was a picture of the elves making toys and Santa standing at a mailbox. It wasn't what Kristi had expected, but it was Christmassy!

Zac held the door open for Kris. They were amazed and overwhelmed at the look inside the barn-like building. It was everything Christmas. Every shelf, rack, and display cabinet featured Santa figurines, glass angels, nativity scenes, and polar bears pulling Santa sleighs. Hooks on the walls had Christmas wreaths and stockings. Christmas trees were filled with every ornament imaginable. Glassed show cases were filled with glittery Christmas jewelry. Christmas-themed sweatshirts, T-shirts, and pajamas with moose, polar bears, and snowflakes could be chosen. Zac picked up a soft and cuddly sofa blanket for Lacey. He could give it to her for Christmas. She always complained she was cold when studying or watching television. He saw a porcelain Santa face with a long very long shredded and braided yarn beard. Grinning he decided to ship it to Mark. Kris handed him some reindeer jerky, also a must-have.

Kristi decided she was in heaven. There were so many things she wanted to purchase. Both of her twin brother's wives loved counted cross-stitching. They would love the reindeer and Santa sleigh kits. She checked off her Christmas list to buy two novel presents gotten for the family, Kristi thought. She picked up three wine stoppers, a moose head with antlers, a wolf head, and a breaching orca, for her brothers—another three checked off the list. Eli would love the tri-fold leather wallet with a moose stamped and dented into the leather. Kris grinned with the thought of putting a hundred-dollar bill inside. What a surprise that would be at Christmas for him. She found a bright red T-shirt she could wear on Christmas Day that would get a chuckle out of her family. On the front of the shirt was written "Dear Santa, It wasn't me!" She saw handmade tiny leather with fur-trimmed mittens for the Christmas tree. She wanted a wooden whale tail fin with red-and-black Athabascan markings on it. And then hand-painted blown eggs shell Christmas ornaments, the fine detail scrolling done in gold paint was exquisite. Kristi frowned with the dilemma of which to buy. She looked at Zac and said, "I can't decide, I want them all." She turned to the cashier and asked, "Do you ship?"

When the sales cashier nodded yes, Kristi said, "I will take all of this and that snowflake Christmas watch in silver too please."

Zac too shipped his purchases home. He selected a picture of the Santa Claus House postcard and wrote:

> Found my mojo in Juneau.
> Santa really is at the North Pole.
> BTW Mrs. Claus is pretty dang hot.
> Zac.

He placed the postcard and the yarn bearded Santa together. He requested that be shipped to California and gave the cashier Mark's address.

After leaving the Santa Claus House empty-handed, they walked over to the fenced-in pasture and looked at the reindeer. Several of them stood with their heads held high; their ivory-colored antlers looked deadly. Kris asked Zac if the reindeer were groomed or were their coats that beautiful.

"I don't know, I live in Florida," Zac said, stepping out of Kris's reach when she tried to slug him in the arm.

It was a little after five when Zac and Kristi walked across the parking lot hand in hand to the bus stop. They waited along with several other shoppers of Santa Claus House. One lady said, "My husband would love you for having the discipline not to buy anything in there."

"Oh no, no, no, no, she shipped everything home. The post office will not be raising the price of stamps this year, thanks to Kris," Zac assured the lady as she tried climbing the steps of the bus with all her parcels. "Here, let me help you, ma'am."

Kris didn't have any problem selecting a seat for the ride back to Fairbanks. Most people headed home out of the city at this time of the day. There were only about six people wanting to go to Fairbanks. When Zac finally sat down, she whispered in his ear, "You are such a sweet Boy Scout. That was nice of you to help that lady."

Zac smiled and squeezed her hand, but he didn't say anything. He rested his head against the seat. He had come full circle. Frank teased him not so long ago about being a Boy Scout. Mark had been concerned that his mojo had been misplaced. He just sent Mark a package letting him know he had his mojo back. And Kris suggested he was a Boy Scout; she even said sweet. He, for the first time in long time, felt contentment. He realized it didn't hurt to breathe anymore. The memory of Sara was a soft spot, no longer an open wound in his heart. He noticed after Kris had gotten done texting her brother, she sat quietly, looking out the window. Zac didn't know if her issue with her ex-husband was a continuation or exaggerated by her vacation. She tried not to talk about it. For the most part, she hid it well.

"Kris, do you want to eat at Pike's Landing for dinner?"

"Yes, that sounds good. I heard someone while panning for gold say the food was excellent there."

It was after seven in the evening when they finally got back to the lodge. After dropping their backpacks at the cabin and washing up, they headed across the parking lot to the restaurant. From the number of cars in the parking lot and the chatter coming from the wood deck overlooking the Chena River, the food must be good, Zac thought.

They were offered a seat open air or in the restaurant. Even though the sun was still high in the sky and the temperatures were a mild fifty-five degrees, Kris decided she wanted to eat inside.

Zac inspected the menu and was very impressed with the wide variety of items to select from. He wanted the king crab legs and mussels. When they first had been seated, someone had just been served the seafood combination. It really looked and smelled great. "What are you ordering, babe?"

The server walked up at the same time Zac had asked Kris about ordering. She said, "Ma'am, sir, what would you like to order this evening."

"I would like the rib-eye steak, medium rare, with fries, and may I have a salad with ranch dressing, please."

"And you, sir?"

"I was going to order the crab legs and mussels, but a steak sounds really good. I will have the same," Zac said.

"Excellent choices, you won't be disappointed."

After the server left, Zac lifted his glass of wine and offered a toast with Kris. He said, "To the last night in Fairbanks. It has been a great vacation. Thank you, Kris, for the adventure." He tapped his glass against hers.

"Thank you. I hope you have had as much fun as I have. Thank you for humoring me and going today to North Pole with me. I had fun."

"I didn't know what to expect today. I realized a while back when you set your mind to an adventure. Wherever you go, it is going to be interesting. You do not disappoint!"

When the server placed their food in front of them, they were, for sure, not disappointed. Not only did the steaks look juicy but it took most of the dinner plate. Their french fries were on a side plate and with a bit of ketchup could be a meal itself. Zac sliced his knife across the meat and pierced a piece with his fork. He slowly lifted it to his mouth. It was the perfect medium rare. The favor was perfection to his taste buds. He noticed Kris wasn't talking. "Kris, how is your food?"

"You might be the food expert, but this is the best steak I have eaten in a long time. It is fantastic." She smiled just as the server refilled their ice water and to check if they needed anything more.

"Yes, will you please let the chef know the food is excellent?" Zac said.

After leaving the restaurant, Zac took Kris's hand as they walked down by the riverfront. Laugher could be heard from the outdoor seating area. An occasional fish breached the quiet water as they looked across the river.

"Such a beautiful night," Kris whispered as she turned toward Zac. She slid her chilled hands onto Zac's face and kissed his lips. They tasted of bourbon. But she didn't mind. She kissed him again.

"You're cold. Let's go sit by the firepit," Zac said close to Kris's ear as he hugged her. He again took her hand. They walked along the river back to the lodge, then followed along the path leading to the firepit. There was no one sitting by the fire as they took two of the empty chairs and pulled them closer to the block enclosed firepit. The sun was slowly dipping behind the trees. Zac once again reached for Kris's hand while watching the fire dance along one of the logs. Between the crackling sound of the logs burning and the water lapping at the shore, it was so peaceful.

Kris wasn't sure if the radiating heat was from the fire or Zac's hand cradling hers. She was feeling very comfortable just sitting next to Zac. The firepit was a bonus treat that very seldom happened in Florida with the continuous warm weather. Funny thing was, when they did get a cool night, why heat it up with fire?

"Is this the perfect night to sit out or what? Not a soul around. I love it," Zac said. There was something primitive about the fire burning as he continued to watch.

It wasn't long before a family of four invaded the quiet serenity of the firepit with a bag of marshmallows and metal fire sticks. Until the parents reached the seating area, the two rambunctious boys played swords with the roasting sticks. Kris grinned, thinking of her older brother's sons; they pulled the same antics. One of the boys grabbed the marshmallow bag and impatiently ripped the bag open, sending marshmallows flying. "Boys, stop," the father growled.

"I think I spoke too soon. Are you ready to walk back to the cabin?" Zac asked Kris as he stood.

"We are sorry to disturb you," the father apologized.

"We were just leaving."

The trees shadowed the cabin as Zac used his key card to open the door. Once inside, Kris noticed the comforter had been turned down, and the bed was ready to be climbed into. There was no time to think about sleep. She had to pull two sets of clothes out for tomorrow, one for their riverboat ride and one for their long flight home. She set her backpack on the bed and set her flight tickets on the credenza. She walked to the kitchenette refrigerator and realized there wasn't any water. Nor was there ice in the bucket. "I'm going to run to the ice machine and also grab a couple of bottles of water."

"Babe, we need to confirm our flights home, I'm going to do mine now. Do you want me to confirm yours also?" Zac asked.

"Yes, please, my ticket numbers are on the credenza. I will be right back."

While Kris was out, Zac decided to contact the airlines rather than just click to confirm his seating on the flights. He took Kris's flight numbers and upgraded her seats to first class next to him. When the flight booking assistant asked if she should put the upgrade fees on the existing credit card, Zac told her no and gave her his card numbers. He had been thinking about the flights on the way back from North Pole city. Their flights were long, and sitting in comfort as opposed to being sandwiched in with two other seatmates made all the difference.

Kris kicked the door for Zac to open since she had her arms full with two bottles of water and a bucket of ice. She had thought about going back to the restaurant and buying two fruit compost cheesecake slices and a bottle of wine.

Zac opened the door and lifted the ice bucket from her arms.

"I was going to bring some desserts from the restaurant, but running all the way over there was just too much of an effort. But I have the next best thing," Kristi said, kicking off her shoes by the door.

"Two bottles of water?"

"No, silly, here I bought you this," Kristi said as she pulled the *Baking with Gold* dessert cookbook and Dredge 8 shot glass candle from her backpack.

"Hey, when did you get this?" Zac asked, looking at the cover of the book.

"Obviously, when you weren't looking, thank you again for the gold. Watch," Kris said as she shook the water globe, and the gold whirled around and around.

Zac lifted the swirling water globe from Kris's hands and set it on the credenza next to Kris's flight information. He kissed her lips and down her neck while he unzipped her jeans and pulled them off with a tug of his foot. He pulled her fuzzy sweater over her head and said, "You wanna take a shower with me?"

"Okay, only if you vow not to use all the soap and shampoo again."

"Me, it was you who washed her hair two, no, three times," Zac said, laughing as he headed for the shower.

The shower time was a lot shorter when they both realized they still had packed to do and an early morning breakfast and excursion to make. Kris emptied the water out of her globe and packed it in between her sweaters. She decided on the outfit to wear on the plane, neatly folding it and placing it in the bottom of her backpack. Her coat was draped over her suitcase to be worn tomorrow if needed. She couldn't wait to get home and wash clothes. Her coat had been dragged across Alaska and jammed in and out of her backpack so many times, it had to be filthy. After finishing up, she walked out to the small balcony with her bottle of water. The lights around the green space between the cabins came on. The crickets and night noises were music to her ears as she stood taking it all in. Zac walked up behind her and pulled her to him wrapping his arms around her. He kissed her shoulder. He inhaled the scent of her lotion. He kissed her neck. Too bad the balcony was not private; he would have loved to make love to her right there in the cool night air.

Kris turned around. She ran her hands up the front of his shirt and wrapped her arms around his neck.

Zac bent down. He slid his arms under her bottom and lifted her. He knew she could feel his arousal as he carried her into the cabin. "It's our last night here," Zac whispered.

He set her gently on the bed and settled down next to her. His shirt came off her body as she pulled his other shirt off him. Somehow Kris could never seem the get enough of his beautiful body. She loved touching him everywhere. She knew her hands drove those gorgeous body parts of his to come to life. But at this very moment, his lips were awakening her body parts. She arched her back, and her toes curled at the sensations his lips were creating. His tongue was trailing down her body as his fingers caressed the soft moist flesh between her legs. She tried to touch his thick shaft, but he moved between her legs. It wasn't fair, but she didn't have the energy to protect. He was driving her body crazy. He knew just where to touch, to lick, to taste. And all she could do was run her fingers through his damp hair.

Zac loved knowing he was driving Kris crazy. His fingers trailed down her body, dipping into her. She arched her back. She ran her fingers through his hair. She pleaded with him. Her hands tried to touch him, but he couldn't let her do that. If she touched the tip of his shaft, his endurance would shatter. He wanted to give her pleasure for as long as he could. But right now, he wanted to sink into her. He wanted her to wrap her legs around him and hold him in place for as long as possible.

Finally, Kris felt Zac slide inside her. She savored the feeling before she wrapped her legs around him. She knew her muscles were about to have a spastic attack when he began moving in deeper and then almost out. She could feel the perspiration trickle between her breasts. She grabbed his buns as she climaxed not once but twice.

Zac felt Kris's muscles contract around him. She called out his name and pulled him deeper into her, if that was possible. It was his undoing. He gave her all that he had. And then smiled when he realized he would give her whatever she wanted. But for some reason, she never said what she wanted. He wanted to think about that, but his thoughts weren't connecting. He was tired, and his focus was drifting. Did she ever say what she wanted? He couldn't remember. All he could feel was the sensation of Kris's warm body beneath his. He decided he should ask Kris what her intentions were. Wasn't that what a father asked while holding a gun? He wanted a drink of water to cool his heated body. But the thought of moving took too much energy. He just wanted to sleep, with Kris in his arms.

CHAPTER 22

Zac woke up feeling parched. He remembered going to sleep thirsty, and nothing had changed. He looked over at Kris and thought about how good they were together a few hours ago. Easing his way out of bed, he grabbed one of the bottles of water sitting on the credenza and headed for the bathroom to take a shower. As he soaped his body, the aroma of brewing coffee mingled with the hot steamy mist of the shower faucet. It smelled heavenly. *Thank you, Kris*, he chanted in his head.

Kristi took a quick shower while Zac was purring over his second cup of coffee. She really couldn't understand how a single cup of mud could make anyone so happy. But she wasn't a Javaholic, so she didn't have that appreciation. However, she did love the scent of brewing ground beans.

Breakfast had a little bit of a change out. Instead of feasting on scrambled eggs, it was specialty omelets prepared by a chef. All the pastries and breads remained; however, the cereals were a little different.

"Yes, I would like bacon, cheese, and onions on my omelet please," Kris asked as she stepped in front of the chef. She had already gotten some fruit and reindeer sausage. All she needed was a slice of toasted wheat bread to go with her omelet.

"I would like ham, cheese, and spinach on my omelet please," Zac stated as he watched the chef pour eggs in a frying pan. He walked over to the ice tray of salmon and pulled a couple of slices off. He needed a bagel and some cream cheese.

When they had received their omelets and finally sat down, Kristi said, "I like how they made small changes, like the cereals are different and the scrambles were yesterday not today."

"How did you know the cereals were different today?" Zac asked.

"Because there are fruity cereal pieces all over the white-clothed table," Kris pointed out.

Zac noticed Jonathan walk in the dining room. He walked from table to table, saying good morning to his group. He then reminded everyone the coach would be leaving at eight thirty from the front parking lot, for the Riverboat Discovery excursion.

Kristi was inspecting her reindeer sausage when Zac asked, "What are you doing?"

"Is Mermaid Isle open on Christmas Eve and Christmas Day?"

"We are open until eight in the evening on Christmas Eve, and we are closed Christmas Day, why?"

"I was just thinking. What if you made reindeer sausage chili or reindeer sausage, mussels, potato, corn, and fish stew for dinner at the restaurant on Christmas Eve?"

"That is an idea. Tell me more," Zac said as he set his fork down to listen.

"Make it totally Christmas. You could even have really decadent cookies and carrot-shaped carrot cake on each table. The dessert plates could have icing written on the side that says 'For Santa.' What do you think?"

"I think you were at North Pole too long yesterday. Actually, I like your idea. I could create an entire menu just for Christmas Eve. You could take pictures of each item. You know the naughty-or-nice scroll? We could make the menus look like that with pictures of the night's specials," Zac said, adding to the Christmas-themed dinner idea.

"Come on, we have to grab our stuff and get on the coach," Kris said, completely losing track of time as they talked about the Christmas Eve dinner idea.

The Riverboat Discovery excursion was just as impressive as each of the other adventures they had taken on their journey. Pulling into the parking lot, Kris looked at the huge building that looked like storefronts out of the 1880s. To purchase tickets for the riverboat tour, Jonathan directed the group into the Discovery Trading Post. The old-time steam paddleboat was scheduled to leave promptly at nine o'clock.

Kristi was delighted to wander through the shops looking at Alaska sweatshirts and T-shirts. But she noticed these were higher quality than most she had seen before. Of course, higher quality meant higher prices. She found a navy-blue sweatshirt that she couldn't put down. It had the Alaska flag in sequins across the front.

"Zac, Lacey needs this T-shirt." It was a black T-shirt with Alaska written in sequins across the front. It was classy but still a T-shirt, perfect with jeans.

"You think so? It is cool looking and black. I think you are right," Zac said as he too wandered around the different sections of the trading post. And then he stopped. He remembered how Kris loved the hand-carved statue on the train staircase ledge. This statue was an Eskimo holding two fish. It was carved by the same man.

"Sir, would you like to see it up close?" The lady reached up on the shelf and gently brought it to the counter for Zac to inspect.

"I'll take it."

"Oh my gosh, Zac, it's beautiful. It almost looks like the statue on the train," Kristi said in awe as she walked up to where Zac was standing.

"Kris, what is your address? I am going to have it shipped to your home."

"Zac, you can't buy that for me. You gave me your gold. You have paid for so many things for me. I'll buy it."

"Too late," Zac said as he handed the lady behind the counter his credit card.

"Thank you. It's beautiful," Kristi said, hugging him.

As they walked along the dock toward the waiting paddleboat, Kristi was amazed at the huge hanging baskets of colorful flowers. It was the middle of May. But she remembered the man in Ketchikan who told her with the long days of summer, all the plants grew large. Kristi stopped to take a picture of a granite boulder with a plaque honoring Captain Jim Binkley. He had piloted riverboats up and down the Yukon River carrying supplies to the miners and native villages. She stood back and took a picture of the *Discovery III*. It was a steel hull with four decks seating, stern drive paddleboat, according to the brochure.

Zac chose seats on the second level. And as the boat pulled away from the docks, he nudged Kris and pointed to the employees on the dock waving.

"Good morning, everyone, for those of you sitting on the lower level and the upper levels, you will be able to see me on the big screens midship. I am currently speaking to you from the second level. My name is Albert. If you haven't eaten breakfast, you will soon be teased by the aroma of homemade blueberry scones and fresh coffee, located on the stern dining area of the second level. I would like to give you a little bit of history of the Binkley family and how the Discovery Riverboat came to play a part of Fairbanks and Alaska's history.

"In 1898, Charlies Binkley along with other stampeders..."

"Tell me, how did you come up with the Christmas Eve dinner idea?" Zac whispered to Kris.

"Yesterday seeing all the decorations at Santa Claus House put me in the Christmassy mood. This morning while I was eating the reindeer sausage, it came to me. It was just an idea. I'm sure you would be able to dream up some really eloquent recipes for your guests on Christmas Eve."

"I could either have pork tenderloin or beef tenderloin being carved by one of my chefs. You know what? I could do a naughty menu of all your ideas since you are killing Rudolph...

"Hey! Well that is true." Kristi laughed.

"And I could put together a nice menu with classic Christmas Eve Entrées. I really like your dessert ideas...instead of a lava cake. I could experiment and make it a white chocolate lava cake. So it appeared to look like snow on a mountain."

"What about a chocolate brownie made in a snowflake mold, sprinkled with powdered sugar served with peppermint ice cream. It isn't real original but still a classic," Kris said, enthusiasm showing in her voice.

"We did that last year, but it was a big hit so why not again this year?" Zac said staring at a beautifully landscaped home along the banks of the Chena River.

"Seaplanes are one of the most necessary modes of transportation here in Alaska. With Mountain ranges separating towns, it would take a day to get to your nine to five job. Look, here comes Keven in his pontoon seaplane, for a greeting before heading off to work. During the summer it is not uncommon to see jet skis up and down the river and in winter snow mobiles racing on the frozen ice."

Kristi took some pictures as the white seaplane's pontoons skimmed the water before heading into the sky.

"On the right of the ship, you will see *Discovery I*. The original stern steam-driven paddleboat that Captain Binkley used to show tourists how Alaskans lived along the Chena River. The boat was also the only way to get supplies to some of the isolated settlements up north of here on the Yukon River. The Binkley family has had a successful stern wheel business for over sixty years now," Albert said.

Zac noticed on the one side of the river a restaurant called The Pump House. It had a deck overlooking the river with ample seating. He wished they had more time to visit some of the restaurants and sample their specialties.

"Captain, please slow the ship down, if you can. Ladies and gentlemen, looking to the right of our ship, you will see that little creek flowing into the Chena River. In July 1902, Felix Pedro discovered gold right there. He was later quoted as saying, 'There's gold in them there hills.' It was the start of the gold rush in Fairbanks. The creek was later named Pedro Creek. And by 1908, Fairbanks became the largest city in Alaska.

"Everyone loves dogs, but coming up on the left are some very special dogs. Please wave to Tekla Butcher! She is standing at Trail Breaker Kennel to talk about her mother, Susan Butcher, four-time winner of the Iditarod Trail Sled Dog Race and her amazing sled dogs."

"Hi, everyone. As you can see, some of our dogs are getting ready for a workout run with our ATV. Our puppies start their harness training as soon as six months of age. From early fall to late winter they will work up to ten miles. During this time, they develop trust between them and their musher. They learn to follow commands and learn to realize their musher will not push them beyond what they can handle during a race. These dogs are not trained to run. They love to run!" Tekla Butcher said into a microphone while dogs sprinted around her and splashed in the water's edge.

Kris took pictures of the dogs and a bit of their workout.

"Did you ever have a dog?" Zac asked as he stood next to her at the window, watching the antics of the dogs.

"Yes, Keith and Kevin tied a wagon to our dog to see if he could pull KC."

"How did that work out?"

"Seven stitches and a broken arm," Kristi said with a grin.

"Please give Tekla and her dogs a big hand of applause. Thanks, Tekla!" Albert said.

A little farther up the river on the right were the most beautiful reindeer grazing in a field of tall grasses and trees with chewed off lower branches. Some had brown fur coats, but one had a completely black coat. He was very striking to see. He held his head high while the others couldn't have cared less if Kristi and others were taking pictures of them.

"We have now come to the end of the river, so to speak. In front of us and as you will see as our captain turns our steamer around, where the Tanana River and the Chena River meet. We have many types of fish here in the Chena River, such as whitefish, king salmon, northern pike, round whitefish, sheefish, burton, and Arctic grayling, but the grayling is a catch-and-release-only fish. All others make the Chena one of the most popular sport-fishing rivers in Alaska," Albert said with pride.

Once the boat had turned around and headed back the way it came, Kris took a few pictures of the beautiful forest thick with spruce, tamarack, poplar, and aspen touching the blue sky.

"We will be stopping at the Athabaskan Native Chena Village. Our hosts will explain in detail as you walk the paths, life along the river during the early 1900s. Folks, it will take a moment to pull the walkways over to the side of the ship."

As Zac and Kristi walked along one of the stone paths, Zac stopped in front of a gray weathered square wood plank building. It had a half moon carved in one of the walls. "Do you suppose that is the outhouse?" Zac asked.

"I'm not going in to find out."

"Everyone who had followed the gravel path from the boat sat down on wooden benches in front of a small log cabin built up on stilts.

Zac wondered what if the benches were just rest benches and not a presentation stop. Everyone sitting there for no reason would be kind of weird, he thought. He studies the cabin while they waited for some action, any action from their host. There was a rack of antlers at the peak of the roof. A girl walked out of the cabin and talked about hanging meat and fish on the outposts of the cabin to dry. There was a hide stretched and drying in the sun. Her presentation lasted ten minutes. She thanked everyone and walked back inside. The group continues on the gravel path to the next log cabin, which was the post office or otherwise known as the general meeting place. It was where everyone came to catch up on the latest news.

Kristi took a picture of the building, including the rack of moose antlers bolted to the peak of the roof. She also took a picture of a stuffed seven-foot-tall bull moose standing near the cabin. The massive creature looked just as majestic as she had seen grazing in the forest in Denali.

A girl with native features came out of the cabin, modeling a full fur coat worn to keep warm during the harsh winter months. Different hides had been pieced together using dyed hides to camouflage the seams. The hood appeared to have been made out of a long-haired furred animal. Kristi took a picture or two of the coat.

"Do you think that would clash with alligator boots?" Zac asked.

Kristi poked him in the ribs as she covered her mouth, laughing.

In the corner of the post office front porch was a bronze monument of the dog Granite with the following caption:

> Greatest lead dog
> in Iditarod history
> led Susan Butcher
> to Victory
> 1986 87 88 90

The original monument had been commissioned by the Providence Cancer Center for Children in Anchorage. A lady in the post office informed all who entered, *Granite*, the book written by Susan Butcher and her husband, David Monson, could be purchased in the post office. David Monson, after Susan's death at the age of fifty-one, from myelogenous leukemia, had established a center in Providence Hospital in Anchorage dedicated to the care and support of children whose parents were receiving cancer treatment.

As Kristi and Zac headed back to the ship, they passed more log cabins, gardens, and the fish wheels that looked like hamster running cylinders to catch fish in.

The ship's journey ended and finally returned to the dock. Zac looked at his watch and was surprised it was a little past noon. By the time the coach returned to Pike's Waterfront Lodge, it would be time to check out.

"There was a lot of historical information given during that tour. It was quite interesting," Kristi said as they were getting back on the coach for their ride back to the lodge.

"Yes, that is true. It seemed like the native Alaskans had to work together for survival, and it has been passed along through the generations. The Alaskan people we have met in all the excursions seem like they have shared community involvement and responsibility. I don't think it was just part of the cruise package. The people here just seemed to want to make sure we had a good experience in Alaska," Zac said quietly.

"I hope you all enjoyed your trip down the Chena River on the Riverboat Discovery. When you get off the coach at the lodge, it will be time to check out and go your separate ways. It has been an honor and pleasure being your guide for the last four days. Thank you. Oh, and, Willard, your very quiet coach chauffeur thanks you also," Jonathan said.

Zac figured checkout would be a madhouse for a little while with everyone leaving. Zac decided to take a quick shower since it would be a good twenty-four hours before getting home. Kristi agreed and was amazed how fast they could shower; she giggled and said, "We sure didn't waste any water today!"

Kristi took one last look around the cabin, making sure they hadn't left anything behind. Zac stepped to the balcony door to make sure it was locked.

"Never having stayed in a cabin before, that was really great. We didn't hear people slamming doors or walking up and down the halls. I liked it," Kristi said as they pulled their luggage to the front desk of the resort and turned in their key cards.

"Thank you for staying at Pike's Waterfront Lodge. We hope you will stay with us the next time you vacation in Fairbanks," said the guest relationships person standing behind the counter.

"Is it possible to store our luggage while we go to Pike's Landing for lunch?" Zac asked, not wanting to drag it across the parking lot.

"Sure, that is not a problem. You have your name tags on them. You will need to show proof of ID to claim them before you leave for the airport, sir."

"Thank you."

Zac was impressed when they walked into Pike's Landing restaurant for lunch. Almost all the indoor seats were filled. There were only two seats vacant at the bar. The hosted greeted them immediately and asked if they would like to dine in or sit out on deck overlooking the Chena River.

"Yes, we would like to sit on deck, please, if that is okay, with you Zac," Kristi said.

"Yes, the deck, please."

After they were seated and handed menus, Kristi said, "I figured we are going to be cooped up on planes for the next twelve hours, so sitting outside will have to sustain us until we get home."

"I totally agree. Do you want to share the Alaskan ice platter? There is peal and eat shrimp, mussels, oysters, and crab legs," Zac said still looking at the menu.

"You know that sounds really good. I think I would like a small Caesar salad to go with it," Kristi agreed.

"Thank you again for the fossilized caribou antler carved fisherman. I can't wait to see it again. That was such a surprise when you found it and then when you bought it for me. Thank you," Kristi said. She leaned over and kissed Zac.

When the platter of iced seafood platter was placed in front of Zac and Kristi, Zac thought he had died and gone to heaven. There were large portions of crab legs and mussels. The shrimps were scattered on top of the ice, looking so appetizing. Zac scooped several mussels and shrimp and placed them on Kris's plate.

"Thank you, I didn't realize how hungry I was until this was placed in front of us." When Zac dished the food onto Kristi's plate, it reminded her of the first time she drove down to The Mermaid Isle. Zac had served her there too. Her heart seemed to do a flip-flop in her chest. She took a deep breath and started peeling her shrimp.

The server came to check on their progress and realized she forgot to bring Kristi's salad. She apologized and was about to bring it when Kristi's said, "No, it's okay. There is more than enough food here. Don't bring it. Just take it off our order, no worries, really."

"This food is excellent. Are you ready for some crab legs?" Zac asked.

"Not yet, but I really only want one, so you go ahead, eat up. What time do we have to be at the airport?" Kristi asked.

Looking at his watch, Zac said, "We have to leave here around three thirty. I hadn't realized that Alana booked us on the same flights coming home until I confirmed the flights yesterday. Our flight leaves at six," Zac said, cracking a crab leg and dipping it in the butter provided.

Kristi was happy they were on the same flights, but she figured she would be stuck sitting next to someone who snored or drooled on her shoulder. She was savoring every bite of seafood on her plate. The mussels were so tender. After cracking the crab leg and eating the sweet meat inside, she was full. She smiled and realized she would probably be the one who snored and drooled on some poor guy's shoulder!

When the bill came, Kristi snatched it up before Zac could reach for it. He had been paying for the meals and some really expensive souvenirs for her. She pulled out her credit card and laid it down on the bill book and closed it.

"Kris—"

"Zac, you have paid for all the meals. I needed to pay for some of them."

"Thank you," Zac said quietly. He remembered she had said the same thing yesterday when she paid for the meal.

They walked back to the lodge and asked for a cab to be called to take them to the airport. The hostess said, "We provide transportation to the airport for guested departing for home."

They arrived at the Fairbanks airport as planned.

"Kris, what is with all the stuffed animals?"

"I know, Alaska has a real thing about showing off their grizzly's and moose." Kristi giggled, looking at a glassed-in stuffed polar bear as they walked through the terminal.

Checking their bags and receiving their tickets, they walked to the TSA checkpoint. After pulling her camera and cell phone out of her backpack, both Kristi and Zac breezed through. And then they waited at the designated gate seating. Zac sat texting the evening manager to see how things were going at The Mermaid Isle. He answered a couple of emails. He texted Frank, since his PI office was by the airport, to ask if Frank could pick him up.

A text came back: "Do you really want Kristianna to see me picking you up? You doofus, text me after she is picked up, then I will come for you. You are paying for breakfast! Frank."

Zac laughed at the message.

Kristi wandered into a couple of the airport shops. She didn't need anything nor have room in her backpack for anything. But it was fun to just look—said no female ever, she thought. As she was walking back to the gate where they would be leaving from, she saw Zac laughing while talking on his phone. He was already connecting with home. It made her sad. Well, in a very selfish sort of way, she admitted to herself. She had loved her time with Zac. She knew she would go through withdrawal. She didn't think it would hit so soon. So she decided she would ignore it as long as possible. She needed to text KC and make sure he was available to pick her up tomorrow morning at nine thirty. She sat down next to Zac and texted her brother. She sent her flight numbers so Betsy his secretary could watch the flight on the flight app and tell him when to pick her up. She was glad he texted back quickly, letting her know he would be there. Kristi looked at her seat numbers again and realized there must be a mistake. Her seats on both flights were in first class. She knew she had told Alana premium economy. She even remembered the seats were halfway down the aisle on both planes next to the window. She decided she better check with the gate desk.

"Kris, is there something wrong. Did you lose your baggage claim number?"

"No, but I think my seats are wrong. I don't want to get booted and stuck here because the seats were double-booked. I'm going to go check," Kristi said as she started to stand.

"Relax, there is nothing wrong with your seats," Zac said as he put his hand on her leg.

"But, Zac—"

"Remember when you went for water and ice yesterday and I was confirming our flights? I noticed your seats were over the wing on both flights. So I change your seats to first class next to me."

"Ohhh, Zac. Thank you," Kristi said as a tear ran down her face.

"I thought you would be happy, but you are crying," Zac said. He hugged her even though the armrest was poking him in the side. "Don't cry."

Their flight was finally called, and they settled into their seats for the six-hour flight. He was still happy he had changed Kris's seats.

He knew once they were home, their lives would be busy. He had so many ideas about menu changes he wanted to experiment with. And then Kris's idea about Christmas Eve needed to be worked out so his Christmas Eve dinner would be fun but top quality as usual.

As they waited their turn to take off, Kris said, "Do you realize it is already nine in the evening in Chicago?"

"Yes, it would probably do us good to sleep as much as we can. We get into SRQ at nine tomorrow morning."

Once in the air, the flight attendant asked if Zac and Kristi would like the shrimp cocktail, the cheese platter, or the meat platter.

"I would like the shrimp cocktail and a glass of white wine. Kris?"

"I would like the shrimp cocktail also and a lemon-lime, please," Kris said. She noticed the flight attendant totally dismissed her and focused on Zac. Her logical side said Zac wasn't hers, but her heart seemed to think otherwise.

The flight attendant returned with their drinks. Again, she handed Kristi's lemon-lime to Zac, and then she handed him his wine once he had sat Kristi's drink on the pull-down table. She next brought the shrimp cocktails served on a bed of ice in a bowl with cocktail sauce in the middle. Zac turned to Kristi and said, "Who is going to put food in your mouth when we get home?" He dipped the shrimp in the sauce and then placed it in Kris's mouth.

"I don't know, I may starve," Kristi said, watching Zac pop a shrimp in his mouth.

Zac noticed when the flight attendant took their order for dinner; she addressed him and not Kris. She removed their plates from their trays after dinner and only asked him if he wanted more wine, again totally ignoring Kris. It didn't make sense to him, but the flight was only six hours. He wasn't tired, but with all the time changes, he really needed to try and sleep. He tilted his seat back and lifted the armrest between him and Kris. He looked at Kris as she too reclined her seat, she laid her head on his shoulder. The scent of her shampoo reminded him of their bubble shower. "Kris, do you need a blanket?"

"No, thank you, I'm good for now," Kristi whispered. She slid her hand down to his knee. She wanted to close her eyes, but looking out the window, the sky was bright with soft white clouds below the plane. It was almost like they were floating on a blanket of fluff. She felt Zac's kiss her hair as he placed his hand over hers. What better place to be than on a blanket of fluff with Zac? Kris slowly closed her eyes.

CHAPTER 23

Zac woke when he felt the plane's speed change. He couldn't believe he had actually slept until he noticed the time was almost two thirty in the morning, Chicago time. Kris shifted in her seat and opened her eyes.

"Sir, is there anything I can get you?"

"Yes, a coffee, black, and a glass of ice water, please." He knew Kris and her love of ice water.

> Welcome to O'Hare Airport
> Departure to SRQ Time: 5:15, on time
> Gate: B10

It was almost three thirty in the morning when Zac and Kristi walked to their next gate. Their flight from Chicago to Sarasota Bradenton Airport didn't leave for another hour and a half, giving them time to look into the darkened shops. Kris mentioned she had picked up some quite unique items in airport stores over the years. But he noticed she must have been very tired as she wasn't at all interested while they walked past high-end clothing boutique and jewelry store windows. All Zac wanted to do was to get on their homebound flight.

"What are your plans for this afternoon?" Kristi asked, trying to stay awake.

"I hope to get a couple of hours of sleep on the plane. Then once I get home, drop off my stuff and head to the restaurant for a few hours of catch up work," Zac said with a yawn.

"But haven't you been keeping up with payroll and texting with your work people?" Kristi asked.

"I have to approve stock orders, which actually means I want to countercheck what we still have in the supply room. I need to reevaluate the menu changes I implemented right before I left. You know, analyze the spreadsheets to make sure it was a productive shift in entrées. Remember some of those ideas you wrote down and emailed me after my walking food tour in Juneau? Well, I would like to see how I can utilize some of those ideas, plus your Christmas Eve dinner concept," Zac said. He actually felt energized just talking about his plans for the rest of the day.

"It sounds like you are going to be very busy," Kristi remarked. To share Zac's passion and enthusiasm for his restaurant would be a lot of work just keeping up with him but extremely satisfying. It was one of the things that fascinated her about him when they first met. He had such intense feelings. The thought of sharing his world gave her a warm feeling in her stomach.

"Apparently, we are boarding. After you," Zac said with a smile as they walked toward the ramp leading to the plane door.

Kris was so happy they were in the last row of first class. She could snuggle against the window and get a couple more hours of sleep. Flying across the night sky was a double-edged sword—she could catch a nap, but for someone like Zac, who was going to spend the rest of the day working, it would take stamina to stay awake.

While the other passengers were boarding, Zac had asked for a glass of red wine. Kristi was surprised but realized it would probably help him to sleep as they soared across the heavens toward home. *Home*, Kristi thought. Part of her couldn't wait to get home. The pampered vacation life was great, but reality was now only a few hours away. Kristi could feel the plane lift off the runway as she thought about what was in store for her once they got home. She would have to deal with Dom and how it would affect Eli. She wished she could delay that fiasco a little bit longer. She realized spending time with Zac actually helped her focus on what made life special.

Zac handed his drink glass to the male flight attendant and asked for a blanket. He noticed Kris had already reclined her seat. She was looking at the flight screen, watching as the plane headed south toward Florida. But he saw her eyes were slowly closing. He carefully draped the blanket over both of them as Kris turned and smiled at him. Too bad they were on a plane full of people. With her soft and dreamlike eyes looking at him, all he wanted to do was make love to her. Instead, he kissed her and held her hand as he drifted off to sleep.

"Good morning, everyone, this is your captain. We are about fifteen miles north of Sarasota Bradenton Airport. It is a balmy eighty-two degrees. The time is seven forty here in Florida. You will be happy to know, while you slept, I did not get a speeding ticket. For you visiting Florida, my lead foot will give you twenty minutes more vacation time. And for all of you returning home, the dishes are probably still sitting in the sink and the bed did not make itself. Sorry. Flight attendants, please prepare for landing."

Once given the all-clear, Kristi and Zac along with almost everyone on the plane turned on their cells and speed-dialed family and friends for a pickup. Kristi turned to Zac and asked, "Do you have someone picking you up or did you park in remote?"

"Actually, when I left, I flew out of Tampa because they had the flight times best for getting to the funeral. I used Uber. But I have a friend picking me up. I have already been informed it's going to cost me breakfast," Zac said with a laugh. "How about you?"

"I just got a text from KC, he is on his way."

While they waited in baggage to see if their suitcases were damaged beyond repair or even made it to the destinations on their claims stickers, Zac pulled Kris aside. "Babe, I want to thank you for our vacation adventure. I really had a great time. If I called you, would you like to have dinner with me one night this week?" Zac said, looking into Kris's eyes.

"Yes, I would like that," Kris said, smiling. She put her hands to his cheeks and kissed his lips. "Thank you." Smiling, she turned and noticed her suitcase was coming around the curve of the conveyer belt. Zac grabbed it for her and then waited while his came within reach.

They walked out into the bright sun just as KC pulled up in his BMW i8. Kristi saw him pop the trunk lid open and watched as he stepped out of the car.

"Zac, this is my brother, KC. KC, Zac."

"Nice meeting you. Thank you for watching over my little sister," KC said and extended his hand. "Kristi, we better leave before security comes after me." He grabbed her suitcase, placing it carefully in his trunk.

Zac hugged Kris one last time as he said, "I'll call you."

Zac saw Frank's dusty SUV pull up in front of him, just as Kris and KC pulled away from the curb. Zac tossed his case in the back seat and climbed in.

"I saw that," Frank said as he maneuvered around tourist leaving the airport. "Glad you are taking me to breakfast, because you, Mr. Boy Scout, have lots of explaining to do."

"Thanks, KC, for picking me up. I really appreciate it," Kristi said as she watched the side mirror as Zac climb into someone's SUV. "What have you heard from my attorney?"

"I thought I was your attorney," KC said as he slowly moved onto North Tamiami Trail. "Dom tried to lie saying he didn't hire the guy who was caught at your home or the blond guy on the ship. However, we have the police report saying he did, and I told his attorney we could get the report you filed with the cruise ship," KC said as he came to a stop at a traffic light.

"But I am sure they never wrote a report," Kristi said sadly.

"Dom doesn't know that. I made it known to his attorney that I have enough evidence for a harassment suit and for it to stick. So we will see. Eli has called me couple of times. He wanted to ditch graduation and come here. I told him to play by the rules until graduation was over. I let him know, you have kept me informed of Dom's behavior. *Whaaat?* Kristi, Eli isn't a little kid anymore. He knows Dom treated you badly. I had to tell him something. So we devised a plan, and he promised to stick with it. Now tell me about this Zac guy." KC grinned.

"What plan did you and Eli concoct?" Kristi asked.

"You are ignoring my question. Tell me about your bunkmate." KC was still grinning.

"He wasn't my bunkmate. Well, yes, he actually was." Kristi squirmed in her seat.

"Kristianna, I conclude you slept with him and had sexual relations with him."

"Leading question, Counselor, and none of your business, big brother," Kristi said firmly.

"Yes! I knew it," KC said as he slapped the gear shifter. "You looked really happy with him just now."

"Don't get any ideas. He owns a very successful restaurant in downtown Sarasota. He puts in about eighty to ninety hours a week. There isn't any time for a relationship. He loves his life as it is. End of story," Kristi said, not wanting to believe the logic in her own voice but being realistic.

Frank refused to use valet parking at the marina. He was just that paranoid. He knew what could happen once he handed over his keys. After parking, as they walked into the exclusive yacht club, Frank said, "Okay, tell me everything. I saw you hug and kiss her."

"You know Mark's dad died."

"Yeah, Mark texted me you flew there before heading to Alaska."

"It was sad, but he had been sick for a while and didn't tell anyone. From there, I flew to Vancouver and hopped on board ship. It was relaxing. I had a great time."

"Didn't you take any excursions? What about Kristianna Romanoff?" Frank continued to question.

"I flew on a seaplane and hauled crabs. I took a helicopter to see the Mendenhall Glacier, which was damn cold, a twin-engine piper to the Arctic Circle, which wasn't as cold as the glacier but close. I rode a train up into the Yukon. Santa does live at the North Pole. I know his address with zip code if you want it. I went horseback riding, a bus through Denali National Park, a paddleboat ride down some river, and I got laid every night," Zac said as he pretended to count everything off on his fingers. He wanted to see the shocked look on Frank's face, hoping the Boy Scout title would be gone for good.

"Are you gonna see her again?"

"I will have the eggs benedict lightly cooked, hash brown casserole with onions, wheat toast, and a Jack and Coke," Zac said to the waiter who was standing there with his mouth open.

"I will have the same but no Jack in my Coke," Frank said and handed the server the menu card. "Zac, you do know it isn't even 9:00 a.m. yet, right?"

"Yeah, I had wine at 5:00 a.m. this morning. I have slept maybe five hours since yesterday morning, and I have a list a mile long of things that have to get done today at work," Zac said, staring at the crystal blue water of Sarasota Bay.

"So you aren't going to tell me about Kristianna?"

Zac looked at Frank and laughed. "She is smart, funny, sexy, and the most adventurous person I have ever met." Zac lowered his voice and said, "However, you know that really mean ex she has? Well, he hired some creep to spy on her on the cruise with intent to take her back to Atlanta."

"No shit?"

"I kid you not. But he fell overboard. We hopped on a charter bus and went to Anchorage," Zac said as he sipped his watered-down Jack and Coke.

"You're pulling my leg, right?"

"No, actually, it's all true. I may see if I can indirectly talk Kris into hiring you to do your PI stuff on her ex. See if you can come up with any dirt on him. She really needs a break," Zac said as the server brought their breakfast entrées and placed the eggs benedict in front of them.

By 10:00 a.m., Frank had dropped Zac off at his penthouse overlooking Sarasota Bay. Before slamming the SUV's door, Zac said, "Thanks for picking me up. I appreciate it. Come down to The Mermaid Isle for dinner some night, my treat."

Zac dropped his suitcase inside the front door of his home. The sun's bright rays bounced off the white marble tile of his spacious living room. He didn't remember the light being so intense, but then he realized, he was never home during the day. He stripped off his clothes, threw them toward the hamper in the bathroom, and headed for the shower. That too had a strange feel to it; Kris wasn't there to share the soap with him. Standing under the mist, he scolded himself. He had too much he needed to accomplish before he could consider sleep tonight. *Stop thinking about Kris.* Zac slammed the water faucet off. Wrapped in a towel, he went in search of some clean clothes and then off to work.

KC's words continued to echo in Kristi's head, the guy found in your yard was arrested. Who found him? Who called the police? How did the police get him to confess he worked for Dom? Since Kristi didn't have any food in the house, she drove to the grocery store and then to the post office to pick up her mail. All the while she was driving those questions kept floating around in her head. Her chaotic thoughts came to a halt when she stopped and ran in the post office to get her stopped mail. There she found eighteen express mailboxes waiting for her, plus the usual assortment of junk catalogs and ads. Four of the express boxes were from Alaska, but the rest were from Eli, addressed to Eli in care of her and her mailing address. She called KC, but he was with a client. It was too early to call Eli; he would still be in school, probably taking finals. She wondered if this was the so-called plan that KC and Eli devised.

It was like Christmas opening each box Kristi had shipped from Alaska. The box from Juneau held the beautiful carved mask, she decided would be hung in the den, and the jade inuksuk in the hall since it was giving directions. The beer steins she would give to all three of her brothers when she next visited them. She saw the box from Ketchikan. The first box she had shipped. She excitedly unwrapped about three feet of plastic and bubble wrap from around the hand-carved sculpture of two natives spearfishing from a kayak that rested on a whalebone base. The card that had been placed along with the carving said the natives and the kayak were hand-carved from walrus bone. It also gave the name of the native who had done the carving and a little history about him. After her journey through Alaska, she appreciated the intricate carving even more. She just wasn't sure where she wanted to place the spearfishing kayakers. Smiling, she started humming deck the halls with boughs of holly as she opened the box from the North Pole. She inspected the beautiful hand-painted eggshell ornaments. She had been worried they would arrive literally scrambled. The Santa Claus House had taken extra care in individually wrapping each ornament. The wood whale fin and the fur-lined hide mittens were so whimsical, they would be cute on the Christmas tree. If the PETA people came to her door, she wouldn't open it. She looked at the counted cross stitch kits for her sisters-in-law and the three different bottle stoppers for her brothers. Sadly, she closed the box and carried it up to her Christmas storage closet. She couldn't remember what else she purchased and had sent when she opened the last box up. Oh, the ulu knives and bowls, she bought one for herself and one for KC. She also bought one for Betsy, KC's secretary, and a family friend as long as she could remember. She hoped George, Betsy's husband, would like the hand-carved wooden salmon. It reminded her of all the times she and KC had gone to George's river house to fish.

She texted Eli, informing him she was home and to call when he could talk. She texted KC, asking why Eli had shipped fourteen boxes from Atlanta to her house. She emptied her suitcases out, washed all her vacation clothes, and was playing with her cat when Eli called her. She put him on speaker while she folded clothes.

"Hey, Mom, glad you are home."

"Eli, I've missed you. Are you done with finals?" Kristi asked. Sometimes Eli was in a talkie mood and sometimes not. It seemed today was a not. She decided to get to the point. "So you and Uncle KC have been talking while I was away?"

"Dad's wife refused to send you a seat invitation to graduation. You won't get to hear my speech. I know you weren't invited to their *grand* graduation party. So I'm not going either. Last week Dad's wife wouldn't let me talk to you. Then some creep showed up at the house yesterday. I heard him and dad arguing about you in Alaska. I called uncle KC." Eli had talked so fast Kristi was shocked.

"Eli, you have to go to the graduation party. You earn it. Show their friends how great you are. You will fly down on Tuesday after your party weekend, and we'll celebrate down here. Now what is with all the boxes you sent?" Kristi asked.

"I think Dad's wife is going to convert my room into a room for her mother. *It* was talking to an interior decorator one day when I came home from school early. They had been in my room," Eli said angrily.

"Don't be totally disrespectful. Go on."

"I called Uncle KC to see if I could stay with him until you got home. But he came up with a better plan," Eli said excitedly.

"And that was…"

"You know It will throw out all my stuff, when I come to Florida. Uncle KC told me to box up my prize possessions and ship them to your house. He sent me the money so they wouldn't realize what I was doing. I gotta go. I hear It coming up the stairs."

Kristi held her now silent cellphone in her hand. She sat on the sofa staring at the sliding glass doors leading out to the pool as if she had never seen them before. They looked different somehow, but exhaustion was setting in. She closed her eyes, thinking of all the burdens Dom had caused his son to endure.

Zac had only wanted to sleep for a moment when he sat down on his bed, which turned into a two-hour nap. He had to rush to The Mermaid Isle so he could get the stock order in before the shipping deadline. He needed that stock, or else he would have to shop non-quality wholesale down the street. The change out in entrées seemed to be holding strong as he looked at the numbers. He posted a notice for a staff meeting for Tuesday. He finally sat down at his too-small office to go through mail and figure out why there were three boxes from Alaska. He could only remember shipping two. One of the boxes was from North Pole; it had the soft chenille Christmas sofa blanket for Lacey. Lying on top were the two packages of reindeer jerky. He hadn't eaten since the eggs benedict with Frank; he was starving. So he ripped open the plastic package and pulled out a slice of jerky. It was pretty good, the flavor was smoky, a little bit gamey but not too bad. The second box held the ulus for the prep kitchen. He would demonstrate how to use it at the Tuesday meeting. Then he read the return address on the third box. He still was confused as to where it came from. He lifted something out completely shrouded in an air bubble blanket. Whatever was inside the packaging was really lightweight. He sliced into the plastic with a knife sitting on his desk as if it was an exquisite fillet. As he lifted a statue of two humpback whales away from the plastic and set it on his desk, an envelope slipped to the floor. His mouth fell open. The whales were perfectly balanced on what looked like a whale spinal cord bone. He bent over to pick up the envelope and pulled out two cards. The first one was the description of the two humpback whales carved out of fossilized walrus bones and were delicately balanced on a fossilized whale vertebra. The card identified the carving as an original from a native with a very long name, a certificate of authentication, and a bear stamped seal. The second note was handwriting in an elegant style unfamiliar to Zac. It said,

> Zac, I saw these graceful creatures,
> Perfect for The Mermaid Isle.
> From Ketchikan,
> Kris.

Zac sat back in his office chair and reread the note. Kris had a way of touching his heart. The artist completely captured the strength and power of the whales. The statue was beautiful. He grabbed his cell out of his pocket and punched in Kris's name, but when the call went to voice mail, he hung up.

Carol, Zac's secretary, walked into his office and said, "Zac, a Mark is...wow, that is beautiful. Was that what was in one of the boxes? Where did you find that? It is perfect for The Mermaid Isle."

"Carol, who is on the phone?"

"Oh, sorry, a Mark someone is on line 3," Carol said as she bent to take a closer look at the whales.

"Carol, do you mind?" She looked up and walked out, closing the door behind her.

"Mark, how goes it?" Zac said as he put the office phone on speaker.

"Hey, thanks, man, for the Santa head, Linda loves it. The kids think since Uncle Zac got to go to the North Pole, they should too. Thanks! Sooooooo, tell me, how was the vacay?" Mark questioned.

"It was great. I got some fantastic recipes. Elderly Athabascan women cook with some weird spices. I took a food sampling walking tour of Juneau. And I hauled crabs in Ketchikan. I walked on the Mendenhall Glacier and a whole lotta other stuff," Zac said.

"I want to hear about your cruise cabin mate."

"What is with you and Frank? Neither of you care about the ten-thousand-dollar vacation I just took," Zac said, shaking his head.

"No, we want to know about the woman who got you to take the ten-thousand-dollar vacation," Mark said. "Now tell or I will fly to that sandpile that you live on and kick your ass until you do."

Zac took a deep breath. He wasn't sure if he wanted to share the magic of his and Kris's relationship just yet. But as usual, Mark would persist until he talked, so he said, "Her name is Kristianna. She has an adventurous streak you would not believe. Do you know she climbed the rock wall on board ship and then challenged me to climb it too? She takes pictures like a pro. She is so very kind. She doesn't need to be entertained. She never asked a thing of me, just enjoyed every day to the fullest," Zac said, smiling.

"Zac, it felt good, didn't it?"

"Yeah, it did," Zac admitted quietly.

"Glad your mojo is intact. I will let you go. Say hi to Lace. Thanks again for Santa. Later."

It was late when Zac rode the elevator up to his penthouse. He walked through the quiet house and again tossed his clothes toward the hamper in the master suite bathroom. He slipped into a pair of black jeans after a quick shower. Standing in front of the floor-to-ceiling windows, looking out over the dark water, he pressed the now-familiar numbers.

"Hello?"

"I just wanted to hear your voice before I go to bed," Zac said quietly.

"Are you just getting home from work?" Kris asked, lying in bed, looking at the ceiling.

"No, I got home a while ago. It just feels strange not seeing you taking pictures of everything," Zac said as he leaned his head against the glass. "Did you get to talk with Eli since you got home?"

"Yeah, he is quite angry that I wasn't given an assigned seat at his graduation. I won't get to hear his valedictorian speech," Kris said.

"He is smart like his mother. I feel bad that you will not get to see the honors of your son's graduation," Zac said. "Thank you for the two-whale sculpture. It is really beautiful. I was shocked when I opened the box."

"When I saw it in Ketchikan, I knew you had to have it."

"Kris, would you like to come here for dinner Tuesday night around six?"

"That would be nice, yes."

"I'll text you my address. Good night, babe," Zac whispered, then disconnected his phone.

CHAPTER 24

Kristi was still feeling the rush of excitement from her late evening phone call from Zac. She was standing in the garage, dragging more of Eli's boxes out of her trunk. KC pulled his car into the empty bay next to hers.

"Whatcha doing, little sis? I brought sustenance!" KC said as he climbed out of the car and held up a pizza box.

"I'm dealing with Eli and your cockamamie plan. Fourteen boxes, seriously?" Kristi said, pretending to be mad. "What kind of pizza?"

"Kristi, are you expecting company?" KC said, staring at a silver-colored sedan that had pulled into her drive.

"Oh my gosh, no, I wasn't. It's Dom," Kristi said.

"Do you want to talk with him?"

"No," Kristi said in a quiet voice.

KC walked out into the sunlit driveway and said, "Dominic." He noticed the man had definitely aged since the last time he saw him.

"KC, I'm here to talk to Kristianna."

"As her attorney, I advise you to leave. If you wish to confer with my client, you will need to have discussion through your attorney. I will call the police and have you removed," KC said, holding his cell in his hand as proof.

"I flew here just to try and make things right with Kristianna. Give me a break. Please."

"I asked you to leave. Don't make this ugly," KC warned.

Kristi watched as Dominic turned and got in his car. She saw KC watching as Dom backed out of the driveway. KC back stepped into the garage tapping the side closure box. He grabbed the now-cold pizza box from the hood of his car and walked through the door into Kristi's kitchen. She watched as KC made a couple of phone calls.

"Detective Burt Kayhe, please…KC Bradlow…Yes…Burt, the home invasion of Kristianna Romanoff's last week. The ex-husband who hired the thug was just at the residence trying to talk to Kristianna. I happened to be here and asked him to leave. I am going to contact the ex-husband's attorney. Due to his persistence, is there any way you could put extra patrol on her neighborhood? You know, possibility more home invasion…I appreciate it. Thanks, Burt.

"Attorney Chester Goodwin, please…KC Bradlow…Yes, pertaining to Dominic Romanoff…Good afternoon, Mr. Goodwin, I will only take a moment of your time. I represent Kristianna Romanoff. Your client, Dominic Romanoff, I have notified you two days ago, has sent or encouraged unwanted contact with persons of questionable character to my client. Approximately fifteen minutes ago, your client, Dominic Romanoff, attempted to make contact with my client other than usual cell or phone discussions regarding parental duties of their child. He arrived unannounced to my client's Florida home address. He was asked to leave. I will file harassment charges against your client if he solicits unwelcome conversation or entry onto my client's personal property again. Thank you for taking the time to talk with me…Sir, I was with my client, Kristianna Romanoff, when your client drove onto my client's personal property. In representing my client, I asked your client to leave…Have a good day, sir.

"Betsy, can you please cancel any appointments I have for this afternoon. Reschedule them for Saturday morning if you have to… Yes, you can happily work remotely from home this afternoon as needed! Thanks." KC laughed, shaking his head.

"Kristi, the pizza, I'm starving," KC said with a grin. He turned and grabbed a couple of plates from the cabinet near the sink, sodas from the refrigerator, and two glasses he filled with ice.

Kristi quickly put her cast-iron skillet on the stove to heat. She placed a couple of pieces of cheesy pizza in the hot pan and watched the crust crisp up. Smiling, she thought how much KC looked and acted like their dad when he was kicking ass.

"What, you date a chef for two weeks and now you are an expert on reheating pizza?" KC teased.

"Shut up."

While they ate their pizza, KC hesitated but then told Kristi the details of the break-in. He decided, for her safety, she needed to know what was going on while she had been away. He said, "George and Betsy have been checking on your cat every couple of days. The other day Betsy drove past your house and saw a guy sitting out on the curb by your mailbox. She really didn't think too much of it, but she told George. They came over for their usual check the next day. The guy had broken into your sliding glass door here by the pool. George caught him coming out of the house. And you know George always carries. He held the guy at gunpoint while Betsy called the police. She also had a couple of your neighbors stand by if the guy tried to bolt. Your neighbor Jeannine wanted to whack the guy with a flower pot and say it was an accident," KC said while he reached for his soda.

First, Kristi listened in horror, then she started laughing imagining Jeannine in her tie-dyed workout pants, throwing a flower pot across the patio. "Jeannine knows karate, why would she threaten him with a flower pot?"

"Maybe because her legs are considered lethal weapons and a flower pot isn't? Anyway, knowing all of this, I was glad you didn't want to talk to Dom. Oh, by the way, he looked like shit. And you, my baby sister, look fantastic. The vacation was good for you, or was it *Zac*?"

"You know I noticed there was something difference about my sliding glass door. Now I know, you had it replaced and that is primer paint," Kristi said with a laugh. She totally ignored his comment about Zac.

The doorbell rang. Kristi stood to answer it, but being leery, she peeked through the peephole in the door. "Hi, George, thank you for dropping the box off. Yes, I heard there was some trouble here, but I was out of town. Thank you. Have a good day," Kristi said and closed the door. George, the mailman, had a way of knowing all the gossip in the neighborhood.

She walked back into the kitchen with the express box and grabbed a knife. She couldn't wait to open the parcel and see KC's expression.

"Yikes, chick with PMS and a knife slice and dice!" KC joked.

"How old are you?" Kristi joked. She walked into the dining room and returned with one of the boxes she had opened already. She handed it to KC.

"You want me to recycle the box why?" KC asked.

"Just open it. It's your souvenirs from Alaska."

"Salmon jerky. Well, that looks better than the alligator jerky you gave to me last Christmas. A Red Dog Saloon beer stein from Juneau Alaska, cool. Oh, and a menu. I take it you ate there? Why did you steal the menu?" asked KC.

"The Red Dog Saloon has so much history behind it. The decor of the place was ole time saloon with a guy playing an old-time piano. There was sawdust on the floor and probably the original bar, tables, and chairs. Oh, and there is a revolver hanging over the bar with a sign that said that Wyatt Earp had checked his gun with the marshals office June 27, 1900. He left for Nome on the twenty-ninth, but the marshal's office wasn't open when he left."

"Oh, that is kinda cool. And what is an ulu? That curved blade looks really interesting," KC said as he looked at the shape of the ulu. After inspecting his new treasures, he hugged and thanked Kristi for thinking of him on her vacation.

Kristi opened the box Zac sent from Fairbanks. She carefully removed the plastic to reveal a statue of a native standing proudly holding two fish. "Isn't it beautiful? He is carved out of fossilized caribou antlers. I read somewhere that only natives of Alaska are granted permission to use fossilized bones like this. Zac bought this for me," Kristi said, smiling while she continued to look at the carved native.

"He's interesting. I am amazed. I wouldn't have thought this kind of thing was your style," KC questioned.

"Alaska was fascinating to me. I can't put my finger on any one thing, but for example, I took like fifty photos of Mount Denali alone. I took over two thousand pictures. The land is rugged but beautiful. The struggles of the people who live there with extreme temperatures, KC, I couldn't do it. The place is amazing."

They spent the afternoon talking about Kristi's adventures and Zac and lounging in the pool. KC hoped Kristi wouldn't realize that he was hanging around to make sure Dom wouldn't return. He didn't want his sister to become a domestic-violence/murder statistic.

Zac got together with Lacey over the weekend. He gave her the souvenirs he had bought her as he traveled across Alaska. She really liked the black T-shirt with "Alaska" written in sequins across the front. She thought the crab T-shirt from Icy Strait Point was cute. She slipped the Jade beaded bracelet on her wrist after Zac explained it was the state gemstone of Alaska. And she loved the silver bracelet he bought for her in Juneau. It had a whale fin charm by the clasp.

Lacey held up her wrist and said, "Dad, it is just like the one you bought Mom. Well, except for the whale fin, but I love it, thank you so much."

Zac told his daughter about climbing the rock wall on board ship and hauling crabs. He said he thought he was going to die both times and laughed. He told her about the vivid blue water stream on the Mendenhall Glacier, and of course he had to taste the water. And the train tracks bolted to the side of the mountain on the trip into the Yukon. They laughed about his walking food tour of Juneau and Kris dragging him to North Pole.

Zac listened to Lacey's decision on summer school, next term classes, her indecision about moving in with her boyfriend, and everything else in between.

"I have to be honest, Lace, I don't approve of your living together situation."

"But, Dad—"

"Hold on, I'm not finished. Hear me out. I love you dearly, and I want you to be happy. I trust your judgment. I won't tell you what to do. I have always prayed your mom and I raised you the best we knew how," Zac said quietly. He knew his eyes were moist. Losing Sara gave him a different perspective on how easily life could be taken from him.

"Aww, Dad, I love you."

Zac stood before his staff on Tuesday morning for his posted staff meeting. He was actually excited about everything he had prepared.

"Welcome, everyone, thank you for coming in early, and for all of you who came in on your day off, thank you. I have a lot to present to you, so let me get started. I hope you all have taken a closer look at the flower centerpiece, which is actually watermelon, papaya, and honeydew melon with orchids and fern leaves that I carved. The other flower arrangement is carved radishes, carrots, cucumbers, and watermelon skins for leaves. I bet you all didn't know I was that talented. I wasn't until I learned in a class on board the cruise. I will teach you, so start thinking up possible holiday centerpieces we could make out of fruits and vegetables.

"This is called an ulu. It was the main cutting tool of the Eskimo natives of Alaska for over three thousand years. No, Ian, not this exact ulu. Anyway, some of you may have heard of the ulu. I would like to demonstrate how to use this multifunctional knife," Zac said as he grabbed a frozen piece of steak and sliced the meat into perfect one-inch portions. He chopped, diced, and removed the skin from a piece of fish with the knife. He smiled when everyone clapped.

He presented a colorful power point of growth and what he would like to achieve in the coming months. He encouraged ideas and praised his staff both servers and chefs for their dedication while he was checking foods dishes and menus across Alaska. And with that, he proceeded to lift the lid on one of their huge stockpots. He ladled out bowls of steamy hot chili and passed them around, followed with ice water and crusty breads. "Tell me seriously and honestly what you think of the flavor of this chili." He asked if anyone had issues they would like to bring up or needed to be addressed.

Someone mentioned that some of the linens for the napkins and tablecloths were coming back from the laundry service with stains on them. Zac asked his secretary to contact the linen service immediately. One of the chefs asked what meat was the base in the chili. Zac smiled and said, "Have all of you finished it? Raise your hand. Would you buy this for dinner at MI?" Everyone but one raised their hands. The one who didn't explained; she had acid reflux, to which Zac apologized for asking her to sample his recipe. He then told them it was reindeer sausage that he had ordered through a gourmet meat shop in Fairbanks. A few people laughed, one person pretended to look in his bowl, calling Rudolf, and some said they loved it. Zac believed everyone enjoyed the meeting as he watched them head to their work stations, talking about the chili and the centerpieces.

Carol, Zac's secretary, came into his office a while later and let him know how much the staff actually liked his meeting. She said she had heard some very positive things.

"Thanks, Carol. Oh, I almost forgot, here is a little something for you, for holding down the fort so to speak while I was gone. I appreciate the emails and updates I could read when I got cell service up there," Zac said, handing her a large box of salmon shaped gourmet chocolates made in Alaska. He was humbled by her sincere appreciation of the gift.

Promptly at thee in the afternoon, Zac placed a sealed container of the extra chili in his car. One of the fruit centerpieces he had carved for the meeting, he carried in a cooler to his car along with the whale carving that Kris has sent him. He turned the volume up on his favorite rock radio station and headed for home.

"Good afternoon, The Mermaid Isle, how may I help you please?"

"Carol, this is Lacey, may I speak to my dad please?"

"Oh, I'm sorry, Lacey. Your dad left for the day. No, he didn't say where he was going. No, he was in a great mood. Have a good day," Carol said as she hung up the phone.

Kristi couldn't count the number of times she had looked at the clock to see what time it was. Since Zac had invited her for dinner at his house, time seemed to almost stand still. She had been stressed with Dom showing up, but KC had luckily been there to defuse that whole situation. But what KC didn't know was, Dom had tried two more times over the weekend to talk to her. He had parked in her drive for about thirty minutes after KC had left late in the afternoon. He rang her doorbell another time while she sat in her den, scanning through photos taken in Alaska. She had already finished compiling sixty of the best pictures of the Arctic Circle for the lady who gave her the six dollars on the flight to Coldfoot. Her cell phone rang yet again; she paused, watched to see if it was him, and then let his call roll to voice mail.

Kristi tried to determine if she was being mean to Dominic. But each time she was about to cave in and answer his call, she reminded herself how he humiliated her when he made a public spectacle of his affair with his secretary no less. The mental harm he did to Eli was beyond reproach. He damaged her relationships with their friends. He trash-talked her with his new wife in front of his son. She didn't want to ruin her day thinking of all the hurtful ploys he had used to destroy her reputation. And now he wanted to talk with her and make things right with her? Just when she was learning to trust someone else, when she was finally finding happiness, he showed up. *Not this time*, she thought.

Kris rummaged through her closet. She had three different outfits on her bed to wear to Zac's house. She didn't want to dress too formal. She was just going to his house. She really didn't want to wear completely casual with flip-flops, even though it was eighty-plus degrees out. She finally decided on a pale blue silky blouse with sequins down the front and white jeans. She was just about to take a shower when the phone rang. *Please don't be Dom*, she prayed.

"Eli, glad you called, what's up?"

"Mom, I'm sitting on Paulson's swing set, but it's okay they know I'm here. I have to tell you. Dad went on a business trip last weekend. He was really angry when he came home. Then he and It got into a screaming fight that made the war in the Middle East look like a spitting match at school. I saw him storm out of the house. Mom, he slammed the back door so hard the glass shattered," Eli told her.

"Eli, are you safe there? Make sure you stay out of their way. Keep a low profile, don't argue with them. You have one week to go, and then you fly down here. Unless you need me to fly up. We could stay at a hotel," Kristi suggested.

"Mom, I will be okay. You know all those boxes I sent to you? I snuck all my important stuff into them and sent them to your house. When I fly to Florida next Tuesday, I'm not coming back here, ever, Mom!" Eli vowed.

"E, I know this is hard for you. But right now, you have to stay focused. Don't let your anger at them take over. If you need me text or call me, and remember to keep your cell close to you and charged all the time. You are really smart. I know you can do this. Just hang on. I love you."

"I love you too. I gotta go. Mrs. Paulson is coming out with a tray of her nasty-tasting cookies," Eli groaned.

Kristi thought about calling KC to let him know that Dom let Eli think he was on a "business trip," but KC was probably with a hot date. Besides, now she was running late.

An hour later, Kristi took the elevator up to Zac's penthouse condo. Seeing how beautiful the building was and the inside of the private elevator, she wished she would have dressed a wee bit more formal. *Oh well, too late*, she thought. When the elevator door slid opened, Zac was leaning against the wall waiting for her. He had on black jeans and a white linen shirt. His black hair curled along his shirt collar. And his feet were bare. She hadn't forgotten how beautiful he was, but standing there, he took her breath away.

"Hi there. Wait, where is your camera?" Zac said as he pulled Kristi into a hug. She felt so good in his arms. For some reason he couldn't wait to show her his house. He wanted to tell her about his work meeting today and his staff's reaction to all his plans for the restaurants and the coming future. "Come in. What can I get you to drink?" Zac said as he stepped back inside the foyer.

"Oh my gosh," Kristi said in awe as she walked into the great room. "Your view of Sarasota Bay and the marina is fantastic. I would never leave this room." She stood staring at the beauty Zac was privileged to see every day. The setting sun in the west had turned the water into a pool of thousands of glittery diamonds.

Zac walked up behind Kristi and put his arms around her middle. He inhaled the scent of Kristi's lotion, which over the last couple of days he missed so much. "The view is what sold me on this place. Come, have a seat and tell me what you have been up to." Zac grabbed the two wine glasses he had waiting in the refrigerator, while Kristi walked to the sofa and sat down. He sat down and handed her the stemware waiting for her reaction.

"Ha-ha, you remembered!" Kristi smiled as she took a sip of ice-cold Pepsi in the elegant long-stemmed crystal wine goblet. "Thank you! Oh, I brought you something," she said as she rummaged through her purse. "Here you go." She handed Zac a thumb drive.

"What's this?"

"Plug it into your television," Kristi said, nodding toward the large flat panel above the fireplace.

Soon picture after picture of their time in Alaska was displayed on the screen. Zac was amazed how she had captured the beauty of the snow-covered mountains until the very majestic Mount Denali came into view. He now understood how she could take fifty pictures of it. It was spectacular. There were pictures of Zac riding the horse, which hated riders but loved him. He liked the picture of him standing next to the Alaska state flag with the North Star and Big Dipper in stars on it. And then he laughed at the picture of him sleeping on the coach. Thank goodness he wasn't drooling.

They were laughing over the pictures when the foyer door opened and Lacey walked in.

"Dad—oh, you have company," Lacey said as she looked at the lady and then her dad, who were clearly enjoying themselves.

"Lacey, come in. I would like you to meet Kristi. She was just showing me the pictures from our cruise. Come have a seat, you have to see Alaska," Zac said, glad his daughter had dropped in.

"Nice meeting you, Kristi. No, Dad, I just stopped in to grab some clothes. Gina and I are driving up to Orlando tonight. She has tickets for a concert tomorrow evening, so we decided to hit Universal tomorrow," Lacey said as she walked into her bedroom for her things. Her dad had left work early. Now she understood why. Dang, he looked happy; it had been a long time since she had seen him smiling like that.

She walked back into the living room after jamming a bunch of stuff into her backpack. She hugged her dad when he stood to walk her to the door. She hugged him again at the door and said, "Dad, don't stay up too late, you know it's a school night." She stepped into the elevator. She laughed as she saw him mouth "smart ass" as the door closed.

Zac was happy Lacey had stopped by even if it was for a moment. He pulled Kris to her feet and said, "Come, let's make dinner." He kissed her lightly, afraid if the kiss lasted any length of time, they would never eat dinner. Would that be a bad thing? He smiled, knowing the answer.

Zac pulled out shrimp marinating in some spices, salad, and cubed sweet potatoes. He set cast-iron skillets on the range and waited while they warmed. He handed Kris his china plates and asked if she wanted to sit on the terrace. He figured the breeze off the bay, and the sun almost set; it would be nice dining out. He watched as Kris place the dishes on the high-top glass table. When she returned, he asked if she would toss the salad. When she turned around, she saw the carved vegetable centerpiece he had displayed at his staff meeting earlier in the day.

"Zac, that is beautiful. Did you carve it?" she asked, taking a closer look, knowing he had to have. The detail of each vegetable's slightly sculpted cuts were amazing. "I wish I had my camera. Oh wait, better yet." She ran to her purse and pulled out her cell. She noticed there were two messages from Dom, which she ignored. She took a couple of pictures of the centerpiece. She watched as Zac pulled a container out of the refrigerator and heated some brown goop in a saucepan. He dished out a small portion into a coffee mug. "Here try this while I cook." He handed Kris a spoon.

Kristi wasn't sure what to expect until one spoon full. "You figured out the recipe for the reindeer sausage chili? This is great. Where did you get the sausage?" Kristi asked excitedly.

"Yes, thank you and Alaska," Zac said, grinning.

As Zac cooked the sweet potatoes and sautéed the shrimp, she took several pictures of him. He was so "in control" in the kitchen. She took the salad and placed it on the table. Zac kissed her as she opened the refrigerator door. She refilled Zac's glass from the open bottle of wine. She stared at the bottle label, it was one she had never seen before, but reading the label, it was a French Loire Valley Sauvignon Blanc. She took a sip. It was tart but smooth.

"Do you like it?" Zac asked as he lifted the grilled sweet potatoes out of the skillet and placing them on a shallow hand-crafted plate and then did the same with the shrimp.

"Yes, it is so smooth. But I think I will stick with my Pepsi. I have to drive home tonight," Kristi reasoned. She followed Zac out to the terrace with drinks in hand, while he carried the shrimp and sweet potatoes.

Kristi enjoyed watching Zac plate their food. As simple as spiced shrimp, a purple cabbage and arugula salad with smoky vinaigrette, and seasoned sweet potatoes were, the colors made the plating beautiful to look at. He picked up a shrimp and placed it in Kristi's mouth. The texture was soft as she bit into it, and then the flavors exploded in her mouth. She looked at Zac. She was unable to talk. It tasted fantastic.

"You don't have to speak. Your eyes tell it all. Thank you, I am honored," Zac said.

The meal continued as they fed each other bites of food. The sun dipped behind Longboat Key, casting the sky in hues of dark orange. The breeze kept the humidity low in the balmy evening as they sat enjoying each other's company. Zac told her about the staff meeting. She complained about her inability to delete any of the two thousand photos she took since she loved them all. She tried to make light of the break-in after Zac asked what had happened. She tried to skim over the bad stuff, but she could tell he pretty much understood what she wasn't telling. She ended up retelling KC's story plus how

Dominic arrived. She regretted her actions after seeing the look of concern on Zac's face.

"Kris, have you thought about hiring a private investigator to see if there is some kind of reason behind Dominic's aggressive and possessive behavior right now?" Zac asked.

"I never thought of that, but it is a good idea. It is just so weird," Kris said, looking across the calm water. "Zac, your dinner was better than anything we ate in Alaska. It was superb. Thank you so much for inviting me," she said as she gathered up the dirty plates. Zac carried the rest of the dishes back into the kitchen. Kris placed the leftover salad and sweet potatoes in bowls in the refrigerator as Zac stacked the dishwasher.

Zac refilled their goblets and sat down on the overstuffed sofa in the living room. He didn't want the evening to end, so he pulled Kris to him. He kissed her and whispered, "I liked you in my kitchen with me this evening."

"Oh really."

Zac wasn't ready to let on; Kris was the first woman he had invited into his home. It had amazed him how comfortable he was with her in his kitchen. He dipped his finger into his wine glass and slowly slid the cool liquid across Kris's lower lip. He saw her eyes soften as she set her teeth over his finger and sucked. He slid his hand along her jaw and into her hair. He tasted the wine on her lips as he kissed them again and again. He felt her arms circle around his neck as she ran her fingers through his hair. When her tongue slid into his mouth, he ran his hands across her breast and down her back. He whispered, "Stay with me tonight."

Kris couldn't remember walking into Zac's bedroom or how her silk blouse had slid off her shoulders, landing in a heap on the floor. But she remembered the soft texture of Zac's linen shirt as she released each button to reveal the tanned and rippled muscles of his chest. She leaned into him kissing his neck and shoulder. She felt his hands as they slid down her back and pulled her bottom to him. She unzipped his now very tight jeans. Although it wasn't her first time with Zac, lying naked on his bed and touching his sexy body was just as exciting as their first time. She loved how he caressed and stroked her. When she thought she was going to climax he found ways to excite her even more. She kissed and licked his body. She lightly ran her fingers up and down and around his shaft, which she knew drove him crazy. She thought her inner muscles would explode when he slid into her. She kissed his shoulder and wrapped her legs around him when she finally felt him shudder and relaxed his body over hers.

Later, he curled Kris in his arms and pulled the sheet over their bodies. She could feel Zac's breath on her neck as she looked out the floor-to-ceiling windows, toward the soft lighting of the marina against the dark night sky. She decided being wrapped in Zac's arms, high above the water, she felt safe as she drifted off to sleep.

CHAPTER 25

Zac watched Kris sleep. He was amazed how calm she was with all the stressors going on around her. Was it her attorney poker face hiding her inner fears? He brushed a few strands of her hair off her cheek as she opened her eyes. "Good morning. Did you sleep well?"

Kristi stretched as she ran her foot down the side of Zac's leg. "Hmm, I kind of miss the rocking of the ship," Kristi teased.

"Oh, then how about we take the boat out Saturday afternoon for a picnic," Zac said, kissing her forehead.

"What boat? You never said you had a boat."

"How could I talk about a thirty-two-foot sailboat when we were on a ship carrying five thousand people? My boat couldn't compete!" Zac grinned. He crawled out of bed and slipped on his black jeans off the floor. He grabbed Kris's hand and said, "Come, I'll show you."

As Kristi turned to get out of bed, she noticed the twin whale carving on his nightstand. It had been dark last night, so she never saw it. "Zac, you brought the whales home?"

"I wanted to be able to look at them before I went to sleep every night," Zac said kind of sheepishly. He walked to the windows. Kris followed as she wrapped the sheet around herself. "See the fifth boat on the left side of the dock over there? That's my boat."

"Wow, that is really nice. Do you take it out much?"

"I used to, but work got in the way. So would you like to spend the afternoon on the gulf, just toying around? Maybe lacey will come, and you two could sun while I do all the work," he said, thinking how fun it would be.

Kristi had planned on being depressed on Saturday since it was Eli's graduation party. She had secretly thought about watching an online video on how to make a voodoo doll that she could pretend was Dom and stab with pins. She laughed and said, "You know, that sounds fun. How about I bring a loaf of Publix fresh bread, some deli meats, potato salad, and other picnic treats? What time do you want to launch the SS *Minnow*?"

Zac laughed at Kris's quick wit. "How about noon? That would give me time to run to the restaurant and make sure everything is running smoothly. I'll pick up water, some wine, and Pepsi," Zac said.

Kristi gathered the courage to finally listen to Dom's voice mail messages she had ignored at Zac's house. It surprised her when his voice said he wanted to send her seat voucher to Eli's graduation, each family received a set number of seats to graduation on Friday. He also invited her to Eli's graduation party at their house on Saturday. Kristi floated in her pool, staring at the blue sky. A month ago, she would have given anything for that invitation. Now she wasn't so sure.

She had taken Zac's advice and contacted the PI she had used for the background check on Zac. She had set up a professional photographer in Atlanta to video the entire graduation ceremony. Standing videotaping the commencement did not require a coveted ticket. He promised her the video overnight express mail for a sort of large nominal fee. She also called KC and told him about the voice mails she had received. He advised her to continue the same mode of conversation that they had always used pertaining to parenting issues, which was exactly what she had already decided.

Kristi excitedly had texted Eli congratulating him on his graduation, Friday morning. She sent his time and flight numbers for his Tuesday flights to Florida. She couldn't wait to see him. She busied herself Friday, making her grandmother's homemade recipe for potato salad to take on the sailboat picnic, Saturday.

She was a little early arriving at the marina. For some reason, traffic had been light, same with the deli line at the grocery store. She carried her beach bag with towel and sunblock in one arm and the groceries in the other as she slowly walked the pier toward Zac's sailboat. She was about to wave when she heard Lacey saying, "Dad, can't you see that Kristi is a gold digger? She is only interested in you because you have money, an established restaurant, a penthouse, and a sailboat."

Kristi stopped abruptly. She felt like she had been struck by lightning. She dropped the groceries on the wood dock, never taking her eyes off Zac. She turned and ran back to her car. She backed out of the parking lot of the marina while tears streamed down her face. She drove over the Ringling Bridge and headed north once she turned onto Longboat Key toward her favorite beach. Her chest hurt, and she was sure her heart was breaking by the time she parked at Whitney Beach.

Her phone rang several times, and text messages beeped one after another, all from Zac. First, she couldn't answer them because she was driving. Then the words *gold digger* and *out for your money* kept ringing in her ears, so she wouldn't answer his texts. She sat on the beach and cried until no more tears would come. She laid her head on her bent knees and looked across the horizon, hoping the entire conversation she had heard was a nightmare. But as she started walking along the warm water, she saw a dolphin breach in the distance and kids splashing in the waves. She knew it was a perfect Saturday afternoon, just not for her.

It was late afternoon when Kristi pulled into her driveway, hoping Zac wouldn't be there. She knew her nose and shoulders were sunburned, and she was exhausted. She didn't even know what she would say if she saw him. She slammed on her breaks. Eli was sitting on her front porch. She pulled the car in the garage while he walked up to greet her.

"Eli! How did you get here? What happened?" Kristi cried as she hugged him.

"Mom, you have been crying, are you okay? Did Dad call you and scream at you?" Eli asked as he pulled his suitcase through the garage and into the house.

Kristi made sure the garage door was closed and locked. She quickly called for a delivery pizza and then sat down. "What happened?"

"Graduation was great. I wish you could have heard my speech. Oh yeah, the mailman delivered this to the door when I got here," Eli said, handing his mom the express mail envelope.

"Okay, go on," Kristi said as she slid open the envelope. Excitement filled her eyes as the CD ROM case fell to the table.

"What's that?" Eli asked.

"That is your graduation ceremony. I hired a photographer to video it for me. Now tell me how you got here."

"Mom, my party friends were arriving. Dad and It were still fighting in the kitchen. You could hear them. So I welcomed everyone and pretty much sent everyone out by the pool. You would have been proud of me. Dad came out and acted all that, It acted like it was her graduation party. So I grabbed all my gift envelopes, picked up my suitcase, and ran out the front door and down the street. Uber picked me up and took me to the airport. I exchanged my ticket for a standby last-minute flight here, which I had to run like hell I mean heck to make it. I called Uncle KC, and he picked me up at the airport. He was going to hang out with me until you got home, but I told him no, I didn't want you mad at him too."

"Was this part of the original plan, you skipping out of your graduation party?" Kristi asked.

"No, that was all me. When Dad started screaming, I knew I couldn't stay any longer. I figured the party was ruined. So I left. Mom, why are your eyes puffy?" Eli asked, staring at her.

"I just had a really bad day, and crying was all I could do."

"Girls," Eli said, shaking his head.

The doorbell rang. Eli stood to answer it, but Kristi asked him to set the table while she paid for the pizza. She feared it could be Zac and not the pizza guy. But she returned to the kitchen with the steamy hot pizza.

"You know you are going to have to let your dad know you are here."

Between bites, Eli said, "I already did. Uncle KC made me call him and apologize for skipping out. I told Dad I couldn't handle the yelling anymore. I thanked him for the party and told him I would call him after you ungrounded me. I said that to make Uncle KC happy."

Kristi started laughing and almost sneezed Pepsi out of her nose; Eli laughed harder. When Kristi could finally speak, she said, "I'm not angry. That was really gutsy. I'm glad Uncle KC made you call your dad. It was the right thing to do. And I'm glad you are here. Have some more pizza, I'll be right back," Kristi said.

When Kristi returned, she was carrying a box, which she handed to Eli.

"What's this?"

"Souvenirs from Alaska," Kristi said.

Eli pulled a Red Dog Saloon T-shirt out first. He liked it after Kristi explained the sawdust on the floor, the stuffed bear chasing a pair of jeans up the wall post to the roof in the Red Dog Saloon Restaurant. She told him of the legend of Wyatt Earp leaving his gun and not returning for it.

"Who is Wyatt Earp?" Eli asked, reaching for another package.

"You will just have to use your search engine to read up on him."

"What's this? Bear poop chocolate candy? Only you, Mom, would buy bear poop candy." Eli laughed. He liked the boxer shorts with the moose walking across the backside. He mentioned that It always bought him the wrong-size underwear. But he figured she did it on purpose. He wasn't sure if he would like the salmon jerky. But said if not, he would sneak it to George. Lastly, he pulled out the moose stamped leather wallet. He ran his fingers over the dented tanned hide. And then he opened the trifold to see ten twenty-dollar bills inside the fold pocket. He looked up and said, "Thanks, Mom." He hugged her.

KC came over for an impromptu graduation party. He had stopped and bought some doughnuts and a cake. They all hung out in the pool, splashing. A couple of neighbors came over to congratulate Eli, including Jeannine, who started to say something about the incident a couple of days earlier. But Kristi shook her head and nodded toward Eli. Jeannine smiled and understood. KC pulled Kristi aside while Eli was showing off his cannonball splashes with a couple of the neighbor girls.

"Kristi, you look horrid. What's going on?"

"Thank you for picking up Eli and making him call his dad. I appreciate that," Kristi said.

"You are evading my question."

Taking a deep breath, Kristi said, "Zac invited me to a picnic on his sailboat. Lacey, Zac's daughter, called me a gold digger because he has a restaurant, a penthouse overlooking the marina, and a sailboat. That I was out for his money." Kristi knew her eyes were welling up again.

"You didn't hear him agree with her."

"But he didn't disagree either. First, I have the crap with Dominic to deal with. Then Lacey will forever dislike me because she will always think that I am trying to take her dead mother's place. I will not be the wedge between Zac and her. It's over. I can't do it," Kristi whispered on the verge of tears yet again.

"I think you should hear him out, sis."

"Well, this is Eli's graduation week. I promised Eli a graduation vacay wherever he wanted to go. I will be back to work as you need me next week. Okay?" Kristi asked.

"Enjoy your summer with Eli. His university life is just around the corner." KC hugged his sister, then waved good night to Eli and headed for home.

Kristi couldn't wait for the neighbor girls to quit drooling over Eli and go home. She was glad he was having a good time, but she really was exhausted. She put extra lotion on her very pink nose and shoulders. All she wanted to do was sleep.

CHAPTER 26

Zac was exhausted. He couldn't remember when he felt so fatigued. He splashed some tequila in a glass and sat down at the table on the terrace. Normally, he loved the view from his balcony. The yachts tugged on their mooring cleats with the ebb and flow of the harbor currents. Fishing trawlers returning with a late haul of fish ordinarily would excite him. Visions of creating a new recipe for the fresh catch usually was his main thought. Tonight, he saw nothing. His introspection returned to Lacey calling Kris a gold digger. He was sure, by the look on Kris's face, she had heard the comment. He remembered running down the dock after her, but her car zoomed off. He had tried calling and texting her, but she didn't return any of his messages. He left his unfinished drink on the table and walked into the master suite, stripping off his clothes, and climbed into bed.

Zac was at work the next morning just like every morning, when the prep cooks came in. They didn't bother him as he took notes, tasted concoctions at the far end of the kitchen, dumped out, started over, scribbled out entries from his notebook, and cooked some more. He knew his sous chef kept a close eye on him and probably reported back to Lacey. She had always found a way to get whatever she wanted from his staff and not because he was the boss. He listened to his phone as he called Kristi every day, her voice telling the caller to leave a message. He felt like he was phone stalking her. He just wanted to talk to her, to hear her voice. He would drag himself home to his empty house late in the evening, remembering her in his kitchen, sitting out on the terrace, laughing and lying between his sheets. Each night he would drink tequila and stumble into bed after the booze had numbed his brain.

Lacey had come home from the beach one afternoon, plopped down on the sofa, and turned on the TV. She thought the Nat Geo channel was showing a docudrama on Mount Denali. There were pictures that panned across the wild beauty of the tundra. The photographer was really good, but pictures of her dad laughing, her dad walking along a dock with a smile on his face, flashed across the screen. He was climbing a rock wall high above the open sea; he was drinking water from a vivid blue stream on top of a glacier. She saw the photo of her dad sleeping on a bus. Kristi had captured the essence of her father. He radiated happiness with her.

Lacey wandered into his bedroom and looked at the carved twin-whale sculpture sitting on his nightstand. She read the note that peeked out from underneath the bone base, from Kris. It wasn't mushy, just something Kristi had wanted her dad to have.

Later that evening, she sat in her dark bedroom, trying to figure out how to fix the damage that she finally admitted she caused. From her bedroom's open door, Lacey watched as her dad walked in from work, poured himself a drink, and stood at the window looking out. She saw him throw the glass against the fireplace and, then not bothering with the mess, walked into his bedroom, and slammed the door shut.

Lacey quietly let herself out the penthouse door. She walked past their private elevator, knowing the hum of the lift could be heard by her dad if he was awake. She walked to the general elevator at the far end of the hall. She waited for her cell service to return as she walked through the entrance doors and sat down on a very hard bench. Did the property manager not want anyone to sit here? *Jeez*, Lacey thought.

"Uncle Mark, this is Lacey. I need your help. I made a bad mistake, and I don't know how to fix it," Lacey begged when Mark, her dad's best friend, answered the phone.

"Relax, Lacey, tell me what happened," Mark said into the phone.

"Dad was taking Kristi out on the sailboat last Saturday. He invited me to come along to sun and swim with them. It made me mad because I could only think of Mom and Dad on the sailboat. Not her. Right before she got to the boat, I called her a gold digger, only after Dad's restaurant, his penthouse, and his money. She must have heard me and ran off. Dad didn't yell at me. I know he hasn't heard from her since. Uncle Mark, I saw the photos that she took in Alaska of my Dad. He was happy in the pictures, and now he isn't. He is back to working long hours, and he smashed a glass of tequila into the fireplace tonight. He doesn't disagree when I try to provoke him. He sits on the terrace late at night and stares out across the bay. Please tell me what to do." Lacey sniffed as tears ran down her face.

"Kristianna Romanoff is a well-established attorney who works in her family's law practice. She is a very wealthy woman in her own right. She doesn't need your dad's money.

"Get one thing straight, Lace. Your father loved your mother with all his heart. He still does and always will. He adores Kristi because she understands the love he has for your mom. As your dad explained it to me, she is the first woman who didn't force herself on him. She doesn't need him, she doesn't ask anything of him, but she does look at life with appreciation. That is what he enjoys about her.

"Your dad sent me a copy of the photos that Kristi took of Alaska. I haven't seen your dad as relaxed as I did in those pictures. Either Kristi is a dang good photographer or he was very happy. I think he was happy. Did you know he sent me a Santa head saying he found Santa at the North Pole?"

"I didn't know that," Lacey whispered.

"Zac drinking tequila means he has hit bottom. I have only seen him drinking tequila at the worst times in his life. I probably shouldn't tell you that. However, I suggest you find a way to apologize to your father. I would say apologize to Kristi, but if your dad can't find her, you won't either. When you apologize, pull it from your heart. Be sincere. It is the only way he will hear you."

"Thanks, Uncle Mark. I appreciate your help. I'll call you and let you know how I do. Bye for now," Lacey said as she hung up the phone and walked back inside.

Zac was leaning against the breakfast bar, holding onto a cup of coffee. He looked like his thoughts were far away when Lacey walked into the kitchen for breakfast. "Hey, Dad, how about I make you my special omelet that you always liked?" Lacey suggested.

"No thanks, I'm good."

Lacey bit her lip, trying to say something from her heart as Uncle Mark had suggested last night. Quietly she said, "Dad, you have always given me good advice. Lots of times I didn't want to hear it, but I did." She wiped a tear as it slid out of her eye with the back of her hand. She took a deep breath. "A couple months ago, I told you to explore life. You listened, you really did. Dad, I'm sorry. I was wrong about Kristi." She saw her dad close his eyes. He didn't move. He just stood there. "If she was out for your money, why would she have wasted her time taking all those beautiful pictures? She would have latched onto you instead." Lacey turned and stood in front of her father. "Please forgive me, Dad," she begged.

Zac grabbed his daughter and wrapped her in his arms. When had his little girl gotten so wise? he thought. "Lace, I love you."

"Dad, you need to go after her," Lacey said as she carefully stepped back into the kitchen. She took some eggs from the refrigerator and cracked them in a bowl.

"I tried. I can't find her. She won't return my calls. She disappeared," Zac said as he walked to the range and placed his favorite cast-iron skillet on the burner.

"Did you go to her house?" Lacey asked as she whisked the eggs, then handed the bowl of eggs to her dad. Her goal was not to cook the eggs as much as getting her dad to talk.

"I did. The house was closed up. I felt like a stalker." Zac laughed to himself, thinking of the creepy blond guy from the ship. He watched Lacey dice some ham and onions like a pro.

"Could you call anyone who might know where she is at?" Lacey questioned as she watched her dad pour the whisked eggs into the sizzling pan.

"I thought about calling her law firm, but they would protect her privacy at all costs," Zac said as he watched the eggs bubble. He turned the range off and let the heat from the cast iron finish the cooking.

"Who else could you call?" Lacey asked as she added her diced condiments and cheese down the middle of the omelet.

"Remember, what was her name from middle school? Bridget Weeks. Her mom sold Kris and me the cruise vacation. I even called her. She said she hadn't seen Kristi all week," Zac said as he folded the omelet in thirds, cut it in half, and plated both pieces.

"Wow, look at that." Lacey grinned. "A perfect omelet!"

Zac smiled and hugged his daughter.

"Now, about the broken glass by the fireplace, Daaad." Lacey grinned as she raised her eyebrows.

"The place is always clean when the housekeeper comes. It will give her something to do," Zac reasoned as he bit into the gooey omelet.

As a graduation gift, Kristi took Eli to several car dealers to choose the car of his dreams. He had insisted on a small jeep in black, even though he humored his mom and shopped around. They ate lunch at a sandwich shop while they waited for the license plate and insurance verification to be completed. Eli said, "Mom, they gave me a hideous old lady car to drive to school. It said I would be more cautious."

"Will you stop calling her it?" Kristi laughed.

"I can't call her by her real name. Inappropriate language is not becoming of a young adult," Eli mimicked.

The first place Eli wanted to show off his car was to George and Betsy's. They had been beloved friends of the family as long as Kristi could remember. Kristi took their souvenirs along when they stopped over. George walked around the little jeep, inspecting it closely as

Betsy gushed over it and congratulated Eli on being valedictorian of his class.

"You will have to come for a cookout at Mom's house. Then you can watch the video of my speech that Mom had made," Eli offered proudly.

"That sounds like a great idea." Betsy smiled. She raised her eyes in approval of Eli's invitation.

Kristi gave Betsy and George the souvenirs she bought them in Alaska. Betsy loved her ulu even though she didn't know what it was. Eli showed her a video on his phone how to cut with the Alaskan knife. She was most impressed but feared she would cut her finger off. George loved his carved wood salmon. He told Eli about the times Eli's uncle KC and Mom had gotten in trouble for ditching school to go fishing for fish just like the carved salmon.

"But, Geo, there aren't salmon in Florida," Eli said, ignoring the warning glares from his mom.

"No, I mean that size, fish," George said patting Eli on the shoulder. "Sorry, I didn't get your slider repainted after the break-in, Kristi."

"You mean the one that the guy got arrested for?" Eli asked.

"How did you hear about that?" Kristi asked, trying to hide the upset expression on her face.

"I figured Dad knew someone down here who told him about it because I heard him telling It," Eli said as he looked from his mom to George.

"Look at the time. I thought you wanted to take the jeep for a spin. We better get going before after-work traffic gets bad. Talk to you later, George, Betsy." She hugged them quickly before climbing into the passenger's seat.

It wasn't long before Eli was happily driving down I-75 expressway heading toward Naples. She wondered if Dom and It had argued over the break-in because one of them hired someone to trash her house and got caught. Oh gosh, now she was calling Dom's wife "It." Kristi grinned. She knew that KC was in touch with the Sheriff's Department. Her brother was not only protective of her; he was persistent in getting to the truth.

With Eli humming to the rock station on the radio, it unfortunately gave Kristi time to think about Zac. Her heart was still bruised and ached, especially in the darkest hours of the night when all was quiet. She had tried to warn herself several times during the cruise. She even pretended she could handle not seeing Zac after their vacation was over, but she was wrong. She missed laughing and talking with him. She longed for him to feed her from his plate. She craved his arms around her in the middle of the night. If it wasn't for Eli's constant reminding her he was happy to be home, she would have lost herself in despair.

"Eli, what do you think of spending the night at a hotel on the beach? We could go swimming in the gulf or the pool or both and then get something to eat," Kristi suggested.

"Wait, Mom, we didn't bring any clothes," Eli said, still gripping the steering wheel and eyes focused on the road.

"Credit cards!"

Kristi and Eli spent several days in Naples, then Marco Island and even Everglades City. They hung out at the beach, swam in the pool, kayaked through the mangroves, rented bikes, and even went parasailing off a boat. They ate cold leftover Cuban and cheesesteak sandwiches for breakfast and doughnuts for dinner. Sandy beach towels were draped over chairs and hung from the balcony railing. Their bodies were tanned darker as the days passed. There were nights when Eli fell into bed so exhausted, he drooled on the hotel pillow. Luckily, Kristi had her camera in her purse before they left Bradenton and snapped pictures of it all.

"Mom, now I understand how you took two thousand pictures in Alaska. Can we go home? I'm exhausted from being exhausted," Eli said still tired as they ate pancakes for breakfast for a change.

After taking a nap under an umbrella at the beach, they headed for home.

Zac received a text from Alana: "She's home."

Kristi had dressed in a bathing suit ready to spend the day in the pool. She dreaded looking at the junk mail that accumulated over the past week. Eli had decided upon scouting out chicks at the beach, when Kristi heard a knocking at the slider door. She walked into the kitchen laughing and said, "What, Eli, did you forget your key?"

Eli was standing at the slider, making funny faces at the glass just like when he was little. "Mom, do you have any junk food, you know like pretzels or chips? Chick watching makes me hungry." Eli grinned.

Kristi gave him his requested, very unhealthy snacks. She was just about to get some cans of soda and ice when she saw him walking toward his new car. She put the cooler back on the top shelf of the pantry, when she heard a knock on the slider again.

"Eli, did you decide you…"

There stood Zac. She was afraid to move, to even blink for fear he would vanish. She slowly slid the sliding door open, never taking her eyes off him.

"I'm in love with you. I can't live without you. I—"

Kristi wrapped her arms around Zac's neck and kissed him. She leaned back and looked into his dark eyes. She pressed her hands to his face and said, "I fell in love with you while cruising Alaska."

Not The End.
The Beginning!

ABOUT THE AUTHOR

Tam Ahlborn is a cardiac and trauma-trained Registered Nurse. There is nothing more rewarding than caring for critically ill patients. With long hours, blood splatters, great bladder control, and no personal life, she longed for a different kind of adventure. Wandering into a vacation destination symposium, she was soon caught up in the wild and beautiful scenes of rugged Alaska. And so, her journey *After Midnight Excursions* began.

CPSIA information can be obtained
at www.ICGtesting.com
Printed in the USA
LVHW090911120420
653138LV00001B/207